# EARTH-TWO

*A romantic fantasy*
*transcending time and dimensions*

## Richard Douglas Taylor

*Jer-Ben Publications, Inc.*

# RICHARD DOUGLAS TAYLOR

This is a work of fiction. Names, characters, places, and incidents are the products of the author's imagination or are used fictitiously and are not to be construed as real. Any resemblance to actual events, locales, organizations, or persons, living or dead, is entirely coincidental.

Copyright 2015 by Richard Douglas Taylor

Published in the United States by: Jer-Ben Publications, Inc.

Library of Congress Cataloging-in-Publication Data

Taylor, Richard Douglas
Earth-Two

ISBN-13:978-0-9789238-3-9 (trade pbk)
ISBN-10: 0-9789238-3-9 (trade pbk)

Printed in the United States

Email comments or queries to rdtaylor@mediacombb.net

10 9 8 7 6 5 4 3 2 1

A special thanks to Jean and B. J.

RICHARD DOUGLAS TAYLOR

# Prologue

Elaine didn't know why she was running across the countryside in the middle of the night, wearing nothing but her raggedy old terrycloth bathrobe tied loosely at the waist. Her bare feet—now bruised and bleeding—seemed to belong to someone else, operating independently of her thoughts. In fact, Elaine wasn't so sure her name *was* Elaine. It didn't seem to define her anymore...at least not at this particular time. Some name like *Phoebe* or *Phebes* kept flashing through her memory. But she had no idea who that person might be.

The only thing the newlywed knew for certain was that something behind her was wrong and she had to get to Four Mile Creek to make it right. The prospect pulled her along over fields of neck-high corn and freshly-cut hay on the outskirts of DeKalb, Illinois.

On the western horizon half an orange moon was preparing to set, having done nothing to light her path anyway. Neither had the fireflies drifting lazily about, blinking off and on, as if also searching for something in the dark.

The fence surprised her, jumping out of the night, catching her chest-high...the top two rows of barbed wire piercing the robe and into her flesh. Falling backwards from the recoil, she leveled three stalks of field corn, landing hard on her back. Unfazed, Elaine scrambled to her feet and blindly scaled the fence, unconcerned with further injury to her scratched and bleeding appendages. As she landed on the other side, the fence tried to keep its victim, snagging the hem of her pink robe with a row of its rusty steel barbs. But it succeeded only in tearing the cotton fabric as the woman forged ahead, her face even more resolute.

When she crossed into an uncut field of alfalfa, a flock of pheasants suddenly flushed into the night, startling her to a dead stop. Gasping for air, a moment of clarity stepped up and slapped Elaine like an angry parent. "What the hell are you doing, Phoebe?" she puzzled skyward to the Big Dipper, hands on her hips, chest heaving. Then she caught her error. "*Phoebe?*" She shook her head in bewilderment. "Who's this *Phoebe*? I'm *Elaine*, for Christ's sake!"

This was totally insane. Every ounce of common sense said to turn around and hurry back to the farm and the conjugal bed. Her husband would wake in a few hours and be worried sick about her. But logic and lucidity retreated as rapidly as the sound of the pheasants' fading wing beats. Blinking straight ahead into the darkness, she hoisted the pink terrycloth robe to her knees, and resumed her course. A dozen mosquitoes that had just honed in on her warmth floundered in her wake.

Among the incessant chirps and buzzes of a Midwest summer night rose the chorus of leopard frogs, growing louder by the second. A few more strides and a pungent odor of wet earth and aquatic life struck Elaine's nostrils. She could hear the soft babble of Four Mile Creek. Her destination and whatever was calling for her loomed only a few feet beyond.

Her pounding heart now outpaced the tempo of her feet, which had quickened in anticipation. The terrain began to slant slightly downward. Her momentum naturally increased even more by the incline, almost beyond her control. Her left foot landed solidly on the cool, damp grass of the ridge. Her right foot followed in cadence. But it found nothing. Only empty air.

As the heartsick soul plummeted the twenty feet toward the welcomed release of death, the night breeze freshened against her face and extremities. Her hair and tattered robe flapped briskly behind her like the DeKalb courthouse flag during an approaching storm. There came the muted sound of a neck snapping, a simultaneous flash of purple. The trickling stream and its rocky bottom should have felt wet and hard, but were warm and soft. Night turned to day. A bright light raced toward her, engulfed her, filling her with a wondrous sense of peace. Ahead on a distant horizon she saw blurred

7

figures…maybe a dozen or so, with still others beginning to appear behind them. None was moving or speaking, yet she clearly heard their welcoming call.

Now irresistibly drawn into the ever-widening channel, Elaine saw large trees materialize out of the haze, along with other familiar objects: picnic tables, a swing set, a shelter house. Children laughing. She recognized the setting. It was the city park on the northern edge of DeKalb. She'd loved going there as a child, but hadn't seen it for many years.

Suddenly, one of the stationary apparitions left the others and approached rapidly, as if on invisible wings. It seemed to be speaking as it flew, but she couldn't understand the words. There was a sense of urgency emanating from its glowing center. Closer it drew, until finally pausing just a few feet away, its features becoming clearer. It was a male figure with broad shoulders and shaggy blonde hair. The square jaw and smiling mouth were so familiar.

And when she saw those sky-blue eyes, her heart leapt in ecstasy.

RICHARD DOUGLAS TAYLOR

# Part One—Phoebe

# Chapter 1

She stood at the end of the boardwalk, her toes dangling tentatively over the edge of the last weathered board. Phoebe had already gone farther than ever before, and advancing one more foot meant stepping onto something she had previously seen only from a distance. She wasn't afraid. Mostly just curious. After all, it was only a beach, even if it did look...*otherworldly*.

Amused by the irony, the diminutive young female easily took the final step. As expected, the powdery white sand pushing up between her toes felt different from on Earth. It was softer, finer, almost tingly. Phoebe bent down to scoop up a handful of the white substance and let it sift slowly through her fingers. Compared to the solid, well-defined lines of her delicate hand, the almost weightless grains with their muted sparkles seemed just this side of fairy dust.

The sea before her offered a degree of mysticism, as well. Her newly-acquired, emerald-green eyes couldn't tell where the sapphire water ended and the sapphire sky began. Even the hint of pink pastel clouds lofting above seemed to reflect perfectly off the mirrored surface. If this were supposed to be the Caribbean Sea, where were the waves? For that matter, where was the wind? Phoebe didn't know a lot about the tropics, but she knew enough. In her previous life as Alyssa, she'd spent her honeymoon in the Bahamas with Ted. Even on the calmest day they could watch the sea roll in to lap the shore at regular intervals. Apparently not here. The surface lay strangely quiet and placid...more like a French Impressionist's painting, maybe a Monet.

Phoebe had viewed this setting many times before from the sundeck of the beach house some thirty feet behind her. But until now the *newly-revised* eighteen-year-old had never given its authenticity much consideration. There were always so many other things to occupy her mind. Sometimes her schooling was so involved, in fact, she could be gazing out across this beautiful vista of sand, sea, and the sky and not see any of it.

Now down here, up close, actually touching the beach, smelling its delicate floral fragrance, it was almost supernatural, especially with that translucent, shimmering luster coating everything. She wondered if she were to close her eyes and shake her head, it might all disappear. But Phoebe didn't want to take that chance. Whatever this was, it was probably Andrew's doing. And that meant she belonged to it, as much as it belonged to her.

To her right the swath of white sand and cyan sea continued for about another quarter mile, arcing in a left-handed crescent before vanishing into the haze. There were people along it, maybe a dozen or so, walking, wading, lounging in the tropical paradise. As near as she could tell, they were all young adults and attractive. Mostly males.

"Undoubtedly Earth-Twos, like myself," she mused, cupping her hands around her temples, as if that would help bring them into a clearer view. Yet similar to everything else in her field of vision, they had this strange, misty radiance about them. Maybe it was just her eyes, reacting to the change they had just gone through…along with her body, mind, and everything else today.

Phoebe had never been out of the bamboo house before, let alone walked along this beach. The young soul probably could have, with Andrew's permission, of course. But like the beach's upper end where she presently stood, it had always been just a part of the inconsequential backdrop, a landscape to be viewed casually from the sundeck.

Phoebe rotated her petite, five-foot-three frame to glance back at the beach house. She was pleased to discover that at least *it* did still have sharp, well-defined lines with no glimmering. She'd never seen it from this perspective before. The simple but charming bamboo-framed structure with its square, thatched roof and breeze-way design was two stories high, the second one being the bedroom loft where she took her therapeutic naps, some lasting for days. The front half of the house sported the sundeck resting on ten-foot stilts, with weathered wooden steps leading down to the narrow boardwalk. The house's back half nestled into a gently sloping hillside of towering palms and leafy rum trees. Multi-colored flowerbeds ran around and under the structure like gravity-defying rivulets. It truly was amazing what her mentor could do with just his thoughts.

11

And there he stood, on that elevated deck: the unimposing, slender figure of Andrew, draped in his usual white tunic with gold braided trim and a silver sash. There was nothing blurry about him either. Just minutes before, he had coaxed her out the door and down the steps. Now, as she hesitated just off the end of their boardwalk, he was gesturing for her to *go on*, both with a backward flip of his hand and mouthing the words.

Phoebe smiled. She loved Andrew. And she had to admit the new astral image he had crafted for her looked quite appealing in the wardrobe's mirror just moments ago. He made sure she retained her signature, honey-blond hair, now lying gently on her naked shoulders in lazy swirls. And she was delighted to keep that sultry, smoky voice she had possessed as Alyssa in that last life. After all, with just a few raspy words rolling up from her throat she could get any man to stop talking and listen…even her mentor, Andrew.

He also made her astral body to be three years older than the one she had been using during her recent post-life evaluation. And it was more developed. *Nicely developed, in fact*, she thought, pulling the bikini bra out a few inches to take another look at her spritely new breasts. They were smaller than when she was Gretchen, but with a much better shape, more like Alyssa's as a teenager. Her face was certainly prettier, too, especially when Andrew had softened the flesh around her eyes and upgraded the irises from hazel to a brilliant emerald-green with gold flecks.

It was at that point Andrew had proclaimed she was now a true beauty…one who would catch the eye of any male worthy of his gender, as well as most envious females. Phoebe assumed this is why he had dressed her in this cute bikini with red-and-white vertical stripes and told her to take a stroll along the beach. He wanted her to prove it to herself.

Once more she looked back at her teacher with the short red hair combed comically forward like Napoleon's. Andrew was still smiling, still encouraging her to move on, with even more insistence this time. She blew him a kiss and slowly started walking down the white sands of what she was told was Magens Beach, St. Thomas in the Caribbean Sea.

# Chapter 2

Already bored watching the repetitive activity of his fellow but fuzzy twenty-somethings in the sea and sand, Leonid lowered the back of the Adirondack chair two notches and lazily stretched out on its soft green and yellow-striped cushion. He had just wandered down the path from his beach house twenty feet behind him. Well, it wasn't exactly *his* beach house. It belonged to Phaidra, his mentor, but it was the only home on Earth-Two he had ever known. The modest, two-story, four-room structure with rounded thatched roof and bamboo supports was also his schoolhouse, his playhouse, his everything-house. Outside of three trips to Earth—giving him the tacked-on classification of an *Earth-Two-3—E2-3* for short—he'd never been anyplace else.

Although his astral body looked about age twenty-three, in mental and spiritual maturity he was still just a pup, requiring a short leash. While Phaidra was out back a few minutes ago chatting psychically with some distant friend, Leonid had sneaked out, tired of his post-life review. "God! How many times do you have to tell me to be more attentive?" he had yelled at her moments before. "I heard you the first twelve dozen times."

The review was regarding his just-completed third incarnation, this one as Jason Warfield, a linebacker for the New York Giants in the early Twenty-First Century. While running wind-sprints during summer training camp, he had suddenly collapsed, sliding face-down across the hot, green turf, dead at the tender age of twenty-three. The shock to his teammates and a few million fans produced the usual uproar over athletes being pushed too hard during days with heat indexes over ninety. But the truth was he had been leveled by a preprogrammed, massive coronary…a fact of which Leonid was not presently aware. He thought it was just bad luck or some hereditary factor. Phaidra knew better, of course, since she was the one who blew the whistle, sending him to the celestial showers. He would learn about such things when he was older. *If he would only listen.*

Thanks to what Jason Warfield's human DNA had constructed naturally during that particular life, Leonid's current astral body was quite impressive, as was his ruggedly handsome face with a broad jawline and azure, bedroom eyes. His only flaws were a slightly bent nose and a scar across his right eyebrow, courtesy of a locker room brawl somebody else started. But he liked those features, believing they simply added to the professional athlete persona.

To be sure, that life and physique were far more enjoyable than his previous one as Hagos, an over-weight, under-paid Ethiopian prostitute in the eighteen hundreds. In light of that ghastly countenance, Leonid had begged Phaidra to let him keep this Jason-the-jock one while between lives here on Earth-Two. As Jason, he had been voted one of the Big Apples' ten most eligible bachelors, never lacking in female companionship. As Hagos, his reflection could break a mirror at twenty feet. Phaidra agreed to his request without hesitation. It was, in fact, one of the main reasons she had so quickly selected that particular body for Leonid's third incarnation. She simply couldn't take any more of the loud-mouthed hooker with more toes than teeth, waddling around the beach house in a bright orange muumuu, chanting in some kind of Afro-Asiatic dialect impossible to understand. Enough was enough.

If Phaidra had possessed the kind of talent and skill necessary to alter Leonid's ugly Ethiopian visage to something more palatable, she would have considered that option, and not rushed him back into the reincarnation cycle quite so fast. He certainly could have used a few more months to study and evaluate the lessons learned from being Hagos. But by Phaidra's own admission she was not very adept at rendering an aesthetically-pleasing, detailed sculpturing of another soul's astral body and face. Her own image, yes. Others, no. Unlike her neighbor, Andrew, up the beach, it was a skill she had never had the desire or aptitude to learn. Consequently, as was true with many young souls in the afterlife, whatever Leonid looked like at any given moment between lives hinged largely on how he saw himself...what he literally envisioned himself to be. And since he was now identifying so strongly with that New York Giant linebacker, his own power of belief was spontaneously coalescing his energy particles into that handsome face and pro athlete body. It was another feature of Earth-Two he did not understand. But few E2s did in the early stages of their existence.

Phaidra's ineptitude at human sculpturing didn't mean she lacked skills. On the contrary, she had a unique talent that kept her in high demand for arranging special welcome-home galas for the recently deceased. These usually involved arrogant souls—such as dictators, politicians, and drugged-

14

out rock stars—who expected throngs of loyal admirers when they came through the channel into the Reception Station. Not only could Phaidra manufacture as many as a hundred humanoid figures at once, she could program them to cheer and clap and mill around like Hollywood extras. It usually didn't matter if they were all basically featureless and fabricated, as long as they stroked the incoming soul's ego enough to help with his transition from Earth back to his home dimension here on Earth-Two.

This talent is why her friend Andrew had asked Phaidra for help in constructing today's charade for Phoebe. He wanted her to conjure up a dozen or so basic images and program each one's movements to be as lifelike as possible. Andrew's job then was to go down the line one-by-one, shaping each one's face and body to look reasonably authentic. Since it was just a matter of visualizing a bunch of energy pixels into approximate position, it was a lot easier than that authentic and far more permanent astral image he had just completed for Phoebe.

As a result, those young people frolicking out here in the tropical setting were a little mechanical and blurry around the edges. But Phaidra and Andrew both felt that from a distance anyway the projected phonies would appear realistic enough to fool Phoebe, when she came walking down the beach in her new body.

# Chapter 3

Joining Leonid under the spreading Spanish elm, Phaidra set a pitcher of iced tea and two glasses between them on the round glass table, and then stood up stiffly. "Sneaked out on me, I see," she said a little miffed, hands on hips, looking down on her wayward progeny.

"I needed a break," he replied, rolling his head to look up at her from behind his black, wrap-around sunglasses. "You're getting to be more of a slave-driver than my coaches were."

"All for your own good, son," she said with that patronizing tone still so often necessary.

Leonid grunted.

Phaidra lifted her eyes to scan up and down the beach. No sign of Phoebe yet. That was good. Leonid wasn't supposed to be here at this time. She hoped it wouldn't interfere with Phoebe's maiden voyage.

"Just don't plan on staying very long," she said sternly. "Have some iced tea and get back in the house. You need sleep more than the sea."

Leonid had already stopped listening. He was too amused seeing his mother-figure in a one-piece tankini swimsuit, rather than her usual purple satin, floor-length tunic that revealed nothing of what was underneath. Ostensibly, she wanted to blend in with the beach scene, even though the attire was very much out of character for her. And it revealed a body that certainly wouldn't be the subject of any pinup taped inside some jock's locker. Her breasts were modest bumps and she had straight lines where most Earth females had curves. Add in a narrow face with high cheekbones, and *slender* was too mild of a word.

Even so, this bald-headed, willowy empress with the classic Greek nose was quite becoming...at least in a charming, understated sort of way. Much of it had to do with those twinkling blue eyes and a mouth that tweaked mirthfully up at one corner, suggesting she knew something amusing you didn't. And in most instances, she did.

Having the same deprecating humor as his mentor, Leonid wasn't about to let this opportunity pass by. While she settled into the other Adirondack chair's cushion, he casually poured himself a glass of the iced tea, took a long

16

sip, and said more to the sea than to Phaidra, "By the way, nice body, babe. Wanna fool around?"

"You couldn't handle me, Junior," deadpanned his fortyish mentor, sliding her hands down her mid-section to smooth a couple wrinkles off the loose-fitting, mustard-colored fabric. Like most entities with the rank and residence of *Earth-Three*, Phaidra was far less concerned with charming the opposite sex. Education was her main preoccupation, for both herself and particularly her one and only offspring. Her present, projected image was exactly as she wanted it to be.

"Hey, I was just throwing you a bone, old girl," quipped Leonid, continuing the good-natured sparring. "Even though you seem to have plenty of your own."

Before replying, for effect Phaidra calmly materialized a lighted cigarette between her fingers, took a big drag and blew a stream of smoke into the air. She then rolled her head slowly to the right and replied dryly, "Listen Leo, I left more broken hearts scattered across terra firma in my forty-five lives than you have hairs on that golden head."

Leonid snorted bubbles in his iced tea glass. "Not looking like *that*, you didn't!" he scoffed, jerking a big thumb in her direction.

That did it. With a coy smile, the almost featureless form suddenly blossomed into a voluptuous body and gorgeous face quite akin to a famous movie star in her prime, pushing out against the pale-yellow swimsuit until the seams were about to split. The platinum blonde hair, full red lips, and little mole on her left cheek verified it.

"You're right," she breathed with pure Marilyn. "Not like that. More like *this*."

# Chapter 4

"Holy shit!" howled the surprised young soul, snapping erect to better scan the exotic vision. In his previous life he was well aware of the Hollywood icon, even though she had died years before he was born. "No friggin' way you were *her*!"

"I was," said Phaidra matter-of-factly. "Now drink your drink and try picking on someone in your own league." She pointed her cigarette toward the slightly-out-of-focus girl in a black and white ruffled one-piece walking past. Phaidra easily recognized her, because of the dozen E2 forms she had created, this was one of the two females. She had programmed her to just walk up and down in the sand as a kind of mobile prop, mostly so Phoebe would think she had some competition on the beach.

Still in awe of his mentor's remarkable past-life as Miss Monroe, Leonid's curiosity got the better of him, and he unhurriedly pivoted his attention toward the cute young thing of about twenty jiggling by. With his index finger he pulled the top of his sunglasses down enough to provide an unobstructed view. She was a typical E2 female with a nice face and body. The bowed nose and olive skin suggested she was fresh in from Tel Aviv…or the upper west side.

"Why don't you go meet her?" taunted Phaidra, as she returned her image to its original slender identity. She assumed Leonid didn't know the passing female was basically a hologram. It would be a hoot watching him try to hit on a pile of unresponsive particles.

"Nah," sighed Leonid, leaning back in his chair and pushing his sunglasses back into position. "She's okay, but…"

"But what?"

The ex-linebacker let out a bored sigh and said, "Well, for one thing she doesn't seem all that real. Probably something you conjured up just to jerk me around. And for another, I don't chase. I let them come to me."

While he may be getting wise to her tricks, Phaidra had to remind herself how immature Leonid still was. He was obstinate and hadn't learned much in his three lives, even with her attempts of intense schooling in between. About the only thing he was well-versed in so far was humanoid sex from both the male and female perspective. Humility and about a dozen other noble traits were still sadly lacking.

"Well, just keep in mind, my young stud muffin," she said, reaching over to tap his tanned leg, "I'm still the one who decides each of your incarnations. So, if you don't watch this *God's gift to women* attitude you picked up in New York, we'll see how you like being a three-toed sloth grinding on a gum tree in Borneo."

The good-natured threat produced a broad grin on Leonid's face. He was just starting to work on a clever come-back, when his attention was drawn to the next entry in the beach parade: an exceptionally beautiful young female adorned in a skimpy red-and-white-striped bikini. And contrary to all the other E2s around here, this one seemed wonderfully genuine.

To Leonid's objectifying tastes, her body was next to perfect—svelte, slender legs, flat stomach, grapefruit-sized breasts, silky, alabaster skin. In her late teens. And the way she walked…not mechanically strutting and wiggling her assets like the previous girl. Her gait was careful, unpretentious, elegant.

But there was something else, too…something he couldn't quite put his finger on. She didn't look familiar, yet she somehow seemed familiar.

Getting interested, the chauvinist linebacker allowed his eyes to slide upward to examine her approaching face in three-quarter profile. That's when her previously downcast head lifted and turned toward him. Those full lips spread into such a sweet, disarming smile, Leonid's head cranked back a tick. In a rush to get a better look, he jerked his sunglasses down so fast they summersaulted off his face. Trying futilely to catch them in mid-air, they awkwardly bounced off his finger tips and landed smack in the lap of his yellow surfer trunks. He quickly glanced back up to see if the passing goddess had seen his fumble. Her smile widened in amusement. Damn! She had.

He barely noticed her honey-blonde hair, because a few inches above that starburst smile were those eyes…those green eyes…those timid, emerald-green, puppy eyes that said, *I'm all alone out here. Please come walk beside me.*

Before Phaidra could stop him, Leonid was out of his chair and jogging toward her, sand and sunglasses winging in his wake.

19

# Chapter 5

Phoebe was mildly surprised by the stares she was getting from the young men—and that one woman—as she walked along the beach. Most seemed to just pause momentarily in their activity to gawk. She hoped it was from them finding her new body attractive and not, god forbid, with some flaw or anything she was doing wrong. More than once she self-consciously repositioned the upper and lower halves of her skimpy, polyester bikini, in case more was showing than should be. Or not enough.

The demure teenager wondered how much longer Andrew wanted her to continue this rather embarrassing strut along Magens Beach. Not much was happening. Just stares.

One couple sitting on chairs under a spreading shade tree just ahead struck her as uncharacteristically in focus…and mismatched. He was a good-looking, blonde-headed male with broad shoulders and tanned, chiseled muscles from neck to toe, while she was much older, rather plain, pale, and shiny bald. *Undoubtedly mentor and student*, she thought, *like me and Andrew*. Phoebe grinned at the all-to-familiar relationship, while holding her attention on the handsome young man. When he suddenly fumbled comically for his airborne sunglasses, her smile broadened even farther. Their eyes met and held for a moment, before she turned her attention back to the powdery white beach stretched out before her.

"Hold up, sweet thing," lifted a voice from behind her. Phoebe stopped and turned around to find that same brawny fellow catching up to her. "Hey, darlin'," he said, pulling up just short.

"Hey, yourself," she replied with a cautious smile, looking squarely into his azure eyes. She wasn't sure of his intentions. After all, nobody else had approached her. And this guy didn't have blurred lines.

"I'm Leonid," he said. "What's your name?"

She liked the confidence in his voice, his demeanor, and the growing fact that he was real.

"I'm Phoebe," she replied, flashing those green eyes at him before timidly dropping them to his hairless chest.

He liked her shyness, that sexy voice, and the strong possibility she wasn't some fabricated apparition courtesy of Phaidra.

"I haven't seen you around here before, have I?" he asked.

"I doubt it," said Phoebe. "It's my first time down here. I live back up the beach with my mentor, Andrew." She motioned backward with her head.

"Yeah, same with me. Right over there. That's mine in the chair, Phaidra."

The two females waved at each other. The older one's mouth cracked into a tight, weak smile. She then changed her wave to more of a *come back here* motion, apparently aimed at Leonid. He pretended not to see it.

"She seems...nice," offered an apprehensive Phoebe, slowly returning her gaze to the young man.

"Yeah, she really is pretty cool," he replied, turning his back completely to Phaidra. "I wouldn't trade her for anyone. Great sense of humor."

"I feel the same way about my Andrew. He's a good teacher. And friend. More like a father, actually."

"Yeah, I guess I could say Phaidra is like a mother, but she says she isn't. Just my mentor. I guess."

Phoebe's eyes got wider. *Mother. Father.* There was always this one question that Andrew would never answer. Maybe Leonid's mentor had told him. "Hey, has she ever told you where you came from?" she queried, hopefully. "How you came to be...you?"

Leonid gave it some thought. "Hmm. Don't think so. Don't think I've ever asked, actually."

Phoebe's eyes shifted off into the distance. The corner of her mouth twitched. Again, no answer. *What's with these teachers and their damn secrets?*

21

# Chapter 6

Leonid took the opportunity for a close-range assessment of her feminine assets. She was petite and nicely put together, just begging to be squeezed. And what a face on this alluring E2! He found himself getting lost in those emerald-green eyes and full, pink lips. And that feeling he knew her from someplace nagged at the corners of his mind. But since she could easily have been one of his many conquests back as Jason Warfield, he saw no reason to pursue it.

What he did consider doing, however, was kissing her right there. Those lips were just begging for it. Then he thought better of that, too. He didn't want to risk turning her off before he had a chance to turn her on with his patented, New York moves. Phaidra had mentioned that sex was free and safe on Earth-Two, but nothing about how exactly it was done…if any differently. So, a little Earth-style decorum and a touch of caution were in order here, at least while they were still in the flirting stage.

"I was a football player in my last life," he stated offhandedly. "Linebacker."

"I'm not surprised. You look pretty healthy."

"Healthy? Yeah, I guess I was…" said Leonid, for the first time showing a little self-doubt, "until my heart exploded at age twenty-three."

"Oh, I'm sorry," sympathized Phoebe, cocking her head. Then she sighed, "But that's not as bad as dying of dysentery at age sixteen."

Leonid studied her face to see if she were joking. She wasn't. Phoebe looked back at him just as intently to see if he were disgusted by that rather unpleasant and possibly unnecessary disclosure. He wasn't. Sensing the kinship of fellow Earth-cyclists who had been to hell and back, they simultaneously burst into laughter. The sexual tension eased considerably.

"Was that *big-D death* from your last life?" chuckled Leonid, rubbing her shoulder lightly with the back of his fingers.

Phoebe appreciated his understanding gesture. "No, my second to the last one. I was a German girl. Sixteen and still a virgin, if you can believe it." Then she added, "Thanks to my father."

22

German? Virgin? Dying at age sixteen? Leonid's memory was clicking. "Your father?" he asked leadingly, getting a little aroused on top of his curiosity. "What happened?"

"He caught me and my boyfriend in the haymow just as we were about to fuck."

Phoebe's round eyes got rounder and wider in surprise. Her hand immediately flew up to cover her mouth. Per Andrew's request, she had been trying to keep those kinds of vulgarities out of her vocabulary lately. What would this young man think? *Damn that Tyree part of her!*

Leonid, meanwhile, was momentarily taken aback—yet hardly displeased—by the sudden obscenity coming from such a seemingly sweet girl. He wasn't aware that Phoebe's first Earth life had been as a foul-mouthed gang-banger on the mean streets of Cleveland, Ohio.

Her mention of the haymow had Leonid's memory now spinning like a potter's wheel. "Your name was Gretchen, wasn't it?"

Phoebe rapidly switched from red-faced embarrassment to open-mouth shock. "Why, yes..." she replied. "How'd you know that?"

"Your boyfriend's name was Gunther," he stated, sitting hard on his growing excitement.

"Yes...it was," she offered, intently scanning his face and her memory.

"I was *Gunther*," announced Leonid, as if she'd just won a prize, spreading his arms wide in recognition.

"Oh, my God!" gasped Phoebe. "It is you. I *thought* you felt familiar."

The two young souls embraced like old friends. The surprise. The coincidence. Some old feelings. Who could have known their paths would cross in this little corner of the Cosmos?

But the truth be known, that particular relationship in old Germany centered almost entirely on exploring the wonders of each other's young bodies. Their few conversations after church and school had rarely extended much beyond hem-haws and pregnant pauses. So, as she now gently pushed away from Leonid, they characteristically fell to those same hem-haws and pregnant pauses. Their chemistry just didn't click, at least for Phoebe.

Eventually they managed to generate some semblance of a dialog, mostly regarding each one's separate life there in Seventeenth Century Deutschland. Phoebe's description of milking cows and forking hay pretty much fell on deaf ears, while she learned that it had been Leonid's first ever incarnation, and that

23

he too had died at an early age, not that long after her. It seems he was kicked in the head while trying to extract seminal fluid from a bull, which apparently didn't care much for cold, impatient hands.

When it inevitably got back around to their failed fornication in the barn, Leonid took Phoebe's hand, his eyes now dripping with innocence. In an all-too-obvious replay of the randy young Gunther, he said softly, "Would you...do you...want to try again?"

Phoebe studied Leonid's face, considering the proposition. Excluding Andrew and a few inconsequential E3s at the Birth Wing, she'd never even known another male on Earth-Two, let alone made love to one. She assumed it worked the same as on Earth...that everyone's important parts would function in this dimension. All Andrew had told her was no one gets pregnant here or contracts any kind of disease. So what would be the harm? She didn't think Andrew would mind. He wasn't really her father or anything...just her mentor.

Or so he said.

The prospect made her tingle, like on Earth, when something sensual and intimate was about to happen. "Why not?" she smiled delicately, giving his hand a congenial squeeze.

The pair turned and began walking down the beach. Away from Phaidra. Away from Andrew. Away from a bunch of animated, intangible E2s, who just kept splashing and frolicking mechanically in the tropical wonderland, not an ounce of brains among them.

# Chapter 7

The proud mentor watched from the bamboo-framed sundeck, as his young protégé eased tentatively along the shoreline in that cute red-and-white-striped bikini he had materialized out of the ether for her just moments before. Andrew had every reason to be pleased. After three tough, but educational incarnations on Earth, Phoebe was developing quite nicely, both mentally and spiritually.

As for her astral body, it was a tour de force, if he did say so himself. All the lives and all the training in between lives he had spent to hone his artistic skills of sculpting the human form had certainly paid off. To his highly subjective eye, Phoebe was now the most beautiful woman, young or old, on any level of the Cosmos, he had ever seen, much less created. Hopefully, her walk along this beach and the stares she was to get from the projected images of fellow E2s would help convince her of the same.

This convincing wasn't necessarily critical...just a little south of important. To maintain this image on her own from this day forward, Phoebe had to *believe* in her new beauty. Believing is everything in Earth-Two, literally. What one believes to be true, becomes reality, the degree depending on the level of the belief. Without a one hundred percent conviction from Phoebe, Andrew would have to keep doing periodic maintenance on both her physical form and her mental perception of it. Otherwise, her self-image could slip back to how she consciously saw herself as any one of her past existences on Earth...or more likely, as a conglomeration of those more impressionable events from all three.

Like that first life. Andrew recalled how difficult it was getting Phoebe back to her original *little girl* persona after being that twenty-four-year-old, two-hundred-pound, African-American male with cold, dark eyes, a perpetual sneer and smut mouth. Even now, she was still having trouble distancing herself from Tyree's rather colorful verbiage at inopportune times.

Her next passing as Gretchen, the big-boned, sixteen-year-old German girl with pigtails, acne and over-developed hormones, was much easier, the transition being from young girl back to young girl.

But this last one, as Alyssa, presented the biggest challenge. If she had died at an early age like the other two, she would have come home projecting a fair degree of youth and vigor. But Alyssa lived to be eighty-seven. She shuffled in, seeing herself as little more than a gray-haired, arthritic grandmother with liver spots the size of silver dollars and sixty-pounds of wrinkled skin hanging off thirty-pounds of porous bones. Andrew had his work cut out for him.

But as twice before, his artistic talents rose to the occasion, not only transforming weathered Alyssa back to youthful Phoebe, but enhancing various characteristics to create this pretty, young girl walking out there on the beach. In turn, his *daughter*—as he liked to think of her, although she was far more than that—kept doing her part as well, accepting and believing in her female identity. And what a confidence boost it was when she viewed herself naked in the mirror just moments ago, seeing how she had been enhanced to the level of an Athenian beauty. Just the fact that she loved her new image meant she should both consciously and unconsciously identify with it from now on, while disregarding any part of her previous three incarnations. Besides, as a final touch, those phony E2s out there on the beach, gawking at the appropriate times, were following Phaidra's programming quite nicely.

Andrew's thoughts were disrupted when one of those images, a male with surprisingly well-defined lines and features, suddenly came out from under a tree and jogged up to Phoebe. Within seconds there was obvious flirting and laughing, with Phoebe twirling her hair and toeing the sand.

"What's this about?" hummed Andrew aloud to the air with a jaundiced tone. "A real E2 wasn't part of the plan."

# Chapter 8

A couple minutes later the nicely-constructed young man and his precious Phoebe were embracing. "Now hold on here," said Andrew, pangs of protective fatherhood welling up inside. "I didn't send you out there to be mauled by some cosmic Casanova." The E3 knew he shouldn't pry into his E2's affair too much, so he told himself to calm down. After all, she was her own entity. She had her own lives to live. Besides, maybe this guy's attention to her would actually help with Phoebe's self-confidence and self-image.

Spontaneous with the hug, a psychic sensation from Phoebe passed through Andrew. It was a feeling of familiarity toward a fellow E2. "Ah, so we must know thee, young man," he posed, feeling a little better about the situation. "Perhaps an embrace of friendship, rather than seduction?"

Andrew did a quick scan of Phoebe's mind to see how she knew the interloper. He had his answer in a nanosecond. That fellow had been Gunther in Phoebe's second incarnation as Gretchen. "Well, it is indeed a small universe," quipped Andrew, shaking his head in wonder. "I'm surprised Phaidra never mentioned you."

Turning his focus back down the beach, the couple was now walking away from him, holding hands. Once again things were not well. "Okay, you two," grumbled the now-very-displeased father-figure, rapping his knuckle on the horizontal railing of his sundeck. "Let's not get carried away here. You're just friends, remember. In fact, you hardly knew each other in Germany...right?" Unsure, Andrew quickly probed his own memory of that particular incarnation of Phoebe's. He had to sort through many experiences and phases until finally coming to that tryst in the hayloft. "Oh, damn!"

The temptation was strong to tune in completely to Phoebe's thoughts, or even influence them enough to strongly suggest she spin on her heels and walk away. Andrew realized his charge was well-versed in the birds and the boys and how sexual intercourse worked on Earth. But he hadn't yet taught her anything about *spiritual coupling* on Earth-Two, and how much more *electrifying* it was. Not that there's anything wrong with it. He just wanted her first time to be with the right E2. In designing Phoebe's upcoming incarnation, he'd researched the probable future for her in ancient Rome. It

27

involved meeting a handsome young man quite symbiotic with Phoebe's spiritual energies. The fellow out there on the beach holding her hand with larceny on his mind and malice in his trunks was not him.

Now the couple had disappeared behind a row of palm trees lining the back edge of the beach. So much for her autonomy. Andrew had no choice but to climb into Phoebe's head. Entering a half-trance state, he sensed they were off the beach, standing behind some bushes, out of view from everyone. Leonid's hands roamed around to Phoebe's back, while hers dabbled with the hard six-pack of his abdomen. Leonid bent his knees and neck to lower his face down to the much shorter Phoebe. He flicked the tip of his nose against hers and she responded in kind. Then their lips came together, lightly, before his teasingly brushed past to nibble on her cheek.

Phoebe's hands slid up Leonid's smooth chest, pausing for a brief inspection of his small nipples before continuing on up to run her fingers through his long yellow hair. He pulled her tight to his chest. Her arms encircled his thick neck. Their lips smashed hard together. Tongues danced. Breaths mixed hot and moist.

Not even bothering with her bra, the ex-New York Giant's large hands slid down along her backside and under the bikini. Hooking his thumbs over the upper hem, he pushed them off the firm mounds of her derriere to mid-thigh. Her eyes fluttered and she moaned softly in his ear. *This was so much like her first time as Alyssa...with future husband Ted...back in high school.*

Phoebe brought her hands down quickly to work at the drawstring of Leonid's baggy trunks. An aura of red and purple particles was beginning to envelop the couple, as sensations neither had experienced before danced at the edges of their young souls.

"Hi there, kids," smirked Andrew, materializing so close to the pair he almost knocked them off balance. "Whatcha up to?

Leonid's head snapped to the left to discover the source of the rude intrusion. It was an older male figure with narrow set, dark-blue eyes and Caesar-type hair only slightly redder than his now-scowling face. Leonid quickly began retying his trunks.

Phoebe was still in a semi-daze, blinking at the sudden sound and presence of her mentor. "Andrew!" she gasped, hastily pulling up her bottoms. "Hi. You scared me. Us." Her head turned back to see how her new-old friend Leonid was reacting to her mentor's interference. He looked embarrassed, a little pissed, and a lot frustrated.

28

A barely audible female voice filtered in through the trees from down the beach in the vicinity of the Adirondack chairs. "Hey, linebacker, looks like it's *you* who got thrown for a ten-yard loss this time."

Leonid ignored her.

Phoebe took a step backwards to have a proper angle for the awkward but mandatory introductions. "Andrew, this is Leonid," she said as politely as possible under the circumstances. "Leonid, this is my mentor, Andrew."

Leonid was quick to offer his hand. He knew all too well what E3 mentors were capable of. "Pleased to meet you, sir."

"And you, young man," returned Andrew, the lack of enthusiasm well balanced between his voice and hand.

Without further discourse, the pretend father put his arm around his pretend daughter's shoulders and began leading her away. "Come along, sweetheart," he said pointedly, his eyes still fixed firmly on Leonid. "It's time for your class in *Sex and the Single Soul*."

"Bye," said Phoebe sadly, waving back over her head.

"See ya," groaned the young stallion, deflating in more ways than one.

# Chapter 9

The walk back toward their elevated beach house began in silence. Phoebe's mind was off in the ether somewhere. Andrew hoped she wasn't too mad at him. After all, it was for her own good. Leonid followed some ten paces behind, kicking sand and grumbling.

When they reached the Adirondack chairs, Andrew stopped to thank Phaidra. Their joint simulation of this *Spring Break* beach motif had accomplished what it was designed to, plus a little extra. And what a coincidence Phaidra turned out to be Gunther's creator/mentor. Who knew?

"I wasn't expecting your real-life protégé to suddenly pop into the picture," said Andrew with a wary smile.

"Neither did I," replied Phaidra apologetically. "I assumed Leonid would stay inside our house, but he sneaked out on me. And when he made his move toward Phoebe, I tried to stop him."

"Well, as things turned out, no harm was done…except maybe to Leonid's ego."

"Believe me, it needs a nick or two," said Phaidra, slowly shaking her head.

Leonid and his wounded pride plopped dejectedly back in his chair, purposely not looking at anyone. Andrew gave a final nod of thanks to his co-conspirator, turned his attention back to his inattentive Phoebe, and resumed shepherding her back to the beach house. As she was obviously still lost in thought of what might have been, he let her be.

Behind them, Phaidra's fading words were barely audible. "O for two, Leo," she said with an exaggerated sigh. "You'll never make the playoffs at this rate."

Halfway up the flight of wooden stairs to the sundeck, Phoebe suddenly perked up, turned around and challenged her mentor with no attempt to disguise her indignation: "What's this bullshit about a class on sex? Hell, I know what sex is."

"I know you do, honey," said Andrew, trying to soothe her ruffles. "But we've never discussed how different it is here on Earth-Two."

"Different?" Phoebe's tone started shifting toward interested. "How different?"

Still one step below her, his eyes level with hers, Andrew placed a fatherly hand on each side of her face. "Well, as you were beginning to find out, it's much more sensual, more stimulating than on Earth."

"That's for sure!" she exhaled, her expression turning fanciful with rolling eyes.

Andrew lowered his hands and gazed off into the distance, typical of any father confronted with having to give his daughter *the talk*. "It's called *spiritual coupling* here," he continued cautiously, "because besides the physical contact of your astral bodies and the...er... *coupling* of your respective...er...*implements*, your spirit energies can actually blend together, as well."

"So *that's* what was happening..." reflected Phoebe, dreamily hugging herself in a slow spin. "Would it have gotten even better if you hadn't...come along?"

"Possibly. And *definitely* with the right man."

"Well, damn it, then," hissed Phoebe, her mercurial mood snapping back to anger. "Thanks a lot, Andrew!"

Feeling the burn of her glare, Andrew led his darling ward by her cold shoulder up the last couple of steps to the sundeck, then into the great room. "It's something we do need to talk about," he said, as they crossed the parquet floor toward the white, carpeted stairs to the loft. "But not right now. You're overdue for a nap. We'll talk when you get up."

Like always, Andrew's touch and power of suggestion acted immediately on Phoebe's psyche. She nodded sleepily and turned to ascend the stairs.

"Hold on a second," said Andrew. Phoebe stopped and peered back over her shoulder. With a simple stare from the teacher, the student's red and white bikini transformed into a knee-length, baby-blue cotton nightie with little pink bunny rabbits. "There. That's better. Have a good sleep, sweetheart."

Phoebe languidly checked out the clothing, smiled in approval, and continued on up to the bedroom, her eyes already half shut. "Night," she said.

Watching her disappear into the loft, Andrew said softly to himself, "Sleep well, my sweet child..." Then as an afterthought, he added to himself, "...*my younger-self.*" That was so easy to forget sometimes.

31

# Chapter 10

Phoebe's creator walked slowly over to the large, glassless window at a right angle to the sundeck. He leaned on the sill and stared out at the colorful array of flowers and foliage along the hillside. It had been quite a day. The training. The intense sculpting that required both of them to stay deep in trance. Her tentative stroll down the beach. His having to prevent that libertine linebacker from popping his precious Phoebe's celestial cherry. At least it was gratifying to learn it was Leonid's second time striking out with her. And what was that vision Andrew had picked up from Phoebe's memory? Something about when Leonid was Gunther...getting killed by some bull who didn't appreciate his touch? Andrew grinned. It seemed Leonid's lack of sexual prowess was not limited to females...or even humans.

But behind the mirth, Andrew also had a strong sense of determination emanating from this Leonid entity. He felt this was not the last they would see of him.

Andrew shook his head back to the moment. There wasn't much left to do in preparation of Phoebe's fourth incarnation...this one scheduled for ancient Rome. A thorough scan of its probable events in The Deep Blue had revealed it was to be a very special one...a powerful one, full of exploits she would both love and hate. It would further define her character and her future. Phoebe would need every bit of her beauty and poise and guile to handle the basic blueprint he had laid out for her, plus all those inevitable random challenges that are never planned or expected.

If the primary events went accordingly—namely her marriage to a saddle maker, being accosted by two Gauls, and a last-minute rescue by a brave, handsome Roman soldier—there was a high probability that very champion with the soul name of Ethan would become the one great love of all her lives...past, present and future. In fact, all vibrations were pointing toward this affair becoming one for the ages.

For some relaxing meditation of his own, Andrew sauntered back out to the sundeck and shoulder-rolled into the hammock stretched between two vertical bamboo poles supporting the half-roof over the deck. Into mind naturally drifted thoughts of his first time with spiritual coupling on Earth-Two and how utterly fantastic it was. Her soul name was Tipphany. He called her Tiff. They were classmates in Advanced Telepathic Communication. She was gorgeous. But so was he back then, when it seemed important to be. They did it where all students do it: in the medatorium in the back of the library at Seth Hall. Sex was so open and guilt-free for them. And with that double-whammy of physical and spiritual meshing…well, it made sex on Earth seem like a conjugal visit with leftover meatloaf. He wondered whatever became of her. Last he knew she was headed for her sixth incarnation as some chieftain's son in the Congo. But that was eons ago.

That memory naturally flowed into recalling his last incarnation on the blue marble. He was a shaman in the mountain region of India, teaching his tribe the art of meditation and connecting with their inner-selves. Yes, it was that life which afforded him enough experience and wisdom to finally qualify going before the Earth-Three Council, where he passed the rigorous testing and was accepted into the realm and status of *E3*. What a great day that was! He had thought nothing could ever surpass it. And nothing ever did. That is, until that glorious time not so long ago.

When he created Phoebe.

# Chapter 11

The *birthing* of a new soul is one of the most intense and challenging endeavors in any level of the Cosmos. It's also quite miraculous, considering the first step involves making an exact copy of the original entity, resulting in two separate but identical souls.

The rules for this undertaking are stringent. First, only those obtaining the level of Earth-Three or higher are allowed to even make the attempt. Without an elevated awareness of the individual self, it would be counter-productive to duplicate it: two *adolescent* souls instead of just one. The blind leading the blind.

Secondly, the E3 must have the strength and capacity to immerse into the deepest of meditative trances and remain there for a long period with complete focus, while his replica is being developed. Not every E3 has the mental acuity to do this. It is as much an acquired skill as an inherited talent.

And finally, it requires an overwhelming desire to take on the heavy responsibility of caring for and mentoring the new self, especially when it is to begin as such an immature fledgling, as he had planned for Phoebe.

The procedure takes place at *The Splitting Image*, a modest, satirically-named little niche somewhere in the ether between Earth Three and Four. You get to this open-air, nondescript plateau only by mentally transporting yourself, which again is an extrinsic ability exclusive to E3s and above. And you can get the coordinates only from a bonafide sponsor, who is usually your own Earth-Four creator/mentor.

Creating a new self—a new soul—commands the assistance of two highly skilled Earth-Four directors. One goes along inside the Replication Pod to perform the actual cloning procedure. The other then accompanies the twin souls inside the Chamber of Exchange. This is where it is decided which of the original accumulated experiences, memories, and personality features the clone is allowed to keep, and which are to be deleted.

In Andrew's proceedings, the cloner called himself metaphorically, if not humorously, *Xerox*. He projected his image as a modest, middle-age humanoid with white hair, a small unisex body. He donned a long-sleeved, light-purple robe from neck to ground tied in at the waist.

The other E4—the one who performs the actual *deleting*—introduced himself as *Eraser*, presumably for the same attempt at a tongue-in-cheek metaphor. He or she looked quite similar to Xerox, with the exception of no hair and a dull-gray robe. During their off hours, what any E4 really looks like depends mostly on their present mood. And who knows what their real names are? There aren't many souls capable of conducting these services, so entities like Xerox and Eraser are always in high demand. Reservation must be made well in advance at The Splitting Image.

Like every other E3 who ever went through the process, Andrew did not remember anything about the initial trance and what happens while in the Replication Pod. So when the deep-purple, egg-shaped pod dissolved around him, and he blinked back into consciousness, the first thing Andrew recalled was lying on his back with Xerox on his left side and a replica of himself on his right. The two souls were identical in every way, from physical features to thoughts and memories. In amusement and complete awe, they locked eyes and grinned broadly at each other, as if in a mirror. In perfect unison they said aloud, "Hey, I am literally *beside* myself!" Xerox just smiled. He had heard that one a million times.

Now the other E4 took over. Eraser helped the twins to their feet and led them to the Chamber of Exchange, a circular, vertical booth of light-blue opaque crystal with just enough height and girth for the three of them. They wrapped arms around one another and touched heads as a prelude to blending spirits and entering another deep trance. This one Andrew did remember. The process was utterly amazing.

# Chapter 12

Spiritually they entered the ethereal region of Earth-Three designed especially for this purpose of identity exchange. But where they materialized was based strictly on a particular fond memory from one of Andrew's past lives. In this instance, Eraser had chosen a small gazebo on a plantation in Nineteenth Century Alabama. It was the actual sixteen-by-sixteen, open-air, cedar octagon where Andrew—as a married father of two young girls—had held many family meetings to iron out problems or to celebrate victories large and small. Eraser selected it to make sure the duplicate parties would feel comfortable and reassured.

Sitting on padded deck chairs and sipping mint juleps, they began a most energizing discussion of how best to design the new soul for the purposes the two Andrews had outlined. It was mostly a matter of deciding how much of the original Andrew's knowledge was to be purposely blocked from the offshoot and how much was to be left in place. Eraser listened intently to the twins' needs and desires, offering advice when appropriate, but leaving the final say to his clients. As in any corner of the Cosmos, it's always best to let souls make their own mistakes.

Once the decisions were completed, Andrew watched as his twin and Eraser stood up in the center of the gazebo and embrace forehead-to-forehead. The E4 put the clone into an even deeper trance, and went to work blocking the necessary features and memories. Andrew recalled how diligent Eraser was to both complete the design according to Andrew's wishes and to make sure the newbie was left with enough faculties to classify as an independent, viable entity, capable of existing and growing on its own.

Like most E3s taking on this challenge, Andrew had wanted a child to rear, a student to teach. He would so enjoy the role of mentor, giving a new part of himself the chance to develop naturally, independently, as it partook in that wondrous and exciting journey through the reincarnation cycle of Earth. But it was also Andrew's intention to mold this new self heavily toward the feminine. It seemed his own gender-oriented Yin-Yang was tipping too far toward the Yang. In the thirty lives Andrew had spent on Earth, he had found being male more gratifying. So much so, in fact, that his last five lives were all as men. Being finished with the reincarnation cycle, this E3 was encouraged by his own E4 creator/mentor to obtain a better balance and understanding of Yin, the female consciousness. This new self was hopefully to be that conduit.

So, just as Andrew had requested, his carbon copy retained most of the feminine qualities he had achieved over the millennia, and virtually none of the many masculine. He christened the new entity *Phoebe*, from the old Greek for "bright and pure."

Not needing any help with the physical aspects, Andrew then used his own acquired skills of matter-manipulation and artistry to easily alter his replicate's image into an adolescent of about ten with a plain but pleasing face. Certain orifices were not yet necessary, so by Earth standards Phoebe was asexual and a-anal. But when he gave it big, hazel eyes with honey-blonde hair tumbling down its back, then dressed it in a simple, white nightshirt, the final product was for all intents and purposes a sweet, innocent, little girl…an empty vessel waiting to be filled.

Standing there looking up at the redheaded man holding her hand and smiling down on her, young Phoebe had yet to do a single thing. Yet Andrew couldn't have been prouder. Or more in love.

In a rite of passage similar to a father walking his daughter to the playground for the first time, Andrew recalled wrapping his arms around his splintered little self and projected away from the Chamber of Exchange between Earth-Three and Earth-Four to materialize in what is commonly referred to as "The Ground Floor," a lower level of Earth-Two. It is here that all new souls are registered in the Hall of Records and given the classification of *E2-0*, signifying they are a citizen of Earth-Two, and have had *zero* incarnations on Earth. It is the creator's task to school his creation, and most do it right away. There is much to learn before taking that first step into the reincarnation cycle.

Once registered, Andrew had propelled himself and Phoebe to this secluded beach house with the Caribbean motif. He didn't want any distractions while he tutored his younger-self in preparation for life in that ominous, slow-spinning, low-frequency dimension affectionately known as *Old Earth*, or *Earth-One*, or just plain *Earth*.

# Chapter 13

Still in the sundeck's hammock, Andrew rolled onto his back and let out a wistful sigh, his thoughts moving past his creation of Phoebe to the close of those initial months of her schooling. It had been wonderful filling her hungry little mind with knowledge. But as those preliminary lessons drew to a close, a disturbing fact was staring him in the face with eyes of hazel green. In his eagerness to balance out his own Yin-Yang, Andrew had let his new creation retain plenty of his feminine qualities, but not nearly enough—if any—of his masculine. As a result, his sweet and innocent Phoebe was *too* sweet and innocent. And there was little chance of toughening her up in this beach house atmosphere of fatherly love.

Oh, he had tried. One time he thought he could frighten her by explaining there were these awful viruses and bacteria all over the Earth and how they could get inside you and make you feel yucky all over. Coughing, vomiting, fever blisters, clogged airways. Instead of showing concern or repulsion by such prospects, the ten-year-old had rolled her little astral body onto Andrew's lap. With her head on his chest she gave him a hug and said, "I won't mind those things, Andrew. I know you'll make them all better."

Another time he used his power of telepathic suggestion to trick her into thinking she had knocked over a carafe of Cabernet that left a big red stain on the white Persian rug. He scolded her like an angry parent to demonstrate how human beings often get angry and raise their voices, if not a hand. "Look what you did," he yelled, pointing at the red stain. "That rug is ruined and it's all your fault!"

Completely unfazed by the chastisement, young Phoebe—who had no concept of misconduct, much less guilt—had just smiled at him with those big hazel eyes and said, "Yes, it does look better with some pretty red color. Can we mix some yellow with it now? How about some blue?"

Andrew put in a telepathic nine-one-one plea to Eraser at the Chamber of Exchange, asking to bring Phoebe back to be infused with a few of his tougher, masculine traits. But Eraser replied they always frown on second chances like that. Taking twins souls deep into trance, listening to desires, analyzing, making suggestions (some of which Andrew obviously had not

38

heeded), then taking the clone even deeper to block some traits and allow others...all the while having to make certain the newbie met all the qualifications for being its own entity. This was tedious and energy sapping. Besides, there were some fifty-seven souls already on the waiting list.

Andrew realized he had little choice but to toss Phoebe into the reincarnation pool and let her learn to swim the hard way. Maybe with the right kind of life she could pick up enough masculine qualities to achieve a fairly decent balance in just one lifetime. It would have to be a dramatically virile one. The less-challenging, ease-into-it environment that most creators opt for their new soul's first life on Old Earth just wouldn't do in this case.

After days of much consideration and consternation—consulting his own mentor and numerous experts in the fields of psychology and anthropology— Andrew finally chose what he felt would be the right kind of human existence for his virtuous, stainless Phoebe. In a word, it would be very *educational*. The prospect of sending her through it, however, pulled at his heart.

He called her over to sit on his knee. "Are you ready for something really exciting?" he asked, brushing a few strands of honey-blonde hair off her plain, gentle face. He realized he had never given her eyebrows.

"Yes!" she replied, bouncing up and down. "What are we going to do?"

"We're going to a place that is soft and pretty. And we will meet two very nice people."

Phoebe smiled. "That sounds like fun. I've never known anybody other than you."

"Oh, there are many other people out there just waiting to meet you," sang Andrew." Many places to go. Many adventures to explore. Many new things for you to learn."

Phoebe's hazel eyes were wide with wonder and excitement, her lips quietly mouthing her racing thoughts. Andrew wrapped his arms around his precious younger-self. After what she was about to go through, he knew this would be the last time he would ever hug this particular little astral body with this particular pure spirit. He craned his neck to kiss the top of her head. Then with an ache in his soul, he gently placed his head against hers.

"Are you ready?"

She nodded with an anticipatory giggle.

"Then hang on, darling," he said with a quiver. "Because here we go."

# Chapter 14

The massive Transition Plaza is actually about half a megahertz closer to Earth than the Ground Floor. Among its many subdivisions is the Birth Wing—a thousand or so small, dreamlike rooms faintly lighted in pastel hues. Its walls and any piece of furniture or fixture within have about as much solidity as downy feathers. Include the delicate aroma of jasmine, plus a soft refrain of wind chimes backed up an angelic chorus, and one is instantly awash in a sense of safety and tranquility.

Each room is operated by two E3s, both far more clearly defined than their surroundings. One is skilled in the art of hypnosis, the other in reading The Deep Blue—the source of all knowledge in the Cosmos—to find the right fetus, place, and time to go.

BW-840—the cloister Andrew had lined up for Phoebe's first incarnation—was manned by Jonathan, a specialist in getting first-timers to relax, and then putting them into a deep trance for the journey. He was a distinguished-looking man of about forty with graying beard, salt and pepper hair, and gentle blue eyes. Like Andrew and most unpretentious E3s, he wore a half-sleeve toga, this one of brushed silver, drawn in at the waist by a platinum sash.

The other attendant was Mishca, a female psychic well-tuned into the last few centuries of Europe and North America. This contradictory free-spirit was imaging around thirty-five, pretty, with bright gray eyes and chestnut hair flowing halfway down her back. Tucked into a burnt-umber gypsy skirt, her white, low-cut peasant blouse accented a healthy chest. She wore more beaded necklaces and bracelets than were necessary, and the bells on her toes were a final statement to not take any of her appearance too seriously.

With a forced Hungarian accent Mishca proudly announced she had a prospect lined up for Phoebe, according to the parameters Andrew had set forth.

"Let's have a look," said Andrew, momentarily leaving his sleepy-eyed, opened-mouth Phoebe, and stepping over to sit beside Mishca on her fluffy, white bench of what resembled kitten fur. Thanks to the psychic's exceptional visionary and projection skills, together they gazed into the big aperture filling that part of the room, suspended in mid-air, just a few feet from their faces. At first it was just a glowing, swirling maelstrom of purple and white clouds. But in a moment it cleared to reveal a dynamic mosaic of probable events in the life of the prospective human.

Accepting the offer to pick and choose at his leisure, Andrew focused in at various stages of the prospective life, paying particular attention to the age of twelve and beyond. At age twenty-four, he saw the potential for a dramatic exit point for Phoebe and made a mental note to make sure nothing prevented it from happening. If things went as the future gestalt suggested, this would be a good time for her demise.

Andrew said he was done with the mosaic, and Mishca refocused her energies to have the circular aperture now reveal the fetus's double helix. It was a spiraling sequence of multiple, colorful orbs that only a well-trained E3 or above could understand and manipulate.

"Anything in the DNA you want to change?" asked Mishca.

Andrew conceptually ran through a short series of scenarios, and then replied, "No, I think that will work just fine. It's her first. The basics will do the job."

As they rose from the bench, a dubious Mishca queried, "Are you sure you want this life? It seems pretty harsh for a beginner." She motioned toward Phoebe. "Especially that babe in the woods."

"I'm sure," said Andrew, stepping over to scoop up his ward, who was now basically asleep on her feet, already in a half-trance by the soothing ambience. "I need to quickly add some masculinity to my darling little self here."

"Why?" queried Mishca. "What's the hurry?"

"No hurry," replied Andrew, carrying Phoebe over toward Jonathan. "It's just our nature."

With the preliminaries completed, Jonathan took Phoebe from Andrew and laid her down on what appeared to be a stream of gently flowing cotton candy in various hues of light-purple and violet. On a lower, fluffy cloud of his own, the psychoanalyst knelt beside the relaxed ten-year-old and started the ritual at a casual pace. He spoke quietly of the wonderful adventure Phoebe was about to experience…how much she would learn…how much she would grow…and very soon she would be back into the waiting, loving arms of her teacher.

For one last moment with her, Andrew moved around to the head of the stream and began gently massaging his younger-self's temples. Jonathan then commenced the systematic suggestions of classic hypnosis, telling Phoebe to close her eyes, relax all parts of her body, release all cares and thoughts.

"As you drift to sleep," said Jonathan, even softer now, "I want you to envision a beautiful, swirling circle of pretty colors opening in front of you. It's very pleasant. It's inviting you to enter. You're curious. You can't wait to see what's inside it."

The psychic Mishca, deep in trance now, was unlocking the actual vortex with a combination of thought-projection and energy-integration. She mentally directed it to Phoebe's unique frequency.

"Do you see it?" asked Jonathan.

Phoebe smiled and nodded weakly, deep in her own trance.

"I want you to move toward the opening. Feel how much it wants you to join with it. Now ease into it. Feel how pleasant it is there. Know its love for you."

The form that had been prepubescent Phoebe began dissolving on the cottony cloud. She was being irresistibly drawn to the fetus. Moving slowly at first, and picking up speed, the human dimension came closer and closer.

Suddenly, it was there, everywhere.

As Phoebe slammed headlong into the womb, time seemed to stop. There was no light, save an ambient pink hue. A low-pitch hum in her head descended even farther to a heavy droning before ending altogether. She could barely move, her arms and legs were stiff. She heard the rhythmic thumping of two hearts, one much faster than the other. She felt the peculiar, human sensations of warmth and moist. Consciousness, as she had known it, faded into nothingness.

Back at Birth Wing-840, the stream of gently flowing cotton candy in purples and violets was now empty. Phoebe was gone. Andrew's heart was proud and breaking.

# Chapter 15

That slide down the birth vortex landed Phoebe in an African-American male fetus in 1984 Cleveland, Ohio. Tyree, was born to a single mother who already had three children, all daughters, ages one, two and three. Neither contraception nor abstinence was in the young mother's realm of awareness.

Without a father's influence and a family barely scraping by on welfare and food stamps, by the age of twelve Tyree was in a street gang called the Sabers. There were ten other members at that time, all dark-skinned, a couple with some oriental blood mixed in, possibly Viet Nam war babies. The ages ranged up to twenty-one. The eldest and biggest was Devon, the leader, weighing in about two-twenty and topping out at six-three in his unlaced Reeboks. The large, crisscross scar gracing his forehead was from exiting his closed bedroom window headfirst at age fourteen, the impetus provided by his father with a request to not return. Devon told his minions it was from a knife fight with two Chicanos a year before he started the Sabers. The black-handled, eight-inch switchblade he was always cleaning his nails with left no doubt in anyone's mind of his story's plausibility.

Although the youngest and only a tween, Tyree was not the smallest member of the Sabers, already a hefty one-fifty, five-foot-eight. The perpetual anger in his coal-black eyes and curled lip made him seem bigger and older.

Devon saw potential in the young buck, and wasted no time in letting Tyree prove himself. The very afternoon of his asking to join, he was directed to the alley off Lincoln Street, where senior citizens often passed by to and from their visits to the market. The first hapless person to come along was an eighty-year-old, black lady wearing a gray, threadbare winter coat and a paisley scarf tied tightly over her snow-white head. Her path was suddenly blocked by Tyree's large, black hand in her face, holding Devon's open-bladed switchblade.

As if born to the part, without the slightest qualm he snatched the seventeen dollars she had produced from her well-worn pocketbook. He even made the sobbing, shaking woman empty her coin purse into his hand.

The initiation successfully completed, Tyree was welcomed into the Sabers.

By the age of fourteen—thanks to eating well and usually free at three neighborhood diners and two 7-Elevens—all too afraid to call the police when the gang would walk out without paying—Tyree had bulked up to only a few pounds and one inch less than Devon.

When a member of their rival gang, the Scars, was spotted shooting hoops at the Lincoln Elementary school yard, Tyree and the newest plebe named Willie were given the assignment of taking him out in a drive-by. Tyree was handed a 38-caliber Smith & Wesson revolver and Willie a Remington, twelve-gauge, sawed-off shotgun, both weapons part of the many profits the gang had procured during a burglary of Sammy's crack house on Becker Street the week before.

Being the first time Tyree had ever fired a gun, all six shots missed badly. The shotgun's pattern was so broad and the distance to the target so far, Willie was equally unsuccessful. Failure not being an option, Devon slapped the young Willie around until he was bleeding from his nose and mouth. When it came Tyree's turn for punishment, Devon's authoritative face was met nose-to-nose by two black, doll-like eyes and a sneer higher and wider than usual, suggesting Devon should think twice before messing with him. So Tyree was let off with a stern warning.

He was lucky. Devon, that is.

# Chapter 16

Two years later Tyree cracked a broom handle across the head of a fellow Saber during an argument over who had to settle for sloppy-seconds with one of the gang's groupies. Devon knew this time he *had* to punish Tyree or lose face with the gang. But since Tyree was now the same size as Devon, and those eyes were as cold and demonic as ever, the leader was smart enough to realize getting physical with Tyree could easily produce embarrassing results. So Devon took the chance Tyree still respected the gang's hierarchy and boisterously ordered him to do surveillance on the Scars headquarters for the next twenty-four hours. Then, just in case that chastisement didn't set well with Tyree, Devon took him aside and with an arm around his shoulders whispered, "Listen, I think those chicken shit Chicanos may be up to something. I needs my best man to find out what."

Devon was right: it didn't set well with Tyree. At the end of his watch—which consisted of sleeping for twelve hours at home and another ten in front of the television—the sixteen-year-old falsely reported to Devon that in the middle of the night he saw someone hide something in a bush behind the Scar's headquarters over on Eleanor Avenue.

"What it look like?" asked Devon quietly, again taking Tyree off to one side.

"I dunno," shrugged Tyree, "kinda like a leather bag or somethin'."

"Can yo tells me exactly where?" asked Devon real friendly like.

"Don't know 'bout dat," bluffed the clever teen. "Would hafta show ya."

"Let's keep this just 'tween yo and me, hear?" said Devon, with that brotherly arm around Tyree. "We'll go out there tonight and look fo it."

"You da boss," grinned Tyree.

The two conspirators met up at midnight at the prearranged spot on the edge of Scar's territory, and Tyree led his gang's leader down a dark alley between buildings in the projects. He stopped at a hedge row of evergreens and pointed at the base of one in particular. When the greedy Devon knelt down to search for the object, Tyree jerked the familiar .38 revolver out of the back of Devon's pants and in one motion put a bullet in the back of his head.

45

The Scars of course got the blame, and via attrition Tyree was promoted to Lieutenant, fourth in command.

By the age of twenty, the sociopathic, baby soul had lied, cheated and murdered his way up the totem to gang leader. He was lord over twelve-to-fifteen members, depending on how many were in the hospital or lock-up at any given moment. The Sabers had built up a mediocre crack-cocaine business, laying claim to and defending well a ten square block area on Cleveland's east side. Their heartless, six-foot-three, two-hundred-pound leader with a .38 Smith tucked in his Levis and eyes that could back down a grizzly pretty much got what he wanted when he wanted.

Three days before his twenty-fifth birthday Tyree got something he didn't want. The local market was out of his Marlboro brand of cigarettes, so in a huff and nicotine fit he foolishly walked alone down Franklin Avenue—the north edge of Scar's territory—to try another store. Halfway there he was spotted by a Scar captain. Halfway back he was cut down in a drive-by with an Israeli-made Uzi. He died right there on the sidewalk, on schedule, in a pool of his own blood.

No one even bothered to call the police.

# Chapter 17

An out-of-focus Tyree picked himself up and continued walking along Franklin Avenue, but it seemed to be changing before his eyes. The sound and motion of the heavy rush hour traffic dissolved, as did the chain link fence along the school's playground on his left. The line of store fronts up ahead got brighter and brighter until he had to squint from the pain.

From Andrew's perspective, Tyree walked into the Reception Station's specially-designed room with the cocky swagger he had long used on Earth. He appeared to be dressed in the same gray hoodie with blue jeans and loosely-tied basketball shoes he was wearing just a few moments ago when gunned down on Franklin.

Andrew was well aware that Tyree's religious knowledge was pretty much limited to God's last name being *Dammit* and Jesus having two middle names: *H.* and *Fucking*. With little concept of a hereafter, Tyree wouldn't be expecting much in the crossover…if he even knew what had just happened to his physical body. So, thanks to Andrew's artistry and homework, the surroundings closely resembled the second floor of the derelict tenement building the Sabers gang used as headquarters.

When Tyree saw Andrew standing there, he thought the man looked familiar. "Where I knows yo from, bro?" he queried, sleepily scanning the hard-faced, white dude dressed in khaki Dockers, a blue denim shirt with the sleeves rolled up, and a pair of light-gray sneakers. "And whatcha doin' in our digs?"

Tyree figured the muscular honky was about thirty and a couple inches and pounds bigger than he was. He had no way of knowing Andrew had just *pumped* himself *up* to outdo Tyree's physique for the occasion. The idea was to make sure the once-fearless gang leader had at least a little respect for his host.

"I came to talk to you," said Andrew calmly, keeping his distance, hands on hips.

"Yo a cop?" challenged Tyree.

"Nope," said the guy who definitely looked like a cop.

47

"Den whadafuck yo wants to jaw wid me 'bout, honky?" asked the defiant, but getting nervous young soul.

Saying nothing more, the big-jawed teacher with reddish hair now in a Marine crew-cut stepped up to come face-to-fuzzy with his wayward student. Andrew grabbed him firmly by his indistinct, celestial ears, looked him squarely in the dusky, ethereal eyes, and said, "We've got a lot of work to do, Tyree."

With that warning, Andrew wrapped his powerful arms tightly around a surprised and speechless Tyree and whisked them both away from the phony tenement building...in a reserved room of the Reception Station...to the beach house on the picturesque shores of the Caribbean.

# Chapter 18

The confused essence of Tyree sat on a swivel stool at the breakfast bar, his head slowly swinging from right to left, up to down, like a bobble head in slow motion. The place looked familiar. Then again, maybe it didn't. That honky behind the bar seemed to be making something with root beer and ice cream. Then again, maybe he wasn't.

Andrew set the float down in front of his progeny and said casually, "Before you were Tyree you were a young child of ten. You were white. Female. Your real name is Phoebe."

"Say what?!" snorted half-asleep Tyree, looking around to see if the dude was talking to some little white girl in the room.

"I'm talking about you, sweetheart," said Andrew a little sarcastically, tapping him on his nappy head.

Tyree inspected his hands and arms for any such evidence. Through the translucent haze he did notice his skin color seemed a bit on the lighter side of ebony. But he wasn't about to admit it.

Andrew walked around the bar, took Tyree by the upper arm, and eased him toward the white carpeted stairwell leading up to the bedroom. Any such placement of a cracker's hands upon his person would normally have resulted in bloodshed. But Tyree went along passively. He was too tired to resist, plus he felt a strange, pleasant feeling from the contact.

*What was there about this dude…and this place?*

In one corner of the bedroom stood the three-foot-tall, gray marble pedestal with a small, mahogany box on it. It looked familiar. Phoebe had often asked about it, but was not allowed to touch. She tried several times to open it anyway, but the latch wouldn't give. In another corner was the wardrobe made of antique ash with a brass handle on each door she also was forbidden to open. Those earlier attempts were unsuccessful, as well.

Andrew placed Tyree in front of the wardrobe, shook him gently to get his attention and said, "Look there. I want you to see something." Andrew left the wobbling Saber and walked over to open the double doors. Inside was a full length mirror.

When Tyree saw the apparition in the glass, he jumped back, bending at the knees and waist in a defensive stance, fists cocked. "What the fuck is that?!" he gasped, now wide-eyed. The part-Phoebe-mostly-Tyree image was an eerie conglomeration of a medium-framed mulatto with brown, kinky hair, dark brown eyes, a moderately-wide nose, and an upper lip owning half a sneer.

"That's you," replied Andrew, matter-of-factly.

"Eat shit and die, muddafucka," he howled, doing a three-sixty to check for that other person somewhere behind him. No goddam way!"

Oh, how Andrew wanted to rap one across that potty mouth!

Tyree raised his right fist in his gang's fraternal greeting to test the ghostly image. It followed right along. "No way!" he said more adamantly. He brought both arms up and flexed his biceps. The image followed suit. "C'mon, man!" He gave himself the finger. So did the phantasm in the mirror. "What kinda bullshit is this?"

Andrew stepped around behind his now-even-shorter protégé and placed a hand on each shoulder, bending down to put his head right beside Tyree's. "You were Tyree on Earth," he said. "But now you're dead. You are in Heaven and your real name is Phoebe. You're my...a...*daughter*."

Tyree just stared in the mirror at his pulsating, blurry image, which now, in contrast, had a crystal-clear, red-headed man with blue-gray eyes right behind him. Dazed, foggy and unable to fathom what this was all about, he was soon reduced to timidly fiddling with the drawstrings of his hoodie, like a frightened little girl.

"If you will concentrate," continued Andrew, employing his power of suggestion, "you can start to see more of the real you. You can see your blonde hair. You can see your white skin. You can see your hazel eyes."

Tyree looked closer, squinting. To his amazement, more vivid hints of those features began to materialize in the mirror. And his outline became a touch more defined.

"Sheeet," was all he could say.

# Chapter 19

Andrew took his stunned student by the arm again and led him back downstairs and across the living area to the sundeck. Once at the railing, he presented the beautiful panorama of the shimmering Caribbean Sea and white sand of Magens Bay. "Look familiar?" he asked, watching his progeny's face for a reaction.

At first, Tyree seemed amazed by the breathtaking scenery. But the more he drank in the sea, the sand, and the sky, the more recognition spread across his face. Andrew watched the brown skin slowly turn to tan, the brown eyes to a mottled hazel-gray, the brown kinky hair to a straighter, longer, lighter brown.

"Look at me, Phoebe," instructed Andrew, gently turning Tyree's head with his right hand. "You know my name. What is it?"

Tyree studied the man's face. An even stronger hint of familiarity flickered in his eyes. "An-a-..." he said with scrunched brow, reaching for the rest.

"You're close," encouraged Andrew. "Keep trying."

"Andru-," he said carefully, then with growing confidence, "Andrew?"

"Very good."

With that name, Tyree suddenly recalled the man's earlier claim. "You're my old man?" he asked with extra sneer.

"That's right," smiled Andrew, starting to put a fatherly arm around his prodigal, confused *daughter*. Tyree brought both forearms up to block the contact. Andrew just smiled knowingly, and abandoned the attempt.

Although some of Phoebe's young, innocent mind was returning, Andrew knew she would not be the same as before. Earlier in the Chamber of Exchange she had been allowed to keep that modicum of Andrew's feminine traits and abilities, but with memory slots left very much empty. And although her earlier times here at the beach house had begun to fill in some of those slots with her own, fond memories of a fun-to-learn, carefree kind of childhood, now more of that void was being occupied by all the experiences

51

from that dark life on the mean streets of Cleveland. In that respect, she was still identifying mostly with Tyree.

They lingered a little longer at the railing, and then he bid Tyree to sit down on the two-person porch swing at one end of the sundeck. Once seated, Andrew maneuvered behind him, reached over the back of the swing and placed both hands on the sides of Tyree's head. He tilted it gently backwards and pressed his own forehead firmly against Tyree's. An accomplished master of relaxed concentration, Andrew immediately blocked out all external stimuli and focused completely on connecting psychically with the Tyree/Phoebe version of his younger self. When his desire to do so reached the required level, the two went into a deep trance. For the first time since Phoebe's creation, their spirits were as one.

As much as Andrew wanted to bring all of Phoebe's previous, sweet persona to the fore, it was paramount to leave a lot of Tyree intact, at least for the upcoming training purposes. Wicked as he seemed to be, the lessons Phoebe learned while being Tyree were a great—albeit harsh—beginning to her education. It had achieved some of the balance he was hoping for: the toughening up of his too sweet, *daughter*.

The current *image*, however, was another matter. Andrew had about all he cared to see of Tyree's narrow-set eyes, perpetual sneer, and slow, *I'm bad* swagger. So, with his powers of thought and artistic touch, he erased all remaining physical traces of the twenty-four-year-old ex-leader of the Sabers, including his clothing. He then enhanced the original girlish face to a prettier, more mature thirteen. He returned her hazel eyes—this time with eyebrows— and gave her the beginnings of womanhood. She needed to identify more with that gender now, as Phoebe—now endowed with what seemed to be plenty of Yang—was going to be a she for many of the next incarnations.

For added feminine effect—something the Tyree portion wouldn't even notice—he dressed her in a virgin-white, floor-length, flannel nightgown with fuzzy pink slippers. After the unpleasant reviews she was about to go through at the breakfast bar, Tyree/Phoebe would be requiring a number of therapeutic naps.

# Chapter 20

Andrew brought himself out of trance, with his younger-self joining the land of the focused shortly thereafter. Taking one of Phoebe/Tyree's light-skinned hands, he led her back into the open-air great room. As they walked, he noticed that *she*—now looking every bit a white, teenage girl in a very youthful nightgown and slippers—was still strutting a little like Tyree. Andrew had to bite his lip. "Well," he mouthed to himself, "you can take the boy out of the hood..." then he added sinisterly, "but you *can* some of the hood out of the *girl*."

Andrew sat his ward back down at the breakfast bar and their waiting root beer floats. Moving around to stand on the other side, he pushed the float toward Phoebe and took his own glass in hand.

"So, what do you think of your first life on Earth?" he asked casually, taking a spoonful of ice cream. He had to keep reminding himself that although she now looked like a cute teenage girl, inside there was still a lot of Tyree.

Phoebe pondered the question as she sucked on the straw. A little surprised by how good it tasted, she released the straw and wiped a drip off her lower lip with the back of her hand. "Very interesting place," she began, with an objective tone that revealed neither Phoebe nor Tyree. "The sensations of hot and cold shoot right through you. So does pain. Having to eat and drink is interesting, shitting and pissing isn't." She took another pensive draw on the straw. "Getting high is a blast, coming down sucks. People are mad a lot. Scared. They hurt each other, sometimes even kill. Money is important. Sex feels good. Anything else you want to know, Red?"

"Did you steal anything from people?" was the next loaded question.

"Sure," she said matter-of-factly. "All the time."

"Did you hurt anybody?"

"Yeah, quite a few." The tone was shifting heavily toward Tyree.

"Did you kill anybody?"

"Some, I guess. Why? What's it to ya?"

"Do you feel guilty about killing those people?"

53

Phoebe thought a moment, then stated sincerely with a hint of sneer, "I don't understand the question."

In their purest form, all E2s lack any semblance of a conscience. In truth, if no soul ever went to Earth, there would be no such thing as guilt anywhere in this corner of the Cosmos. It is a commodity manufactured originally in that low frequency dimension as a means to control each other, to keep people from doing harm to one another. This is vital, because it enables a bunch of frightened souls to coexist in less than ideal conditions of which they believe they are powerless. No wonder it is always such a joy to die and come home to the safety and serenity of Earth-Two.

But if one is to use the reincarnation cycle of Earth, it's mandatory to grasp the concept of right and wrong. Laws must be followed, if one doesn't wish to come zooming back to Earth-Two at a very early age life after life. This idea was purposely blocked from Phoebe in the Chamber of Exchange. As Eraser had suggested, it would be better if Andrew's younger-self learned such things on her own, in the school of hard knocks. And dropping that innocent soul into Tyree was certainly that, even though it taught her practically nothing about guilt.

That was about to change.

Andrew directed Phoebe's attention to the fifty-five-inch, Samsung flat-screen on the wall behind the bar, where normally a large mirror might be. She knew what the television screen was, having burgled a few in Cleveland. Then, with a technique only an E3 proficient in thought projection can do, he dipped into The Deep Blue, fetched the sequence of Tyree mugging the old woman, and put it on the screen. He selected the perspective of a third person at street level.

"Remember this?" asked Andrew.

54

# Chapter 21

Phoebe was amazed at what she was seeing and how she was seeing it. "Jesus! That's me. How the hell did you do that?!"

Andrew ignored the question and repeated his own.

"That's who I had to mug for my initiation into the Sabers," she said with no emotion, as if pointing at a photo in the family album. "The old bitch only had a few bucks."

The image zoomed in on the terrified face of the eighty-year-old, social-security-dependent woman. Andrew cranked up the volume so her pleas and sobs were clearly heard. He then turned it down again so Phoebe could hear his next question clearly.

"What does her anguish mean to you?"

"It means I was doing my assignment," Phoebe said with a shrug. "The way Devon showed us. I had the old woman so spooked she gladly coughed up her cash."

"What do you think she was feeling right here?" asked Andrew.

"Well, how the hell should I know?" countered Phoebe quickly, a lot of Saber still coming through. "I'm not the bitch."

Again it pained Andrew to hear such crassness come from such a sweet looking mouth. He casually slipped off his stool and moved in behind Phoebe. Thinking she might be in for a fight, she instinctively tried to spin around to defend herself. But he had the smaller girl by the shoulders before she could fully pivot. And the sensation from his gentle hands indicated this Andrew dude wasn't necessarily mad.

Still ahold of her from behind, Andrew bent forward to place his forehead against the back of Phoebe's head. "Close your eyes," he said softly. "Relax and let yourself drift away with me, as we did out on the sundeck." The small head fell limp, immediately under his influence. "Only his time I want you to go inside that old woman you saw on the screen. I want you to become a part of her. I want you to feel what she is feeling as she is being robbed." He waited a moment and asked, "Are you there?"

When he felt Phoebe's head nod ever so slightly, he projected his thoughts with more intensity, taking Phoebe deep into the old woman's consciousness.

"Do you feel her terror, Phoebe?" he whispered. "Do you feel her fear of being hurt or killed?"

Phoebe nodded a little harder, trembling slightly. Andrew let the scenario play on until a soft *gasp* signaled the message was getting across to his juvenile delinquent. He slowly coaxed Phoebe out of her trance, lifted his head from hers, and walked back behind the bar. With elbows on the counter and his face just two feet from hers, he asked, "So what do you think about that woman's feelings now?"

Phoebe shook her head back to reality. Her hazel eyes danced between his and the television screen, which now was showing the old woman on her knees, face in hands, crying in the aftermath. "That didn't feel so good," she said with a hint of sadness. "It wasn't like anything I've felt before. Even when I got into fights I wasn't at all afraid. I was mostly just mad. I wanted to pound on the asshole and protect myself. I didn't feel any kind of fear the way she did."

Andrew let Phoebe stew in her own juices awhile before leading her back upstairs for a badly needed sleep. As he tucked in the conflicted young soul, he said, "A nap will do you good. Many answers will be there when you awake." He brushed aside the honey-blonde hair and kissed her white forehead. Phoebe didn't react. "Anything you need before I go? he asked quietly."

"Yeah," she said, pointing toward the corner. "What the hell is in that goddamn box?"

# Chapter 22

In the following weeks Andrew used the wide screen frequently, going through each pertinent episode of Tyree's wanton life of crime, from the burglaries and muggings to rapes and murders. He would have shown scenes when Tyree was given love or displayed any of his own, but there were none. Even Tyree's mother (a first time Earthling herself) was sadly lacking in compassion for anyone but herself. And while Tyree thoroughly enjoyed his numerous sexual encounters, they all centered strictly on his narcissistic, self-gratification. No love or empathy was ever involved. Pretty much as Andrew had planned.

Each class would end with a nap and the same question about the box. Andrew knew these sessions could accomplish only so much. For Phoebe to truly understand caring about others and the basic concept of right and wrong, she needed to learn it first-hand. She needed another visit to Earth.

On the last day of class Andrew treated his young Phoebe-Tyree composite to the contents of that mysterious box. He brought it downstairs to her as she sat waiting anxiously at the breakfast bar, spinning around on the swivel stool. He had her dressed in blue shorts and a yellow tank top with white sneakers.

She had envisioned the box containing anything from a diamond necklace to a magic wand to a pearl handled pistol. So, with great expectations she flipped up the gold latch and opened the lid.

It was only a small scroll.

"What the fu…heck is this?" she asked indignantly, at least trying to be a little more vigilant with her language, as her mentor had requested.

"Go ahead, read it," encouraged Andrew.

With a sigh of exaggerated disappointment, Phoebe unrolled the parchment, scanned it, wrinkled her forehead, and read with no enthusiasm, *"Earth is your schoolroom."*

She repeated it to herself, then lifted her eyes to meet Andrew's. "Huh?" she said, gesturing with a listless sweep of her arm around the bamboo house's great room. "I thought *this* was my schoolroom. At least, there's sure been a hell of a lot of schooling going on here."

Andrew motioned for them both to sit down on the tan, patent leather couch. Twisting sideways to face Phoebe, the slender man in the khaki Dockers and white pullover sweater placed his left arm on the back of the couch and his right hand on her knee. She sat in the basic, cross-legged yoga pose, staring down at the scroll, as if the message might begin making sense.

"Phoebe," he started, wanting to call her sweetheart, but knowing the Tyree portion wouldn't care much for any term of endearment, "this beach house is indeed where you have learned a lot. But we've used it mostly for discussing and reviewing what you experienced on Earth as Tyree. And we will use it again after more of your incarnations. But Earth is a great place to learn about many things you need to know, to grow, to become wiser."

"Why can't I learn these things right here on Earth-Two?" she asked, still irritated. "From what little you've told me about it, and the even less I've seen, it's a pretty cool place."

"You could to some degree. But you can't really learn about Earth without being on Earth.

"So what's the big deal about being on Earth, anyway?" whined the Phoebe portion. "You just say I need to go without telling me why."

Andrew looked at the ceiling to find the right words. "It's where most Earth-Twos go to experience different things in a way they can't experience them here on Earth-Two," he said, trying to keep his explanations at an elementary level. "You could say you need lives on cold Earth to show you how warm our reality is here. Earth teaches this by contrast. It is your best classroom."

# Chapter 23

Realizing his student was still as young as she looked, Andrew ran through a list of examples in his mind, searching for one that Phoebe/Tyree could better understand. "Here on Earth-Two," he finally continued, finding one he liked, "did you know you can have just about anything you want? And without paying for it?"

"Really?!" said a skeptical Phoebe. "For free? Anything?" She had only Tyree's experiences on Earth to call upon. There, if you wanted something, you had to steal it. Or as a last resort, pay for it with stolen money.

"Yes, anything."

"What could I get?"

"Whatever you want. Go ahead, ask for something."

Phoebe slipped off the couch and started walking in strange, wide circle…a cute little girl with a gangbanger's swagger.

"Oh man, I don't know…" she said, debating. "There's so much. So many things." She paused by the breakfast bar. It reminded her of Tuffy's Tavern, Tyree's favorite hangout with the beer glasses and popcorn and ashtrays. *Ashtrays.* They reminded her of the cigarettes Tyree was on his way to buy when he was mowed down by the Scars. "I know," Phoebe chimed. "Cigarettes. Marlboro Reds. Soft pack."

"Easy enough," said Andrew. "But are you sure? Cigarettes can be bad for your health. Remember, they got you killed in Cleveland."

"Just give me the goddamn cigarettes," she said, impatiently snapping her fingers, almost salivating.

Andrew plucked them out of thin air and tossed the pack to his delinquent daughter. They had been his favorite too during one of his incarnations long ago.

Feverishly she tore open the pack and popped one between her lips. "Light."

Andrew stepped closer to ignite her cigarette with the flame coming out of his fingertip. Too engrossed with the prospect of a long-overdue nicotine buzz to notice any of this magic act, she took a big draw and inhaled deeply.

Immediately her eyes pinched shut as she hacked a plume of smoke signals across the room.

"Holy shit!" she wheezed between coughs. "That is strong! What the fuck?!"

Andrew couldn't hold back an outright guffaw. It may have been Tyree's mind and memory that wanted the cigarette, but they were Phoebe's clean, untarnished, thirteen-year-old lungs.

She gladly allowed Andrew to take the Marlboro from her fingers and flick it somewhere into neverland. He waited until her hacking subsided, then asked, "Is that all you want? Wouldn't you like something a little more...expensive?"

Phoebe was back to circling and strutting again. "More expensive, huh...let's see...cough...okay, how about a fur coat? A *mink* fur coat. Cough. A *white* mink fur coat."

Andrew had to consider how much of that request came from Phoebe and how much from Tyree. But since Phoebe on her own wouldn't have much knowledge of such luxurious outerwear, he suspected it was all from Tyree. A quick mental peek inside Phoebe's memory from 2008 Cleveland provided the answer.

Andrew visualized. When he opened his eyes his protégé was encased in a beautiful, white coat of the finest albino mink, complete with floppy hood and a wide black belt. Andrew thought it was befitting attire for the leader of the Sabers, if not an uptown pimp.

"Absolutely awesome!" gasped Phoebe.

Andrew watched the elated youngster parade around the room, inspecting every visible inch, while rubbing her hands and face over the soft texture. When he thought it possible to have her attention again, the wise mentor continued the lesson.

# Chapter 24

"You really appreciate that, don't you?" offered Andrew.

"I sure as hell do," sang the Tyree side of Phoebe. "I had wanted a coat like this ever since I saw Germane wearing one the last time I went to his place to buy our monthly stash of crack."

"So, why didn't you get one?"

"You gotta be jivin' me, man," hooted the black man in a white girl's body. "It takes big bucks to buy shit like this on Earth. And tough to steal."

"So, you think it's rather nice here on Earth-Two, where you can have things like this anytime you want them, and for free."

"Damn straight!"

Andrew placed both hands on the sides of his student's face and looked squarely into the hazel eyes. Here came the lesson.

"Do you realize that the main reason you are so pleased with this coat right now is because you've just returned from a place where it wasn't possible to have anything this nice just by wishing for it?"

"I guess that's right," mused Phoebe. "So?"

"*So*, if I had given you the coat *before* your trip to Earth, do you think you would have appreciated it as much as you do now?"

She gave that some further thought. It made sense. "Probably not."

"This is one reason you E2s go to Earth: to learn to appreciate how much better you have it here. It builds character. It builds your spirits. And it's mandatory, if you ever want to make it to Earth-Three status, like me." Andrew dropped his hands from her face and walked away toward a window.

"You said that is *one* reason," she called after him. "What are the others?"

Andrew stopped and turned to face her, leaning against the window sill. "You probably wouldn't understand them yet," he sighed, baiting his student.

"Try me," challenged Phoebe, moving in to get the answer.

After a calculated period of thought, Andrew said, "Okay. All souls— you and me included—are created curious. We can't help ourselves. We have this inherent urge to explore, to learn new things."

"I'm not very curious," stated Phoebe with a shrug.

"No? Why do you think you've been dying to know what's in the mahogany box for so long? A few minutes ago you were curious to see what you could get for free. You just now followed me to the window to find out what other reasons there are for visiting Earth."

"Okay, okay," conceded Phoebe, sheepishly. "I see your point. So, what's that got to do with going to Earth time and again?"

"Very simple, my friend. The Earth dimension, with all its faults and slow humming frequency, is just too fascinating of a frontier to pass up. It's a veritable cornucopia of experiences and adventures just waiting for us to explore. Think of all you learned…how much wiser you are after being in the Earth dimension as Tyree."

That hit home. Phoebe could feel the expansion her mind had experienced from those twenty-four years on planet Earth. Some voids being filled. She felt wiser, more certain of herself.

No more questions came from Phoebe, bordering on overload. She plopped back down on the couch, seemingly contemplating the concepts. Andrew let her sit there a while, rubbing her cheek on the soft fur over and over. If nothing else, it was bringing more of Phoebe through than Tyree. Andrew hoped some of his demonstration and answers were sinking into his sweet, thirteen-year-old murderer.

# Chapter 25

After a while, Phoebe rolled onto her back and crossed her ankles over the back of the couch. She blinked at her father and said pointedly, "By the way, I've been meaning to ask you where I came from. The first memories I have are of this house. Nothing before. How did I get here?"

Andrew wasn't particularly surprised by the query. It was inevitable sooner or later. Better to address it later. "There are many things I can't explain to you right now, because you're too inexperienced to understand," he said, sitting beside her. This time there was no baiting. Her eyes narrowed on his. Her lip started to curl into that sordid Tyree sneer. Andrew felt he had to toss her something conciliatory before the leader of the pack was back and ready to rob the Seven-Eleven. "But you will understand after a few more trips to the Earth dimension. I promise."

Phoebe's face lifted a little. She was beginning to relish the idea of going back to that violent planet. Exploring. Getting more answers. Filling more voids. "Well then," she said, dropping her legs across her tutor's lap and sitting upright, "what *is* my next life going to be?"

The hint of enthusiasm in her voice pleased Andrew. "I'm glad you asked," he said with his own tone of excitement. "As a matter of fact, I've found the perfect human for you."

"Cool. Tell me about it."

"Sorry. No."

Phoebe was stunned by yet another rejection. "C'mon! Why the fu--. Why not?"

"Take it easy," soothed Andrew, patting her knee. "There's no point telling you, because once you go down the birth canal again you won't remember anything anyway. Just as when you went in to become Tyree."

"Yeah, I was wondering why we don't remember that?" said Phoebe, the anger spinning momentarily back to good old *curiosity*.

"Because that's the way some folks a lot smarter than we are designed it to work," he said. "While experiencing an incarnation, you become that human being. Its brain becomes your conscious mind. You are locked in it. You are purposely blocked from knowing who you really are. Otherwise, you wouldn't get the full benefit of the experience...of being hungry...being cold...being afraid. If you knew all these human struggles were just a matinee creature-feature from which you could walk out at any time into the sunshine, you wouldn't take any of it seriously."

"There'd be no reason in even going," contributed Phoebe, obviously getting the point.

"Exactly," piped a proud Andrew. Then he added with a wry smile. "Besides, if all the souls visiting Earth suddenly remembered how great it is here, there would be mass suicides, followed by a stampeding exodus back here to Earth-Two. We'd be overrun by fuzzy apparitions literally dying to get away from Earth."

Phoebe laughed and joined in, "They'd be crawling all over our beach and sundeck."

"We'd have to chase them off with cattle prods," grinned Andrew.

The two shared a moment of amusement and a small connection. Andrew completely understood the feeling. Phoebe wasn't sure.

It was time. The soul who had undergone thirty lives in the earth dimension rose to his feet, walked to the center of the great room and beckoned his E2-1 to join him. She left the fur coat behind. It quickly disappeared.

As he watched the image of a pretty, thirteen-year-old girl slip off the couch and walk toward him in shorts and t-shirt, that comical half-swagger helped Andrew remember once again that the twenty-four-year-old gang leader was still very much in there.

It became even more evident when—before taking the waiting embrace—Phoebe/Tyree looked up at the man with ivory skin and reddish Caesar hair and asked, "Will I enjoy it? My next life?"

Andrew just smiled patronizingly.

"C'mon, you old fart," she said with an impatient Tyree tone. "You won't tell me where I came from. You won't tell me where I'm going. You can at least tell me if it will be enjoyable, damn it."

Again, that mouth. Andrew bent down to place his lips right next to his wayward daughter's ear, so the sinister smile on his lips would not betray his words.

"You will learn a lot, my dear student," he whispered. "A *lot*."

# Chapter 26

The human being Andrew very thoughtfully got Phoebe into for incarnation number two was a female named Gretchen in the late sixteen-hundreds. Her parents owned a dairy farm near Berchtesgaden in southern Germany, which she and her two younger siblings helped work when not in school. The chores consisted of milking, forking in hay, and, when they were older or bad, scooping up manure. Gretchen helped her mother in the kitchen, as well. Another job she didn't much care for.

Her parents were honest, loving people, and were very strict, demanding their children—and especially Gretchen, the oldest—to have exemplary manners, temperaments, and above all else, morals. Consequently, the headstrong, self-absorbed girl with plenty of Tyree's less-than-desirable traits left intact frequently found herself over a parent's knee, receiving the business end of a wooden spoon or hairbrush on her bare behind.

The first chastisement for the brown-eyed brunette came at age four when she defiantly took an icebox cookie off the kitchen table after being told not to. That single punishment didn't do anything to alter her larcenous ways, but she didn't care much for icebox cookies thereafter. It took a couple more incidents of thievery and punishment before she began to see a connection.

Her next lesson dealt with violence. Gretchen was seven when her younger brother, Hermann, pulled her hair so hard a few strands came out by the roots. Gretchen retaliated by fetching a nearby copy of Nietzsche off the end table by her father's chair and placing it forcefully upside Hermann's head, knocking him head over heels. That earned her the wooden spoon and her first taste of shoveling cow manure...with a spatula. Gretchen decided that maybe she shouldn't hit Hermann anymore.

Slapping her sister, Hilda, a few months later for calling her an ugly poop face produced the hairbrush plus some needed clarity that the previous spanking wasn't about striking Hermann in particular, rather the act of violence itself. This lesson, as well, was slowly sinking in.

It really hit home at age twelve when, after lighting her father's pipe for him on the front porch one summer evening, she tossed the still-burning match onto the family cat as it nuzzled against her stockings. She didn't have feelings one way or another for the feline. She was just curious what would happen when fire met fur. Gretchen quickly found out when the cat streaked off across the yard, screeching and trailing a plume of smoke and pungent burning hair. She learned even more when banished to her room for a month, allowed out only for meals, school, and to do double chores. She was also giving the sole responsibility of nursing the cat—which lost a patch of fur and suffered a second-degree burn—back to health. That punishment certainly made Gretchen think twice before causing harm to another creature or sibling.

Gretchen entered her teen years as a rather plain-looking, big boned fraulein with long braided hair, a reddish complexion with plenty of pimples, and an overly-mature pair of mammary glands. It was the latter that attracted some of the boys, one in particular named Gunther, who lived just a half mile down the road and seemed to have quite the infatuation with her. Awkward flirting at school and church meetings soon progressed to petting in the forest, which in turn led to that August night in the haymow.

The hormonal rendezvous abruptly ended when Gretchen's father caught them in the preliminaries with Gunther's pants down and Gretchen's dress up. The big knife and threats of neutering sent the bare-assed boy flying out the barn window one story up and Gretchen into solitary confinement in the milk house for twenty-four hours. The dairy farmer didn't know that was about the worse thing he could have done to squelch his oldest daughter's sexual desires. Still reeling from the coitus interruptus with Gunther, plus having little else to do there among the milk cans, Gretchen taught herself the joys of self-fulfillment. By the time she had finished her incarceration, the young German girl and her overactive endocrine gland couldn't wait to sneak off with some boy again.

Unfortunately, that would never happen. Seeing that Phoebe had learned as much as she needed about right and wrong and crime and punishment in this particular life, Andrew allowed the first of four potential exit points to open, and he directed Gretchen's inner-self to step in. She got a severe case of dysentery from drinking out of the wrong milk can while in isolation, and died from dehydration two weeks later at age sixteen.

# Chapter 27

With no friends or family members dying before her, and being a semi-serious Protestant-in-training, Gretchen had no expectations to be met in Heaven by anyone other than Jesus. Andrew accommodated her with that holy façade long enough to quell her anxieties over dying so wretchedly, then he blinked them both out of the Reception Station's private room and back to the beach house.

The fuzzy image lay passively on the patent leather couch in the great room, her head propped up with a lavender, down-filled pillow. Still identifying entirely with Gretchen, she saw herself dressed in the pale-green, full-length dress with puffy half-sleeves and off-white apron she wore almost every hour of the day. Sticking out from under the skirt were two shoeless beige stockings with dirty soles and a big toe poking through the hole of one. Her brown eyes kept opening wide then closing half-way in a syncopated rhythm, trying vainly to focus on the large ceiling fan at a 45-degree angle above her. She wondered how the windmill behind their farmhouse in Germany got up there in the rafters.

Andrew took the opportunity to dissolve the milkmaid togs from the dazed girl in exchange for satin shirt-and-pants pajamas…again in preparation for those necessary restorative naps between sessions. He also used his energy-manipulation techniques to return her image to that of pre-Gretchen, only prettier. Her body had earned slightly wider hips, a narrower waist, and longer legs. The large breasts that got Gretchen into trouble were reduced to a size more in balance with her slender body. Phoebe was graduated to fifteen-years-old, an age more symbolic of the level of education she had reached.

With the physical image of Phoebe back in focus, it was time to work on the mental and spiritual aspects. Andrew pulled a footstool up to the couch beside Phoebe and took her left hand in both of his.

"Do you recognize me?" he asked, beginning the usual sequence of Q&A.

She looked hard at his face, straining to focus. "Yes," she said with a degree of certainty.

"What's my name?"

"She thought for moment, then announced the answer: "Andrew.""

"That's right. Do you know where you are?"

"I think I'm on our farm, but this room doesn't seem right."

"No, this isn't your farm. You are not on Earth any longer. You are back in Heaven. This is the beach house you live in while here."

Phoebe sat up and looked around, blinking. Recognition washed across her face. "Yes," she said smiling. "I remember this place."

"Now here's a tougher one," warned Andrew. "So give it some time before you answer." When Phoebe nodded, he asked, "What's your name?"

A plethora of thoughts swirled through the young girl's mind. She saw dairy cows and familiar faces, young and old. There was a black man, a gun, an old lady. A beautiful beach with white sand and turquois water. A full length mirror. A small wooden box.

"I was Tyree," she finally said. "But now I'm Gretchen."

"Very good," said Andrew. "You have been both of those personalities, and they are a part of you. But now you are back to your true self. Your real name is Phoebe."

"Phoe-be," she repeated with a slow whisper, analyzing the possibility. "Phoebe. Yes, I remember. *Phoebe*."

# Chapter 28

All in all, the preliminary recovery process was much easier this time. And after a long nap in the loft, Phoebe was back at the breakfast bar, slurping on a cherry smoothie Andrew made for her with the blender. Out of nostalgia, he liked occasionally doing things the Earth way. Ironically, Phoebe remarked it tasted *heavenly*.

Looking beyond the physical changes, Andrew could see and feel quite a difference in his young student. He had to remind himself that this hazel-eyed nubile across from him was now a spiritual composite of Phoebe, Tyree, Gretchen, and himself. *It will be interesting*, he thought, *to see what this concoction brings forth.*

"How did you like your life as Gretchen," he asked, shoving a plate of icebox cookies toward her. (For expedience sake, he had conjured these from the ethereal.) She curled her lip at the prospect, but took one anyway.

"It was okay, I guess," she replied, carefully nibbling on the edge of the cookie. "My little brother and sister were brats, always whining and wanting this and that and getting me in trouble. Milking the cows was okay, but I didn't care at all for shoveling shit."

Andrew stifled a laugh. He wasn't sure which of her two past lives that four-letter word came from. Probably both. "Did you learn anything about stealing there on the farm?"

"Yeah, it wasn't so easy this time. I was always getting caught. Seems Mother or Father was always around. I didn't get away with much."

"What would happen when you got caught?"

"I'd get my ass beat," she said, rubbing her bottom, as if it were still sore. "That wooden spoon and hairbrush hurt like holy hell."

"What do you think your parents were trying to teach you?"

That one took some thought. "Probably that I shouldn't take things that weren't mine or that I wasn't supposed to have.

"So, is stealing right or wrong?"

"Wrong, of course."

"Why is it wrong?"

"Because if you get caught you get punished."

Well, at least she had learned the crime-and-punishment aspect of the lesson. The right-and-wrong concept obviously was still hanging on the fringes somewhere. Andrew decided to come in from another angle.

"Remember when you took your little sister's dolly from her and threw it in the river?"

"She deserved it," said Phoebe/Gretchen flatly. "She made me so mad. I wanted to go fishing by myself, but Papa made me take Hilda with me. And then all she did was throw rocks into the river and scare the fish. I told her to stop, but she just kept doing it. So I grabbed per precious doll and tossed it in the water."

"Did it bother you that it made Hilda very sad?"

"Of course not," she said with a shrug. "Served her right."

"But it was her favorite doll. She cried for days. Didn't that make you feel even a little sorry?"

"Why should it? "said Phoebe, though a mouthful of cookie. "It wasn't my doll."

Andrew could see his younger-self had little concept of morality, much less empathy or the ability to see things from the other person's perspective. This was not unexpected, considering the impact narcissistic Tyree had on her at the outset and was still quite present. So, if she were to climb the Cosmic ladder faster than he had, it was evident her next incarnation needed to be something special, something almost as dramatic as the life as Tyree.

Again Andrew asked for advice from his usual available sources, and was pleased to be provided with a basic blueprint that seemed quite viable, at least in theory. When he presented the needed characteristics to his favorite psychic, Mishca, at the Birth Wing, they sat in front of the *Window on the World* to see what might be available. In very short order they came up with what both agreed would be the perfect next life for teaching Tyree-Gretchen-Phoebe another valuable lesson.

If it worked out, where other souls often took as many as three trips to gain such missing qualities, she just may do it in one.

# Chapter 29

The digital clock on the night stand was beeping 7:00 a.m. A slender female hand snaked out from under the teal, 800-threadcount sheet, feeling for the snooze button. On the fourth blind attempt it found it and the annoying noise stopped.

Alyssa rolled over and pushed the heel of her hand into her husband's warm back. "Time to get up, sweetie," she mumbled into her pillow.

The man mechanically swung his one-ninety frame to the sitting position, rubbed his stubble with both hands, and stood up. He slowly turned back and looked at the lump still in bed. "Are you ever once gonna fix Lucy's breakfast and take her to school?" he asked, making no attempt to hide his disgust.

"You know I'm not a morning person," Alyssa replied by rote, rolling back to her left side. The first light of dawn was creeping through the crack in the curtain, hitting her face. She pulled the sheet over her head.

"Yeah, well let's see how you like *this* morning," he said under his breath, as he headed for the master bathroom.

Two hours later Alyssa shuffled into the kitchen wearing a robe and slippers to pour a cup of coffee. She was pleased to see that Ted had done the dishes before he left. Such was not always the case. She popped a slice of bread into the toaster and sat down at the table to read the morning paper. A white envelop was propped up against the sugar bowl. It was addressed to her.

"Probably an apology from Ted for being such an ass lately," she mumbled, as she flipped up the unsealed flap and withdrew the piece of paper. It was his handwriting.

*Alyssa,*

*I dropped Lucy at school. She has dance class afterwards. You'll have to pick her up at the front entrance at 4:30. I have a meeting. I won't be coming home anymore. I've moved into the Super 8 by the Interstate until my apartment is ready on Wednesday. Our lawyer has already mailed a copy of the divorce papers to you. You should have them today. I'm filing for joint*

*custody. Sorry. It just isn't working out for us. Tell Lucy I love her and will
see her very soon.*
    *Ted.*

    Alyssa just sat staring at the page, stunned. This had to be some kind of cruel joke. Ted wouldn't really leave her. He loved her. So what if she wasn't the most beautiful woman in Springfield. So what if she couldn't put any weight on her ninety-five-pound frame? It wasn't her fault. This is how she looked when he knocked her up seven years ago after prom. She took excellent care of herself, working out at the health club three days a week, visiting the beauty salon at least once a month, bathing in perfumed bath salts every day. He wouldn't be able to live without screwing her once a week. He was always saying she was fun in bed. Well, he hadn't said it lately, or maybe for a few years, but it was still true. He usually made sure she had an orgasm before he finished. She always liked that about Ted. Well, okay, it had been a while since they made love. That was okay, she had her vibrator.

# Chapter 30

Marcie Sandafeur picked up the kitchen phone on its second ring.

"Ted's left me!" said the sobbing woman at the other end.

The name *Ted* and that sexy, smoky, signature voice told Marcie immediately who this was. Alyssa.

"What? You've got to be kidding," she replied semi-sincerely. This was no real surprise. "When? Why?"

"This morning. He left me a note on the kitchen table. I have no idea why?"

*I do, you self-centered bitch*, Marcie thought to herself.

She listened to her next-door neighbor cry and moan for a few minutes, interjecting an occasional question or sympathetic word. When the tirade finally ended, Marcie gladly hung up the phone and went back to mopping the floor, whistling "You Don't Bring Me Flowers Anymore."

The white Princess phone on the nightstand rang. It rang again. Then again. Finally the sleepy woman rolled over and picked it up. "Hullo."

"Ted's left me!" spat the angry voice at the other end.

"Who?" asked Judy Foreman, still half asleep.

"Ted!" was the sharp reply. "He left me this morning."

Judy sat up in bed and switched hands with the phone, giving herself an extra moment to clear her head. Who did she know married to a *Ted*?

"What do you mean he left you?" she queried, hoping the answer may provide a clue or two.

"He left me! He walked right out on me. With nothing more than a note on the kitchen table. Says the divorce papers are coming today in the mail. That goddam, selfish bastard!"

"Yeah, the bastard," parroted Judy, still with no idea who this was.

For the next two minutes a cacophony of self-pity, self-righteousness and husband-hating expletives rang out from the ear piece. When a lull finally offered Judy an opening, she quickly said, "Take that asshole for everything he's got. Gotta go. The tub is overflowing. Bye." She hung up and shuffled into the master bathroom. "Who the hell *was* that?!"

For the rest of the morning and half the afternoon, Alyssa called everyone she knew from her address book, which consisted largely of people she'd met at the health club and beauty shops, plus a couple neighbors. Most knew who she was because Alyssa started announcing her name at the beginning of each call. A few still couldn't make the connection.

The rapid-fire phone calls were interrupted when the clank of the mailbox beside the front door sent her double-timing to retrieve its contents. As promised, her copy of the *Petition for Dissolution of Marriage* was there in the magazine rack.

Her next phone call was to a lawyer she picked out of the Yellow Pages. She and Mr. Jensen had a brief discussion on the phone, then after a shower and make-up she left to meet him. As she parked the 1975 Volvo station wagon on the side of Jensen's office, it was three-thirty and distant flashes of lightning lit up the western horizon. When she pulled back into her garage it was five o'clock and raining heavily.

Alyssa walked into the kitchen, tossed the copy of her counter petition on the table and grabbed a beer out of the refrigerator. She popped the top, poured it into a glass and sat down at the table near the wall phone. Who should she call first with the news of her counter petition?

As she reached for her address book, she felt something was missing. It wasn't Ted. He usually didn't get home until about 5:30 each day. "Well, he won't be fixing supper tonight," she said out loud with a hiss. "Guess I'll have to fend for myself...and Lucy. *Lucy?*"

Alyssa hurriedly pushed aside the papers on the table to find the note from Ted. Her eyes zeroed in on the first line, telling her to pick Lucy up at school after her dance class at four-thirty. She glanced at the clock on the wall. It screamed *five-fifteen*!

# Chapter 31

When the Volvo station wagon pulled up front of the elementary school, Lucy was sitting alone on the steps in the rain. It looked like she was crying, but Alyssa couldn't tell for sure, since every inch of the seven-year-old was soaking wet.

That's when it happened.

Through the sweep of the wipers rhythmically clearing the vision of her only child sitting there, alone, in the rain, trembling, and frightened, something snapped inside the mind of Harrison High School's 1969 vice president of the Drama Club. She saw the reality of the immediate future. She saw that poor, innocent little girl growing up without her father, or just seeing him every other weekend. She saw Lucy crying herself to sleep at night, missing the person who usually tucked her in, who read to her, who got her dressed and fixed her breakfast and took her to school and picked her up afterwards and fixed her supper and played with her. He wouldn't be there for her much anymore.

Alyssa's heart broke in two, tears gushed and streamed down her cheeks. She had never felt so much pity for anyone before, including herself.

In words backed by emotions she didn't know she possessed, one of the worst mothers in Springfield, Connecticut pledged aloud to the universe, "From this moment on, everything I do will be with Lucy's best interests in mind." As she heard her own words echo back to her, a strange sense of purpose swept through her. Something so new felt so right. Alyssa would never be the same.

"Oh, baby, I'm sorry," shouted Alyssa, splashing through the puddles to sweep her daughter up in her arms. Clutching the soaked, crying little urchin like the most precious thing in the world she suddenly was, the distraught mother carried her to the car and set her down in the passenger's seat, not in the back, as usual. She ran around to other side and slid in behind the wheel.

"Where's Daddy?" asked a quivering Lucy between sobs.

"He'll be home later, honey," said Alyssa, fetching the red plaid blanket from the backseat. She took off her own light cotton jacket and wiped Lucy's face and hair, then wrapped the blanket around her shivering daughter.

"Tonight, it's just you and me for supper," she smiled, kissing her on the cheek. "What say we get a pizza? Then later we can watch a movie."

Becoming a good parent wasn't an instant transformation for Alyssa, but she was off to a good start. The little girl she used to resent for ruining her life, for waking her up every couple hours to nudge Ted to fetch her bottle or change her diaper, was now the center of her life. Alyssa had a lot to learn, but at least the foundation was there.

She and Ted stayed civil for Lucy's sake, each marrying someone else in the next two years. Alyssa found she could actually love a husband and happily gave birth to a little brother for Lucy. She began to see the virtues of motherhood, finding caring for others quite rewarding and fulfilling.

She crossed over from Alzheimer's at age eighty-seven, the grandmother of four.

# Chapter 32

The old woman floated into the white light, not sure if this was another of those realistic dreams of Heaven she had been having lately or if this time she had really crossed over. The sense of peace and love permeating her very center was reassurance this was finally the real thing.

Alyssa was met in the Reception Suite by six pets and a couple old friends previously passed from Springfield. But her attention immediately fell on her mother, who had died when she was only nine. To the observer, it was rather humorous seeing a decrepit, eighty-seven-year-old daughter hugging her beautiful, twenty-something mother. Andrew knew he could have transformed Alyssa's astral body to when she was age nine on Earth. But he assumed the two souls would be so involved spiritually they would easily recognize each and not care at all about appearances.

Andrew waited patiently at his art studio, working on a painting of the Chicago skyline he had recently started. When he got the telepathic sensation that Alyssa and her mother had caught up and it was time for her to move on, he willed himself back to the quaint little coffee house façade he had prepared for them at the Reception Station. After happy good-byes between Alyssa and her mother and promises to get together again real soon, the eighty-seven-year-old woman suddenly found herself wrapped up in the arms of a nice, younger man. His vibration and face seemed familiar, but she couldn't put a name on him. Andrew simply gave his bewildered, wrinkled progeny a hello kiss and whisked her off to his beach house at St. Thomas.

* * * *

Alyssa sat on the edge of the bed in her granny gown, looking out the open window at some palm trees, still dazed and confused by where she was. Behind her, Andrew quietly opened the doors to the wardrobe, exposing the full-length mirror. The first time they did this, black Tyree did not enjoy seeing himself with hints of a blonde white girl around the edges. Such simply was not acceptable in the hood, especially to the leader of the Sabers.

It took a lot of reorientation before the Tyree portion would accept that image of the thirteen-year-old Phoebe he was reflecting.

The shift of Gretchen back to Phoebe was much easier, because Gretchen didn't mind having her physical image transition from a plain, brown-eyed, brown-haired, sixteen-year-old, acned fraulein to a petite, hazel-eyed, much prettier blonde of the same age.

But since Phoebe was still identifying with an eighty-seven-year-old body, this transition was going to be different. And a lot more fun.

Andrew took Alyssa/Phoebe by her liver-spotted, boney hand and led her slowly to stand in front of the mirror. Once in position, he asked her what she saw.

"Me," the old woman said flatly, slowly running a hand down the side of her leathery face. "Just old, white-haired me." She didn't notice the lack of arthritic pain in her joints or that she was standing quite erect.

"And what is your name?" asked Andrew.

"Alyssa, silly. What did you think it was?" She glanced back at the man behind her. "Who, by the way, are *you,* young man? I seem to recall you kidnapping me from the coffee shop. You do look familiar."

"I'll tell you in a minute," dodged Andrew. He moved behind her and placed his hands on her shoulders. "Do you remember what you looked like when you were a teenager, Alyssa?"

"Oh, my goodness," laughed the old woman. "I was kind of pretty back then. At least, one boy seemed to like me."

"Would you like to look like that again?"

"Goodness me," she twittered, "of course I would. Who wouldn't want to be young again? But that's not possible, you silly man."

Andrew gently pressed his fingers to Phoebe's temples and bent down to place his face next to hers. "Let's just pretend for a moment that it is possible," he said, both looking at their reflections. "I want you to focus on yourself there in the mirror and envision what you looked like at age sixteen."

With Andrew's hypnotic help, it was easy to do. In a half-trance and her eyes still open, Phoebe watched her sallow, craggy face suddenly blend to creamy smooth. Her cloudy eyes brightened to clear blue. The short, thin, white hair was now thick, peroxide blonde and in a ponytail.

"Oh, my word!" she exhaled, in utter disbelief. "Look at me! I'm young again!"

"You certainly are," smiled Andrew. "And you can stay this way, if you want to."

"Really? Can I? Oh, good Lord, yes! I want to keep looking like this. Yes. Yes."

Suddenly, the revitalized Alyssa reached down, grabbed the hem of her granny gown and whipped it up to her neck. She gasped. It was all there: the body of her youth, from the perky breasts to the flat tummy and the smooth, toothpick thighs. She spun around to throw her arms around Andrew. "Bless you! Bless you!" she cried. "This really is Heaven, isn't it?!"

# Chapter 33

A grateful student is a much more willing student. So, in one short session Andrew had Phoebe completely remembering who she was, who he was, and why they were here in the beach house on Magens Bay.

With three rather extreme lives under her belt now, the Phoebe-Tyree-Gretchen-Alyssa composite had developed into a tolerable, actually pleasant-to-be-around entity. She was even a bit self-conscious now, probably from the quite understandable confusion about who she really was at this point. Fortunately, this insecurity made her even more charming; not to the point of the innocent child of her beginnings, but certainly more than any of her previous identities individually. Andrew knew how important this was, because the more attractive she was in thoughts and deeds, the more it would help maintain the beautiful exterior he was about to sculpt for her.

Phoebe lay back on the leather couch in her favorite position, her feet up on its back, her hands behind her head. Andrew had her clothed in tight, orange capris slacks and sleeveless green blouse, apropos of what Alyssa often wore as a teenager in the American sixties. He humorously played along adorning himself in plaid bell-bottoms and a miss-matched purple paisley shirt with orange butterfly-collar. The outfit was so horrendous, Phoebe never noticed his high-top Italian shoes with zippers and platform heels.

Andrew pulled the footstool up to beside Phoebe and sat down facing her. They had already been over most everything pertaining to her life in Connecticut, and in a few days she would be off again to the Birth Wing for an incarnation even more special than any of the other three. But before they went, he wanted her to see the next message in the box.

"I have a surprise for you," he grinned, holding something behind his back.

That got her attention. "What is it? I want to see it," she said, lifting her head, but staying supine.

When he handed her the mahogany vessel, Phoebe sat right up and flipped it open. She eagerly fetched the scroll and unrolled it.

"Read it aloud," said Andrew.

**"It is more blessed to give than to receive. Jesus."**

80

"Does that make any sense to you?" asked her mentor.

"Oh, it sure does!" Phoebe nodded with her sexy, raspy voice. "That moment in the car when I rushed to pick up Lucy in the rain? That was an epiphany for me." Phoebe/Alyssa was off the couch and walking around the room. "In a flash I went from not caring about anybody but myself to wanting to do everything and anything for my sweet daughter. I mean, what a revelation! It turned my life around. It was fucking awesome!"

Something still needed to be done about her language. But it was understandable. So far, his sweet younger-self had incarnated as a bastard, a brat, and a bitch, with the first and last having a rather foul mouth. Andrew toyed with the idea of dropping her into the body of a Tibetan monk for about fifty years. But he settled for a mild suggestion to *please tone down the language*. He didn't want to squelch the natural progression of his E2-3's development or override any of her past lives that defined her up to this point.

Besides, the next life he had on her agenda consisted of being such a desirable beauty in ancient Rome, she'd have no reason to curse about anything. Well, at least not until her eighteenth year. And especially those last few weeks of her life, when she would meet and then lose her soul mate. And violently, no less. His name in that incarnation would be Flavius, a handsome Roman soldier. His real name, his soul name, was Ethan.

# Chapter 34

Andrew wished himself out of the hammock (even on Earth-Two hammocks are hard to get out of by conventional methods), and walked over to the railing of the sundeck. His mind was still recalling his creation of Phoebe and her ongoing development. Despite some of the mistakes he had made along the way, he felt reasonable confident his younger-self's spirit had grown enough to handle the upcoming Rome adventure. So, the last step had been to fashion her physical appearance for the trip. Andrew had looked forward to doing this since the day he created her at The Splitting Image. It was to be his finest masterpiece.

Since that physical transformation had occurred earlier this very day, the events were crystal clear in his mind. He had asked her to come back to the couch and join him in a sit-down hug, followed by Andrew nonchalantly pulling her forehead to his. In an instant the beach house's great room had become Andrew's celestial art studio. They were still facing each other, but now straddling a small bench. Phoebe remained in trance. Andrew was also, but his senses were keen and focused on the job at hand.

Like working with soft, pliant clay, Andrew applied all his skills of an artisan to mentally change the sixteen-year-old face and body of Alyssa to that of an eighteen-year-old Phoebe, along with her honey-blond hair. He upgraded her hazel eyes to a brilliant emerald-green with gold flecks. He tweaked the cheekbones, nose, lips and jawline just enough so her face took the contour and features of an Italian contessa. The only part of Alyssa he left untouched was that smoky voice. It was a classic by itself.

In a final touch, Andrew altered the flesh around Phoebe's eyes to make them a little rounder, a little sadder, more like that of a beagle puppy. From checking The Deep Blue for some insight to the likes and dislikes of her future soul mate, he learned this would help make Phoebe irresistible to Ethan during their Roman incarnation, seeming vulnerable and in need of male protection.

"Look at me, sweetheart," Andrew had said, when they came out of trance, back in the beach house. He pushed her gently away to arm's length to focus on her face. Indeed her eyes were just as he had envisioned. "I want you to see something. I think you'll be pleasantly surprised."

Ignoring Phoebe's insistence to know right now, Andrew had led his precious daughter upstairs to the wardrobe mirror. He purposely placed her just three feet from it, and then slowly opened the doors to expose the full-length mirror.

"Hey, is that me?" she had gasped, gawking at the vision, feeling her cheeks, nose, lips and chin.

"It certainly is," beamed Andrew, bursting with pride at his handiwork.

"Well, thank you, Andrew!" Her smile was a mile wide. "I'm really pretty, aren't I?"

"Wait, there's more," said Andrew.

Her green blouse and orange capris from the 1960s had suddenly disappeared, leaving her completely naked.

"My word!" she exhaled, a lot of old lady Alyssa coming through. "You've made me...*sexy*, I guess you'd call it." She turned this way and that to view all sides of the delightfully delicate, statuesque body. "I love it!"

Andrew had to resist telling her just how beautiful he found her to be. So, he casually mentioned that she was very attractive and would turn a lot of heads. He knew that if things went according to plan, in a few minutes she would be finding this out first-hand.

When it seemed she had fully inspected every inch of herself unclothed, he had blinked that red and white striped bikini into place.

"Oh, now that's cute!" she had remarked. "I had one like this as Alyssa, when Ted and I were dating. Only it covered more than this one does."

"I remember," said Andrew, again taking her hand and heading back downstairs. When they reached the doorway to the sundeck, he said, "I want you to go down the stairs and walk along the beach now."

Phoebe had stopped. "Why? What beach? *Our* beach?"

"Yes, and well beyond," he said, leading her onto the deck.

"But I've never left the house before," she had said, a little hesitant, "let alone go down *there*. Why now?"

"Just to have a nice walk and enjoy the Caribbean air," he said, gently pushing her down the steps. "And to show off your new body."

Easing down the steps, Phoebe's head turned back to throw another questioning look at her mentor.

"Go," he smiled. "Enjoy yourself."

# Chapter 35

Finished recalling Phoebe's history from creation to that stroll down the beach, Andrew refocused on the present moment. There really wasn't much more for him to do. He had sculpted her exterior to the point of becoming an incomparable beauty. He had set up the Magens Beach ruse to increase her self-confidence enough to maintain that self-image completely on her own. And he had just psychically reserved their usual suite at the Birth Wing for her all-important fourth incarnation, this one in 387 BC Rome. All that was left to do was make sure Phoebe was mentally ready for the biggest adventure of her young existence.

As if on cue, down from the loft stumbled a sleepy Phoebe, yawning and stretching life back into her body. She looked for her mentor in the breezeway great room. Not there. Then she spotted him standing at the railing of the sundeck, his back to her.

"Wow," I feel like I've been out for days," she said, coming up behind Andrew and giving him a hug. He turned into her and returned the gentle embrace. He kissed the top of her honey-blonde head, and tilted it back enough for inspection. Even with a web of sleep lines down the left side of her face, she was still the most beautiful thing he had even seen.

"You did sleep a long time, sweetheart," he said. "You needed it."

With one more yawn, Phoebe eased free from his arms and bellied up to the railing to look out over the sand and the sea. It was picturesque and so peaceful. She slowly turned her head to the right, beginning to recall the little walk she had previously made along the beach's white sands. Something started stirring inside her. That's when the memory of Leonid and their interrupted intercourse among the bushes down there slammed back into her mind. Her mood immediately shifted from serene to caustic.

"Andrew!"

"What, sweetheart?" he asked, inspecting her current state of dress, yet unaware of the glare he was receiving from his daughter figure, "Would you like me to put something on you other than that nightie?"

"Sure," she cooed sarcastically. "How about my sexy little red and white striped bikini. Leonid and I have some unfinished business, if you recall."

"Okay, I deserved that," smiled Andrew sheepishly, lifting his head to face her. "But I had my reasons."

"Really? Let's hear them." Phoebe's newly constructed gentle eyes were showing faint hints of Tyree around the edges.

"I don't know if that is really necessary…"

"Hey, I was about to experience something really fantastic," she whined. "Like never before. On my own. And you had to butt in. I think at the very least you owe me an explanation."

Andrew started to put his arm around her. She quickly pushed it away. Tyree.

"And don't go laying that voo-doo shit on me that makes me all passive and sleepy. Just tell me."

Andrew took a step back to study his younger-self's determined face and fervent demand. On the one hand, he did owe her. And this was the perfect opportunity to explain why he had stepped in to spoil that potentially very pleasing encounter with Leonid.

On the other hand, doing so would inevitably lead into revealing certain aspects of her next life that she would just forget all about anyway the moment she sailed down the birth vortex. So what was the point of telling her now?

And on the third and final hand, Andrew considered how enjoyable it would be to watch Phoebe's face light up when he revealed the best part of her upcoming incarnation: meeting her soul mate. The worst parts, of course, would be left unspoken.

"Okay, sweetheart," sighed Andrew. "I'll tell you."

"Thank you!"

# Chapter 36

Andrew took her small hand in his and led her to the center of the great room. He backed away a couple steps and blinked. The cotton nightie with little pink bunny rabbits was instantly replaced with a simple white tunic ending just a few inches above her ankles. It was belted at the waist with a burgundy cord.

"What's this about?" she asked, inspecting the garment. "It's like what you wear most of the time around here, except rather bland and tacky."

"It's apropos to your next incarnation," said Andrew."

Phoebe's eyes lifted to stare hard at her mentor in disbelief. "You've never told me anything about an upcoming life before. Does this mean you're going to now?"

Andrew stepped up to his darling daughter and gave her a kiss on the forehead. "Yes," he said. "I am."

"Why?" asked a curious Phoebe. "I'm pleased. But why suddenly this time?"

"It leads into why I stopped you from coupling with Leonid," replied Andrew. "Besides, I think you're old enough now to understand a few more things."

"Well, *good*," said Phoebe, emphatically. "That means a lot to me."

"You've earned it."

"So, why am I wearing a *tunic*, I think you call it?" she asked, spinning around.

"It's typical dress for both men and women of ancient Rome."

"Is that where I'm going...ancient Rome?"

"It is indeed."

"Hmm..." She again lifted the tunic to feel the fabric and study the cut. "So what will I be there."

"Beautiful," smiled Andrew.

"I figured that," she grinned back. "Especially after all the work you've done on me lately. I mean who will I be and what will I do? What's my purpose?"

This time Phoebe allowed Andrew to place his arm around her shoulders and lead her over to the breakfast bar. With none of his *voodoo*, he guided her onto her usual swivel stool, and sat beside her on his. He casually materialized a plate of figs in front of her on the countertop.

"What are these?" she asked, taking one and smelling it.

"Figs. A common staple where you're going. Try one."

She took a nibble. "Sweet. Chewy. Not bad." She popped the rest in her mouth. "So, what will my name be?"

"Octavia."

"*Octavia*," she repeated thoughtfully. "I like it. Sounds kind of...mythical." Phoebe took another fig off the plate and studied it. "What will I look like?"

"Similar to how you look now. Very pretty. Refined."

"Good," she remarked, spinning on her stool. "I like looking like this."

After a couple more spins, she stopped and placed her right elbow on the countertop to support her head. She peered intently up into the face of her mentor. She wanted to get the full effect of his answer to her next question.

"Any men in my life?"

# Chapter 37

Andrew couldn't keep from grinning. "A couple men," he teased. "You'll have a father and a little brother."

"You know what I mean," she scolded, playfully slapping his arm.

Mirroring Phoebe, Andrew placed his left elbow on the counter to support his head and come face-to-face with the wide-eyed, raised-brow teenager.

"Yes, sweetheart," he replied in complete candor. "There most definitely will be a very important man in your life. In truth, there is a high probability he will become your soul mate."

The breath left Phoebe's astral lungs. "Really?" she gasped.

"Really," smiled Andrew.

Phoebe began to tingle all over. She slid off her stool and started wandering around the room. "Wow," she said, shaking her head, trying to absorb the possibilities. "I'll have a real lover. A *soul mate*."

Andrew slid off his stool and stepped up behind Phoebe to wrap his arms around her. Placing his mouth right next to her ear, he whispered, "This is why I stopped you from having spiritual coupling with Leonid. I wanted your first time to be with someone who truly loves you, who wants you for you and not just your astral body. I wanted it to be with the one, great love of your life."

Phoebe spun in her mentor's arms and encircled his torso. "Thank you, Andrew," she said, hugging him passionately. "I should have known you were only looking out for me, like always. I'm sorry for getting mad at you."

"It's okay, sweetheart. Under the circumstances, I would have been mad at me, too."

"So, when do I meet him?" she asked, new energy coming back into her smoky voice. "Where will it be? What's he look like? Will we have an Earth wedding? Will we have children like I did as Alyssa?"

"Take it easy," cautioned Andrew. "There's no need to be told all about a story you are going to write for yourself very shortly. Besides, many such details are yet unknown. They will be determined by your own decisions as you course though the life."

"Can you at least tell me his name?" sighed a decompressing Phoebe.

"I could," sighed Andrew. "But you'll forget it the second you leave Earth-Two and enter the fetus of Octavia."

"I know. I know," nodded Phoebe impatiently. "But maybe it will be imbedded deep in my soul, and will help me recognize him when the time comes."

"Maybe it will," humored Andrew, although he knew full well there was some truth in her hopeful musing. Nothing one learns is ever forgotten, even if it seems lost forever. Besides, the way their encounter was designed, there was no chance in Heaven or Hell that she wouldn't recognize her one great love.

"So, tell me."

Andrew smiled warmly at his anxious daughter and said, "His name in this Rome incarnation is Flavius. He is a soldier. But his real name, his soul name, is Ethan."

"*Ethan*," she breathed, as if daring to speak of deity. "Ethan. I love you already."

# Chapter 38

The year was 387 BC, when the Gauls were in the process of sacking Rome. As they pushed their way southward through the city, most of the Roman legions were unable to withstand the onslaught. But a few were still intact and organized, as they fought to maintain strategic positions and storehouses.

Ethan, now with the Earth name Flavius, along with three other soldiers was sent to defend a large horse stable in the southeast corner of the city. It was reported that some Gauls were already infiltrating that area, and if they got control of the stable and its four dozen horses, yet another section of Rome would be in jeopardy.

Upon arrival at the front of the stable, the four Romans were challenged by five Gaul warriors. When the dust cleared, the only one left standing was Flavius. As he finished making sure his enemies were dead and his only surviving comrade had a tourniquet on his hemorrhaging leg, Flavius heard a woman's screams coming from the far end of the stable.

With the urging from his wounded friend and sword drawn, he ran towards the cries to find two more Gaul soldiers in an empty stall, intent on collecting their spoils. They had already peeled the surcoat from the defenseless woman, and had her naked on all fours in the straw.

Charging into the stall, a swift forward stroke of Flavius's sword departed the closest man's head from his shoulders. The body slumped to the side in death throes, blood gushing freely over the wall and straw. An immediate, two-handed return caught the second man just above the left ear, crushing his skull. He slumped to the other side, also dead before hitting the floor.

Surprised by the sudden rush of violence, the stable wench—actually more a girl in her late teens—rolled onto her side, quickly fetching the brown tunic to cover her nakedness. Seeing the two, blood-spurting, convulsing bodies at her feet, she started to swoon, but was able to catch herself on one elbow before going completely prone on the dirty straw.

When her eyes cleared, they cautiously climbed upward to survey the ominous figure in the stall's entryway. He was well lighted by the morning light coming in over her shoulder from the single window. She recognized him as a Roman centurion by his silver armor and helmet with a red crest. He was still in combat stance, chest heaving, sweat glistening on his square face, blood dripping from his black blade.

The terror in Octavia's eyes gave way to curiosity, then softened to a glimmer of gratitude. "Thank you, sire," she spoke, barely above a quivering whisper. She pulled her tunic closer to her chest.

Those gentle, barely audible words—contrasting the screaming rage in his head—slowly drew Flavius's attention from the harshness of mortal combat and the bloody carnage. Blinking away the sweat in his eyes, he tried to focus on the trembling, half naked image in the corner of the stall. But light from the window glaring in his face made it difficult to make out her features.

It didn't matter. Winsome or plain, the young female was terrified and in need of his help.

# Chapter 39

Sheathing his weapon, Flavius stepped into the stall to kneel beside the wench he had just rescued. With the light from the window now at a better angle, he almost gasped at her beauty. The moist, alabaster skin was flawless, the emerald-green eyes were big and soft, the nose was unusually small and straight for a Roman's. And those lips! Flavius swore that was the most voluptuous, sensual mouth the gods had ever fashioned. If his heart and mind hadn't still been coming down from a battle high, he may have entertained the prospect of enjoying some spoils of his own, taking her in his arms and kissing her right there.

"Are you all right?" he asked, plucking pieces of straw from the honey-blonde hair.

"I'm fine," she lied, forcing one corner of that mouth into a smile. Her still-frightened eyes scanned upward from her champion's strong, hairless arms to center on his half-shadowed face. Flavius could have been as homely as a troll under a bridge and she would not have minded. Instead, she beheld a man with a broad jaw, full lips, and curly blonde hair. Quite attractive, in a rugged, war-weary sort of way. But when she saw those piercing, sky-blue eyes, her heart banged hard inside her chest. She wanted to offer herself right then and there to the most handsome man she had ever seen.

Lost in the moment, she instinctively reached up to touch his face. It was warm and wet with two days' worth of stubble. But mostly it sent a sensation through her fingertips like nothing she had felt before.

The young, strapping Roman soldier was lost in a stupor of his own. The world of war suddenly seemed far out on the fringe, a distant thunder. He wanted to know more about this fabulous creature, to walk with her hand-in-hand somewhere peaceful, to sit under a tree and kiss her cheeks, her forehead, her chin, her lips.

The sound of approaching horses made Flavius suddenly remember their tenuous situation. "We must go," he said firmly.

His words snapped her back to reality, as well. Sensing the urgency, she quickly rose to her feet, turning her bare backside to the young male. He should have averted his eyes, but couldn't, as she slipped the brown frock over her head and down to the backs of her knees. Hanging loosely from her shoulders, the thin fabric trembled like a leaf in a breeze, suggesting the delicate damsel was not steady enough to remain on her feet. Flavius rushed up behind her and in one motion scooped the feather-light girl up into the cradle of his powerful arms. Caught by surprise, she gasped, instinctively throwing her arms around his neck and pulling herself tightly to his armored chest.

They hustled out the door at the near end of the stable. As he had hoped, Flavius's horse had made its way down to the paddock area, and was patiently waiting for its rider. The Roman centurion wasted no time mounting his loyal steed and pulling the girl up behind him.

"I'm Flavius," he casted back over his shoulder, as he maneuvered the horse around the paddock and toward an open field.

"Octavia," she returned, sliding her frail arms under his armament and around his warm, firm abdomen.

Just a few minutes ago, the brave soldier was willing to die defending Rome. But both of their lives had suddenly become very precious to Flavius. He didn't know if they could get out of Rome's suburbs without being stopped by the enemy, he knew only they had to try. He dug his heels into the horse's sides.

As luck would have it—plus a little help from another dimension—the three members of a Gaul outpost along the way decided to take an afternoon nap so deep that thundering hoofs racing just a hundred feet from them went unnoticed.

By nightfall the young pair had made it far south of the Seven Hills of Rome to the farm of his Uncle Cladius and Aunt Adel in the Latium Plains. They were welcomed with open arms and bade to stay as long as they wished.

# Chapter 40

At supper that first night, Flavius and Octavia sat across from each other, stealing occasional glances between mouthfuls of mutton, red potatoes and wine. Uncle Cladius and Aunt Adel picked up immediately on the sexual tension in the room, and enjoyed a private unspoken conversation of their own with winks and smiles.

After the meal Octavia helped Adel with the dishes, while the men sat on the front stoop smoking pipes of Turkish tobacco Cladius had obtained from a merchant a few months back in Rome. They talked of the war and whether Rome would ever be the same under the rule of the Gauls.

When the ladies joined them, Cladius quickly gave up his seat to Octavia, and steered his wife back into the house. "Let them have some time alone," he whispered.

The two young Romans sat in silence, looking out across the starry night, listening to the concert of crickets and tree frogs. The war and the events of earlier that day seemed years behind them.

Finally Octavia broke the ice. "I wish to thank you again," she said with her eyes cast downward, "for saving me from those Gauls."

"I'm glad I could be there for you," he replied modestly.

She squirmed in her seat, recalling he had seen her completely unclothed, and on all fours, no less. "They most certainly would have killed me afterwards," she said, trying to keep the shame from her tone. "I owe you my life."

Besides a brave warrior, Flavius was raised a gentleman. It would be against his principles to take advantage of any young woman in such a vulnerable state. But her face, even in the faint lantern light slicing weakly through the kitchen shutters, was beauty beyond description. Plus, he did hold vividly the image of her creamy nakedness on the floor of the horse stall, made only more magnificent by the contrast of the two sweaty Gauls about to ravish her from behind. Then there was the vision of her standing with her back to him, her delicate contour silhouetted against the morning light.

Now here she was, completely in his debt. How could he not take advantage of such a perfect situation?

94

"I would gladly have but a kiss from you in payment," he said quietly to her bowed head.

With a barely audible whimper, Octavia suddenly rose from the chair and stepped toward the door. "It is what you deserve, my champion," she said woefully. "And far more. But I cannot. I'm sorry."

She opened the door and disappeared into the house.

Flavius sat in disbelief, crestfallen. A sure thing had just descended into an improbability. She was untouchable. She had a secret.

He wanted her more than ever.

# Chapter 41

In the following weeks Flavius helped his uncle around the farm, tending the vineyards and olive trees, plus the sheep and cows. Octavia stayed at Adel's side, learning to cook, garden and sew. She slept in the spare bedroom, while the young soldier had to settle for a pocket of blankets between straw bales in the barn's loft. Anytime their paths crossed during the day and at mealtimes, Flavius would look at her with hungry eyes, his blood pumping hot. Her return glances spoke of equal desire, but behind a veil that said it must never happen.

Then came that hot, sunny day he had sneaked down to the small stream everyone used for bathing. He knew Octavia had gone there just moments before. He parted the river willows with his hands in time to see the purpose of his voyeurism step gingerly into the shallow water, completely uncovered. The sun glistened off her creamy shoulders and the top of her boyishly firm gluteal muscles. The backs of her slender legs were smooth and soft, devoid of muscle definition. Most of this he had seen before in the stable back in Rome. But it was nowhere as stimulating as this.

He watched her kneel down in the flow of water warmed by the August heat and begin soaping her hair, face and body with one of those cleansing bars Adel made from a mixture of sheep tallow and scented olive oil. He used one himself earlier that morning in this very creek. He liked the smell...even better now as it drifted to him on the wisp of a breeze.

When it was time to rinse, the young lady dropped to hands and knees, then stretched out to lie face-down in the foot-deep flow. Obviously loving the sensation against her skin, she took her time before slowly rolling onto her back to wash away the last of the soapy lather. When she finally rose to the standing position, she was facing in the direction of the hiding Flavius.

It would be years before Botticelli painted The Birth of Venus, but it would not do justice to the masterpiece that stood before him. Framing her face in a thousand dripping strands, her honey-blonde hair now masqueraded as brunette. Water droplets on her round, full breasts sparked like tiny diamonds encrusting two erect nipples. As she began to walk toward him, her

96

slender hips rotated effortlessly, the front of her alabaster thighs proving smooth and faultless.

When Octavia heard the soft gasp come from the river willows, she stopped. Her eyes leveled to spot Flavius peering through the boughs. She did nothing. He stood up to unabashedly face her, his eyes flashing with desire. She made no attempt to cover herself, standing still, hands at her sides, her lips parted, her eyes sad and longing. The handsome Roman warrior stepped through the willows into the water. The beautiful Roman stable girl stepped slowly toward him, her arms starting to rise. Their eyes never left each other's.

Three paces from the long overdue encounter, she suddenly stopped, dropping one hand, raising the other higher, the palm facing Flavius. "I cannot," she said once again, almost sobbing. "I'm married."

The words were a steel blade to his heart. He stopped his advance, his mind raced. So that was it. That was her secret, why she kept avoiding him. *Married.* But if this is true, where is her husband? Why hasn't she jumped on a horse and ridden back to him, wherever he is? Why is she still here, looking at the man who saved her like she longs to be in his arms till the end of days?

Without another word, the delicate eighteen-year-old turned a few degrees to her left and waded quickly past the much taller, statuesque Flavius. She collected her tunic and sandals, slipped them on over her still-moist body, and headed up the hill toward the farm. A quick glance back revealed a tear trickling from an emerald-green eye.

# Chapter 42

That night at the supper table the conversation was sparse and muted, only between Cladius and Adel. Flavius kept his gaze on Octavia, who kept hers on the plate of her untouched food. When she finally did look up at him, her eyes and parted lips revealed more than ever she wanted him, but was afraid. Her eyes fell back to her plate, her chest beginning to heave.

Flavius suddenly rose to his feet, knocking the wooden stool backwards. It startled the other three, their eyes snapping upward to peer quizzically at him. He circled to the opposite side of the table and plucked the panting Octavia from her chair and brought her high into his arms. Her arms immediately encircled the brute. She buried her face into the side of his neck, a pitifully poor and highly insincere complaint lifting from her muffled lips. He carried her off to the spare bedroom and slammed the door behind them with a backward kick.

What emanating from that chamber for the next six hours not only kept Aunt and Uncle awake, it caught the attention of more than a few telepaths on Earth-Three.

The following morning brought the inevitable guilt from Octavia. As the two Romans lay uninhibitedly exposed on the bed in each other's arms, she explained that only three months ago she was married to the twenty-year-old son of the owner of a leather shop just half a mile from the stable where Flavius had saved her. Times were tough, so while her new husband labored in the shop helping his father make bridles and saddles, she worked for the Roman army as a stable girl, feeding and grooming the military horses. She didn't mind the work, having come from a poor family herself. When that small band of Gaul soldiers came thundering into the area, she was carrying buckets of oats to the horses.

"Curtius is a good man," she said, her head resting gently on Flavius' smooth but scarred, muscular chest. "He's handsome and caring and I suppose he loves me. But in bed, well..."

"Things come up a little short?" Flavius finished for her.

Octavia giggled, embarrassed.

A big hand came into her view. Its little finger lifted above the others, forming a small, downward hook. Both beautiful people burst into laughter.

98

Octavia pulled herself on top of him and gave him a playful slap. "You're so bad!" she smiled, her face turning a little red. He returned the slap on her bottom and the couple almost got it going for the fifth time, or was it the sixth? But there were still many things in need of discussion, clarification. She gave him a big kiss and rolled off onto her back with a sigh.

"Do you love him?" asked Flavius.

Octavia thought a moment then said, "I don't know. I suppose I do in a way."

"Do you want to go back to him?"

Again she paused to ponder the concept. "I feel I should. After all, we are married. I promised to love and obey." She rolled onto her side, and propped up on one elbow. She brought her left hand up to his face, looked him lovingly in his sky-blue eyes and said. "But after you, my handsome champion…"

His heart sang. He pulled her tender young body tightly to his own and kissed her more passionately than ever before.

When the kiss ended, her head slid down to rest again on his chest. His heart was pounding like a galloping horse. "I've already committed adultery," she said, "and I may end up in Hades. But I don't care. I'm so in love with you nothing else matters."

# Chapter 43

For the next few weeks Flavius and Octavia were almost inseparable. They asked permission and it was granted to sleep together in the spare bedroom. They enjoyed walking across the meadow hand-in-hand. They would sit for hours in the olive orchard talking about their likes and dislikes, dreams and desires. The more they learned about each other, the more in love they fell. The more they made love, the less they could wait until the next time. The passion of these two gorgeous specimens pushed the limits of what humans are capable of experiencing.

If allowed to run its course, perhaps the infatuation would have slowly tempered to a more natural level, typical of young love. But as *destiny* would have it, such was not to be. A band of Gaul warriors, looking for Roman renegades from the city, happened upon Flavius as he was chopping wood one hot afternoon. The battle scars crisscrossing his shirtless chest and arms suggested he may be more than the simple farmer he claimed. The threat of slashing his beloved Octavia's throat quickly coaxed a confession from Flavius.

He was executed then and there in front of her.

Just before the sword plunged downward to pierce his heart, Flavius gazed into his lover's tear-filled eyes and swore aloud for all to hear they would meet again.

"And soon," replied Octavia, the words catching in her swelling throat. "Very soon."

Somehow, both knew their oath was more prophesy than pledge.

For harboring a fugitive, Uncle Cladius's left foot was unceremoniously amputated. Aunt Adel may have suffered the same misfortune, but she was in the haymow where Flavius used to sleep, hiding under a bale of straw. The Gauls didn't wish to waste any more time searching for an old woman nobody really cared about.

Unfortunately, such was not the case with Octavia. She was far too beautiful to waste. The leader of the horde announced she would be taken back to Rome and sold into servitude...undoubtedly for a very high price.

As the Gauls partook of the farm's food and wine before their journey back, the one in charge of watching Octavia (yes, you guessed it: Leonid incarnate) was so infatuated with her beauty, he put a hand over her mouth and started dragging her into the fig orchard.

Kicking and squirming, she managed to sink her teeth into the meat of Leonid's thumb, causing him to release his hold in pain. Gagging on the taste of dirt and dried blood, she let out a scream that did not go unnoticed. Before Leonid could even get her tunic pushed up to her hips, two of his compadres were hauling him off the thrashing Octavia and fighting each other to take his place. This brought more men, and within minutes an all-out skirmish had six Gauls trying to wrench Octavia away from each other. It took the shaft of their leader's spear laid smartly across a couple heads to break up the melee, and poor Octavia soon found herself draped across his saddle and galloping north toward Rome. Leonid rode a few lengths behind in the dust, cursing and rubbing the lump on his bleeding head.

Two days later Octavia was auctioned off as a domestic slave to a prominent Gaul for an exceptionally large bag of gold ingots. But before the grossly overweight and gaseous magistrate could enjoy the fruits of his acquisition, Octavia skulked into the kitchen her first night there and slit her wrists deep with a carving knife.

* * * *

If Flavius and Octavia thought nothing could possibly top that flesh-on-flesh, tongue stroking tongue, breasts to chest, climaxing penis inside climaxing vagina they had experienced on Earth, they were in for a most pleasant surprise. Just moments after Octavia took her last breath and entered the light, her lover was front and center waiting for her. Their reunion in the honeymoon suite specially built for them in the Reception Station instantly became the event souls still talk about on Earth-Two, as well as most regions of Earth-Three. In fact, to honor it for eternity, a renowned E3 artisan was commissioned to do an animated mural to hang in the Reception Station lobby. It depicted our unabashed, naked lovers, writhing in each other's embrace, sending a whirlwind of multi-colored fireworks and lasers flashing across the nexus, as feathers fluttered down like large, white snowflakes from the wings of two circling angels, humping each other on high.

# Part Two—Ethan

# Chapter 44

The diminutive, nineteen-year-old waitress of an American-Polynesian blend continued slowly wiping the same spot at the end of the tiki bar's slate countertop. She knew it wouldn't get any cleaner. It just gave her the best angle to keep a wistful eye on that magnificent looking man sitting at her table forty feet away. Dressed in a silver jogging suit with black trim, he was tall and built just the way she liked her men. Pookie put him about twenty-four and at least an E2-5—meaning he had been to Earth five times. He had a powerful jawline, straight nose, curly blonde hair cut just below the ears, and, oh, those sky-blue eyes!

But it was more than just his god-like good looks. This young soul had an allure about him…a captivating aura that had Pookie fantasizing about offering herself up to him right then and there…heart, soul, and astral-body. Those strong arms encircling her. Those full lips pressing against hers. That joining of her essence with his. He would certainly sweep her off to corners of the macrocosm she never knew existed.

With spiritual coupling being so free and fabulous on Earth-Two, Pookie didn't understand why he had given her little more than a sideways glance when she sauntered up to take his order earlier. Her Earth-Three mentor had put a lot of time and thought into sculpting this round, light-brown face with big chocolate eyes, full, pouting lips and long, straight black hair that she presently had wound up in a French twist. She knew her body was virtually flawless, as well. Didn't he see her ample breasts pushing up from beneath her florescent-green Samoan wrap-around, as she served him his cappuccino? Didn't he watch her perky cheeks wink alternatingly at him from beneath the tight, silky fabric as she walked away?

Obviously her customer was preoccupied with something. He just sat there in the high-back wicker chair, drumming a steady tattoo on the smoked-glass tabletop, looking out over the beautiful scenery, while apparently seeing none of it. Under the table the white, patent leather cross-trainer tapped nervously on the gray slate floor. He hadn't touched the cappuccino-*easy-on-the-milk* she had delivered ten minutes ago.

Since Pookie had just started working here a few days ago, she didn't know Ethan was a frequent visitor, usually coming in just to get away and think about things. He indeed had a passion exuding from him, partially the result of an exceptional curiosity, a burning drive to find the answer to so many unanswered questions: *What is Earth-Three like? When will I be able to zip around from place to place in the blink of an eye like my mentor, Macailah, does? How does she just think things into existence, like this silver jogging suit I'm wearing? Will I find any of these answers in that next mahogany box?* And of course the ultimate puzzler that had been haunting him for as long as he could remember: *Where did I come from?*

In whole or in part, most young denizens of Earth-Two have such questions. But you can go to the far edge of Chroma and back and not find any soul as determined to uncover the answers as Ethan. He simply *had* to know. And he would not be denied. The heart wants what the heart wants. And Ethan wanted it even more.

"In due time," Macailah kept telling him. "When you're a little older."

Since there was supposedly no hatred on Earth-Two, Ethan had to settle for *disliking* those patronizing words intensely.

But to contemplate these celestial puzzlers was not the reason for his visit today and his nervous preoccupation. Ethan was lovesick. All he wanted was his precious Phoebe back home safely. She was due to come through the Reception Station in just a few hours, and he was beside himself in anticipation. He hadn't seen her in what seemed like an eternity.

On top of being uneasy, he was also admittedly frightened, a rare commodity in this highly evolved dimension. But he had good reason. Whether his soul mate would make it back safely or not could depend largely on how well he played his role. Forgetting what he was supposed to say or how he was supposed to act could be disastrous this time. After all, he'd already messed up once before. Big time.

103

# Chapter 45

That screw-up was after their previous incarnations in DeKalb, Illinois, shortly after World War II. The plan had been to become high school sweethearts, marry, have a passel of kids, and grow old together. It was to be a clichéd, vacation kind of life, one they had told their mentors was much deserved after the traumatic existence and violent deaths they had previously experienced in ancient Rome. Their mentors had agreed. Or so Ethan and Phoebe thought.

But as they were to discover, no agenda is indelibly etched on some parchment in the Hall of Records. Coincidence and an occasional nudge from the ethereal are always a possibility to keep destiny volatile and interesting. If Ethan (not his name in that DeKalb life) had turned left as he exited Hoover High School after classes that April day his junior year, he would have bumped into Phoebe (not her Earth name either), sending her books spilling to the ground, commencing their designed destiny.

But for some reason Ethan turned right and was ambushed by Mary Lou Benton, his current girlfriend, asking for a ride home. Thirty minutes later they both lost their virginity behind the school's bus barn in the fold-down seats of his rusty '48 Nash Ambassador, purchased just the day before for seventy-five dollars.

That event ended up sidetracking Ethan to Chicago after graduation, where he sought his fortune as a stock broker. Neither that profession nor his marriage to Mary Lou worked out, and Ethan—to the horror of six eye-witnesses—inexplicably and absent-mindedly stepped into the path of an oncoming bus on Lakeshore Drive, being instantly killed at age thirty-two.

Phoebe, meanwhile, had also missed out marrying her soul mate and having children. With no other prospects, she had agreed to marry an impotent, Republican farmer with eight hundred acres of prime cropland on the outskirts of DeKalb. This handsome young man—whose soul name, by the way, was of course *Leonid*—hadn't started out impotent, and in fact was quite cocksure of his sexual prowess during their short courtship. But there had been no way for him to prove it, since his virginal fiancée insisted they wait until their wedding night to have intercourse. As *fate* would have it, on that very night poor Leonid suddenly couldn't perform. They had tried everything, but to no avail. Phoebe hadn't been wild about marrying him in the first place, and this was now the frosting melting sadly off the wedding cake.

In a peculiar sleep-walking daze she was compelled to leave their nuptial bedding at three in the morning and run across farm fields to launch herself down a steep ravine half a mile away. They found her twelve hours later with a broken neck in the shallow stream of Four Mile Creek. Her distraught, inconsolable husband told police he had no idea what his bride was doing wandering around the countryside in her bare feet and pink bathrobe at that odd hour of the night anyway. He didn't think his temporary phallic failure had anything to do with her actions, so nothing along that line was forthcoming. Besides, it was nobody's business.

(Leonid's running scorecard for doing it with Phoebe: Oh for three.)

# Chapter 46

Phoebe's cross-over from Earth back to Earth-Two three weeks after Ethan's was just as easy as his. Being Methodist agnostics there in DeKalb, both returnees didn't know if there was some kind of heaven waiting for them, but they had hope. Consequently, rejoining the afterlife held very few surprises, especially when their Reception Suite closely resembled a familiar corner of DeKalb's city park, complete with picnic tables, sandwiches and lemonade. This was a long-standing façade specially constructed for any of DeKalb's fresh-dead, who were expecting some type of pleasant environment up there in the clouds. Being generic, it worked well for folks of virtually any religious or atheistic belief.

When Ethan had come through, he was met by his previously-passed and much-loved Illinois grandparents, his baseball coach, his childhood dog, and Jesus. The Messiah was actually Macailah, Ethan's celestial mentor on Earth-Two, again doing her part to fulfill Ethan's expectations as much as possible. Such well-meaning deception is not an uncommon practice in the suites of the Reception Station. The important thing is to make the transition from Earth to Earth-Two as smooth and comfortable as possible for the returnees, many of whom arrive in a confused or even terrified state. Loved ones—real or facsimiles—were almost always used at the conclusion of a soul's first half-dozen or so incarnations.

After some joyful reunions and partying, Ethan's confused mind was clear enough to realize he was much more than that thirty-two-year-old stockbroker spread-eagled on the grill of a Chicago bus. From there the memories came flooding back, and soon Macailah had him reoriented to his true reality. After all, this DeKalb life had been Ethan's fifth go-round in the reincarnation cycle and therefore his fifth trip back to the Reception Station. It was almost old hat for him at this point.

Then it was just a matter of waiting for his beloved Phoebe.

When she spirited into the same city park theme three Earth weeks later, the plan was to have her met first by a beloved grandparent and some old family friends. Then would come Joan, her best friend from DeKalb High, killed in a car accident just after graduation. During a sleepover freshman year they had pinky-sworn to meet each other in Heaven someday, and they

106

remained inseparable right up until Joan's death. So Phoebe was certainly expecting Joan to be at the reception. However, that entity had since reincarnated back to Earth. Upon learning this, Ethan had pleaded with Macailah to disguise him in the image of Joan. It would be fun tricking Phoebe, plus this way he'd get to kiss and hug her sooner than planned, and under the guise of someone else. He promised to keep tongue out of it.

Macailah reluctantly agreed, and they laid out a simple plan: after hugging and catching up with Phoebe, he—as Joan—was supposed to fade out of the vision, regain his own handsome image, and patiently wait for Phoebe on the periphery. Once she was done meeting with family and friends and had regained most of her Earth-Two memory, she would, of course, be looking for her beloved Ethan. That's when he was to whistle and wave at her from the oak trees at the fringe of the park. Recognizing him, she would naturally come running to smash and couple with Ethan in their usual uninhibited and carnal manner. Keeping this public display of affection out of sight would hopefully avoid embarrassing themselves and everyone else at the welcome-home party.

As it turned out, they should have had someone else play the part of Joan...someone less in love with Phoebe, someone less desperate for her return. When the frustrated farmer's wife first materialized in the tunnel after breaking her neck in a last ditch effort to find what was missing in her life, Ethan was so anxious for his beloved, he completely forgot the plan and sprinted straight to her. The Joan façade Macailah had so diligently created for him peeled off in layers, evaporating into the nexus like so much flash paper.

When Phoebe saw those familiar sky-blue eyes, her soul recognized her treasured Ethan before her mind could, and she instinctively leapt to meet him. The reunion was so excruciatingly steamy and passionate, everyone else in DeKalb's City Park quickly turned their backs and sauntered off to someplace else, figuratively with hands in pockets and whistling nonsensical tunes.

Phoebe didn't mind having to wait a little longer to see those old relatives and friends. Reuniting with Ethan made her temporarily forget all about them and whatshername from high school.

# Chapter 47

That was the DeKalb fiasco. This was now. Phoebe's return today would be quite different. And potentially dangerous. Ethan had to play a role far more important than being some long-lost, high school friend. It would require hitting his marks, perfect diction, and this time *total restraint*. If he were to virtually rape her again in the Reception Station's façade, Macailah had warned he may lose Phoebe forever.

To broaden their horizons, Phoebe and Ethan had boldly decided to spend this particular trip to the blue marble as Arab males in Twenty-First Century Afghanistan. Phoebe (named Ackmed) was the son, while Ethan (named Ali) was the father. The inherent love these souls shared just naturally formed a strong father-son bond there in Kandahar.

But it was dashed a few Earth months ago when Ali (Ethan) was killed by a Predator drone attack aimed at an al-Qaeda hideout next door to the restaurant he was patronizing. Devastated and full of hate, Ackmed (Phoebe) became an easy recruit of the Taliban.

Presently, at age nineteen in the year 2010, Ackmed-Phoebe was about to blow himself up—in the name of Allah and jihad—next to a police station in Kandahar where U. S. Marines were training Arab recruits. Because of the promises made by the cleric extremists, after his crossing, the impressionable young Arab was expecting to be met by a disciple of Muhammad, some virgins, and his father, Ali.

In some ways, the role Ethan was to play this time would be easier, since he had been Ali. That existence was now part of his very being, and the memories were still quite fresh in his consciousness. Of course, he would need Macailah to re-envision himself in that Ali image, because he wasn't yet able to do that himself. No E2 was. Then Ethan was to act like her father, Ali, while hiding the fact he was her lover...her heartsick, pining lover, who—as was becoming a habit—wanted to jump her celestial bones at first sight.

But what if he became so anxious he blew his cover...*again*? Due to that event at DeKalb city park, Macailah had warned that anything like that again, too fast, too soon, under these extraordinary conditions, and Phoebe—coming in as a highly-focused and determined Arab male who had just executed a terrifying suicide mission and blown her human body into pink dust—could experience a serious degree of confusion. It could send her spinning into a belief system of self-delusion that is much harder to recover from. She could even become a permanent resident of that netherworld dimension no one likes to talk about. The thought of being without Phoebe longer than necessary was bad enough, but losing her altogether was beyond his realm of comprehension.

*Thank goodness for Macailah*, thought Ethan, finally allowing a few of the tense muscles in his shoulders to relax. His knowledgeable mentor had agreed to take charge of everything. She would be playing the part of the holy man; she would be responsible for securing the virgins; she would deck him out in the appropriate visage and apparel; and she had already constructed an adequate Arabic setting in the suite they had reserved in the Reception Station. Ethan's only job was to be Ali until Ackmed could be made to understand he was actually Phoebe and was home. Then the long-overdue love fest could begin.

# Chapter 48

Tired of worrying, Ethan stood up from the wicker chair and looked out across the stunning vista. Carved into an overgrown hillside, this small, airy tiki bar rested on a ridge a few hundred feet above a plush, green valley of a tropical rain forest. About a mile away was a giant waterfall, whose mist gave off a spectacular prism effect as it cascaded down to crash against massive, smooth boulders at the bottom. From there the turquoise water flowed horizontally, feeding the stream that wound through the valley.

Behind him was the path he had walked in on. Ethan had been teleported to its starting point by Macailah, who said she'd be back soon to join him for a drink before the two headed to the Reception Station for Phoebe's arrival. The dirt trail was about a hundred yards long, winding through the jungle of elephant-ear plants and broad-leaf evergreens before opening into the tiki bar's main seating area.

The floor and the bar's counter were all fashioned out of warm, dark slate, while the six tiki torches sat atop bamboo poles. A large awarra tree provided the only overhead structure, currently the sanctuary of various tropical birds, including a couple scarlet macaws squawking and preening above Ethan, while Iggy the Iguana foraged for crumbs at his feet. The combination of steel drums and harp may seem an odd tandem to the uninitiated, but the soft composite was very soothing, as was the scent of spring lilacs lying gently on the air.

Ethan hadn't built any of this. He wasn't yet capable of doing anything remotely like it. But he was welcome to come here anytime he wanted, as was anyone who shared the same retreat fantasy as the entity who did construct it long ago.

Ethan returned to his wicker chair and unconsciously resumed tapping on the table top. Within seconds the darling and more determined Pookie—now showing a lot of leg through a slit in her dress that wasn't quite as high earlier—approached Ethan's table once again. She hovered for a moment above the shaggy blonde hair, imagining what it would be like to run her fingers through it. The fine male specimen under it didn't seem to notice her presence…for the *third* time!

110

"Is there anything else I can get you?" she asked, purposely bumping the table lightly with her hip. The mild tremor running up his arm brought Ethan out of his stupor. He turned in the direction of the feminine voice. His gaze scaled up the floral print to the cleavage, then on up to the full lips, stopping at the big brown eyes. He didn't recognize her.

"Oh, hi," he said, sitting up a little straighter, "You're new here, aren't you?"

Pookie wanted to say, "Hey, dude, I took your order for that special cappuccino, you know, the one with *just a little milk*, the one you still haven't touched. I made it special for you. I brought it to you. I bent over so you could look down my dress. I walked away slowly and seductively. Now I'm at your table for the third time, and I have to practically knock it over to get you to look at me."

But instead she smiled warmly and said, "Yes. This is my first week. My name is Pookie."

# Chapter 49

"Hi, Pookie. I'm Ethan." His large, powerful hand extended to meet her small delicate one. She quivered.

"Is Tovia still here?" asked Ethan, looking around. She'd been the waitress at the bar for as long as he'd been coming.

Pookie was a little hurt that the topic had shifted so quickly to her ex-coworker. But the good news would be fun to share. "She went in yesterday," she announced, with a tone of pride for a fellow Earth cycler.

"Well, good for her!" chimed Ethan, shifting in his chair to face Pookie more directly. "That's great. Did she say what she was going to be?"

"I was so busy trying to learn my job the last few days that I didn't get much chance to talk to her," confessed Pookie. "But I heard the boss tell someone she was going to be a Hollywood actress in the Twentieth Century."

A knowing smile spread across Ethan's face. "That explains why she wanted to practice at waitressing here," he quipped. Ethan then noticed the sheepish look on Pookie's face. He quickly put two and two together. "Ah, et tu, Brute? Sorry."

Pookie blushed and ran a finger along the edge of the table. "Yeah, me, too. But I probably need to learn more about waitressing than Tovia did. I think they said her blueprint has her being successful, landing some big movie roles for MGM or some famous studio. Not me. I'm going to be designed to have a tough time of it. Maybe get a commercial or two, at best. My mentor feels I need some experience in rejection and frustration."

"Well, that's just great," said Ethan sincerely. "You certainly don't need much experience in courage."

"Thanks. It's only my third trip down to ol' Terra Firma. How many has it been for you?"

"Six."

"I thought as much. What were you in your last one?"

"I was an Arab…in Kandahar…I…

The topic of that particular incarnation on Earth brought Phoebe slamming back into Ethan's mind. His eyes dropped from the pretty brown face and began staring off in the distance again. Realizing she was hopelessly back to square-one, Pookie shook her head slowly in defeat and returned to the bar to resume the duties she had been neglecting. Her lessons in frustration and rejection scheduled for the next life had begun a little early.

Ethan's third chakra started pulsating again, as the upcoming play rematerialized like a movie's opening scene fading in from black. *I can do this*, he thought to himself. *How tough can it be? Phoebe will come through without a hitch. After all, I've got the best mentor on Earth-Two. She'll pull me through it.*

Ethan felt better. He lifted his now cold cappuccino high in a toast. "Here's to you, Macailah!" he said aloud, bringing the cup down to his lips.

# Chapter 50

"And here's to you, too!" chimed Macailah, suddenly appearing in the wicker armchair beside him, causing Ethan to spill some of the drink down the front of his jogging togs.

"Don't do that!" scolded Ethan, trying to catch any more of the brown liquid at his chin. "You're always doing that." In vain he dabbed at the wet spot with his fingers, then added for the umpteenth time, "More to the point, *how* do you do that, damn it?"

Macailah just smiled and leaned back in the chair to take in the ambience of the quaint tiki bar. It was indeed a remarkable work of visual creation. It reminded her of a similar establishment just down the beach from one of her own thought-constructed, tropical hideaway mimicking the Cayman Islands.

Pretending to be more perturbed than he really was, Ethan turned to face his mentor, his most valued friend, his mother figure. Macailah was donned in her usual half-sleeved, floor-length tunic, trimmed in gold braid. Even in dim light the silver-gray fabric shimmered like flowing water back-dropped by filtered moonlight. Around her waist was the gold sash, tied at the side to dangle along her left thigh. Her feet were wrapped in bronze-colored leather sandals.

There was nothing vain or pretentious about Macailah's choice of clothing. It's how most E3s dress to distinguish themselves from others, particularly their E2 progeny, who, until they "grow up," usually *are* a little vain and pretentious.

It was hard to say what age Macailah projected herself to be. Her visage carried the wisdom of a middle-age woman, with milky, glowing skin and a shiny, bald head. Much smaller in stature than Ethan, she exuded a gentle femininity, with soft, brown, compassionate eyes, narrow shoulders, and fingers long and delicate.

One thing that never changed about Macailah was her infectious, signature smile, accented by that right-front tooth canting ever-so-slightly outward. Her appealing image, plus the calm confidence she had cultivated from thirty lives on Earth and a lot of tutoring since, afforded Macailah a charisma that just gravitated souls to her in search of wisdom and serenity.

With his thumbs jammed into the fabric of his silver pull-over, Ethan purposefully protruded the brown coffee stain in his mentor's direction. Head tilted back, Macailah was lost in the brilliant plumage of the macaws above until a not-so-subtle "Ahem" slowly turned her focus to her young progeny and those raised eyebrows.

"You can do that yourself," Macailah said dismissively. "And you need the practice."

"You're the one who made the mess," countered Ethan, smug in the rare occasion of the pupil chiding the teacher. "You clean it."

With a sigh, Macailah casually squinted at the coffee stain. It disappeared as quickly as it had come. Ethan cracked a smile and settled back into his chair, quite pleased with himself.

Macailah kept her gaze on the profile of her favorite other-self a while longer. She couldn't help but admire her own handiwork on that handsome image and how Ethan was now able to maintain it completely on his own, even after just getting back from being a dark-skinned Arab. The young soul had certainly grown quickly. It wouldn't be long before Macailah could begin answering some of Ethan's many questions. And in particular, the one thing he seemed most determined to know: the origin of his existence.

# Chapter 51

When Macailah had splintered herself to make Ethan, the primary goal was to create a predominately male entity infused with even more curiosity and drive than she had herself. She wanted to develop an explorer, an inquirer, a lover. Just as Andrew felt he needed a stronger connection with femininity, Macailah knew she would be more complete with some extra essence of male in her soul. She also relished the idea of having another protégée, a son, to raise and guide into the wonders of the Cosmos. Ethan would be her second.

As always in the Chamber of Exchange, Eraser had the two halves and himself embracing under the small crystal dome. They sailed off to land around a small campfire in the woods, a favorite memory of Macailah from many lives ago. Still equal in every characteristic, the first thing they decided upon was to name the clone *Ethan*, a moniker from the Chroma dialect meaning *Seeker of Truth*. Then came the decision of which traits and memories of Macailah's the replica would have blocked and which would be saved. When finished, Eraser took the clone into the deep meditative state to complete the process.

At its conclusion, Ethan came out of trance now his own being. He had retained only a few of Macailah's learned attributes, while blocking most. First and foremost, he had all of Macailah's desire to explore. While such is indigenous to all souls—otherwise what's the point in even existing, if not to expand in knowledge—Macailah's was stronger than most. So, when Ethan's burning curiosity was combined with a generous allotment of impetuousness and desire, there would be no stopping the young voyager.

As for memories and experience, Ethan held only a shadow of Macailah's and not a single one of his own. This left him mentally, spiritually, and virtually a babe-in-the-woods.

At this point Ethan still looked exactly like Macailah. One of the many skills Macailah had cultivated over the millennia was that of an accomplished artisan, particularly in sculpturing human features. Consequently, she not only saw her new-self as fresh clay waiting to be molded, but desired him to have a better-defined, masculine astral body with which they both could identify from early on. So, with prodigious vision she enacted matter-manipulation to shape her progeny into a seven-year-old, asexual eunuch with plain, almost plastic features. Macailah knew that later on, as Ethan grew in experience and knowledge from his training and a few lives on Earth, there would be natural changes made to portray his evolving self-image. But for now, at least, he would be her ideal of what most mothers want their prepubescent, darling sons to resemble: obedient little dolls.

With all aspects of his new essence now complete, the adorable young man stood there like a deer in the headlights. That taller woman, with a bald head and crooked tooth smiling down at him, seemed quite familiar, and the strong affinity he felt toward her was curious. But he was too drowsy and uninformed to pursue the thought further.

Young Ethan became even less alert when Macailah wrapped her arms around him, putting him instantly into a trance. His eyes cracked open at *some* area called "The Ground Floor," where he was registered by *some* kindly old man at *some* place called the Hall of Records, and was given *some* classification known as *E2-0*. Whatever that meant. Then just as he was almost fully awake, those arms came around him again. That was the last thing Ethan remembered until waking up in yet another place equally immersed in the realm of the unknown.

# Chapter 52

For Ethan's initial training Macailah chose the seclusion of her visually-constructed, snow-covered chalet with a view of the Swiss Alps. Superficially huddled in a clearing at the base of an alpine mountain, the two-story A-frame had a great room with floor-to-ceiling windows, a steel fireplace surrounded by black brick masonry, and dark-stained knotty pine furniture with down-filled cushions. A wrought-iron, spiral staircase led up to the loft and the chalet's only bedroom. There was a bathroom, but its main purpose was as a visual aid when the subject matter dealt with certain constitutionals on Earth.

Most classes were held sitting cross-legged on over-stuffed throw pillows before the orange glow of the fireplace. Along with a reasonable IQ and working vocabulary during the cloning, Macailah had let Ethan retain the basic knowledge of life on Earth-Two, so that topic wouldn't have to be covered as much in the training. Consequently, the subject matter invariably involved some aspect of the Earth dimension and what it will be like existing there.

As was to become typical of Ethan, almost every teaching point was interrupted with a barrage of questions. "What do you mean this would *feel hot on Earth*?" he asked, holding his smooth, almost formless hand in the fire. "What exactly is 'hot?' What is 'feel?' I don't understand this thing you call 'pain' or what it does. And what's in that box over there in the corner?"

Macailah explained that while in human form, any activity that can cause damage to any part of his physical body—such as sticking his hand in a fire—would immediately send a strong sensation of discomfort along the nerves to the brain. Being the control center of the human, the brain would respond by telling the arm to pull the hand out of the fire, or it may be altered in such a way to not function properly thereafter.

To which Ethan's reply was, "What are nerves? Where is this brain thing? What is damage? What is discomfort? Oh, and in case you didn't hear me the first time, what's in that box?"

So the first part of this inquisitive seven-year-old's training was devoted to the human body. To better make the points, Macailah would cleverly use her artistry to add texture and definition to each of Ethan's particular body parts under review. He was also given a qualified nervous system, so if he now stuck his hand in that fire, it would hurt like hell.

By the end of *Anatomy for Dummies*, Ethan's image was well-defined and looking almost every bit a human child of seven. The following course-study dealt with the finer points of bodily functions on Earth, so Macailah had to add a non-functioning penis and anus. The young lad found the latter particularly amusing, because to see it he had to stand on a chair in the bathroom and look in the mirror upside down while bent over peering between his legs.

The functions of breathing and sweating seemed silly to him, and he jokingly called urination and defecation "a *waste* of time." This brought a smile from Macailah, partially for the play on words itself, but mostly to learn her offspring was developing a sense of humor, not unlike her own. If there was one thing any soul needed to get through the tougher times of existence, it was a sense of humor.

The final series of subjects dealt with sex and procreation on Earth. Just as this subject matter is of high interest to human teenagers, so it is among most young souls, especially during their first dozen or so incarnations. It is, after all, an intricate part of creation, love, and sharing in any dimension. As for Ethan and this particular topic, his questions came faster than Macailah could answer.

# Chapter 53

Macailah knew they had come to the end of "grade school" when Ethan floated the inevitable query. The young student, now looking more the age of nine and draped in an off-white tunic like his mentor, had been unusually quiet after their last session.

Mini-Macailah paced the great room of the chalet, eventually stopping to gaze out one of the floor-to-ceiling window. There in the clearing, framed by the beautiful backdrop of snow-laden pines, two whitetail deer were nibbling on the bark of a young sapling. A bright red cardinal, perched on the birdfeeder, was disemboweling a sunflower seed. A few sparkling snowflakes danced in the hazy morning light.

It was a picture postcard setting that by physical standards wasn't really there. It was instead a vision Macailah had placed in Ethan's mind as an introduction to a few of Earth's indigenous creatures, plus to provide a sense of serenity during his intense schooling. Ethan wouldn't discover this façade for a long time. But today it didn't matter, because he was too preoccupied to appreciate the beautiful hallucination anyway.

"Why bother going to Earth?" he finally said, spinning slowly around to face the answer. "From what you've taught me, it's not all that great of a place."

Macailah wasn't always prepared for her protégé's many questions, but she was for this one. All E3s who have new selves to teach are ready.

"Do you find your life here on Earth-Two to be pleasant?" Macailah asked.

"Yes, of course I do," Ethan immediately replied. "It's wonderful."

"Tell me what you mean by *wonderful*," said Macailah.

A little surprised by the question he thought was self-explanatory, Ethan paused a moment then replied, "Well, it's *really* wonderful, I guess. I don't know what you want me to say."

Macailah moved to one corner of the great room where that wooden box rested on its marble pedestal. Ceremoniously, she took the box in her hands and turned toward Ethan. The student leaped into the air.

"Really!" he shouted. "Do I finally get to see what's in there?"

Macailah walked to her salivating youngster and handed him the eight-by-four-by-four-inch mahogany box. Ethan took it tenderly and glanced at his mentor for confirmation. He had tried so many times to open the thing. Would he actually succeed this time? Macailah nodded in the affirmative.

Much to his delight, the golden latch lifted and the lid rotated smoothly on its golden hinges. Inside was a small scroll. Ethan quickly fetched the parchment and mindlessly flung the empty box over his shoulder. Macailah stopped it in mid-air and floated it back to its pedestal. Ethan unrolled the scroll with trembling hands and peered intently at the words.

*"To truly appreciate something, you must experience its antithesis."*

Ethan stood there in silence, mulling over the message. His face went from determined to blank to puzzled. "What's *an-tith-e-sis* mean?"

"The opposite of something," said Macailah. "Like beauty to ugly."

Ethan's face went back to puzzled, then came a glimmer of understanding. "To truly appreciate *wonderful*," he began, slowly nodding as the concept revealed itself, "I have to experience things that aren't wonderful. Things that are the opposite of wonderful. Just being told about it isn't enough."

Macailah nodded.

Ethan began circling the room. "To find out how wonderful my life is here on Earth-Two," he thought out loud, "I have to go to Earth-One where it's not so great. That way I'll really appreciate it when I come back."

"Exactly," beamed Macailah.

"And I'll bet going to Earth is the best way to get smart fast," he said, stopping right in front of his teacher, looking up into those soft brown eyes. He tugged on Macailah's sleeves. "And the more times I go there, the smarter I'll be, right?"

Macailah nodded with a weak smile. It wasn't exactly how she would have put it, but knowing her impetuous Ethan, it was good enough.

"Wow! This is great! I'm ready," added Ethan enthusiastically. "Let's do it. Let's go now!"

With a sigh of resignation and a touch of pride, Macailah hugged her growing child in preparation for the journey.

*Look out Earth-One*, she thought to herself. *Here comes Ethan.*

# Chapter 54

When Macailah and Ethan arrived at the assigned room in the Birth Wing, they were met by Marlese, the E3 psychic Macailah had enlisted to find an appropriate life for Ethan during prehistoric times, a fairly common period for first-timers. Many such psychics in this afterlife profession prefer to present themselves as gypsies, and Marlese was no exception. Straight out of a carnival side show, this voluptuous thirty-something had enormous hoop earrings dangling out from under the ivory-tinted scarf covering most of her brown, wavy hair. The obligatory peasant blouse in a teal paisley almost went with the solid tan, flowing floral skirt. No surprise her brown eyes had a touch of mirth about them, because her arm—tattooed with a hodge-podge of suns and moons and stars—was draped over the cloudy crystal ball Marlese sardonically used for a paper weight on her fuzzy, cluttered desk. The real instrument for peering into the Earth dimension, of course, was the sparkling hole in the air behind her, currently flashing snippets of Ethan's future life like a Kodachrome slide show.

"See what you think, Macailah," she said, rising from behind her desk and walking over to the hole in the air. She sat on some type of floating cushion of a blurred, but vibrant violet. Macailah slipped in beside her on her own cushion to study the mosaic of probable futures for the human candidate. When a particular event at age sixteen revealed itself, Macailah thought that would be an excellent exit point for Ethan and made a mental note.

Next, Marlese brought into view the fetus's DNA double helix. "Anything you want to change?" she asked.

Macailah shook her head. "This will work just fine. It's Ethan's first body. Things will naturally work out on their own."

*And you'll take care of the rest*, grinned Marlese under her breath.

Off to their left, standing beside the standard-issue bed of glowing, colorful particles, patiently waited Abe, the other E3 in attendance, a typical hypnotherapist specializing in first-timers. Either Abe took his work seriously or his head-to-toe Lurch outfit from the Adam's Family was as much tongue-in-cheek as Marlese's crystal ball paperweight. Macailah guessed the later;

122

you'd need some flippancy to break up the monotony of doing the same thing over and over, day after day.

"If you're ready, then," signaled Abe, "we can begin."

Macailah led an anxious Ethan to the glowing bed and had him lie down. Abe knelt beside the young boy and asked him how much he desired visiting the Earth dimension.

"A lot, replied Ethan, enthusiastically.

"We don't have to do this, you know," baited Abe. "You can get up, walk away, and stay right here on Earth-Two forever, never having to go to Earth-One. It might be kind of mundane after a while, and you won't advance very fast, but it's a nice, safe existence."

"No! No!" pleaded Ethan, sitting up. "I want to go. I really do!"

"You're anxious to learn aren't you, young man?" observed the long-faced, handsome but pale Abe.

"Yes, more than anything!"

"That's good. You'll go far. I can see you are already making your teacher proud."

Convinced there was more than enough desire in his young subject, Abe gently pushed him back down. In a soothing voice he explained how wonderful Ethan's new adventure was going to be and how he would learn so much and grow from the experience.

As Abe placed the youngster in a deep meditative state, Marlese focused all her energies on the now-glowing, purple aperture. In an instant it became the standard spiraling wormhole into the Earth dimension, and just that fast Ethan was gone.

# Chapter 55

Macailah recalled how overwhelmed she was by emotions at that point of Ethan's departure to Earth. It was like watching the school bus take your child away to his first day of kindergarten. You stand there, smiling through the tears, proud and missing him already.

"Will you be staying for the birth?" asked Marlese.

Macailah flicked at the corner of her eyes and nodded. Knowing the procedure, she rejoined the psychic on her cloudy bench. While Marlese shifted the time frame to the moment of birth, Macailah focused in, both with her eyes and on what her progeny was sensing. Into view came a young Indian woman, lying on her back by the glowing embers of a fire. On the fire was a small urn of steaming water. The domicile was a circular hut supported on birch poles that joined at the peak, forming a small hole to let the smoke out, as it curled upward from the embers. The walls were solid and strong, made of brush and gray mud. Stretched across the small opening, two beaver pelts sewn together served as the door.

Obviously in the delivery process, the grunting woman, a piece of rawhide between her teeth, was being propped up by a male, presumably the expectant father. He wore light-colored pants and moccasins made of elk hide. His black hair was tied back in a braided pony tail. His face and torso were hairless and reddish brown.

The expectant mother's deerskin dress was pulled up to her waist, her exposed skin glistening with sweat, her hands clutching the buffalo hide she lay upon. Two midwives were in attendance, one with her hands at the ready between the arched legs, the other mopping the mother's brow.

In a rush of red placenta and white umbilical cord, out popped Ethan right into the hands of the midwife. The other midwife quickly severed the cord with a sharp stone and tied the knot. Once wrapped in a woven receiving blanket, the crying infant was held up for all in attendance to see, then handed to the exhausted mother.

The new father beamed with pride and wonder. However, as the teepee walls echoed with the ever-increasing wailing of the newborn, he absentmindedly dropped his wife's head to cover his ears. No baby in the tribe had ever made just an ear-piercing, prolonged screeching.

Back in Birth Wing 510, Macailah immediately sensed a high degree of discomfort from her young progeny.  She felt his cold.  She felt the pain of bright light in his eyes.  She felt his discomfort and anger.  She felt his stringent demand to "Get me the hell out of here!"

# Chapter 56

Ethan found himself a member of a Paleo-Indian tribe about 15,000 years ago at the end of the last glacier age in what is today New Mexico. At birth he was given the name Eecautu, which means "screaming hawk." But by the age of two it was changed to Chucenaca (chew sen' a ca), which loosely translated to "one who charges forth without grace." He was the second child born to his 17-year-old mother; the first one being still-born a year earlier. She loved him very much and tolerated his impetuousness far better than his overbearing father, who was determined to teach the inattentive youngster to hunt the local quarry of beaver, buffalo and mastodon.

Quite frankly, young Chucenaca wasn't much good at anything. He was decent looking with a nice physique, but he lacked in motor skills, intelligence, and spatial concepts. It wasn't anything Macailah did in designing the blueprint, just the nature of this particular human being. Besides, as this was Ethan's first trip to Earth, he didn't have any intuitive or unconscious knowledge to draw upon. He had to learn everything by trial and error...mostly error. As a result, his knees and elbows were perpetually scabbed or bleeding. Bruises decorated his arms and shins. Splinters were his constant companion.

At age thirteen Chucenaca discovered something he *was* good at. While washing his five-foot-four, naked frame in a community brook his tribe shared with the one to the north, a young girl about his age came down from the north bank to bath herself. He had met her here before, the last time about two years ago. Back then they had shared greetings and laughed a little while throwing stones upstream, trying to hit the muskrat hut. She hit it three times. He never came close.

Her name was Teeshopa, which meant *dancing fawn*. And today she looked different: taller—a good five-foot—more mature, and oddly more attractive. She waved at him and sat down on the stream's bank to slip off her moccasins. She then stood up, reached down to her ankles, grasped the hem of her doeskin frock and in one motion abruptly peeled it up and off.

Chucenaca stood knee-deep in the stream, transfixed by the vision. Where nothing had been before on the girl now perched two round breasts about the size of apples. Between her wider hips was a patch of dark hair.

Between his legs was a rapidly developing reaction.

Teeshopa giggled as Chucenaca stood dumbfounded, staring down at the stiff appendage. He instinctively grabbed it with both hands and spun his back to the now-laughing cause of his affliction. With a face even redder than before, the poor confused and embarrassed young Indian splashed out of the creek and up the bank, still clutching his erect member. He scooped up his clothing, tripped on a pant leg, and summersaulted onto his back. The howls of laughter from back in the stream gave him extra impetus to return to the running position and disappear over the hill.

That night Chucenaca was introduced to the wet dream. It occurred again the next two nights. Finally he discovered he could control the event manually. Teeshopa was always the haunting subject.

# Chapter 57

It had been only five suns since his last washing, but he told his mother he needed one anyway. If Teeshopa was there, he realized she may laugh at him as before. But he was willing to take that chance. He had to see that exotic creature again.

Teeshopa had been having her own tingles and dreams. She wanted to meet up again with that comical, but strangely fascinating boy, so she too was bathing more often at the creek.

For the next few weeks they kept missing each other, sometimes by only minutes. Then on the night of the full moon, both awakened from slumber with a strong urge to go down to the water. They met at midstream, both naked, excited, and not sure what to do. Under the bright lunar light the two hormonal humans looked each other up and down, still an arm's length apart. He could just make out those fascinating orbs on her chest, and she could barely see that topic of her dreams for the previous three weeks. They didn't speak, mainly because neither had any idea what to say.

Finally, Teeshopa reached out her hands and Chucenaca accepted the offering, taking hers in his. The two intuitively pulled together, nose to nose. Their lips touched. They kissed softly, awkwardly. His left hand released from her right hand and slid upward to clumsily explore her breast. It was exquisitely firm and warm. He massaged the nipple between his thumb and middle finger. She took his rigid penis in her free hand and instinctively began to stroke it. It exploded all over her arm and torso.

The spell was broken. They both backed up one step, now in even deeper uncharted territory. Teeshopa rubbed the strange fluid between her fingers, studied it, smelled it. Then she casually bent down to wash it off. Meanwhile, concern was running through Chucenaca's mind. Did she find his discharge disgusting and him along with it? Would she turn and run away, never to come here again?

Sensing her friend's anguish, Teeshopa came back to the upright position, sloshed forward two steps in the cool, shimmering water, and wrapped her arms around him. He gladly returned the embrace, releasing a gentle sigh. Something poking her lower stomach signaled the young buck was back in business. He instinctively bent at the knees until his genitals lined up with

128

hers.  Feeling a most delightful sensation from the pressure, she instinctively thrust her pelvis forward.  The penis slipped begrudgingly into the tight, wet vagina.  Teeshopa winced.  Blood trickled.  Eyes rolled.  Hearts pounded. Groans of newly-discovered sensations filtered upward to brighten the stars.

* * * *

The teenagers enjoyed each other many times thereafter and eventually joined in matrimony.  Teeshopa was barren, so no children came from their frequent copulation.  That was okay, as it wasn't in the cards for Ethan to experience fatherhood this soon in his reincarnation cycle.

The glorious sex notwithstanding, it was a tough life.  Sixteen years provided Ethan with all he needed to learn about breathing, pain, pleasure, hot, cold, and especially those annoying gastro evacuations.  That left just one more physical experience.

Death was achieved when Chucenaca unconsciously took the *exit point* Macailah had previously planned for and was now available.  It consisted of being gored by a bull mastodon, who took issue with that poorly-aimed spear stuck in its hind quarter.

Ethan left the blue planet the same way he had entered it: screaming in terror.

# Chapter 58

He was immediately met at the mouth of Suite 927 in the Reception Station by the loving encirclement of Macailah, who was disguised as an elderly Paleo-Indian chieftain from Chucenaca's tribe, having died just a year before. The familiar image and vibration were instrumental in calming Ethan's distress. Macailah wasn't sure how to decorate the suite to be familiar surroundings to Chucenaca, and she wasn't sure it even mattered. So she simply spirited the now-semi-comatose youngster back to the Swiss chalet before he even had time to look around.

Due to Ethan's incessant desire for knowledge, it took only one brief session before the five-foot-four teenager, who smelled of wood smoke and red meat, had most of his old memories back, now enhanced with many new ones. His appearance, however, was another matter.

"That was awesome!" yawned Ethan, winding down the stairs from the loft after a very long sleep. "A lot of things about Earth are unpleasant, but some are fantastic."

Macailah had to smile, as her slightly out-of-focus, half-naked younger-self stumbled across the room, still looking every bit Chucenaca in his deerskin diaper.

"Like Teeshopa," he continued. "She was really great! I miss her. Will she be alright? Will I see her again?" Before Macailah could answer the first questions she was hit with another: "And that copulating thing, as you call it. Wow! I mean WOW! Can we do that here on E2?"

The requests from Ethan to do another knowledge-building stint on Earth were relentless. Macailah wanted to keep her progeny—now upgraded from an E2-0 to an E2-1 for having one incarnation under his belt—at the chalet for some more training, but Ethan was so determined he couldn't focus on anything else. Realizing it was pointless to deny, plus maybe it would be a good learning experience, Macailah finally agreed.

"Before we go, don't you at least want to see what's in the box this time?" queried Macailah.

She didn't have to ask twice. The E2-1 raced over to the corner and lifted the box carefully off its pedestal. He opened it, took out the scroll, put the box back on its platform, and read the words out loud.

***"Everything you do and learn is shared by all."***

Ethan cranked his head back toward his teacher. "Is that true? Everything?"

"Yes, everything."

He started walking purposefully toward Macailah, his face growing taut. "Does that mean everybody in the universe watched me make a fool of myself that time in the stream with Teeshopa?"

"Hold on, my friend," cautioned Macailah, stopping him in mid-step with hands gently on his chest. "Nobody was watching you. Very few souls are capable of prying into your private affairs and even fewer would care to."

"But you care," Ethan said, pushing away from his teacher. "So I bet you were watching, weren't you?"

"I didn't watch you at any of those times," she stated softly. "I was vaguely aware. I could have, but I didn't. I had better things to do."

The salve soothed Ethan's indignation. But it didn't stop the questions. "So, how are you capable of spying on me when no one else is?"

Macailah tapped her student on his left temple. "You and I have a special connection."

"Huh? What kind of a connection? How's that work?"

Macailah thought a moment, then replied, "Later. When you're older."

Before steam could start coming out of Ethan's ears, she quickly added, "Listen. What the message means is whatever any soul learns or experiences, whether on Earth, here on Earth-Two, or wherever, that knowledge automatically goes into The Deep Blue."

"The Deep Blue?" Yes, this was certainly diverting Ethan's attention. "What's that?"

"It's where everything is stored, every thought every soul has ever had, every event large and small in any dimension, every time you laugh or stub your toe. It all goes here."

Ethan tried to absorb the concept. Realizing he couldn't, but seeing great potential for this *Deep Blue* thing, he switched to, "Can anybody access it?"

"Yes, if you know how to do it."

"Could I?"

"No."
"Why not?"
"It takes some training."
"Will you teach me?"
"Yes, but not now.
"When?"
"When you're older."
"Damn it!"

# Chapter 59

Using the psychic airwaves, Macailah called ahead to make a reservation at the same room in the Birth Wing, and have Marlese looking for prospective fetuses again in the prehistoric era. It was only Ethan's second trip. They needed to keep it simple.

When they arrived, Ethan was still the fuzzy self-image of a teenage Indian and completely oblivious to that fact. Macailah didn't see any point in altering it, with so little time between incarnations.

They were met by some bad news from the psychic: there weren't many choices right now; all the more desirable bodies were already taken.

"I don't care," claimed Ethan fervently. "I'll take anything as long as there is potential for learning and copulation."

Macailah just shook her bald head. Marlese muffled a snort, pretending to look too closely into her fake crystal ball.

Via the usual process, Marlese and Macailah put their minds together to look through the catalog of availabilities, while Ethan looked over their shoulders, completely mesmerized by the window on the world.

"Here's a Cro-Magnon male with cerebral palsy being born in early Paleolithic Europe," announced Marlese with very little enthusiasm.

"I'll take it!" said Ethan without hesitation.

Macailah scanned the future for this prospect. "Oh-oh," she said. "His reproductive system never develops properly. He's not capable of ever having sexual relations. But it will be a good learning experience."

"No thanks," said Ethan. "What else you got there?"

"Here's a boy a thousand years earlier in the south of France...."

"I'll take it!"

"...who has a bad heart and dies at age 11."

"Beaver shit," said Ethan, an expression he learned from his Paleo-Indian father. "What else?"

"There really isn't much right now," said Marlese. "If you could wait awhile I'm sure we can find something suitable to your educational desires."

The five-foot-four, reddish-brown teenager in the deerskin diaper paced back and forth in Birth Wing 510, hands on his hips. "Okay, fine. Do what you can. I'll take anything with an active copulation life."

"Wait," mocked Macailah, "I see there's a male rabbit being born right now in 1792 Amsterdam."

Ethan stopped pacing and glared at his mentor. But he did consider the possibility. Only for a moment.

The search continued, but the only fetus with any sexual potential was a female Inuit in Greenland circa 500 BC. A check of her double-helix showed all the tools were present and healthy for making love, but she would not be at all attractive.

"That could work," said Ethan with his usual optimistic enthusiasm. "Being female I can see what copulation is like from the other side…like it was for Teeshopa. I'm sure she was enjoying it as much as I was."

"Hold on, young stud," cautioned Macailah, speaking from the voice of thirty Earthside experiences. "There are implications here that do not lend themselves to the kind of sexual fulfillment you shared last time."

"I don't care. I can work around it. Besides, you've taught me that Earth women hold a power over men…that basically any woman can have sex anytime she wants, while men have to beg for it, right? So as long as my implements are working, I don't see a problem being this woman. I want to go. Pleeease!"

Again, Macailah knew all too well the futility of resisting. In fact, trying to do so could result in Ethan discovering that no one can prevent another from doing anything they want. Free will is an inalienable right to every soul of any age in every corner of the Cosmos. So if that chip off the old block was determined to dive headlong into that fetus, consequences be damned, there was nothing Macailah could do to stop him. Besides, on the positive side, it was a good way to learn some life lessons quickly. And while there was no time limit for advancement, she knew how badly Ethan wanted to qualify for E3 status. It was his nature. It was her design. An incarnation like this one might do wonders after all.

"Okay," said Macailah, with a secretive wink to Marlese. "But don't say I didn't warn you."

# Chapter 60

Konoma was the third-born to an Inuit family in the icy tundra of northern Greenland.  She was a plump, energetic, happy child, eager to help her parents and grandparents with any endeavor.  She loved making string dolls with her little sister on the warmer, second level of their igloo, and had a Woody Woodpecker laugh that once had the whole clan laughing with her.

Those, unfortunately, were about the extent of high points in Konoma's life.

As she lumbered into adulthood, her weight increased to borderline obesity.  This was fairly tolerated by others, because the Eskimos were a hefty people by nature themselves.  But from chewing on seal and caribou skins too energetically and at too early an age, her permanent teeth grew in crooked and compacted.  This caused numerous cavities, which in turn caused halitosis so severe people would slide a few feet away anytime she talked.  Her father tried to marry her off at age 13, but found no takers, even with the dowry of a beautiful elk-skin parka and two sled dogs.  Her bent nose and wall-eyes only added to the deficits.

The saving grace for Konoma was her highly-active libido.  The first male brave enough to take advantage of the free whalebone necklace she offered and the promise to keep her head turned with her mouth shut, was a virginal 14-year-old boy almost as homely as she.  Both found the warm encounter on a cold Arctic night highly stimulating, and the word spread quickly throughout the tundra that Konoma was a decent lay willing to pay.

Eventually, her reputation was good enough she no longer had to offer incentives.  In fact, out of the goodness of their hearts, if not sympathy, some would leave a little gratuity as they crawled out of the small igloo her father, grandfather and two brothers had gladly and rapidly built just for her.

So many sexual encounters sex with so many males inevitably led to Konoma contracting an STD, probably from a visiting Norseman.  In the spring of her twentieth year, syphilis blessedly and on cue sent her back to Earth-Two and her waiting mentor.

# Chapter 61

When Ethan-Konoma wound down the spiral stairs of the Swiss chalet after an even longer sleep this time, Macailah again had to stifle a smile. On the comedic side, waddling across the room in her white polar bear parka and sealskin boots, Macailah's blurry progeny was still identifying with the plump, repugnant Konoma. The facial expression flickered back and forth between depression and excitement, confusion and composure.

On the more serious side, Macailah was quite proud. Her young splinter had impetuously dived into an existence with very little forethought or fear of the consequences, all in the name of sexual gratification and wisdom. But as the following sessions on the throw-pillows by the fireplace revealed, he had emerged noticeably wiser, having just been through a litany of lessons, from physical abuse to humility, low self-esteem to apathy, illness to depression. But none of this squelched his enthusiasm and quest for knowledge.

To emphasize that point, Macailah allowed her curious student to fetch the mahogany box and see what was inside it this time.

The scroll read: **"The harder the lesson, the greater the reward."**

Ethan knew exactly what it meant and felt even more encouraged. Physically, however, he had morphed into an interesting-looking blend of Konoma and Chucenaca...just as he saw himself. He had black, straight hair resting on broad shoulders, dark-brown eyes, a bent nose, fat lips, a chunky body with man boobs, and things between the legs that would qualify the young soul as a hermaphrodite on Earth. Here on E2, in the seclusion of the chalet, it meant next to nothing.

That played a large part in Ethan's far more interesting third incarnation. With two lives under his belt, and feeling he had learned quite enough about cold, ugly and embarrassment, thank you, he asked to do a complete one-eighty this time. He didn't care what, just as long as it centered on sex and was much more pleasant. And he was willing to wait this time. But not too long.

This gave Macailah an idea. Behind Ethan's back, she and Marlese set out to find just the right parents and time frame. There wasn't much in the prehistoric era—Marlese's current realm of expertise—but she was happy to expand her horizons. In doing so, they found just what they were looking for:

a fetus about to be born to a well-to-do, handsome couple in Third Century Greece.

As Marlese kept the double helix swirling bright and clear, Macailah—with a notable degree of expertise—tweaked the nucelotides just right to create what she today feels was perhaps her finest genetic work. The result was Ethan's powerful, Adonis-like features, from wavy, golden hair and sky-blue eyes to the high cheekbones and broad jawline. Below the neck was a chiseled physique any Earth-man would envy and most Earth-women would be drawn to. Oh, and he was well endowed.

All this was to facilitate Macailah's half-serious, half tongue-in-cheek blueprint for Ethan as an Athenian gigolo named Arion. After what her younger-self had been through the last two times, he had earned a lifestyle of hedonistic decadence.

And enjoy it he did. It wasn't long before every person in Athens--married, single or otherwise—knew about the handsome young stallion, who could bring you a full hour of heavenly bliss for just a few drachma. By age twenty-one Arion had appointments as often as twice a day and was becoming a very rich man-whore.

But alas, this most enjoyable existence ended soon thereafter at the hands of a dagger-wielding husband who had this strange inclination to come home an hour early that day. So, for the third time in as many lives, the very young soul thought his demise came from pure happenstance. But for the third time he was wrong...and purposely made none the wiser.

On the plus side of this death, so enamored with Arion's features, Ethan begged to keep them as his signature image while between lives from here on. Rather proud of her artistry manipulating the DNA and a little post-life sculpturing, Macailah acquiesced. She even took particular pains to have the image remain perfectly intact during Ethan's fourth trip to the planet. This was important because his good looks were to play an intricate part in meeting and winning over a special young female.

The location was ancient Rome. The beautiful young woman was called Octavia. Her soul name was Phoebe.

# Chapter 62

As Macailah's thoughts came back to the present, she noticed Ethan was again slowly drumming his fingers on the slate tabletop of the tiki bar. "You ready to go?" she asked.

Ethan glanced over at his mentor, nodded the affirmative, and stood up. "Let's do it," he said, a mixture of bravado and worry in his voice.

Macailah rose and stepped over to Ethan. With no words necessary, the two embraced.

"Just relax and give it over to me," whispered Macailah, as she had many times before. "Join with my spirit."

That was always easy for Ethan to do. For reasons he wasn't yet allowed to understand, he felt that strong association with his mentor. Anytime they hugged like this, elation washed over him like a warm rain. Everything seemed right with in his world.

"As before," continued Macailah, "focus on that statue of H. G. Wells at the entrance to the Plaza."

* * * *

Also located on the Ground Floor of Earth-Two, and one step closer to Earth, is the Transition Plaza. Not unlike any modern mall in style and layout, it is a circular multi-plex of numerous Birth Wings, Reception Stations, Recovery Rooms, spas and shops. From millennia of practice and operation, whatever might be needed to facilitate the departure and arrival of souls to and from Old Earth is found here. And to say it is busy would be a gross understatement. Anyone who has ever been to Las Vegas during the first Saturday of spring break agrees that the atrium itself is more congested than the terminal at McCarran airport.

Their first stop, "The Drama Pool," was no exception. But it was well managed and had plenty of dead thespians anxious to play any kind of a role. The casting agent who waited on Macailah and Ethan looked the part, complete with bouffant hair, horn-rimmed glasses, and a pencil behind her ear.

The brown riding pants with Adidas running shoes were a brow-scrunching non sequitur.

"We have whatever, whoever, and however you need them," she stated matter-of-factly. "Each actor is at least a three-bee" (E3-B).

When Macailah said they were looking for two Arabic virgins, the agent immediately transformed herself into a sixty-something madam with purple hair and a too-tight red dress drowning in cheap sequins. Stroking her pink boa, she cocked one eyebrow at Macailah and said, "See, you definitely have come to the right place. I'm a Class B myself. Call me *Miss Chelsy*."

That reassured Macailah. While Class Bs from Earth-Three were not yet capable of generating someone else's image—as was Macailah, herself a Class AA—they were more than good enough to form and maintain their own self-image projection. That's all she was looking for.

After hearing the requirements, the casting agent-now-madam Miss Chelsy marched a dozen handpicked actors into a screening room, then left Macailah and Ethan to conduct their interviews. All twelve virgin-whore-wannabes showed off their skills by transforming into various shapes and personages, each trying to outdo the next. Macailah and Ethan eventually settled on two eager drag queen types that not only were quite capable of shape-shifting and holding the disguise, but seemed the least likely to overact.

# Chapter 63

Their next stop, a middle-eastern clothing store named *Habib's,* was not busy at all.  Most of the arrivals in this section of the Plaza were North American Christians, Jews, or atheists, who therefore were expecting to be met by God, Jesus, Moses, Satan, or Woody Allen.  Meanwhile, Phoebe, a five-time Westerner—now living a life as an Arab coming from the Middle East sector and expecting Islamic figures after crossing—was a bit out of the ordinary.

"Welcome, welcome!" bowed Habib, appropriately dressed in fine Turkish silk from toe to neck, topped by a burgundy turban.  "It is a pleasure for me to be serving your needs."

Macailah again explained the requirements, and the kindly Habib fell all over himself trying to accommodate them.  First, he showed Macailah a variety of clothing worn by Islam sheikhs, a role Macailah had already decided to play, in line with Ackmed's expectations to be met by a holy man.  She eventually settled on a modest, brown robe and matching skullcap.

As the clothier held both items up in clear view, Macailah used her visionary skills to copy the ensemble onto herself, replacing her usual gray-silver tunic and gold sash.  Standing in front of a mirror, she then gave herself a masculine face and a full head of gray hair with matching beard and mustache.  The final touch was a pair of coal-black eyes.

"How do I look?" she asked Ethan in her new masculine voice, popping the skull cap into place.

"I'll tell you, if you tell me how the hell you do that," he replied with his usual exasperated whine.  His mentor's power over just about everything never ceased to amaze him...and make him all that more determined to earn his Earth-Three wings.

Ethan was next to be outfitted.  For this Macailah had to consider how he—as Ali—was dressed the last time Ackmed saw his father.  That, unfortunately, would be as his body was brought home from the destroyed restaurant.  So Macailah dipped her consciousness into The Deep Blue to observe Ali as he lay on his bed just before being washed and wrapped in a shroud for the burial ritual.  After taking a mental picture, she refocused back on Habib, explaining in great detail what she was looking for.  As it was a fairly common ensemble for that time and place, Habib had no trouble rounding up each piece and dressing them onto a mannequin.

Having Ethan stand beside the dummy, Macailah again used her visual creation to easily replace the silver jogging suit with Ali's last known outfit.

When done, Ethan observed himself in the full-length mirror. "Ah, I remember this well," he said, turning side to side. It was one of his favorites, a rather stylish cotton jubba with tan jacket and matching pants. Under the jacket was a white, high-collar, button-down shirt. On his head was a white turban. Still picturing the image of Ali on the slab, Macailah added the full black beard and mustache.

"Perfect," exclaimed Habib. "But you two may want to add a little color to your skin. You're a bit pale for Arabs."

Embarrassed by the oversight, Macailah quickly cast a deep brown tan to both their facades.

A final inspection in the mirror brought back a flood of memories for Ethan, when he was the Afghan father to his beloved Phoebe. He began to feel surer of himself and the upcoming charade.

That left the two virgins. But rather than being encased from head to toe in black burqas of that time and place, they both suggested spicing things up a bit by wrapping their newly-concocted, full figures in white satin, leaving uncovered their comely, ebony faces with black eyes and full ruby lips. A few jewels around their necks, wrists and ankles seemed a nice touch, too. Macailah weighed the concept a moment, and then agreed, figuring it would do no harm. If everything went according to plan, there probably wouldn't be any contact between them and Ackmed anyway. All they had to do was stand there looking ready and willing to grant a young dead Arab his every wish.

# Chapter 64

The last stop was the Reception Station itself. Going through the huge, revolving smoked-glass door, the foursome found themselves in what could best be described as the expansive lobby of a grand hotel. No imagination or energy had been spared in creating the ornate décor of gold-plated pillars and walls, accented with diamond-encrusted planters and ceiling tiles. This was offset by rich mahogany vertical panels, a Rosa Aurora Classic marble floor and a wide variety of foliage interlaced throughout. Songbirds flittered and chirped from the treetops. A pair of magnificent Belgium tigers lounged by the huge fountain. Exotic African antelopes drank from the pool. Soft, angelic music permeated the air.

One never minded coming to the Reception Station's atrium.

While the others absorbed the tranquil ambience, Macailah walked up to the front desk to confirm the suite she had reserved for Phoebe's return. She had no trouble remembering the handsome, flamingly gay clerk named Luther, who was decked out in his usual silk shirt in an explosion of bright colors and wore those twin diamond earrings the size of grapes. In turn, Luther quickly recognized her from earlier visits. The hug was warm and the dialog lively.

"So, who is Ethan coming back as this time, Macailah?" he queried pleasantly.

"Not Ethan," she replied. "The arriver is Phoebe."

"Ah, yes…Phoebe," he repeated with a nod, now looking down at the touch-screen and busily poking it with his fingertips. "I remember her coming back from her DeKalb *trip*." When Macailah purposely stone-faced him, he quickly apologized for the cheap play on words.

"No apology necessary," laughed Macailah, now going along. "And she didn't *trip* to her death, she *jumped*. You would, too, if you were trying to get away from this E2 stalker named Leonid."

Luther tapped his screen a few times, pulling up the standard video and bio of Leonid. "Speak for yourself, girlfriend," he breathed, eyes wide. "He's de-lish looking. Send him my way."

"I'm sure Phoebe will let you have him," said Macailah, leaning forward enough to see Luther's screen. "Apparently he's been a pain in her ass since day-one." After a polite few seconds, Macailah tapped Luther on his platinum head. "Now, if you can tear yourself away, can we get back to Phoebe?"

With a sigh, Luther returned the screen to the video and bio of Phoebe. "Well, as far as females go, this girl has become quite the beauty, indeed. Your handiwork, Macailah?"

"I can't take the credit for that one," she sighed with a broad smile. "Just Ethan. I've never met Phoebe's creator, just heard about him. Name is Andrew. We thought he might show up for Phoebe's return today, but no sign of him yet."

"Oh, that *is* Ethan over there by the fountain," chortled Luther, motioning in that direction. Macailah affirmed it was. "Well, now, that fine mess of thought particles has certainly developed into a handsome young man. Especially after his second life as that Inuit woman. No offense, Macailah, but that was one ugly bitch."

"I had nothing to do with that DNA," Macailah quickly said. "He got that by diving headlong into the body without listening to me."

"Well, you have done yourself proud with him now. He's *gorgeous*."

"Thanks. It's the image he wants while between lives from now on. And I don't have to help him maintain it at all anymore. He completely believes in himself."

"How wonderful," said Luther, resting his chin on his fist and gazing longingly again at the distant Ethan. "I assume he's along today to help you bring in Phoebe?"

"Correct."

"Her lover?" asked Luther, coyly.

"You have no idea!" sighed Macailah, shaking her head slowly.

# Chapter 65

"Oh, but I do," countered Luther with a crafty smile. He pointed over Macailah's shoulder to a rather erotic mural on the wall of a recessed area of the main lobby.

It's hard to make an E3 blush, but Macailah just did. "Oh, my God," she winced, studying the animated work of art from floor to ceiling. There were spiraling fireworks, humping angles, and a naked Ethan and naked Phoebe engaged in a twisting, thrusting episode of unadulterated spiritual coupling.

"It's really quite beautiful," said Luther, studying it more closely. "I wonder who the artist is."

Getting over the initial shock, Macailah turned her focus away from the mural's content to zero in on the artist's style. Well, I'll be," she mused. "I'm pretty sure that's Renoir's work."

"Oh, do you know this Renoir dude?" asked Luther casually, still far more interested in the animated mural.

"Yes," reflected Macailah. "We were classmates in a number of art classes at Seth Hall. A fair talent."

"Yes, not bad," mused Luther, bending his head this way and that to better study the ever-changing positions of the animated lovers.

"Oh wait a minute," Macailah suddenly blurted. "I can't let Ethan see that. It will rip his heart out. He's pining enough already for Phoebe. I need to keep him as calm as possible for her return today."

"I think it's okay," said Luther, stretching over the counter to better scan for Ethan. "He's well past it…still over there by the fountain, petting a tiger."

"Great," breathed Macailah. "Quick, let's finish up here."

Luther dropped his attention back to his screen. "Okay," he said. "Yes, you have reserved Suite-361. And I see you've already done some work on it."

"It was rather simple, just a plain Islamic prayer room."

"So I see. Our records show this was not your usual artistry, Macailah," he quipped. "Is your life getting easier or are you getting lazier?"

"Maybe a little of both," smiled Macailah.

Luther glanced back down at his touch-screen. "Okay, your Gatekeeper's name is Samuel. One of our best. Hmm. Seems you're going to need him…this looks like a rather precarious return, huh, dear?"

"Afraid so."

"Well, don't you worry. Samuel will get you set up and make sure everything is in alignment. All I need from you is your signature, sweetheart."

Quite familiar with the procedure, Macailah placed the index finger of her right hand on the same touch screen and watched the green light flash in the upper left-hand corner. A pretty, asexual image with a pleasant voice appeared on the screen. "Thank you, Macailah. Good luck with Phoebe's return and please come again soon. We so enjoy your visits."

# Chapter 66

After offering a hearty thanks to Luther, Macailah rejoined her waiting group. Ethan and the two *virgins* followed her through another revolving glass door, down a long, glowing hallway of polished silver to a door marked *S-361*. It had no knob or handle. Macailah placed the same finger in the middle of the shiny black door and it swung open.

The foursome was greeted by the gentle face and demeanor of Samuel, dressed for effect like a 1930s magician, complete with top hat and tails. With a bow and sweep he invited them to enter and move to the middle of the barely-lighted room of indeterminate proportions and content.

Once in place, Samuel did something from behind a dark curtain, and the room gradually illuminated to reveal the prayer hall of a mosque. In contrast to the elaborate atrium they had just left, it was quite small and bland. There was a soft beam of light spilling through a single dome in the ceiling and a little more from two arched windows, one on each side of the room. Right next to them was a mimbar, where an imam would sit to deliver a sermon.

"What do you think?" Macailah asked.

Ethan glanced around the small room. As they had discussed during the planning stage, it was just enough to look authentic, yet not so elaborate to have Ackmed lost in its splendor, thinking he really had obtained Paradise for his misguided act of terrorism.

"It looks good," he stated. "Your usual fine job."

Familiar with Islamic customs, Macailah took her place on the mimbar. "It might be better if Ackmed-Phoebe sees me sitting here," she remarked. "He expects a holy man; and based on his strong, Muslim indoctrination, he should be greeted by me first."

When Ethan agreed, Macailah continued with the scenario, "I'll rise and beckon him to me. I'll embrace him and reassure him. There is no hurry. We'll let Ackmed-Phoebe go at his own pace. When I feel he's ready, I'll direct him toward you, Ethan-Ali-father. He will undoubtedly rush over to you. That's when you tell him everything is alright and he's completely safe, and you love him...as his *father*. And *only* as his father." Macailah glared hard at her protégé.

146

Ethan nodded sheepishly, memories of messing things up back in DeKalb's fake city park were still fresh on his list of embarrassing fubars.

"This can't be stressed enough," cautioned Macailah, stepping closer to make the point once again. "If Phoebe's memories start coming through too soon, as they might, her Ackmed portion may begin to *feel* you as his lover as well as father. If that process starts, take it very slow. Stay in character. Don't let the Ackmed portion get confused."

Ethan nodded pensively, his solar plexus chakra beginning to throb again.

Then Macailah added a little louder, "You virgins remember you're basically window dressing. Young, virtuous Ackmed will probably be too intimidated to approach you anyway. Sorry. And if any part of Phoebe is materializing," Macailah added humorously, "she certainly won't want anything to do with a couple of Arab hookers.'"

"His-her loss!" one of them replied in mock indignation.

"That's okay," said the other with a lisp, winking at the first one while wagging a limp-wristed hand. "We're covered."

The group rehearsed a few minutes longer, until Samuel announced that Ackmed was only a mile from the police station. It wouldn't be long now…just a few more minutes. The tension in the room rose considerably. As Samuel instructed, all four pretenders faced toward the far wall from which Ackmed-Phoebe would arrive, at present showing no signs of being anything other than a sand-colored, featureless partition.

Off to the left, Ethan nervously shifted his weight back and forth, as he practiced his lines in Persian. Farther on the left, the two virgins fussed over each other, adjusting necklines and jewelry. At the fore, Macailah got herself into character by reading various passages from the Koran in her masculine voice. She'd done a number of impersonations before, but this was her first Islamic sheikh.

For some well-timed comic relief, Samuel let off a puff of smoke in the room and said in his best Wizard of Oz voice, "Pay no attention to the man behind the curtain." Macailah and the hookers laughed. Ethan didn't get it. He'd never seen the movie.

Just seconds before zero hour, Samuel casually announced that Ackmed had gone off course. The car was moving away from the police station. It may be another minute or two.

# Chapter 67

Ackmed's white-knuckles were squeezing the sawdust out of the steering wheel, as the beige, 1995 Mercedes sedan maneuvered slowly and steadily through the crowded streets of downtown Kandahar. Breaking clear of the marketplace and the hordes of shoppers, Ackmed's stomach was so tied in knots he threw up in his mouth for the third time.

His mind raced with jumbled thoughts—from his dead father he couldn't wait to see again to his live mother whose heart he would break…from the clerics who strapped him into the car to the American marines he was supposed to blow up. Envisioning the virgins awaiting him in just a few minutes in Paradise gave the nineteen-year-old some semblance of calm. But the image of his beautiful, healthy, young body exploding into a cloud of pink mist and red chunks mixed with steel and rubber car parts brought breakfast up once again, this time all over his lap.

Emptying his stomach actually cleared Ackmed's mind somewhat. He began to question his hatred of the United States for killing his father. That drone wasn't actually targeting him, Ali just happened to be in the wrong place at the wrong time. The West was attempting to squelch terrorism, which Ackmed and his family had despised as much as they did. And what did those marines ever do to him? They were probably American boys his own age, just doing what their government told them to do. Did they deserve to die just for trying to train some Afghan recruits at the local police station, just for helping his country become a better place?

In a fit of conscience, Ackmed frantically tore at the seatbelt and yards of gray duct tape that had him strapped in. No chance. He glanced at the single, silver switch screwed into the dashboard he was told to flip after he crashed through the station's barbwire and steel posts barricade. No, throwing it now would kill many innocent bystanders, as his route took him though a heavily populated residential area all the way to the objective. Not throwing it was no option either, as he knew a back-up timer was rigged to detonate the explosives in case Ackmed did change his mind; this would occur approximately 30 seconds after the time it had been so meticulously determined he should arrive at ground zero. And the clock in the dash said he was right on schedule.

Sweating profusely and hyperventilating so fast he was on the verge of passing out, Ackmed turned onto the narrow street that led straight to the police station, just four blocks away. His heart sank. There was nothing he could do.

Suddenly, a vision flashed through his mind. It was the map he had studied so diligently, the street map of Kandahar, the map that had his suicide route marked in red. But now it also showed with a special glow the Arghandab River a little less than half a mile beyond the police station. Ackmed's pulse raced. Could he make it there before the explosives automatically detonated? If he could, the chances were very good he would be the only one losing his life this day.

Half seeing the map, half seeing the real world outside his dusty windshield, Ackmed cranked the steering wheel to the right and pulled onto a side street. Another two blocks and he turned back to the left. As the map vision had promised, he was on a secondary dirt road that lead straight to the Arghandab River. He slammed his foot hard on the accelerator. The engine roared. The seconds were ticking.

The road ended abruptly at the river bank. In a cloud of dust the Mercedes launched into the air going seventy miles per hour over the water. Ackmed's heart soared right along with it, light and free. He felt no anguish, no fear. An incredible peace enveloped his very core.

What a wonderful feeling!

What a beautiful white light!

# Chapter 68

"Here he comes!" announced Samuel, from his trance behind the curtain.

The unremarkable gray wall suddenly blossomed into a circular glow of soft, white light. A ghostly human form with ill-defined edges materialized in its center, at first stationary, then moving slowly forward, apparently looking side to side. As it reached the center of the room, just a few feet in front of Macailah, it stopped, its blurry image beginning to sharpen. It was indeed a human, its black eyes wide with wonder, its mouth open in stunned silence.

As it focused on the imam sitting before him on the mimbar, the image's expression turned quizzical, searching. The gray-bearded sheikh in a brown robe and skullcap rose to his feet, opened his arms and in perfect Persian said, "Welcome to Paradise, my child."

With a little hesitation, a more in-focus Ackmed took the final two steps to embrace and be embraced by the Islamic holy man. Throughout the embrace, his nineteen-year-old image grew clearer. Sparkles of joy and relief dislodged from the region of his head and heart, flittering outward in an array of vibrant blue mist.

When the exchange of positive energy reached its maximum and leveled off, holy-man-Macailah placed his hands on Ackmed's shoulders and gently turned him ninety degrees in the direction of Ali. "There is someone you might know, Ackmed."

"Father!" cried Ackmed, rushing to Ali-Ethan's waiting arms. They hugged hard and long, sparks dancing freely from both, their spirits entwined in pure joy. The love was overwhelming. Macailah beamed with pleasure for both her younger-self and his soul mate. Over in the corner, tears rolled down the cheeks of both virgins.

Macailah would later take the blame for what happened next. With all the planning and rehearsing, with all the careful attention to detail, one thing had been overlooked: Ethan's eyes should have been *black*, not *sky-blue*. When she had psychically dipped into The Deep Blue to see how Ali was dressed before being prepped for burial, of course the dead body's eyes were closed. So, Macailah hadn't even considered his eye color.

Being dressed in the exact clothing Ackmed had last seen his father wearing, plus the beard and the brown skin, from a distance Ali-Ethan looked every bit the father he had been for nineteen years. But up close those sky-blue eyes became evident, causing something to stir inside Ackmed's unconscious. He pushed away from his father just enough to study his face more closely. His hands came up to stroke the otherwise familiar brown face.

Unfortunately, impressionable Ethan—blindly lost in the passion of finally being reunited with his beloved mate—completely forgot himself and took that gesture to mean Phoebe was positioning herself for a kiss, as the pair had done so many times before. And that is exactly what Ethan-Ali did, wet and steamy, full on the mouth, tongue down her throat.

Most religions don't condone tonsil-hockey in public, much less between father and son. And Islam frowns on it even between marrieds. Ackmed quickly pushed himself away, his eyes dancing, his mind racing. He searched for rationale. His very fiber teetered between loathing and ecstasy. His self-image began to flash in and out between Eastern male and Western female.

Still seeing only Phoebe in his mind's eye and in a state of confusion himself, Ethan-Ali held out his arms. "Sweetheart. Phoebe. It's me, Ethan!" he pleaded, walking after his back-peddling lover.

From a son's perspective, his father was now coming after him with weird eyes, compelling words, and an amorous tongue about a foot long. And to make matters worse, Ackmed was feeling a strange attraction for him.

*By the beard of Allah, this is incest!* The young Arab thought in terror. *This is blasphemy! This is grounds for damnation in Jaheem!* Ackmed began to see shadowy apparitions dancing about the room. They had come for him. The light was fading. Guilt and excitement filled his stomach. Joy and disgust battled for his heart. Horror seared his mind.

In the blink of an eye, Macailah was between Ali-Ethan and Ackmed-Phoebe. She motioned for her protégé to keep his distance, and then turned to the confused entity, who was now oscillating between the two identities even more, its outline returning to less-defined.

"Ackmed, it's okay," said the holy man, in a calm, comforting tone. "You are safe. Nothing can hurt you. You're in Paradise. Everyone here knows you and loves you. And you know them."

It wasn't working. Macailah's words went unheard. Ackmed-Phoebe was fading away.

151

# Chapter 69

While not a common topic of discussion, Earth-Two has other vibrations, or frequencies, or layers, if you so choose. As previously noted, the Ground Floor could be said to be a half of a megahertz "below" or away from the main level. But there is another region below that one. Some would call it *Purgatory, Limbo,* or even *Hell.* But perhaps the more appropriate moniker would be *The Gray Zone.* It's not necessarily a bad place. It's just an area that certain souls may drift into, if they are too conflicted to accept the validity of their real Home in Earth-Two.

This is where Ackmed-Phoebe was heading.

The soul doesn't create the basis of the environment it finds itself in. It was here long before. The bewildered spirit only "decorates" it to some degree with its expectations, augmented by the intensity of its fear and confusion.

Fortunately, most stays here are temporary. A few of the less severe cases may come back to Earth-Two on their own, eventually resolving their issues or simply finding the accommodations of The Gray Zone less than desirable. Most, however, require the guidance of an Earth-Three specialist, trained in such matters of recovery and reorientation. And the sooner the guide can get there the better. Without redirection, the dislodged soul may come to accept this netherworld as its true reality, and lose all incentive to leave. That is a much more difficult condition to rectify.

Macailah had just such a case a short while back. Her very first clone—named Korlin—had designed his sixth life to be a devout Roman Catholic in Milan, Italy after World War I. When Korlin found his wife cheating on him in their own bed, he completely snapped. He walked into his study, pulled his Uberti revolver from the drawer, walked back to the bed chamber and fired all six bullets into the copulating couple. Since Mussolini had reinstated capital punishment in 1927, Korlin was executed by firing squad in the spring of 1929.

When he came through the portal, he was fully expecting to find himself mired deep in fire and brimstone. So, although he initially entered into the same level of love and serenity that Ackmed-Phoebe just had, his powerful Catholic expectations sent him straight toward his own version of Hell.

Well prepared for the event, Macailah went right along with him, holding his hand, dressed as his church's bishop. That act alone prevented Korlin from getting as deep into the concept of Hades as he probably had imagined. Also instrumental was Macailah's expertise in rapidly "painting over" Korlin's expected environment with a less harsh version.

Like space, time as we know it doesn't really exist on Earth-Two, or Earth-Three, or anyplace in the Cosmos, for that matter. But if one were to put a label on how long it took Macailah to convince Korlin that his harsh surroundings were the result of his own beliefs, it may have been days. In small doses, the wise, well-traveled mentor kept upgrading Korlin's setting with her own trappings, making things brighter and warmer, all the while counseling her younger-self with gentle explanations and encouragement.

The final stage of the therapy found the pair in a psychiatrist's office with an Eighteenth Century Venetian motif. Korlin was pretty much convinced by now that he was a good soul who deserved at least some degree of Heaven, and Macailah's visage had morphed into a male with a Freudian goatee and round spectacles. She so loved playing roles.

Mirrors had purposely been avoided throughout the entire recovery period, as they would only reinforce Korlin's belief that he was an Italian murderer. So, there at the end, with Korlin now on the verge of remembering his true self, it was time to see for himself. Macailah had guided her progeny to the wardrobe and had him stand facing it as she opened the doors. The full-length mirror inside reported back to Korlin his true, spiritual self. Stroking the familiar face and hair as one would a lovable puppy, his consciousness was instantly refilled with any missing pieces of his six lives and many experiences. Korlin was whole again. The nightmare was over.

The knowledge gained was invaluable for Korlin, Macailah, and The Deep Blue.

# Chapter 70

Ethan paced up and down the silvery hallway like an expectant father. Behind the white door he kept passing was his beloved Phoebe, who—as far as he knew—still thought she was Ackmed. With her was Macailah, his trusted mentor, who—as far as he knew—was doing something to bring her back. Also in there was some soul named Andrew, who—as far as he knew—was some benevolent doctor from this hospital who had come in to help.

Wanting desperately to help out, but also afraid he would make matters even worse, Ethan wasn't too upset when Macailah told him to wait outside until he was called. He was also told to stay in character as Ali...and by all means to maintain those black eyes Macailah had now given him. So the distraught E2-6 wandered aimlessly through the halls of the Reception Station's Recovery Wing, having nothing to do but pause momentarily to gaze at the many art masterpieces lining the walls. He was especially enamored with one work entitled "Bather Standing," by some artist named Renoir. The woman's pose and honey-blonde hair reminded him of Phoebe as Octavia...standing naked in that stream...at Uncle Cladius's farm...south of Rome...a couple incarnations ago.

"Maybe when we get through all this," he mused nostalgic, "we can get this Renoir fellow to do a portrait of us."

"Can you tell me your name?" asked Andrew, his chair drawn up close to the hospital bed Ackmed-Phoebe was occupying. The nineteen-year-old Arab, wearing a basic, white and blue, floral-print hospital gown, was lying back at a forty-five-degree angle and covered to the waist with a multi-colored, crocheted blanket. Staring off in the distance, the dazed patient blinked a couple times, then replied, "Ackmed?"

"Very good," said Andrew. "And do you know who I am?"

The patient's eyes slowly lowered to the image the voice was coming from. He appeared to be a typical Arab physician with olive skin, beardless face, dark eyes and wearing light-green scrubs. "You're a...doctor," was the reply.

When Ackmed-Phoebe's gaze lazily slipped off into the distance again, the doctor projected the color of his own skin to be a couple shades lighter.

"Do I look at all familiar?" he continued.

Again Ackmed-Phoebe studied him, squinting more. "Maybe a little."

"Very good," said Andrew. "That's all for now. Just go back to sleep."

When the patient gladly obeyed, Andrew looked at Macailah and with a nod of his head motioned back toward Ackmed-Phoebe. "What do you think?" he asked.

Macailah moved in closer, craning her neck to better study the patient. The black hair was beginning to show traces of highlights. The skin was no longer dark-brown, just brown. Lifting one eyelid revealed a softer shade of black with a hint of green. Two small bumps were pushing out from the hospital gown's chest region.

"I'd say eighty-twenty Ackmed," concluded Macailah.

Andrew concurred. He rose to his feet and motioned toward the door. "Am I correct in assuming that soul out there in the hallway belongs to you?"

Macailah smiled sheepishly. "Yes, that's my Ethan," she replied, bowing to the entity who had come in to help recover Phoebe. "And I'm Macailah."

"Wonderful to meet you, Macailah. I'm Andrew."

The two hugged briefly. Macailah felt a connection, but couldn't place it at the moment. Andrew, on the other hand, was aware of everyone's relationship. Of course he knew Ethan was his precious Phoebe's lover and that Macailah was Ethan's creator. He also knew that up until this moment Macailah didn't know who he was. She thought this doctor was just a kind E3 coming in to help bring Phoebe back to reality. He would tell her soon enough. But for now it was fun keeping the little secret. Earth-Threes enjoyed playing games with each other. It was always too easy with the ignorant Earth-Twos.

"And if I'm getting the vibrations correct," continued Andrew, "Ethan and Phoebe are lovers."

"Oh, yeah," laughed Macailah.

"And in this Afghanistan incarnation they were father and son."

"Yes. Ethan was the father, Ali."

"I see..." mused Andrew. "Would it help to bring in Ali now?

"It might," Macailah replied cautiously.

155

# Chapter 71

When the white door finally opened, Ethan-Ali rushed in, only to be blocked by his mentor, still in the role of the Arab sheik. "Hold on a minute, my impetuous child," she cautioned. "We need to go over a few things first."

"Sure. Okay," hastily agreed Ethan-Ali, looking past Macailah for a glimpse of Phoebe-Ackmed, still unconscious on the bed. "How is she?"

"She's stabilized," assured Macailah, with both hands on Ethan's shoulders. "We feel she's pretty much out of danger. Some of Phoebe is present, but she's still identifying mostly with Ackmed."

To make sure she had Ethan's attention, Macailah placed her delicate hands on the taller man's bearded face and gently pulled it down until their eyes met. "As Ali, you need to make amends with Ackmed," she stated firmly. "You need to explain your overly-affectionate actions. Do you understand, *Ali*?" Ethan-Ali nodded.

While Macailah continued to coach her anxious younger-self, over in the corner Andrew had produced a hand-mirror with a flick of his wrist. He used it to monitor the subtle changes he was making toward his own natural image. His skin, eyes and hair all lightened another shade, the latter beginning to show red highlights. The light-green scrubs remained.

When everyone was ready, Andrew took his place standing at the foot of the bed. Macailah pulled up a chair to the left side, while Ethan-Ali took the one Andrew had previous occupied on the right. Gazing longingly at the odd image of his Arabic male Phoebe, the yearning soul softly reached out to rub the uncovered arm. "Wake up, young prince," he whispered, as Macailah had suggested. "It's me, your father."

Ackmed-Phoebe's eyes cracked open and rotated toward the familiar voice. His father often called him "young prince," especially when Ackmed had done something worthy of praise. Ackmed-Phoebe's eyes widened when they saw Ali. "Hi, Father," he said with a weak smile, still a little groggy.

Although Phoebe's image was mostly that of a young Afghan male to everyone else in the room, Ethan could feel the true vibration of his beloved, which, from his perspective, naturally changed her visage closer to that of Phoebe. Pangs of desire started rising in most of his seven chakras. He couldn't help himself. He lifted a few inches from the chair to slide his hand farther up the arm...his mouth heading toward hers.

At that moment, he detected some interference coming from across the bed. A quick glance in that direction found a scowling Macailah, followed by the unspoken demand to *back off*!

"Ackmed, my son," said Ethan-Ali, lowering back into the chair and removing his hand, "Please forgive me for kissing you earlier in the mosque. I was so happy to be reunited with you, I got carried away."

Ackmed studied his father's face with its now-black eyes.

"It's true, my child," added sheik-Macailah from the left. "Your father missed you so much that the sight of you made his heart soar."

Ackmed rotated his head to face the holy man. He remembered him from the prayer room when he arrived from Earth. Ackmed smiled.

Sheik-Macailah scooted a little closer and took Ackmed-Phoebe's right hand in his. "I checked with Muhammad about the kiss, Ackmed," he continued. "He said it was all right. In fact, He said it was wonderful to see such love a father can have for a son. He blessed both of you."

A big smile of relief spread across Ackmed-Phoebe's face. "Oh, Father!" was all he could say, reaching out for Ali.

Ethan-Ali was quick to rise and meet the embrace. As he basked in the warm essence of his cherished Phoebe, he was slapped with a double bolt of caution and intense stink-eye from the other side of the bed. Difficult as it was, he released himself from Ackmed-Phoebe's arms. "I have to go take care of some business," he announced, almost choking on the lie. "I'll see you soon...*Son*." He rose and walked toward the door, as instructed.

By now the nineteen-year-old Arab male was projecting about seventy-thirty Ackmed-Phoebe. Memories were working their way back into his consciousness. Seeing that person he loved so deeply moving away from him was particularly heart-wrenching. "Please, don't go...er, Father!" he cried, stumbling on the last word, not so certain it really applied.

Ethan-Ali stopped his retreat and took a yearning step back toward Phoebe. Another glare from Macailah, spun him right around again. "We will see each other very soon," he proclaimed without looking back, to hide his anguish. "I promise." The white door opened and he disappeared behind it.

# Chapter 72

Andrew quickly suggested another nap would do wonders, and Ackmed/Phoebe was once again in a peaceful, restorative sleep.

"While we have a few moments," began Andrew, "I'd like to commend you on the fine job you did in diverting Phoebe away from the abyss. She could have been lost to us for a while."

"Well, thanks," said Macailah, smiling modestly, "but I don't deserve much of the credit."

She explained that she knew how much Ethan wanted to be reunited with Phoebe, and how distraught Ethan was for sending her over the edge. Macailah also revealed that it was as much her fault for forgetting to give Ethan-Ali dark eyes. So, in a panic herself, Macailah spontaneously sent out a distress signal that spanned every sector from here to Earth-Four. The next thing she knew Phoebe was in a coma and they both were whisked away from the depths, landing smack into this specially prepared hospital room. The logistics and timing were more than she could have done herself under those adverse conditions.

As she finished, Macailah suddenly picked up the vibe from her fellow E3. "Well, of course," she laughed, now enlightened. "You're Andrew. I didn't make the connection when you introduced yourself. My mind must have been elsewhere. Phoebe is yours."

"Andrew smiled, "My pride and joy."

"And it was you who came to my rescue."

"On the wings of a panicked father."

Macailah shook her fake, skull-capped head. "The whole time we've been here in this room, I've assumed you were just some Good Samaritan from Recovery. As fast as you got there...your ability to pull her out of the abyss...and the degree of love you've been projecting towards Phoebe...I should have known."

"I was going to tell you when we had a moment," grinned Andrew. "I hope you don't mind my little deception."

"Not at all," chuckled Macailah. "It's what we do, isn't it?"

158

The two shared the private joke, then Macailah asked, "So, what do you think about this torrid love affair our other-selves are having? Have you ever seen anything like it?"

"Never, replied Andrew. "She's a chunk off the old soul in many ways, and I certainly have my passion for love and lovers. But the way those two E2s can send up sparks rivals anything we do on Earth-Three."

"Yes, I let Ethan have a good slice of my impetuousness and passion, too," said Macailah. "He discovered sex during his first incarnation and couldn't stop harping about it. He was so anxious to get back to Earth for some more, he—against my warning—dived right into being an Eskimo woman who was so repulsive she had to pay for it."

"*That* was a lesson," said Andrew with a snort, now puffing on a pipe.

"Most certainly," said Macailah. "He learned some things about humility, self-esteem, and the like. But he also came back hornier than ever. He begged to be a good-looking man for the next one. So I turned him into a Greek god and dropped him into ancient Athens as a gigolo."

Andrew threw his head back and laughed.

"Oh, it gets better," continued Macailah. "For the exit point, I nudged a husband to come home early and sneak into the bed chamber. Ethan was back with me in mid-thrust.

Now both E3s were cackling.

# Chapter 73

It was enlightening for Andrew to hear a brief history of Ethan's amorous exploits leading up to meeting his Phoebe. From that point on he already knew about the latter part of Ethan's fourth trip to Earth as a Roman soldier, because it was when Ethan came to Phoebe's rescue in that stable. As she was about to be raped, Andrew detected her distress signals and flew to be by her side, trying to quell her fears the best he could without interfering. Once Ethan arrived, Andrew knew she was safe and in good hands, at least until Phoebe's cries of anguish at Ethan's execution later brought Andrew back to comfort her again.

Andrew blew a stream of pipe smoke into the air. "It would seem your young man's sexual propensity stems from a series of events where his passion is cut short at its apogee," he surmised. "And as infatuated as they were with each other, having him executed right before her eyes at the crest of their desires was really the cherry on top."

"You are exactly right," nodded Macailah. "If they'd had the rest of that Rome existence to marry and grow tired of each other...or even just a few more months to let the shine wear off, maybe their passion would have waned."

"I wanted to be there with you during Phoebe's return from that Rome incarnation," added Andrew. "But I was detained trying to comfort my latest offspring during his first stint on Earth. He hadn't gotten his gravity legs just yet, and had fallen down a gorge and become wedged between two big rocks. I had to babysit him until he died of exposure."

Macailah shook her head knowingly. "Kids."

"Tell me about it."

Getting back on the subject, Macailah concluded, "It's probably better you weren't there when Phoebe arrived. I'd spent considerable time and effort constructing a beautiful honeymoon suite for them, complete with rose petals and circular bed, heart-shaped Jacuzzi, the works. And all they did was...well, have you seen the mural in the Plaza's lobby?"

"I have," confirmed Andrew with a deep sigh. "I told Renoir he needs to get a life."

Andrew turned his attention to the empty space between them. With a blink and a nod, a small table with two glasses of *Dom Perignon 1957* materialized. He handed one to his fellow E3, and took the other. He held it high, and Macailah followed suit.

"Well, my beautiful friend," toasted Andrew, "together you and I have intentionally and unintentionally helped generate a love few souls ever experience."

"May it continue to flourish and be a beacon to young lovers in every corner of the microcosm."

Suddenly, an ominous vision of Leonid's frustrated face flashed across Andrew's consciousness. He shuddered. But he clinked Macailah's glass anyway.

After a reflective moment, both mentors rose from their chairs to check on the patient. The face was peaceful, shifting ever so slightly back and forth between Ackmed and Phoebe. He/she was really quite attractive, with full lips and a light brown coloring to both the complexion and hair. Satisfied with the progress, they settled back into their seats.

"So, tell me all about Phoebe," said Macailah, leaning toward Andrew in interest, her elbows on her knees and hands clasped. "I'd love to hear her background."

Always pleased to talk about his favorite progeny, Andrew leaned back in his chair and blew a perfect smoke ring toward the ceiling.

"Well, her first incarnation was as a gangbanger named Tyree..."

# Chapter 74

Andrew tapped the pipe's cold ash into his hand and neatly flicked it into thin air. He stuck the stem back between his teeth, and glanced over at Macailah.

"And here we are."

Macailah sat quietly for a moment, soaking up the fascinating history of Phoebe. "Interesting," she mused. "On the surface their meeting in Rome looks to be purely random. I mean, I saw it in the probable future for Ethan, and I guided him in the right direction. But beyond that, I did very little to make it happen. I just put a few Gauls to sleep so our lovers could get by an outpost undetected. Did you do anything?"

"Not really," replied Andrew, shaking his head. "I may have helped get her that job in the stable, because I saw it was paramount to later meeting her soul mate. And I may have had something to do with this *particular, horny, obsessed E2 named Leonid* failing to take Phoebe for his prize after they executed her lover. But other than that, I let nature take its course."

Macailah hadn't witnessed that part of the Rome ending. She had been quite busy calming Ethan's terror at having just been executed by the Gauls at Uncle Cladius's farm.

"So, when we put their two histories together," continued Macailah, "and look at how they seem to mesh just right in so many ways to create a love, a *passion* that, well, you know…"

"Yes, I know what you mean," replied Andrew.

"…you have to wonder if maybe there isn't a greater power at work here."

Both mentors contemplated the premise a while, before Andrew concluded, "Well, *They* do move in mysterious ways."

The two E3s smiled knowingly.

It was time to walk over and check on the patient. Still asleep, she was showing about sixty-forty Phoebe-Ackmed. They agreed it should be easy sailing from here on.

Having changed back to his full, Andrew-self with red hair and dark-blue eyes, he sat on the edge of the bed and gently shook Phoebe's shoulder. Her

162

eyes slowly cracked open and followed the hand up the arm to the man's face. "Hey, teacher," she smiled weakly.

"Hey yourself, sweetheart," he replied with a grin. He bent over and kissed the light brown forehead. "Have a good sleep?"

Phoebe stretched her arms way out and brought them flopping down beside her on the bed. "Yeah, I did. Was I out long?"

"Just a little while. You really needed it. You've been through a lot lately."

Phoebe's pale-green eyes blinked rapidly as she collected her thoughts. "Yes, I have, haven't I?"

# Chapter 75

Andrew had her sit up in the bed, saying he had a few questions he wanted to ask her. When she was in position and her attention fully on her teacher, he began.

"What's your name?" he asked.

Her eyes flicked right, then left. "Ah, Phoebe," she replied with a tone that implied, *Duh*!

"Do you have another name that is in your head right now, that may belong to you?"

Phoebe searched the ceiling for an answer. "Yes," she said thoughtfully. "Ackmed."

"Very good. And who exactly is Ackmed?"

"He is me…was me. No, is me," she battled. Then it became clear. "He is who I was a little while ago in Afghanistan."

Just then the memory of racing down the dirt road to launch out over the river as the bomb was about to explode flashed in front of her. She grasped the imaginary steering wheel and cried out. Andrew quickly leaned in to wrap his arms around her and pull the trembling girl to his chest.

"It's okay," he whispered, stroking her hair that was reverting back to a darker shade. "It's over. You are safe. You are in Heaven. I'm here. You did well."

It took a few more minutes and soft words before the terrifying episode began to subside. Phoebe pushed back from Andrew, searching his face for something, anything. Andrew decided to try diverting her attention.

"You remember being a farmer's wife in DeKalb, don't you?

Phoebe found the memory and nodded.

"And being a mother named Alyssa?" he quickly asked.

She thought a moment. "Yes."

"And Gretchen?"

Phoebe smiled and nodded.

Andrew left it there. No reason to bring up Tyree and risk the slippage of a few four-lettered words to embarrass him in front of Macailah. "And what's my name?"

Phoebe smiled weakly, "Andrew, of course."

164

From the other side of the bed, Macailah saw what Andrew may have been too involved to notice: Phoebe's hair was now more blonde than brown, her eyes quite green, and her skin just slightly off-white. Consequently, Macailah saw no further need of her imam persona. She blinked it away in exchange for her favorite silver-gray tunic, bald head, soft, brown eyes, and signature smile with that right-front tooth canting one degree outward.

Andrew noticed the sparkling activity of the wardrobe change and glanced over at Macailah. Macailah smiled and nodded toward Phoebe, with an unspoken *Look*. Andrew peered back at his progeny to discover her astral image was almost eighty percent back to being Phoebe.

"Okay, one more question," said Andrew, saving the best for last, knowing what it would spark. "Do you remember being Octavia in Rome?"

Phoebe's memory snapped to one hundred percent.

"Where's Ethan?" she demanded, quickly scanning the room.

# Chapter 76

"Where's my man?" Phoebe threw the covers off her legs and started to push her way past Andrew, who was still sitting on the edge of the bed. "I want to see him."

"Just a minute, sweetheart," said Andrew, holding her in place. "Ethan is right outside the door waiting to see you, too. But we have to go over a few things about your life as Ackmed first. There are a lot of lessons to be covered."

"Oh, can't that wait?" whined Phoebe. "I need my Ethan right now!"

There was a whimper from the other side of the door. Macailah sent a mental message for Ethan to stay put a little longer.

"Well, maybe you can," said Andrew. "But I have to ask you some questions that can't wait. They are too important. Okay?"

Phoebe looked deep into her teacher's eyes. She knew he was sincere. She trusted him. "Okay," she said anxiously. "Ask away."

"First and most obvious," started Andrew, "I assume you know who Ethan is."

Phoebe laughed sarcastically. "Let's see...I think he's the one I can't wait to join with in passionate and unbridled spiritual coupling."

There was a louder whimper, followed by a banging on the door.

"Okay, but who was he while you were Ackmed in Afghanistan?"

"He was my father, Ali," she replied impatiently, looking past Andrew to the closed door.

"Excellent. And when you returned from Earth, was Ethan there, in the Reception suite, as your father?"

Phoebe's answer was not so quick. "Yes, he was," she said thoughtfully. "He was actually both Ethan and Ali. It was a little confusing."

"It was," confirmed Andrew, stroking the side of her face. "Do you remember anything special happening when you hugged your father?"

Phoebe's eyes narrowed. "Yes...Father was acting like he was going to make love to me, and that frightened me. Yet, I wanted him to, and that *really* frightened me. It went against Islamic law."

"Are you frightened about it now?"

"Oh, not at all," Phoebe stated confidently.

166

"So you understand it now? And you're okay with it?

"Oh, certainly. It was just my beloved Ethan anxious to reunite with me. And me with him."

"Then what happened?"

Phoebe thought a moment. "I don't remember anything after that," she said, shaking her head.

Andrew looked at Macailah. Macailah looked at Andrew and shrugged. They both looked at Phoebe. Her emerald-green eyes were pleading.

"Okay," sighed Andrew. "I guess we can do the rest of the reorientation later." He bent down and kissed Phoebe on the cheek. "You can see Ethan now."

The nineteen-year-old beauty jumped up and started bouncing on the bed like a child waiting for the okay to run downstairs Christmas morning. The two *parents* moved toward the door, smiling and shaking their heads. Before opening it, Andrew turned back toward Phoebe and asked, "Would you like me to dress you in something more appropriate than that hospital gown?"

"That won't be necessary," was her reply, as the gown suddenly dissolved, leaving her completely naked. Andrew was both surprised and pleased that she had done that on her own. Truth was, Phoebe hardly knew that she had.

Macailah opened the door and Ethan flew in, literally! All his clothing, even his beard and black eyes dissolved into gray dust in his wake. He streaked straight for his waiting Phoebe, her arms spread in invitation, her mouth open in exhilaration, her head tilted back in excited anticipation. They collided in mid-air above the bed, twisting and tumbling in an explosion of ecstasy, colorful particles pin-wheeling outward from the center of their joined spirits.

Macailah and Andrew paused in the doorway to psychically share in the joyful passion. After all, the two entities rapturing above the hospital bed were still very much a part of themselves.

Being time to leave the pair alone, Macailah and Andrew moved out into the hallway and closed the door. But then in afterthought, Macailah opened it again and called, "Please try to keep it down a little, you two. There's already one commemorative mural of you two making love, hanging here in the Reception Station's lobby. We don't need another."

# Part Three—Cohabitation

# Chapter 77

The young lovers sat on the Persian rug in the middle of their great room, both dressed in very simple, short-sleeved, knee-length pullover nightshirts, hers in pink, his in blue. They could have chosen anything more stylish from the walk-in closet full of clothes that Andrew and Macailah had made for them. But thin, cotton shirts were about the only clothing they could create on their own with matter-manipulation. Besides, they had just made love on the rug, and they might again at any time. The nightshirts were easy to fling aside or just dissolve into thin air.

Inside their two-story log cabin, Phoebe and Ethan were facing the only wall in the great room that didn't have floor-to-ceiling windows. It sported the fireplace with bookshelves on either side, presently void of books. The color of the wall at the moment was basic ivory.

"I like it okay," said Phoebe. "It goes with the oak mantle and bookcases. But if it were just a touch more on the tan side..." She squinted hard and the wall turned to a light-brown. Phoebe smiled, pleased with herself.

"Yeah, I like that," said Ethan, studying the new hue. "And if we changed the oak mantle to some kind of stone...." He squinted, but the wood turned only to a mottled texture, like the result of a termite infestation. Phoebe laughed. Ethan turned it back.

"That's okay, honey," she said, kissing his cheek. "We're learning."

"Speaking of which," said Ethan, standing up. "Macailah's coming in a minute to take me to class. I want to change before she gets here."

His words were no sooner out than both Macailah and Andrew materialized by the fireplace. Macailah was donned in her usual gray-silver tunic with the gold sash and piping, Andrew in his usual white tunic with the purple trimmings. Both were grinning.

168

"Well, to what do we owe this pleasure?" chimed Phoebe, jumping to her feet and rushing over to hug the entity she always considered her virtual father. Ethan followed suit, almost engulfing his mother-figure.

They hadn't seen their two mentors together since Macailah and Andrew were here at the cabin putting the finishing touches on Phoebe and Ethan's love nest. It was their gift to the happy couple in celebration of each one's tenth incarnation, the last one appropriately having Phoebe and Ethan as lovers in 2030 London and finally getting an Earth wedding. They came back to Earth-Two together at age forty-six, when their hovercraft malfunctioned, crashing into the statue of Eros at Piccadilly Circus, instantly killing both, as planned.

When asked what kind of house each would like and where, of course Phoebe wanted something like the Magens Bay bamboo beach house she was raised in and still visited for special tutoring by Andrew. Ethan in turn loved the Swiss chalet for the same reasons. So they compromised on this log cabin in the foothills of the Ozark Mountains in southern Missouri. It had a no-banister staircase with wooden planks leading up to the only bedroom, a wood-burning fireplace, and a breakfast bar between the kitchen and great room. The inside walls were mostly cedar panels with bamboo posts here and there for a hint of the Caribbean. The floor was hardwood parquet, covered with heavy throw rugs from various countries.

Outside was a ten-acre, glove-shaped pond with one finger coming right up under the deck at the rear of the cabin. The water was crystal clear and easily revealed huge largemouth bass and rainbow trout working along the shorelines at any given moment. White swans and various species of geese and ducks were frequent visitors to feed on the smartweed along the edges.

Beyond the pond and around the area was a rolling meadow of well-manicured Kentucky blue grass with patches of wildflowers sprinkled throughout. For vertical contrast the landscape was dotted with strategically placed spreading oak and maple trees, adding shade and definition to the spectacular vista.

On the other side of the cabin sat a basketball court, tennis court, baseball diamond, 18-hole golf course. And, of course, right off the back steps was a two-level swimming pool with waterfall and attached Jacuzzi. All of these were encased and interlaced with a fabulous garden of tropical plants, trees and marble statues from about every era on Earth.

It had taken Andrew and Macailah a lot of time, imagination, matter-manipulation, plus ever-changing minds of their two progeny to complete the entire homestead. But all agreed it was well worth it. Phoebe and Ethan loved their new home and actually used all of the facilities quite regularly. Their joy of sports stemmed from their ninth incarnation as twin sisters on Italy's woman's basketball team, which qualified for the 2024 Summer Olympics.

"I can't believe you both just dropped in to say hello," said a suspicious Phoebe, bending backwards in Andrew's arms to watch the answer come from his thin lips.

"Intuitive as always," he said, his dark-blue eyes showing a slight twinkle. "And you are correct. We have a nice surprise for you."

# Chapter 78

"Yes," said Macailah, "come sit down here on your new couch." A three-cushion sofa of the finest brushed lamb suede instantly materialized in the middle of the great room.

"Well, hey," said Ethan, casting a sideways glance at Phoebe to see if she were as underwhelmed as he. "That's a nice present. Thanks."

"Yes, thanks," added Phoebe with as much enthusiasm as she could muster, considering the letdown. It wasn't worth both Andrew and Macailah coming here just to deliver a couch, she thought, even though they did need one.

"Please, sit down, both of you," said Andrew, motioning toward the new piece of furniture. Phoebe and Ethan obediently took their place side-by-side on the silky-smooth middle cushion. "We have something to tell you. Something you have wanted to know for a long time."

"Where we came from!" screamed Ethan, flying right back off the couch and almost hitting the ceiling twenty feet above him. "Yes! Yes! Finally!"

"Calm down and come down," ordered Macailah.

A still inflated Ethan floated slowly back down beside Phoebe. "Sorry," he grinned, barely realizing the scope of what he had just done.

With Ethan seemingly settled and both their faces beaming with anticipation, Macailah said, "Okay, yes. Andrew and I have decided you both have reached an adequate level of experience and wisdom to understand the process of your true beginnings."

This indeed was something they both often asked to know, but were constantly put off. *You're too young to understand. When you are older. In good time. Be patient.* Now the time was finally here!

"All right," giggled Phoebe, bouncing up and down. "Tell us."

"We're dying to know," added Ethan, still unconsciously levitating a few inches above the cushion.

Andrew and Macailah looked at each other, politely asking the other who should break the news. Andrew nodded toward Macailah.

"You think of us as your teachers, right?" she said matter-of-factly. Phoebe and Ethan nodded. "We're more than that." Macaila watched their faces turn quizzical again.

"You're our parents, aren't you?" surmised Phoebe, sitting up straighter. Both she and Ethan had been suspecting this was the case for some time now.

"In a way, yes," said Macailah. "But in a way, no. We are more than your parents."

Phoebe and Ethan sat staring at Macailah, then at Andrew, then back to Macailah. Confusion was etched on both faces. They searched every corner of the logical portion of their minds for some other option.

"If not our parents," asked Ethan, his hands gesturing out at his sides with palms open in vexation, "what else is there?"

"Go ahead, Andrew," offered Macailah.

Andrew walked forward and knelt down on one knee in front of Phoebe. He took her hands in his and said softly, "Sweetheart, you are a part of me. You are in truth *me*, and I am you."

Phoebe's eyes danced all over Andrew's face, her lips mouthed the words she had just heard. She had heard them alright, but the concept had yet to register.

Macailah stepped forward and stood before Ethan. She offered her hands. Ethan numbly took them. He was as perplexed as his wife. Macailah pulled him up to stand in front of his mother, who apparently was much more than that. "Ethan, it's the same for us," she said quietly, looking up at the taller soul. "You are a part of me, and I of you. I literally made a copy of myself to create you."

The room fell silent.

# Chapter 79

To ease the tension, Macailah playfully conjured the sound of crickets, while she and Andrew waited for the inevitable questions. The younger ones continued to wrestle with the concept.

"I am a part of you," Ethan finally stated, half as a question, half as a statement that was beginning to sink in.

"Yes."

"Which part?"

Andrew took over. "When we created you…when any soul creates a new soul like you two, at the outset he or she makes an exact duplicate of himself or herself."

More crickets.

"But I am hardly a mirror image of you," said Phoebe with a scrunched brow. "There is no resemblance at all and never was."

"Yeah," agreed Ethan, looking at Macailah. "I don't look anything like you. And I never did, even before you gave me this awesome…er…pleasant-looking image."

"At the very moment I divided in two, said Macailah, "you were exactly another me, an exact duplicate. But having two identical Macailahs or Andrews was not the goal. We wanted another self, a new self with very few similarities, so that one of us—in this case, you, Ethan and you, Phoebe, would grow into your own self, have your own identity."

"Why would you do that?" asked the ever-questioning Ethan. "What benefit does it serve you?"

Macailah looked over at Andrew and they both smiled.

"Oh, the benefits are beyond measure," whispered Andrew. "Teaching a new soul and watching it grow in wisdom is reward in itself. But add to that the fact that the new soul is a part of you, and the joys are tenfold."

"Not to mention these joys are instantaneous," added Macailah. She paused for effect.

"Instantaneous?" asked Ethan, just as Phoebe was about to. "What do you mean?"

"Being a part of one another," explained Macailah, we are spiritually connected...a kind of invisible umbilical cord, if you will. Consequently, at an unconscious level, Andrew and I are aware of everything you are doing, seeing, feeling, experiencing, learning."

Ethan and Phoebe looked at each other with very wide eyes. "You mean you've been spying on us our entire lives?!" Phoebe almost shrieked.

Flashing before their eyes were all the embarrassing things each young soul had done during their lifetimes in what they assumed was private. And *Oh, My God!*...here came all the times the pair had made love...right up to the new position executed a few minutes earlier on the Persian rug here in the living room...the same rug their *parents/mentors/other-selves* were now standing on!

"You see everything we do, even in our more private moments, like when we make love?" howled Ethan.

"Well," said Andrew drolly, "the way your energy waves streak across the Cosmos, most of Earth-Two and half of Earth-Three are aware when you two make love!"

Macailah pursed her lips to stifled the smile.

"I don't think that's so funny," spat Phoebe.

"I don't either," said Ethan. "Those are personal moments and nobody else's business." Ethan was back on the couch, with his arm protectively around Phoebe.

"Hold on, you two," cautioned Macailah, still biting a lip, one hand waving dismissively. "We most certainly do *not* spy on you guys. In fact, we never have unless it was absolutely necessary."

"When was it ever *absolutely necessary*?" demanded Phoebe indignantly. "Give us one example."

# Chapter 80

Andrew didn't have to think long. He looked straight and hard at Phoebe. "Remember when you were Ackmed and your father, Ali, died, and you were wailing for Allah to take away your pain?" She nodded slowly. "You were in such a state of grief you unconsciously sent a super-charged signal shooting through the channel between you and me. I immediately sensed your pain and came to comfort you. Not to mention I talked to you in your dreams every night, like we do during all of your incarnations."

Phoebe just stared blankly, soaking in the explanation.

"Remember when you were driving down the streets of Kandahar strapped to a bomb?" Andrew continued. "Your terror again signaled me. I analyzed your vibrations, your feelings, your situation, your needs. I saw that you had had a change of heart and wanted to avoid blowing up the U.S. marines at the police station. So I used our psychic connection to show you the street map with the river and a route to it highlighted. Remember? We went over that river bank together. I was holding you in my arms. I gave you that sense of calm a second before the car exploded."

Phoebe burst into tears. Ethan squeezed her hard, tears flowing freely from his eyes, as well. "I had no idea," she said between sobs. She reached out for Andrew and he obliged, wrapping both Phoebe and Ethan in his embrace.

"And when you were heading for The Gray Zone with me unable to pull you back," added Macailah, "it was Andrew who swept in to rescue us. He even constructed the hospital room you woke up in. He then nursed you back to reality."

Not much was said in the following moments, just tears and hugs, followed by more tears and hugs. Both Ethan and Phoebe were now basking in the glow of discovering they had never been alone all their lives. They were perpetually surrounded by the love of something greater than themselves. They were and always would be protected. They indeed had connections in high places.

Macailah saw no reason to relate any of the few times she had come to comfort Ethan in any of his incarnations, mainly because none were anywhere

175

as dramatic as Phoebe's…not even being gored by that mastodon when he was a clumsy Paleo-Indian male in 13,000 BC.

Once everyone had regained their composure, Macailah stood before the other three on the couch and continued, "Now that you know our spiritual connection with you, young ones, also know this: anytime you want to block your thoughts or shenanigans from us, simply request it. It doesn't even have to be out loud. Just think it: *Go away, Macailah* or *Buzz off, Andrew*. That closes the door to *your room* and we *parents* can't tell what's going on in there."

"The same holds true if you want to block out the entire Cosmos," added Andrew. "A simple, *I wish to be alone*, instantly throws up impenetrable walls and affords you complete privacy. Even God will honor your request."

# Chapter 81

Phoebe and Ethan looked at each other, obviously relieved. Then another question began forming on the brow of the insatiable Ethan. "Say we had requested you to stay out of our business. But then suddenly fell into some kind of peril where we really needed you, but were unconscious or in too much terror to remember to call for you. What then? Are you still blocked?"

"Just the fact of your peril would break through any barrier," said Macailah. "Remember, as parts of the same self, we are always spiritually connected. You may have previously asked for our eyes and ears to be temporarily closed to you, but you can never block off our hearts. If you really need us, the power of your emotion supersedes all, and we are there."

"That's really good to know," sniffled Phoebe. "Thanks!"

"Yes, thanks," said Ethan sincerely. Then his tone of gratitude quickly changed to one of skepticism. "But, just to be clear…you guys have no idea what Phoebe and I were doing here just minutes before you arrived. Right?"

"Sweetheart," said Macailah, leaning down to give him a patronizing pat on the cheek," all we sensed was a faint, distant vibration of joy from you two. And we hardly gave it a second thought. We have neither the time nor inclination to babysit all our younger-selves during their waking hours. We have enough of our own goals and endeavors to keep us quite busy."

Before that clarification could even sink in, Ethan was firing off another inquiry. "*All your younger-selves*?" he piped. "There are others like us, other pieces you've broken off?"

"A couple," said Macailah.

"So, we have brothers and sisters?"

"In a sense."

"Wow! Cool! Can we meet them?"

"You will sometime. Like you, they are quite busy with their own education. Meeting them now would only be a distraction for all of you."

Andrew could see Phoebe's green eyes lighting up with a question. He already sensed what it was and urged her to ask it. They needed to stop Ethan's barrage and get back on topic.

"I'd like some more information on how we were created," she said. "How exactly does that work, anyway?"

"We anticipated your query," smiled Andrew. He glanced over at Macailah, who turned to face the fireplace. She blinked once and an eighty-inch, wide screen television appeared resting on the mantle.

"We brought footage."

With considerable activity and murmurs of anticipation, the two elders joined the two youngsters on the couch. Courtesy of Andrew, out of thin air all were supplied with a twenty-ounce bottle of Pepsi and a big bowl of popcorn. Lots of butter.

"Now, if you prefer," said Andrew. "We could do each of you separately. I could take Phoebe upstairs into the bedroom and watch her birth, while you two did Ethan's down here."

A duet of protests instantly followed, each saying they most definitely wanted to see the other's creation.

# Chapter 82

By the time the popcorn bowls were empty, Phoebe and Ethan had watched the whole cloning process of each other, from the initial dividing to just before whisking off to the Ground Floor to register as new souls. They were utterly astounded.

On the lighter side, Ethan thought Phoebe was really cute as a ten-year-old girl with honey-blonde hair, standing there like a deer in the headlights right after coming out of the trance in the Chamber of Exchange.

"Well, at least I looked like *something*," she laughed. "You looked like a featureless, department store dummy waiting to be dressed in kid's clothes."

The mood was sky-high, as everyone chatted about their favorite piece of footage and how the two offspring had developed in so many ways since their creation. Of course, Ethan had to know if he and Phoebe could copy themselves and have "babies" of their own. It didn't surprise him to learn that only E3s are capable or even allowed to try.

"You can't even get to The Splitting Image as an E2," said Macailah, with her arm around the waist of her favorite splinter. "It takes a number of skills you have yet to learn, plus the recommendation from an E3 sponsor."

"Namely, you," surmised Ethan.

"Namely, me."

Poor Macailah was then barraged with the usual questions of what it takes to reach the level of E3, and how long it might be before he could apply. Her reply was the standard, "Be patient, my son, it will come," followed by the typical deflation of Ethan.

Andrew said he needed to go, and gave good-bye hugs to Macailah and Ethan. When he folded his arms around his diminutive Phoebe, she pressed her head hard against his chest and said, "This feels even better now, knowing we are a part of each other. It's like you are my father and I'm your daughter. Would it be okay if I called you *Father*?"

"I would like that very much," said Andrew, giving her an even tighter squeeze. "I've thought of you as my daughter since the day you were created. Even for us *parents*, it's difficult to grasp the miracle that created you, and

179

that you are actually a piece of ourselves. I just naturally keep seeing you more as my daughter."

"As I soon did of you being my father," said Phoebe. "You always seemed more than my teacher."

Andrew brushed back the honey-blonde hair and kissed her forehead. "Au revoir, mon beaute filles," he said, and disappeared.

"As for you, mon fils," smiled Macailah. "You do have a class to get to. But in light of what you've learned so far today, I could take you another time, if you and Phoebe wish to talk."

Ethan looked at his lover, recumbent on the couch, smiling at nothing. "Oh, you go ahead to class," she said with a mischievous look, waggling the tv remote. "I want to see some more of my big, strong, virile husband when he was a ten-year-old eunuch."

# Chapter 83

As she had a half-dozen times before, Macailah dropped her younger-self at the entrance of Seth Hall, then disappeared to who knows where. But before she left, she admonished Ethan to keep his new-found discovery of where he came from completely to himself. Other E2s were not to know such things until their mentors deemed it so. He agreed.

Ethan walked up the marble steps, down the brightly-lighted hall of gold and mahogany panels with a large skylight every twenty feet. He was wearing cut-off jeans and a textured cyan t-shirt, one of the many articles of clothing created for him by Macailah and hanging in his closet at the cabin. He wasn't confident enough to chance wearing something of his own creation…for fear of it evaporating into the nexus at the most inopportune time.

He took a sharp left turn at a small, turquois sign sticking out of the wall marked *Astral Projection 102*. Without breaking stride he passed through the foggy doorway into the small classroom abuzz with chatter. The ten, light-gray, padded recliners were already occupied with nine fellow students. Ethan filled the tenth, his usual.

The instructor was a strikingly comely woman of about thirty named Sendy. She wore her typical full-sleeve, floor-length tunic of a glowing, sparkling purple, with silver braids at the hem, waist, and neckline. Atop reddish-brown hair that curled in at her neck sat a black beret at a jaunty angle. Besides the crystal-blue eyes, the most endearing feature of Sendy was the asymmetrical mouth that had an endearing, upward tick on the left side. She always seemed on the verge of saying something humorous.

"We left off last time," she began, walking among the chairs, "with a discussion of how your ability to focus sharply on the desired destination is paramount to the success of the journey. A sudden lack of concentration and you could find yourself face down in Okefenokee Swamp." The class laughed. "How many of you did the assignment and practiced at home?" All raised their hands. Ethan kept his up when all others had dropped. "Yes, Ethan," she said, stopping by his chair.

"Isn't it possible to project without even thinking about it?" he asked.

"Go on," prompted the wise teacher, suspecting this would provide a nice segue to the main topic for today.

"Well, I was sitting on my couch when my mentor, Macailah, said she was finally going to answer a question I had wanted to know for a long time. I was sure what it was, and was so excited I suddenly found myself twenty feet in the air."

The class laughed again, this time with a hint of envy.

"Emotion," announced Sendy, walking back to the front of the group. "The catalyst of so many things you can do here on Earth-Two, or anywhere else for that matter. It's as much a part of projection as concentration. Yes, Callie."

The cute brunette to Ethan's right, lowered her hand and said, "Emotion is the fuel, concentration gets you to the right location."

"Exactly. So that's what we are going to work on today. Ethan, would you please come to the front? You seem to be the perfect guinea pig, er, subject for a demonstration."

A few good-natured hoots and fist-bumps accompanied the popular Ethan to the front. He lowered his large frame into the overstuffed, tan recliner beside Sendy. It wasn't his first time here.

# Chapter 84

"Okay, Ethan" started Sendy, "try to describe what exactly you were feeling when you projected into the air at home."

"Well, I was elated, like never before," he began slowly. "And it came on very quickly, like I didn't have any control over it."

"Can you tell us the cause of your elation?"

"Ah, well, I'd like to," he stammered, "but I had to promise not to tell anyone."

"Are you sure," she prodded facetiously. "You're among friends here. We all love you."

A murmur of affirmation and encouragement rose from his fellow classmates. Marcie, the gorgeous blonde with the short skirt in the front row, slowly crossed her legs and winked at him.

Ethan took a breath and let it out. "Like I said, Macailah said she was going to tell me something I had wanted to know for a long time. I've been dying to know the answer and I just took off."

"What was it?" yelled someone from the back, when Sendy didn't follow up.

"Sorry," said Ethan. "Can't tell you. It was private."

"That's right, class," chided Sendy, putting an end to her teasing of Ethan, which was just as much a test. "Such things are strictly between you and your mentors. When it's time for you to know certain things, they will tell you. Learning it from a classmate is just hearsay, and may not apply to you anyway."

Sendy spun on her heel, turning her back on the group. She stared at nothing pensively, hands on her hips. When the students started to twitter, she turned back around. She fetched a pad and pen from the podium and wrote something down. She tore the sheet off the pad and folded it. Then Sendy disappeared, literally, only to reappear a nanosecond later at a cross-beam in the rafters about 15 feet above the class.

"Up here," she announced. Everyone looked up to watch her place the note on the top of the beam. Then in a flash, Sendy materialized back on the floor. There was a smattering of applause. It wasn't the first time the attractive instructor of astral projection had demonstrated what her students were here to learn.

"Okay," she said, "I want all of you to lie back in your recliners, close your eyes, and focus on that piece of paper up there in the rafters. The first one to read what it says gets the Sendy Special after class. Go!"

After a few moments nobody had done much of anything beyond projecting a few phantom particles of themselves up to the beam. That is, with the exception of the perpetually curious Ethan, who had about one quarter of himself in the rafters.

"Oh, did I forget to tell you what's on the paper?" teased Sendy. "It's an answer to.....wait for it....*who made the Cosmos.*"

# Chapter 85

It didn't matter that the note was suddenly surrounded by various degrees of apparitions. Only one was there one hundred percent, tearing open the folded paper. Ethan read it and suddenly found himself back in his chair, pissed. He was immediately surrounded by the other nine students. Ethan casually handed the note to one of them, who scanned the words as anxiously as Ethan had.

It read: *I don't know. I wish I did.*

One by one the note was read by the students, each time followed by a grunt, sneer, or in one case, a clearly audible, "Shit." When it made it back to the author, Sendy glanced at it and flicked it into neverland.

"If any of you ever finds the answer," she said, "let me know, okay?"

Everyone took their seats, including Ethan back to his.

"I apologize for tricking all of you," said Sendy, "but it served a purpose. When you thought the reward was something you really wanted, one of the strongest emotions we have, *desire*, kicked in and propelled you toward the objective. The stronger the desire, the closer you came…one of you, a little more than the rest." The class turned toward Ethan and lightly applauded. He sat there with his head down, face flushed, still pissed.

"Hey, don't take it so hard," nudged Callie next to him. "You get the Sendy Special. And if that's not enough, there's always the Callie *Super-Special*."

Ethan looked into the brown eyes of the smiling brunette. He could see and feel how much she wanted him. For the briefest of moments he imagined meeting her down the hall in the so-called *Meditation Room* of the library for a short go-round. She was every bit as pretty as Phoebe, and her inner-slut would be fun to explore. But she wasn't Phoebe.

Coming back to reality, he patted her hand, the one already on his leg. "Thanks, Callie," he said with a tone of polite rejection. "I'll keep that in mind."

With a cocked eyebrow and half smile, she slowly dragged her hand across his thigh and returned it to her own lap. They both turned their gaze back to the front.

"That's enough for today, class," announced Sendy. "Next time we'll cover the number one factor that blocks you young souls from flying around the Cosmos on your own. Be thinking about what that might be."

As everyone rose to leave, Sendy motioned for Ethan to join her by the podium. "I know you're disappointed, Ethan," she said, taking his large left hand in both of her much daintier ones. "And I apologize again, especially to you, for leading you on. You have a beautiful curiosity and a drive like few others. Don't let go of your goals."

Ethan smiled sadly and gave Sendy's hands a gentle squeeze. "Somebody must know," he said. "Any idea who I could ask?"

"I honestly don't know," she said, shaking her head. "That kind of thing is far beyond my no-pay grade."

They both smiled at Sendy's little quip; no one is paid for any service or product they provide on Earth-Two or above. It's always done out of the love they have for doing it, as well as gratitude for someone finding it desirable enough to use or possess it.

She pulled Ethan close to her and said, "Now c'mon. You've won the Sendy Special again. This is one thing I do know something about."

Ethan grinned and followed Sendy's lead, wrapping their arms around each other. He closed his eyes and let his mind go free to enjoy the wonderful meshing with her essence. Doing it with an E3 was always like recharging his batteries. And it came with a soothing sense of belonging to something so much bigger than himself. It may not be as strong and loving as with Macailah, his other-self. And it had very little sexual connotations, as with Phoebe. But it was wonderful nonetheless, and with a special vibration, uniquely Sendy.

# Chapter 86

When the five-foot-two Phoebe walked into the classroom late, all heads turned, including the teacher's. The usually-modestly dressed, twenty-year-old was today bedecked in a skimpy, white sports bra that ended just below her rib cage, and a pair of red, satin shorts barely covering her shapely behind. Both articles of clothing were snug enough to suggest the size and shape of what they so seductively covered, and loose enough to force imaginations to figure out the rest. On her feet were white canvas tennis shoes over pink ankle socks, but only the females noticed them.

On Earth-Two there's nothing unique about good-looking souls, especially among the younger set. Few want to look anything less than attractive here, although some may have mentors lacking in body sculpturing skills as good as Macailah's and Andrew's. Others that fall short may still be carrying the self-image of a recent Earth life in a less-than-attractive body…or simply have strange ideals of what attractive is. Regardless, sex is as much on the minds of these young souls as is their desire to learn. And since no one can get pregnant or contract any disease here, the act of love is freer, less inhibited, and much more enjoyable. In many cases, it's even encouraged.

But while the tactile sensation and ensuing orgasm derived from sexual, physical contact on Earth is indeed wonderful, a much higher realm of pleasure between the participants is achieved here on Earth-Two. This occurs when the essences of two souls completely surrender to one another, temporarily becoming as one…sharing, knowing, enjoying their differences and similarities. Termed *"spiritual coupling,"* it is best achieved chest-to-chest, but front-to-back can also produce satisfactory results. Depending on the desire behind it, the sharing of two souls in this manner—in tandem with all the physical sensations—exceeds anything found in that other, slowly vibrating dimension of Old Earth.

So, if many young souls here on Earth-Two are at least reasonably attractive, what was it about Phoebe that made her so desirable to all the males and half the females? For starters, she was simply drop-dead gorgeous by anyone's standards, thanks in part to Andrew's artistry. That cute nose and sad, emerald-green eyes made you just want to hug the daylights out of her. Those full lips with their perpetual smile had the males longing to kiss her and watch her eat large pickles. And that perfectly proportioned, petite body drove them to fantasizing about slowly unwrapping her package and laying her down on a soft bed with twelve-hundred-thread-count sheets of Egyptian cotton.

But Phoebe had something more. Some say it's the way she walked, proud and confident, yet with an air of fragility. Others say it's her soft, sexy, raspy voice that can quiet a crowd before her first sentence is completed. All agree her personality certainly belies her looks: she genuinely cares about you and what you have to say; she has a great sense of humor loaded with witticisms and self-deprecation; and you could spend an entire week with her and not once would she give any indication of knowing how beautiful she was, inside and out.

And one more thing made Phoebe so desirable.

She was spoken for.

# Chapter 87

"Damn, girl!" teased Meshaun, as Phoebe was about to take her seat at the front of the class next to the devilishly handsome black guy. "You're gonna cause a riot in here dressed like that."

Phoebe stopped in her tracks and bent over enough to inspect herself as much as possible. "What's wrong with how I'm dressed?" she asked innocently.

"Well, for starters, those shorts are really short," he whispered. "And with those legs you're gonna have every hormonal hound dog in here howlin' at your moon."

Phoebe's face turned a little red itself. In a modest attempt to cover any exposed portions, she ran her hands around the front and back of her upper thighs and quickly sat down. "Ethan and I were playing tennis when it came time for class," she explained. "I just forgot to change. Is it really so bad?"

"I'll protect you," smiled Meshaun.

"Phoebe leaned toward him and whispered with a curled-up nose, "And who'll protect me from you, Meshaun?"

Their jovial flirting was suddenly interrupted by a faint voice in both their heads: "Greetings, class." It was undoubtedly the instructor.

*And greetings to you, too, Robert*, projected Phoebe and hopefully most of the other fifteen students in the telepathy class.

Audible giggling swept through the students, followed by a now-audible statement from Robert in front of the class, "I see we are making some progress."

The very dignified man of about forty-five wore the standard, floor-length, half-sleeved tunic of an E3, this one in cobalt-blue with a cyan sash. He had long, straight black hair down to his shoulders with a white headband just above his brown eyes. The mustache and short goatee matched his hair.

"As we've learned," he continued, stepping behind the podium, "telepathy is a two-way communication. You can project a message to a friend until you are blue in the face, but if he or she is engaged in some activity that requires their full attention, they may sense little or nothing. But have them in some mindless chatter, like students before a class begins, and even a semi-focused message can get through, as most of you just witnessed."

There was some mild chuckling.

Robert moved a few feet to his left and leaned on the back of one of the two armless, straight-back chairs, upholstered in a charcoal-colored fabric. "Now image how strong the link can be if both the sender and receiver are open to a transmission." Robert paused, looking into the half circle of students. "Leonid, would you come here please."

The class buzzed as the six-foot-four, blonde-headed, broad-shouldered, barrel-chested young man straight from the Trojan War lifted from his chair and walked to the front. It was no coincidence he had the rugged look of a gladiator, since three of his five lives on Earth were in one type of arena or another, including as a linebacker for the New York Giants. He got along with the other students well enough, but he seemed to carry a chip on his shoulder for some unknown reason. Only Phoebe knew what it was.

# Chapter 88

Robert directed Leonid to move the two chairs as far apart as the small room would allow, and have them facing their respective walls, away from each other. He then called for Phoebe to come to the front and bring her pad and pen. She could sit in whichever chair she wished.

*Oh, why me? Why today?* she thought to herself.

"You go girl," encouraged Meshaun.

Once-again the self-conscious girl in the skimpy outfit rose and quickly walked toward the chair on her right, the pad and pen held behind her to cover any part of her derriere that may be protruding below the short shorts. The class was all atwitter, especially the males. Some nerd-type even wolf-whistled. Phoebe was happy to hurriedly sit and not be facing the group. Robert had Leonid sit in the other chair.

"You two know each other, of course," said Robert.

Leonid smiled and nodded. Phoebe just nodded, wanting this over as soon as possible.

Leonid was still determined to *do it* with Phoebe, having failed four straight times to date, three of those during incarnations on Earth and once while here on Earth-Two. And as long as she was so committed to Ethan, he knew it would be difficult. But that hardly meant he was giving up. He did have a plan, which involved stepping completely out of character and pretending to be a sweet, wonderful guy.

Phoebe, on the other hand, had always found Leonid quite attractive, as well. And they certainly did have a history. She actually felt sorry for being the subject of all his frustrations. If she wasn't so in love with Ethan, well, who knew what might happen?

Robert handed a small flash card to Leonid with instructions to not look at it yet and to not let anyone else see it. It read simply, "Hi. How are you today?"

"Okay, class," began Robert. "I want you all to tune into Leonid. When I say so, he's going to look at the card and project that message to Phoebe. Phoebe, sweetheart, you will try to keep your mind open and receptive to anything that may come only from Leonid. You and the rest of you will write

191

down the first things that pop into your minds. Everybody ready? Go ahead, Leonid."

Leonid looked at the card, absorbed the words, pinched his eyes shut, and projected the message to Phoebe. She immediately jerked in her chair as if hit by an electric shock. She saw a vision of Leonid and her, both naked, wrapped in an embrace, floating in mid-air. Then she saw his mouth open and say sinisterly to her, "Hi. How are you today?"

Phoebe wavered in her seat a moment, then wrote something down on her pad. The sound of pens scratching on pads wafted up from the other class members with some odd chirping scattered throughout.

"Everybody done?" asked Robert, scanning the group. There was a chorus in the affirmative. "Then sign your papers and bring them here and drop them in the box." He set a small green shoebox with no lid on the floor. One by one the students complied, while Robert walked over to collect Phoebe's paper.

# Chapter 89

With everyone back in their seats and Robert at the podium with the green box, he announced he would first read Phoebe's. He opened the once-folded paper and read aloud, "Hi. How are you today?" He then took Leonid's flash card and held it up for all to see. He repeated the message, exactly the same as Phoebe's: *Hi. How are you today?* Everyone clapped.

Phoebe quickly rose from the charcoal chair, took a short, comedic bow, and returned to her regular seat next to Meshaun. She hadn't written down everything Leonid had transmitted to her. She could only hope no one else received any or all of Leonid's unwritten, lurid message.

"Very good, you two," said Robert, sending Leonid back to his seat…the ex-linebacker/gladiator never taking his eyes off Phoebe. "See how easily a telepathic message can pass from one to another under the simplest of conditions with just a little bit of focus? Now let's see how those of you on the periphery did at intercepting a message that wasn't meant for you."

Phoebe cringed. Leonid started to, but then thought, *Hey, what the hell?*

Robert plucked the first one out of the box and read it aloud, "How are you?" He looked up at the redhead in the front row and said, "Good, Elsa. Very close." He picked out another. "Hi, Phoebe," he read aloud. "Not bad, Sasha. Just focus a little harder next time." The third one, from Michael, read, "I want you, baby!" Robert set it aside without reading it aloud. The one from Jacob read, "You have the sexiest body I've ever seen." It joined Michael's. Sally's was a rather description drawing of two people copulating.

"Ooo-kay," said Robert, tossing the box onto the floor. "That's enough of that. It seems a telepathy class is not the best of places to be projecting secret thoughts."

Half the class, mostly the males, broke out in laughter. The other half—the less psychic ones—had no idea what the joke was about.

Phoebe slumped as far down in her chair as possible.

With his thoughts of making love to Phoebe now a matter of public record, Leonid felt like slumping in his chair, as well. But since the cat was out of the bag, he figured he might as well go all-in…make the best of the situation. He had nothing to lose and maybe a lot to gain. He took in a breath and rose to his feet.

"I'm so sorry, Phoebe" he said with phony sincerity, his ruddy complexion showing a hint of forced red. "I didn't mean to send anything other than the words on the flashcard." For effect, he looked down to gather another heartfelt thought. "It's no secret you are a very attractive girl, and I'd be lying if I said I didn't think about making love with you."

That brought a chorus of sweet "awws" from the ladies and lounge-lizard hoots from the men. Phoebe's red face dropped straight into her hands. She wished she were in Advanced Astral Projection class so she could project herself the hell out of there.

Soaking up the attention, and not one to pass up a chance to enhance his charm, Leonid rotated to the group and said, "Hey, I'm only non-human."

# Chapter 90

When Andrew dropped Phoebe off at home, she found Ethan fishing out on the pond in some fancy boat she knew nothing about. She walked out on the hundred-foot-long dock to wave and yell at him across the water. Ethan immediately fired up the two-hundred-horse outboard motor and roared in toward Phoebe, the brand new, twenty-foot bassboat skimming across the rippled surface at seventy miles-per-hour. One hundred feet out he throttled back and the tri-hull came down off plane to slowly gurgle up to the dock.

"Hi, Hon," he said, jumping up to the front deck to stop the bow from bumping into the pylons. "How do you like it?"

"It's beautiful," she replied, looking the craft over. It was made of silky-smooth fiberglass, painted in azure-blue with silver flecks. It had four seats, two in the lower section behind consoles, and one on each raised deck, front and rear on pedestals. The whole inside was carpeted with light-blue Astroturf. "Where'd you get it?"

"The older-self of a classmate builds these things," he said, tying the boat up to the dock. "Someone named Forest something. I guess he made them as a business in one of his lives."

Ethan leaped up on the dock, took Phoebe in his arms and gave her a big kiss. "Wanna go for a ride," he grinned impishly. "We could do it out in the middle of the pond in one of these deck seats."

The prospect sounded enticing, and Phoebe's knees were going a little weak in Ethan's embrace. But at the moment her curiosity needed stroking more than her fanny. "This soul makes boats for just anybody?" she challenged, pushing away slightly to study his answer.

"Well, I don't suppose he does it for just anyone," surmised Ethan.

"Then why did he make one for you?"

"As a favor, I guess."

"A favor from him or your classmate."

"My classmate. We get along real well."

"What's your classmate's name?"

"Callie."

That rang a bell. Ethan had mentioned her before. "So what did you do for *Callie* that deserved such a nice favor?" Her tone was becoming more accusing, as was her weak smile.

"Nothing really, hon," said Ethan. "We're just good friends. We sit next to each other in Astral Projection. I'm better at projecting than she is, and I help her now and then. What can I say? She must like me. She offered, I accepted."

It was unfortunate for Ethan that Phoebe's psychic abilities were on the increase. A fairly strong impression of a sexual attraction between her man and Callie flashed through her mind. She could understand it; he was the sexiest hunk this side of the ethereal Rockies. And while it was obvious all the ladies wanted him, there had never been any doubt that Ethan was interested only in his beloved Phoebe. Until now.

Phoebe peeled away from Ethan and walked quickly down the dock toward shore. "Don't you want to go for a ride?" Ethan called after her.

"Not now," she called back over her shoulder. "I have a headache."

Since Ethan knew Phoebe was not designed to have headaches, or any kind of physical pain for that matter, she obviously was angry. That in turn made him a little mad, because, *hell*, he hadn't done anything with Callie. He may have thought about it, the way she keeps flirting with him in class. But he would never do that to Phoebe. She had to know that.

"I hope your *headache* gets better," he yelled sarcastically after her.

As Phoebe reached shore and turned toward the cabin, out of the corner of her eye she notice the black, brand-new, shiny SUV parked in the backyard. Behind it was an equally-new boat trailer. Her retreat paused in mid-step long enough to shake her head, then resumed at a faster pace.

"Oh, damn," breathed Ethan.

# Chapter 91

Things were a little icy in the following days. They spoke cordially, and they certainly didn't make love. Ethan didn't know how it was affecting Phoebe, but their lack of intimacy was beginning to play on two of his primary chakras. And her purposely parading around the house completely naked half the time was driving his cosmic libido crazy. But since he felt it was undeserved punishment, he refused to let on how much it bothered him. In fact, he started strutting around the cabin unclothed himself.

To Ethan's surprise, when Macailah arrived to take him to Astral Projection class, it wasn't by the usual method. Instead of suddenly popping in to whisk him away like a pair of sunbeams, she pulled up in the driveway in a canary-yellow 2013 Lamborghini Veneno.

"What the f….!" exclaimed Ethan, coming out the door of the cabin. "Where'd you get this?"

The passenger side door swung straight up like a big wing, bidding Ethan to enter. He slipped into the firm leather seat and gawked at Macailah. Instead of her usual tunic, she was decked out from neck to ankles in an authentic yellow, NASCAR jumpsuit, complete with patches and insignias of everything from Pennzoil to Mountain Dew.

"A bunch of us attended the Indy 500 this year," said Macailah casually, "and I thought, hey, it would be fun to zip around at two-hundred miles per hour with the roar of seven-hundred and fifty horses under the hood. So I looked up my old friend, Ferruccio, and we built this beauty, copying it from the original on Earth. They made only three of them."

"Ferruccio?" queried Ethan.

"Lamborghini. He built the first one in the mid-nineteen-sixties and I was his chief engineer. In the fifteen-thirties he and I were husband and wife in France."

Ethan just shook his head. Nothing much surprised him anymore. Besides, it was beyond what he wished to absorb, considering there was a more pertinent question pending at the moment: "So, what are we doing sitting here in a car? I have to get to class."

"And you shall be there in a few minutes," replied Macailah, pouring the coals to the engine and fishtailing down the orange brick driveway in a blaze of smoke and screaming tires.

"I don't understand," yelled Ethan over the din, pressed hard against the back of the seat. "Isn't Seth Hall in some other dimension or something? We always have to project ourselves there…or you project and I hang on."

"I figured it's time you started taking yourself to class," hollered Macailah, shifting into fifth gear with a squeal. "You're a big boy now."

"I like *that* idea," said Ethan, relishing in the independence he'd been thinking about lately. "I like it a lot. But how am I supposed to do that? I can project across a small room, but that's about it right now."

"Do you think you could learn to drive a car?"

"Duh. I've driven many of them on Earth. But as far as I know there are no roads between here and Seth Hall."

"Well, there are now," laughed Macailah. When she saw the dubious look spread across her younger-self's face, she added sardonically. "Hey, if I can build something as complex as your log cabin, and give you that Adonis face and body…"

Ethan had his answer. All he could think of was when he would be able to pull off miracles like this himself. But even that soon gave way to his current problem back at home.

# Chapter 92

After a few miles of just listening to the V-12 engine purr along at two-hundred-and-ten miles per hour, Macailah asked, "Everything okay with you and Phoebe?" She had sensed something was amiss a few days ago, but it wasn't strong enough to elicit any interference.

"Na, it's really nothing," he replied. "She thinks I'm messing around with another woman, but I'm not."

"What would give her that idea?"

Ethan explained about the boat and SUV and how Phoebe's gotten fairly psychic these days with her telepathy class, and how she picked up on Callie and his flirting.

"Hell, she should know I love her and would never have carnal doings with another woman. And even if I did, it's not that big of a deal, like on Earth where everybody is paranoid. I'd still love Phoebe just as much, still live with her, still plan lives together, still miss the hell out of her when she went down, and go nuts waiting for her to come back."

It was easy for Macailah to sense Ethan's sexual frustration. "I assume she's cut you off," she said, wanting to smile, but repressing it. She'd been a male thirteen of her thirty lives. She remembered the feeling.

"Yeah, and it's beginning to work on me," sigh Ethan. "Any advice?"

"Oh, no," said Macailah emphatically. "Not from me. This is between you and Phoebe. In fact, it's about time you two had a spat." She patted Ethan on the leg and smiled, "All that constant lovey-dovey has been getting nauseating."

The humor was not wasted on Ethan.

Instead of driving up to the front entrance of Seth Hall, Macailah pulled into the small parking lot, which was virtually empty. Most students arrived for class the same way Ethan usually did: on the *mentor express*, not in a vehicle.

As they both got out, Macailah tossed him the keys.

"There you go," she said, flashing that winning smile with the canted tooth. "From now on it's your ride to and fro."

Ethan's mouth opened but nothing came out. Everybody seemed to be giving him vehicles these days. But along with everything else, the main issue of the moment was whether he could find his way *to and fro* after this.

"There are two buttons on the GPS," replied Macailah to the nonverbal question written all over his face. "One says *Home*, the other *Seth Hall*. I trust you can figure it out."

With that, she was gone.

# Chapter 93

As Ethan walked down the hall to class, he was tempted to turn around and drive back to the cabin and take Phoebe for a ride. Maybe she'd be so impressed, she would forgive him and they'd do it right there in the Lamborghini. Then again, she'd probably be even more upset that he was the recipient of yet another beautiful mode of transportation. He was supposed to be learning how to transverse the Universe with just his thoughts.

He shuffled through the door and plopped down in his assigned recliner.

"Hi, Handsome," cooed Callie, bumping his shoulder with the back of her fingers.

He glanced over at his classmate. His eyes widened. She was looking exceptionally fine today. Maybe seductive would be a better word. She was wearing a pure-white cashmere one-piece that loosely covered from the bottom two-thirds of her ample breasts to about six inches north of mid-thigh. The whole thing couldn't have been more than a total of two feet in length. She had some kind of yellow flower in her hair that accented her big brown eyes, which by the way, were really sparkling about now. Ethan tried not to stare. He failed.

"Did they deliver your new boat and SUV?" she asked, knowing full well they had. Her mentor never let her down.

"Yeah, it's great," Ethan replied, perhaps with less enthusiasm than Callie deserved. "Thanks."

Callie leaned toward Ethan as far as her recliner would allow, offering a blatant view of her cleavage. "I'll bet Phoebe liked them too, huh?"

"She didn't say much about it, really," said Ethan, actually telling the truth.

Callie liked the signs she was reading. Perhaps her plan was unfolding as she hoped. "I've always wanted to learn how to fish," she lied. "Maybe you could take me out in your new boat sometime and teach me." Her eyelids fluttered.

The thought was not repulsive to Ethan, especially in his present state of forced celibacy. Besides, it would be the least he could do for her getting him the rig. And she was certainly very attractive. He had thought about coupling with her before. Could he hide it from Phoebe? No way.

"Maybe," he smiled dismissively.

Sendy welcomed the class to another session. Ethan welcomed the interruption.

"We left off last time demonstrating how the stronger your desire to project, the faster and more complete the results," said Sendy, wearing the same tunic as always. Most E3s have moved past looking sexy. "I also asked you to think about what might be the main factor that blocks so many of you young souls from rocketing around like we E3s can. Did anyone come up with an answer?" Ethan raised his hand. "Yes, Ethan."

"Focus," he said. "You have to maintain your focus."

"Very good. Anybody else? Yes, Jude."

"Imagination," a voice said from a recliner on the other side of the room. "You have to be able to picture exactly where you want to go. Have a clear idea of what the target looks like."

"Also very good. But what else is there that could inhibit both your focus and your ability to envision the goal?" The class fell silent. Then Callie raised her hand. "Fear?" she said cautiously.

# Chapter 94

"Fear. Exactly," commended Sendy. "Nothing messes with your progress, your education, your development, your collecting knowledge like worthless old fear. On Earth it's a constant, you live with it every minute of the day. You have to in some ways to survive. But there's no reason to fear anything here. Nothing can harm you. Nothing can cease your existence. Yet all those incarnations of Earth are so ingrained in all of you, you still carry fear on your back like a frightened monkey."

"Way to go, Callie," whispered Ethan, leaning toward her. He was impressed with her insight.

"Thanks," she whispered back, tipping in his direction. "Fear has been my bugaboo in a certain area lately. So I decided to go for it."

Ethan knew what she meant, but pretended not to.

Before Callie could tell if her quarry had picked up on the innuendo, Sendy chirped, "Let's try a demonstration. Ethan, would you come up front here again, please?"

The class twittered with some words of encouragement. Ethan was the logical choice. He ambled to Sendy's side and spun to face the group, looking studly as always, today in stone-washed jeans and a gray, sleeveless sweatshirt...again from his closet. She motioned for him to sit in her tan recliner, directing his attention to a marble pedestal located at the other end of the room. There was nothing on it. Sendy then reached under her podium and produced a small, wooden box. A murmur rose from the class; everyone knew about these boxes; they were a part of their training for incarnations on Earth; each mentor had one in his domicile.

Sendy held the mahogany box close to her chest, closed her eyes and immediately disappeared, only to reappear a nanosecond later in front of the pedestal. Polite applause. She placed the box on the stand, closed her eyes, and returned to her original location behind the podium. More applause.

"Believe me," she said, holding up her hand to stop the mild adulation, "that was second nature for me. And you can do it, too, right now, as Ethan will demonstrate.

"Huh?" said Ethan, nervously pushing himself up in the recliner.

"You've already shown you can project to the rafters, why not scoot a few feet over to the box?"

"Well…"

"I know what you're thinking. That was different. You were motivated by the belief there was something you very much wanted to know on that piece of paper, weren't you?" Ethan nodded, happy with the excuse. "Well, how do you know there isn't something just as desirable in that box?"

Ethan's eyes lit up, his curiosity kicked in, just like the instructor knew it would. He was so predictable.

"So, go ahead," she said with a wave of her hand toward the box. "Project yourself."

Encouraged, Ethan closed his eyes and envisioned himself standing beside the box. His confidence level was high. The picture was very clear.

# Chapter 95

Ethan's concentration was suddenly broken by clapping, yelling and whistling from the other class members. He opened his eyes to find himself standing right next to the pedestal with the box. He blinked and shook his head in case this was still just his imagination. It wasn't. He smiled and threw his arms into the air in a victory salute. More cheering from his fellow students, each all the more encouraged that they should be able to do it, too.

When Ethan started to reach for the box, Sendy quickly said, "Hold on a minute, Ethan. You can't look in there just yet. You have to do it again, for good measure."

*Hey, no problem*, thought Ethan, feeling pretty cocky. He strutted back to the recliner and settled his six-foot-two frame into the cushions once again. At that point Sendy walked to the other side of the room and wheeled the mobile, six-by-six-foot partition over to half way between Ethan and the box. She turned it broadside to Ethan, so he could no longer see the pedestal and the box.

"Okay," said Sendy. "Do it again. Project yourself to the box."

Ethan hesitated, blinking.

"Go ahead, just like last time," encouraged Sendy. "Just because you can't see it doesn't mean it's not there. You know it is."

Determined, Ethan closed his eyes and envisioned his target once again. He told himself it would work. He focused hard on the box.

This time there was no cheering, no clapping, just a few groans. Ethan opened his eyes and found himself standing on the same side of the partition, one foot from it. He looked back at Sendy, then at the class in general, as if someone would tell him what went wrong.

"I don't know what's the matter," he moaned. "I thought I was doing everything just like last time."

Sendy stepped in. "Can anyone say what may have caused the problem?"

Remembering this was supposed to be a demonstration of fear, almost everyone's hand went up. As Callie was the first to propose it earlier, Sendy felt it was only fair to give her first crack.

"When there was nothing in his line of sight," Callie began, "it was easy for Ethan. But the barrier blocked his view of the table and box, and that made him lose confidence, made him fearful of failing." She paused, realizing she had just demeaned the guy she wanted to couple with. She quickly gathered a new thought. "And if Ethan—the best of us and the bravest—balks at a barrier, what are the rest of us going to do in that situation?"

A soft refrain in the affirmative rose from the class.

"Would you agree with Callie's assessment?" asked Sendy, turning to Ethan.

He pondered the concept a moment, then replied, "Yeah, that's a good part of it. But to be perfectly honest, I think it had more to do with my being afraid of passing *through* the partition. I thought maybe my particles would get mixed in with it or I may even get trapped. I know it seems crazy, but it did cross my mind."

"How many of you agree with Ethan's assessment?" asked Sendy. Most hands went up, Callie's the highest. She felt off the hook and even a little vindicated.

# Chapter 96

"Ethan hit the nail on the head," said Sendy, beginning the lecture. "I've set up this experiment hundreds of times and not one student has ever been able to get to the box the first time with the partition in the way. And it's all about fear. Fear of failure, yes. Fear of looking foolish in front of the class, yes. But until you've tried it, as Ethan just did, you don't realize the real fear comes from passing through a solid object on your way to the target. Will you get stuck in it? Will it become a part of you? Will you become a walking placard so wide you'll never be able to pass through any door again without turning sideways?"

The class laughed.

"But think about something, Ethan and the rest of you," Sendy continued more pointedly, placing her hand on Ethan's shoulder. "The only way you would ever get lodged inside that partition or any solid object is if you *meant to*. If it was your desire to. If you concentrated and focused all your energies to become a part of it."

While the class murmured and nodded with that revelation, Sendy removed her hand from Ethan, bowed her head and disappeared, only to immediately reappear inside the six-by-six-foot partition. Like some Alice in Wonderland playing card character, her face protruded from the upper center of the board, grinning and looking sideways at her class. Her hands extended just beyond the right and left borders, as did her feet down below, now walking the partition around the room. The students were clapping and howling with laugher.

"What do you think, class?" she yelled above the din." Do you like the new me?"

Sendy, the comedic partition, broke into an Irish jig, spun around a couple times, then stopped and did a deep bow, as if made of flexible rubber.

The classroom went crazy.

"Now watch this," she offered, closing her eyes and bowing her head. Just that fast she was back to normal, standing beside the partition.

Even louder applause and whistles.

Motioning for things to quiet down, Sendy turned to Ethan and said, "So even if you did end up inside an object, you could get back out of it just as easily, couldn't you?"

Ethan grinned and nodded.

"So, would you like to try it again?" she offered, motioning toward the chair.

"Love to," he replied without hesitation, jumping back into the seat.

# Chapter 97

Sendy repositioned the partition so it was back to being perfectly between Ethan and the box on the pedestal. Ethan closed his eyes and concentrated on projecting to box, now having no misgivings of passing cleaning through the partition.

His concentration was suddenly broken by loud cheers and accolades. He found himself standing right next to the box, one hundred percent intact. Ethan executed a hardy first-pump and spun a three-sixty. His arms went high in the air in victory. He was so elated he forgot to even see what was in the box.

The entire class rose to its feet to give him a standing ovation. In her own state of euphoria, Callie came racing between the recliners. From six feet away she launched her five-foot-three astral body to crash into Ethan's, her arms up high around his neck. She kissed him hard on the mouth. Bending backwards to absorb the impact, his arms instinctively wrapped around her waist, lifting her off the floor. Her firm breasts smashed against his chest, her already-too-short one-piece riding up to expose the bottom half of her denuded behind. The entwined couple was immediately serenaded with a cacophony of hoots, whistles, cheers, sighs and groans.

Before the encounter could escalate into a shameful exhibition of spiritual coupling right there in Astral Projection class, Ethan released his hold on Callie and gently lowered her to the floor. Sky-blue eyes fixed on big brown eyes, each tattling their passion and desire. But mixed with Ethan's were overshadows of embarrassment and apprehension.

"Let's go *meditate*," breathed Callie, her chin pressed into his sternum, her eyes gazing longingly up at him.

Before Ethan could change his garbled stammering into an intelligible excuse not to, she leaped back up, grabbed a handful of his golden locks in each hand, and kissed him again, this time with tongue attacking his teeth, palate and tonsils. She thrust her pelvis hard against his.

The class's laudation elevated to a crescendo when Ethan's muscular frame turned and walked out the foggy door with his hands firmly on Callie's butt, her arms wrapped around his head, her legs entwining his waist, and her face buried in his neck.

Suddenly, another couple locked up in a kiss and embrace, followed by another, then another. Recliners became beds. Those students not participating intensely watched the ones who were. Chaos enveloped the den of iniquity.

"Class dismissed," announced Sendy, rolling her eyes skyward.

# Chapter 98

Ethan sat slumped behind the wheel of the Lamborghini, staring out at nothing. The car was still in Seth Hall's parking lot, right where Macailah had left it. His mind raced with thoughts of Phoebe, of Callie, of what just happened and what would probably happen in his very near future.

Was it really his fault? What healthy young male could resist some sexy, healthy young female throwing herself at him like that? Outside of Phoebe, no one had ever done that to him before, at least not on Earth-Two.

How do you say no, when she attacks you like that…lures you into the Meditation Room…peels off her only article of clothing right in front of you, revealing the talents of an Earth-Three artist as well trained as his own Macailah, who obviously knew how to sculpt beauty? How do you resist when she strips off your shirt and pants and latches onto you like you've just come home from the war? How do you pass up a good coupling when your true love has denied you any loving whatsoever for days and your libido is running wild like a road-runner in heat?

Would he be able to hide it from Phoebe? Not a chance. Even if she weren't almost a full-fledged psychic, she'd know the minute she looked at him. No, he'd just have to fess up and beg her forgiveness. But if she had given him the cold shoulder for the just the *suspicion* of flirting with Callie, what would she do when the suspicion became reality and flirting became coupling?!

He was so screwed.

"Too bad I'm not human right now," he sighed, driving out of the parking lot. "I'd wrap this thing and myself around a tree."

# Chapter 99

Ethan skulked in the back door and through the kitchen, heading for the great room. He couldn't decide if he wanted to find Phoebe home or not. It didn't matter, because she was standing in the middle of the Persian rug, her hands on her hips, facing him like a peeved parent an hour past the teenager's curfew. Except this parent was wearing nothing except black bra and panties.

It was strange to see her dressed this way, since underwear serves no purpose on Earth-Two, other than for show. So, was she showing off to torment him, as she had been doing for days, or just wearing a these for the sake of trying something different? He had to admit that after getting used to her strutting around the house naked most of the time lately, she looked extremely alluring in the skimpy outfit, leaving something for his imagination.

"You like this?" she demanded, presenting her body with an outward sweep of both hands. "Does this turn you on?"

That settled it: it was to torment him. Ethan swallowed. "Yeah, you look great, baby."

"Is Callie's image better than this?"

"Oh, no way, honey," dripped Ethan, hoping there might be a chance of talking his way out of this. "You've got her hands down."

Phoebe squinted and the bra and panties disappeared. Ethan gasped, partly that she could do that with something other than a thin cotton shirt, partly because that body always did that to him, and partly because this might be a good sign.

"Come here!" she ordered pointing at the floor. Literally in a blink of an eye, Ethan zipped from the breakfast bar to standing one foot in front of Phoebe. It surprised both of them. He started to reach for her.

"Unh-uh," she cautioned, pushing his hands away. In a return motion she grabbed the hem of his sleeveless gray sweat shirt and derricked it up and off. Phoebe then pulled his stone-washed jeans down to his ankles and waited for him to kick them free. When she stood back up, she allowed his hungry hands to slide around to her back. Hers followed suit, clutching his rock-hard buttocks and pulling him toward her. Her breasts smashed against his abdomen, her head tilted back, her emerald-green eyes locked hard onto his sky-blues, her full, moist lips parted. Ethan's mouth drew down toward hers, his entire body heaving in anticipation.

"I know you did it with Callie," she whispered into his panting mouth.

Ethan froze.

Phoebe pushed him away abruptly. There was nothing sexy about her right now.

"Did you really think we were going to make love?" she hissed, backing away even farther. "After you spread your essence over another woman you think I'm going to say, *oh that's alright, baby, I understand…you were just horny, because I was mad at you and wouldn't make love to you…I can't blame you…so, here, let me make it up to you…take me…have your way with me.* Is that what you think was going to happen here?"

Ethan could only stammer. He'd been doing a lot of stammering today.

"Well, let me tell you what *is* going to happen, lover," she said curtly. "I'm going upstairs to put on the sexiest, hardly-there piece of clothing I can find. Then I'm going to call Andrew to take me to Telepathy class. I have a sexy classmate, too. His name is Leonid. Remember me telling you about him? He makes Brad Pitt look like a wet fart on Old Earth. He wants me. And after class he's going to have me."

With that, she spun on her heels and sashayed away, pausing at the foot of the stairs to give her adorable behind an extra wiggle. "Say goodbye to this, Ethan," she called back.

Then the nude ascended a staircase.

# Chapter 100

Phoebe was the last one to enter the classroom, just as she planned. She was dressed to kill them all, but she had only one victim in mind. And she wanted to make sure he was there and watching when she swished between the chairs on the way to hers at the front.

The class beauty was wearing nothing but a flimsy, beltless sundress that hung loosely from the top of her cleavage to about mid-thigh. Canary-yellow with a floral pattern, it was almost too sheer. A gust of wind could blow the entire dress over her head. The shoes were white t-strap platforms that, again, no one noticed, not even the women this time.

Being the instructor and the one true telepath in the room, Robert immediately picked up on Phoebe's intentions.

The maid on a mission eased slowly into her chair and crossed her legs, causing the dress to ride up, revealing an exorbitant amount of thigh. She felt Robert inside her head. She glared back at him, mentally sending the message, "I know that you know. So let's get this show on the road. I have things to do."

Robert smiled weakly and walked behind his podium.

Meshaun leaned over and whispered, "Hey, if you're selling, I'm buying."

Phoebe gave her black classmate a sideways glance. His face and vibration were dead serious. The pursed lips and gentle shaking of her head sent the reply clearly: *Sorry. Not today.* Meshaun knew that rejection undoubtedly could be extended to *not ever*. The fire may have drained from his libido, but he still couldn't take his eyes from wistfully scanning her cleavage. Phoebe turned her attention back to Robert, who at this point seemed preoccupied with organizing his class notes.

"Hello, students," came Robert's usual parapsychological opening, his notes now in order. Those who picked up the telepathy replied in kind.

"Last time," he said, now aloud, "we learned how mental transmissions are radiating from each of us on a constant basis, even if we aren't consciously trying to communicate with someone. So our most private thoughts are potentially known to everyone." Some students snickered. Leonid squirmed. Phoebe's lips creased to a half smile.

"Fortunately, this doesn't mean these thoughts are received by everyone. Not by a long shot." Robert looked straight at Phoebe's black neighbor, who eyes were now massaging her crossed legs. "If they were, Meshaun here could have the slightest depraved thought, and the entire population of Earth-Two would be pointing its collective finger at him...labeling him a perverted deviant."

Meshaun's attention snapped to the instructor. He had heard only the last few words. *Did he say I'd be labeled a pervert?*

"No, this doesn't happen," continued Robert. "In fact, it can't happen."

*Thank God!* Meshaun thought to himself...and half the class. His expressions had run the gamut from comprehension, to nervousness, and now finally to welcomed relief. To keep from projecting any further lascivious thoughts of Phoebe, he now kept his eyes and attention riveted on the instructor.

# Chapter 101

"So, why aren't all your thoughts immediately accessible to everyone?" continued Robert, moving away from the podium and his notes. "Well, first off, ninety-nine percent of the souls on E2 don't care one whit what you are thinking. They don't care, because they don't know you.

"Secondly, we all have a natural, built-in barrier, a firewall that blocks this otherwise steady bombardment of other people's thoughts. I can't tell you what it is or how it works. I don't know if anybody does. But thank God it's there. If it weren't, your head would be a constant swirl of noise, literally millions of thought-particles bouncing off the inner sanctum of your consciousness. It would be impossible to latch onto and register a single one, let alone have any thoughts of your own."

Robert walked between the chairs and stopped beside Leonid. The brave gladiator was already sweating. Robert knew why.

"Third, you must be at least somewhat tuned into a person's wavelength to make heads or tails of the thought they are projecting. Otherwise, it's just noise, like a faint ringing in your ears. Your mind would discard it before it even came close to understanding it. Not being a familiar frequency, it would make little or no sense to you.

"Of course, in this class, we all know each other, so we are familiar with one another's wavelengths. And when we purposely zero in on one member in particular, does this mean we can read all his thoughts?" Robert put his hand on Leonid's moist shoulder. The class laughed.

"Not all of them," grinned Leonid sheepishly. "At least I hope not."

"Why not all of them?" asked Robert, removing his hand and looking at its dampness with mild disgust.

"Because the sender still has to purposefully transmit the message or image," said Leonid. "No send, no receive."

Until now, Phoebe had been launching images at Leonid of her kissing him, massaging his broad shoulders, letting him fondle her breasts. Now she upped the ante. Focusing more intently, she transmitted pictures of them together in the Meditation Room. She had him flinging her sundress up off her body, leaving her stark naked before him. She had him feeling his navy-

216

blue muscleman shirt being ripped from his bulging torso, then his denim cut-offs jerked down to his ankles.  With even higher intensity she projected their bodies smashing together, twisting, writhing high in the air.

# Chapter 102

"And what if," asked Robert, "the sender transmits to a particular party, but he is not presently tuned into the sender's wavelength?"

Leonid was so distracted he didn't even hear the question. He was receiving the full impact of Phoebe's projected imagery now, partly from the extreme desire behind the transmission, and partly because the moment she walked into class he had been wide open to receiving anything Phoebe might send his way.

Also suspecting something between these two might be in the offering, half the class was getting enough of it to be amply distracted themselves. This was evidenced by the variety of muffled laughter, oos and ahs, snorts and pants building in the classroom.

Smiling himself, Robert walked back to the front and said, "Those of you who are laughing or panting the loudest get A's today. Those snickering get B's. And if you are just sitting there wondering what's going on, your telepathy needs some serious work."

Amidst the rising disquiet, Phoebe stood up and swayed to the back of the room. She stopped well short of the exit and turned around, her flimsy dress flaring in some phantom breeze.

"Leonid," she called firmly, pointing straight at him with both index fingers.

His attention had never left the source of the erotic visions. He had even slowly turned around in his recliner, coming up on his knees to follow Phoebe as she glided past all members of the class.

"Come!" ordered Phoebe.

Leonid was out of his chair and sprinting toward the beckoning woman. The fine specimen of manhood was gushing flop sweat. The front of his pants a pup tent. What he had dreamed and schemed for eons was finally going to happen. Often ignoring the advice of his mentor, Phaidra, he had carelessly jumped head-long into so many incarnations based on little more than a longshot at making love to this illusive beauty. He was chased out of the haymow by her father in old Germany. There was that coitus interruptus by her mentor, Andrew, on Magens Beach in the Caribbean. He'd tried to rape her after his fellow Gauls had killed her soul mate in ancient Rome. He wasn't able to consummate his marriage to her in DeKalb, because for some reason he suddenly couldn't get it up. He didn't even want to think about that last incarnation as Fifteenth Century French betrotheds, trying to make love, but each time getting so excited he exploded before penetration. Eventually she left him for a lesbian lover.

Now, the frustrating agony of all those failed attempts was blessedly coming to a quick and unexpected end.

Phoebe took the hand of the wide-eyed, panting Leonid and led him toward the door. Before passing through the fog, she turned back to the class and said, "Please continue with the lesson. We'll be back in just a minute..." She looked down at the stain on the front of Leonid's pants. "...or less."

# Chapter 103

Dressed in his favorite blue jogging suit with white cross-trainers, Ethan leaned against the floor-to-ceiling window, looking out over the west side of Macailah's chalet. Myriad thoughts swam though his mind, one of them why he was looking at a metropolis skyline instead of snow covered pines. The last he knew this was supposed to be the Swiss Alps, not a Chicago suburb.

Oh, well. Nothing his older-self did surprised him much anymore. He just wished he knew how it was done. Maybe that would be the "special something" Macailah promised when she was to arrive in a few minutes.

Ethan's primary thoughts were, of course, about Phoebe. He still loved her. But would it ever be the same again? Granted, what he did was wrong. But what she did was beyond wrong. It was unforgiveable. He was drawn into a spiritual coupling by a clever, manipulative seductress intent on having him, and too beautiful to resist. He was not in control of the needs of the male. Meanwhile, Phoebe was the perpetrator of her sexual tête-à-tête with Leonid. She had complete control of the situation. Even if it were out of revenge, she went too far to punish him for his moment of weakness.

To keep from startling her obviously preoccupied young-self—as she often liked to do—Macailah materialized at the back of the chalet and walked into the great room, announcing her pending presence with a muffled cough. Ethan was so deep in thought he didn't notice the arrival until he saw the classy woman's reflection in the window. He smiled and turned to receive the embrace from his bald-headed mother with that infectious smile.

"Hi, favorite creator," he said.

"Hi, favorite appendage," returned Macailah. "How are you doing at this time?"

"I'm okay," said Ethan evenly, dropping his arms back to his sides. "Lot on my mind."

Macailah nodded her understanding and said, "Listen, why don't we zip over to the cabin and fetch the Lamborghini, so you'll have something to drive around while you're here?"

"Now that you mentioned it," mused Ethan, looking back out the window, "where exactly is *here*? What is what I assume is Chicago doing out there on the horizon?"

"C'mon," said Macailah, pulling her progeny away from the window and extending her arms for the projection hug. "I'll explain on the drive back."

"Oh, I don't know," cautioned Ethan, turning away. "I don't want to risk running into Phoebe right now."

When Andrew had dropped Phoebe back at the cabin after her telepathy class and Leonid tryst, the inevitable argument and finger-pointing ensued. It ended with Ethan storming out of the cabin, having no idea where to go and how to get there. The GPS in the car would only take him to Seth Hall and he was afraid to just drive off to anywhere. So he had sent a distress call to Macailah, who flashed in to whisk him here to the chalet, not bothering to even consider driving the yellow sports car.

"You really are upset with her, aren't you?" said Macailah. When no response came from the shaggy blonde with hard-set, sky-blue eyes, Macailah extended her arms back to hug mode and said, "It's okay. She's not there. She's staying at Andrew's beach house. She didn't want to remain in the cabin any more than you did."

# Chapter 104

When the yellow 2013 Lamborghini Veneno left the blacktop and turned east on Highway 64, Ethan finally felt comfortable behind the wheel. As Macailah had said, Phoebe wasn't at the cabin and this was the road to Seth Hall he had been on before. He revved the tachometer up to 5,000 rpms for the third time and shifted into fourth.

"So, Seth Hall is in Chicago," surmised Ethan, as they cruised past mansions, ranches, golf courses, and lakes.

"Close enough," confirmed Macailah. "Elmhurst to be exact."

"So, where's the cabin we just left?" asked Ethan a little indignantly. "It's supposed to be in the Missouri Ozarks, but now it seems to be in *eastern Illinois*, for god's sake."

Macailah directed Ethan to pull over into a roadside fruit stand. She would need the student's full attention. "Want an apple?" she asked, opening the big-wing door and climbing out. "The Braeburns are delicious here."

"No thanks," said Ethan, irritated by the delay.

When his toga-draped *mother* rejoined him in the car, Ethan repeated the question of where exactly was the cabin. Macailah took a bite of the red apple, wiped a little juice from her chin, and through the side of her mouth with the least amount of fruit wedged in it said, "The cabin is where it's always been, just a few miles outside of Elmhurst, Illinois. You just thought it was in the Ozark Mountains in Missouri."

"I don't understand." said Ethan, shaking his head.

"It's wherever Andrew and I want you and Phoebe to believe it is."

Another blow to rationality. Ethan had to digest that concept. "What? Are you saying you hypnotize us…play some kind of mind game with us?"

"In a manner of speaking, yes," confirmed Macailah, taking another bite of the apple.

Another long pause. "So, it's not real?" proposed Ethan, clearly getting upset. "None of this is real?"

"Oh, it's real, all right. Very real," smiled Macailah. "It's as real is this apple." The apple suddenly turned into a bright yellow banana. "Or as real as this banana."

Ethan wasn't all that impressed. He'd seen these kinds of transformations many times before. He could even do some himself. Well, for the moment only with simply things like paint and thin cotton t-shirts, but he was learning.

Since that little parlor trick didn't seem to make any kind of point, Macailah turned the banana back into her half-eaten apple. "Look at the fruit stand," she directed. "How real do you believe it is?"

"Well, of course it seems real to me, but I suppose you're going to say it's just an illusion you've hypnotized me into believing."

"Hypnotized? Sort of. Illusion? Not in the sense you are thinking."

"Please explain," said Ethan, still studying the validity of the fruit stand.

Macailah closed her eyes and envisioned a Tyrannosaurus Rex ten feet in front of them. She knew it was a dirty trick to play on her confused splinter, but what's life without a little excitement?

"Holy shit!" screamed Ethan, jumping right out of his leather bucket seat and hitting his head on the car's padded ceiling. "Where the fuck did that come from?" He laid on the horn. Two customers and the attendant at the fruit stand looked over at the two people in the yellow sports car. The driver seemed agitated. They gazed for a moment, then returned to their business with the peaches.

"It's all in your head, Ethan," yelled Macailah, above the horn and his screaming. "It's all in your mind."

"You did that?!" howled Ethan, now cringing as far down in his seat as possible, the ugly creature with enormous sharp teeth swaying its head from side to side in a hideous grin.

"Yes. Not bad, huh?"

"Then get rid of it, goddamn it. Right now!"

The giant lizard turned and looked straight at Ethan. It winked a scaly eye and disappeared as quickly as it had appeared. Ethan didn't know whether to laugh, cry, slap the trickster, or congratulate her.

"I got that from one of my favorite movies in my fifteenth...no sixteenth incarnation: *Jurassic Park*."

"Jesus H. Christ!"

"And if you think that's scary, you should have seen what my mentor did to me," mused Macailah.

223

# Chapter 105

A limp and exasperated Ethan was now lying sideways, his head resting against the driver's side armrest, muttering, "How does she do that?" over and over to himself.

"Like I said, it's all in your head," continued Macailah. "Or to be more precise, it's what I put in your head."

"So, I'm the only one here who saw that thing?" Ethan mumbled.

"I saw it too," she said matter-of-factly. "I certainly should have, since I created it. *In my mind.*"

"What about those people there at the fruit stand? Didn't they see it?"

"Do they look like they just saw a seven-ton T-Rex?"

Ethan sat up to study the three people's movements and demeanors. They acted as if nothing out of the ordinary had occurred. He turned in his seat to face the perpetrator of his terror and the source of his confusion head on.

"Why didn't they see it?" he queried with a most suspicious tone. "If you created that dinosaur for me to see, why didn't they see it, too?"

"The only souls who can see one of my mental creations are those who have blended with me, who recognize my wavelength, and who I choose to see it. And even then, they would have to *want* to share the vision."

"Ah, ha!" gleamed Ethan, his index finger pointed skyward. He had his mentor now. "I didn't agree to see the frigging lizard. You didn't even ask me, did you? So why did I see it? Huh? Huh?"

Macailah placed her left hand on the back of Ethan's neck and pulled him gently toward her until their foreheads met. "You forget, young grasshopper," she said softly. "You are a part of me. In some ways we share one mind."

Damn that Macailah and her soft words that always made sense...and that warm, loving touch that radiated through Ethan's body and made everything suddenly seem okay.

"In other words," laughed Ethan, "I'm easy to fool."

"For me, the easiest," smiled Macailah. "After all, I'm just fooling myself, too."

Ethan fell pensive, a thousand more questions swirling in his head. Eventually a small spot of something on his blue jogging pants caught his attention. "So, what about my clothes?" he finally asked. "Are they real or imagined?"

"They are real."

"This car."

"Real."

"Your chalet? Our cabin?

"Real. Real."

"The Ozark Mountains?"

"Imagined."

"The Chicago suburb?"

"Real."

"So, while Phoebe and I were living at the *real* cabin," deduced Ethan, "everything around us—the mountains, the pond, the basketball and tennis courts, the golf course—were all fake."

"Oh, no," said Macailah. "Just the distant mountains. If you two had ever roamed far out to explore, you would never have reached them."

"Sort of a dream-world mural, huh?"

"Close enough."

"So, was that the same thing with the view outside the chalet when we were supposedly in the Swiss Alps?"

"The vast majority of it, yes," said Macailah. "One of my finer imageries, if I do say so myself. I got away with it because you were so young then, you didn't know any better. You didn't really care what was outside the chalet. You never wanted to go out other than that one time to feel the snow...which I had to quickly make you think was cold and wet. No, you were quite content to stay indoors and just learn."

"Now that I think about," mused Ethan, "the scenery was always the same, wasn't it? Morning, noon, and night. Day after day. The same snow-laden pine trees, the same two deer, the same cardinal. Pretty clever there, old soul."

Macailah couldn't help but crack a prideful smile.

"But everything around the chalet now is real, right?" assumed Ethan. "That really is Elmhurst and the Chicago skyline?"

"Yes."

"And it's been there this whole time, right?"

"Right."

"And so has the cabin."

"Yes."

That look of suspicion was spreading across Ethan's face again. "Seems pretty convenient that everything—from the cabin to the chalet to Seth Hall—is within a few miles of each other and always has been."

"Actually, my observant young self," said Macailah, "*many* things are centered in this immediate area. You'd be amazed how many. It's an energy hub."

Phoebe suddenly flashed across Ethan's mind. "So, where is Andrew's beach house Phoebe was always talking about? She said it was somewhere in the Caribbean."

Macailah pointed to the north. "About four miles that way."

# Chapter 106

Phoebe was lying on the bed, staring at the ceiling, clutching one of the feather pillows to her chest. Wearing baby-doll PJs with bunny slippers, and her honey-blonde hair in short, double ponytails, she looked every bit a sad little girl, exactly how she felt.

She had awakened from a long nap a while ago, and had been wrestling with her thoughts and emotions ever since. She ached for Ethan, or at least for what they had before they cheated on each other.

*Damn it. Ethan started it.* She would never have hooked up with Leonid if Ethan hadn't succumbed to Callie's wiles. "Why did he, anyway?" she spat aloud, squeezing the life out of the pillow. "I have everything over that little tart: face, body, personality, not to mention a long and passionate history with Ethan. Okay, so Callie really came after Ethan, relentlessly. And he is an E2 male. Seems few of them can resist any set of astral tits waved in their faces."

Phoebe and Ethan were just settling down together in that great log cabin in the Ozarks that Andrew and Macailah had worked so hard creating it for them. They had plans for more incarnations: she was going to be his father in one, his sister in another; he wanted to be her college teacher in one, her mother in another. All for rounding out their souls, all for working toward the many experiences and knowledge and balance they needed if ever to make it to the level of Earth-Three.

Phoebe rolled over onto her stomach and buried her face in the white down comforter. She replayed her feelings at that moment she had sensed Ethan's infidelity with Callie. *Damn telepathy!* Then she recalled how she tormented him with the black bra and panties, then her nude body, then taunting him only to push him away and say this pretty package was going to be opened by Leonid, not him.

*Shit!* She did to Leonid the same thing Callie did to Ethan, luring him down the sacred halls of Seth Hall and screwing his brains out in the Meditation room. Males are so easy. Ethan didn't have a choice. But she did. She didn't have to do it. But she did.

Andrew came up the stairs into the bedroom and sat down on the edge of the bed. "Are you alright?" he asked with fatherly concern.

"I need a good spanking," came her muffled whine from the comforter.

"Sweetheart," he said, rubbing her back, "you're too old for a spanking."

"You think so?" she asked, turning her head enough to see him out of the corner of her eye. "I don't! I feel like I'm three years old and just got caught stealing a cookie."

Andrew saw the obvious Gretchen connection from her second Earth life.

"Let's see..." he said, doing some math in his head. "Tallying up all your Earth years so far, you're about 520 years old."

"Arghh!" cried Phoebe, burying her face back into the bedding. "You're supposed to make me feel better, not worse!"

"Why don't you two just get together and talk things out?" suggested Andrew.

Phoebe rolled onto her back to better face her mentor. "I don't know if I could forgive him," she said sadly. "And I seriously doubt if he would ever forgive me. Besides, he's probably already shacked up with that bitch. What's done is done. Phoebe and Ethan are no more." With a whimper she did an exaggerated flip back to face down.

# Chapter 107

Andrew gazed sadly at his young-self. The love she and Ethan had was one for the ages. Everyone knew about them, and he was so proud she was a part of him…a virtual chip off the old block. But passion is passion and can certainly work both ways.

Andrew gave Phoebe a fatherly pat on the bottom, stood up and said, "What you *do* need is a nice surprise. If you'll come downstairs, I'll show you something that I'm certain will amaze you."

Her interest piqued, Phoebe turned over and sat up. "Really? What?"

Andrew held out his hand. "Come."

He led her down the stairs, across the great room and out onto the deck. As they pulled up to the railing, Phoebe gasped at the panorama before her eyes. Instead of the expected white sands and crystal blue waters of the Caribbean, she beheld a manicured golf course with a huge lake, expensive-looking houses scattered along the perimeter, and in the background a metropolitan skyline.

"What the….?"

"Welcome to Chicago," said Andrew, extending a hand toward the skyline. "Well, actually a suburb of Chicago."

"How'd we get here?" asked a stunned Phoebe.

"To tell you the truth, we've always been here. Just the scenery has changed."

For the next hour Andrew explained in detail the same thing Macailah was telling Ethan four miles to the south in the chalet. She found the concept scintillating, and it did take her mind off her troubles. So did the throat-burning, alcoholic potable they were drinking while sitting at the breakfast bar. Andrew called it a *Headlong into a Black Hole*, his own concoction.

"What I don't understand," mused Phoebe, swirling the ice cubes against the side of her glass, "is how some things can appear and disappear with a blink—like an article of clothing or a particular color of paint on a wall—while other things—like this beach house or the city of Chicago outside the window—seem so real, so permanent."

"Good question, my dear," said Andrew. "And if you don't mind, allow me to answer your question with another question."

"Please. Go ahead."

"Okay: Where did you get those PJs you're wearing?""

"Out of the closet. Why?"

Andrew shut his eyes and concentrated. Phoebe suddenly found herself wearing a simple, lavender, cotton jumpsuit. Inspecting her new togs, she asked sarcastically, "Am I supposed to be impressed? You've dressed me many times before."

"Is the suit real or imagined?" proposed Andrew.

Phoebe felt the fabric of the sleeve. "It's seems pretty real to me."

"It's imagined," said her mentor. "It's only in your mind."

"So, I'm what, dreaming that I'm wearing a lavender jumpsuit?"

"In a sense, yes. I put the image in your head. It's in mine, too. Remember, you and I are of the same mind, virtually."

# Chapter 108

Phoebe digested the concept. "So, if Ethan walked in here right now, would he see the jumpsuit?"

"Yes. He is already in our circle...on our wave length. Any friend, classmate, or anyone who has met you would see it...as long as I wished them to, of course."

"What if a complete stranger walked in? Would he see it?"

"No. He would see you only in your PJs, which are real. The jumpsuit isn't."

"Why one and not the other?"

"Because I opted to make your baby-dolls permanent, as I did everything in your closet, for that matter."

"Could you make this jumpsuit permanent?"

"If I wanted to, yes."

"Why don't you then?" tested Phoebe.

"I don't want to."

"Why not?

"It's too tacky and not really your best color."

Ignoring the pale attempt at levity, Phoebe took a sip of her drink. It still burned. "Well, how do you go about making something real, anyway?"

"It takes a lot of training and concentration."

"Could I learn to do it?"

"In time, certainly."

"How much time?"

"However long it takes you to reach the level of Earth-Three."

"What? Only you guys can do it?"

"For the most part, yes. As part of your training as an E2, you learn the basics of matter manipulation. You'll be taking those classes pretty soon. Becoming proficient at it is one of the perks of reaching E3 status. Then once an E3, you are taught how to make objects permanent. It's pretty intense training. You couldn't handle it yet."

231

"Matter manipulation," repeated Phoebe. "I suspect that's how I can create my simple nightshirts and change the color of paint on my walls. But I've been wondering how exactly that works."

Andrew pondered the viability of explaining something to a neophyte that he hardly understood himself. This was something perhaps better left to the instructors and classes she would be taking some time in the not so distant future.

Then again, she may be old enough now to grasp the general concepts. Worth a try. He was as anxious for his younger-self to reach E3 status as she was.

# Chapter 109

"Well," said Andrew, starting slowly, thoughtfully, "there is energy all around us: here, there, everywhere, in us, beside us. It's like being under the sea, only instead of water, we are engulfed in a sea of energy waves and particles. We are even made up of those same particles, as is everything in the Cosmos. Follow?"

Phoebe nodded. "Yes. Please, go on."

"Our thoughts are of the same energy. In fact, it would be completely in bounds to say that everything in the Cosmos is actually *thought energy*."

"Thought energy?"

"Yes. When you *think* about it, it makes sense. No pun intended. Take your jumpsuit for example. Right now it is basically thought energy. It exists only in your thoughts and mine. It has gone no farther. Yet, because you *think* its covering your body, in that respect it is real, completely valid. Meanwhile, in a different reality—the reality of solid, permanent objects—it would be classified as something imaginary, something I created in my mind and planted it in yours. Still with me?"

"So, far. Keep going."

"Actually, everything in the Macrocosm starts out as a thought. Nothing just suddenly exists. You can't create something out of nothing. It must be based in something, and that *something* is pure energy. Your jumpsuit, again for example: it was easy for me to create it. I just pictured it vividly in my mind, and a bunch of energy particles are plucked right out of the *sea* to oblige my imagination. I did the same with your baby-doll PJs initially."

"But you said the jumpsuit is imaginary, while my PJs are real," interjected Phoebe. "How'd you make the baby-dolls real?"

"That's the next step, the one it takes a lot of training to master. By going into a much deeper corner of my mind, I stay very focused, while visualizing the object to solidify, to become authentic. When done correctly, my mind literally seizes those energy particles and spins them to a higher frequency. They naturally coalesce...bond together into a molecular structure that becomes permanent. At that point the object is automatically registered with The Deep Blue, where it becomes completely valid and can be perceived by all. It can never be destroyed or even altered by anyone, including me."

"The Deep Blue?"

"Oh, let's not go there just now," warned Andrew. "Suffice it to say it is the Cosmos's *databank*…where all knowledge…where everything that is and ever was…is stored."

# Chapter 110

Phoebe's E2-10 head was nearing overload. Signaling for a pause, she mulled the concepts over for a moment, and decided it was all she could absorb for now. Well, right after a couple more questions.

"What do you mean it can never be destroyed?" she challenged. "You're always making things, like my clothing, disappear right off my back. That doesn't strike me as being very permanent."

"The clothing may have disappeared, but that doesn't mean it doesn't still exist. It does. If I had previously validated it, I could only send it someplace else, like back into your closet. Or I can just send it to The Deep Blue, where it waits to be recalled at any time."

"You also said it couldn't be altered. What if I wanted you to change my red and white striped bikini to blue and yellow?"

"Then I would have to make an entirely new bikini. And if I validated it, you would now have two."

"And the red and white one would be hanging in some closet in The Deep Blue, right?"

"Yes, they both would, just as both would hang in *your* closet."

Phoebe slipped off the bar stool and shuffled back to the sundeck to take in the Chicago vista again. So much to consider. So fascinating. She watched a foursome of golfers putting on the closest green. A red-tailed hawk circled lazily on the upper air currents. A couple vehicles eased along on a distant highway.

"So, is everything out there real?" she finally asked, still drinking in the scenery and concept.

"All of it," replied Andrew, walking up to stand beside her and share the view.

"And you did all that yourself?"

"Hardly," laughed Andrew.

Phoebe turned to study her older self. "You mean there are some things you can't do?" she mocked. "I don't believe it!"

"Oh, I can create your jumpsuit, and then just as easily send it back to the energy pool from which it came." To demonstrate, Andrew blinked and it disappeared, leaving Phoebe in her baby-dolls. "And I can almost as easily make any of your clothes permanent. With a lot more effort I built this beach house and helped Macailah build your log cabin. But when it comes to something as massive and complex as a city like Chicago, well, that's out of my realm of expertise. I helped with a couple minor projects on its south end, but civil engineering on such a large scale is not my forte. Other E3s specialize in such matters and have spent years constructing this city and others like it."

"So, Chicago wasn't built in a day either," proposed Phoebe flippantly.

"Correct. It took a lot longer than a day to build both this one and its counterpart on Earth. And the methods were quite similar. As Chicago on Old Earth went up board by board, brick by brick over the centuries, E2's Chicago followed along, staying in step. But while Earth's buildings require manual labor, Earth-Two's use mental labor. Each wall, each door, each window, sidewalk and fountain and tree and bus stop and movie theater…all were constructed piece by piece, mental image by mental image from skilled E3s."

"What projects did you do?" asked Phoebe, actually sounding interested.

"Oh, nothing really. I helped with the botanical garden on Sixth Street and a couple parks. It was part of my *energy manipulation* training. I did okay, I guess. I was young. I had a very patient supervisor."

236

# Chapter 111

"So, is this Chicago an exact duplicate of Earth's?" asked Phoebe.

"From the outside looking in, it's fairly close," replied Andrew, walking over to the breakfast bar. Phoebe took one more look out the window, and then followed. "But behind the façade it's quite different. Most buildings are empty from the second floor on up, since there's no need for insurance, financial planning, a Chicago Board of Trade, banks, loans, and a few thousand other businesses that would have no meaning or use here. Meanwhile, virtually every structure on the ground floor is occupied by anything from restaurants and clothing stores to yoga classes and automobile makers; things we do use and enjoy."

"Say I want a car," said Phoebe, recalling Ethan's yellow Lamborghini suddenly appearing in their driveway, thanks to Macailah. "Do I just walk into one of those car shops and drive away with one?"

"It depends on what you want."

"Let's say a little red sports car, a Lexus."

"Then you find an E3 that specializes in Lexus. If he doesn't already have what you're looking for, ask him nicely and he'll probably make it for you and to your exact specifications."

"Does he just think it into existence, like you do with cocktails and PJs?"

"Basically, yes. But creating a car involves a lot more concentration, time, talent, and above all know-how. The creator has to know what he's doing."

"Is that how Macailah made that Lamborghini for Ethan?" Phoebe asked. "Instead of using some kind of super visionary prowess?"

"Exactly," said Andrew. "She told Ferruccio what she wanted and he suggested something special, like his 2013 Veneno, of which only three were made on Earth. He knew every nut and bolt of that car by heart, so he was able to whip it out in less than hour. Macailah told me it was amazing watching it materialize piece by piece. If she had wanted something different, she and Ferruccio would literally have put their heads together, joining their spirits.  She would envision it, he would see it and start constructing it while she supervised."

"I know we don't use money here, so how do you pay someone for doing that for you."

"Your wanting their product or service is all the payment they need. They love what they do and are tickled you admire their work.  It justifies their passion.  You'll understand when you become an E3."

*Passion.*  Phoebe fell silent.  There were more questions she'd like answered, but her thoughts had snapped back to Ethan and her aching heart. How could something so wonderful be over?  How do two souls meet under the harshest of circumstances, be denied each other's love, be separated time and again, only to come crashing back into each other's arms each time in untold passion?  There's even a mural of them making love, hanging in the Reception Station's atrium, for the love of God!  How is all that thrown away in a few moments of self-inflicted stupidity?

# Chapter 112

Phoebe turned toward her mentor and leaned into his chest. "I need a hug," she whimpered. Andrew gladly obliged, wrapping his essence around his darling young-self. Phoebe wallowed in the familiar sensation. Some of her pain diminished. Things seemed better, but not completely.

"Do you think Ethan would take me back?" she said barely above a whisper."

"He'd be a fool if he didn't," replied Andrew, giving her an extra squeeze.

Phoebe eased away from the embrace and began walking to nowhere in particular. "Could we call him and see if he'd agree to meet me somewhere?"

Due to her own improving clairvoyance, Phoebe was pleased to discover Andrew was already sending the request to Macailah along the psychic airwaves.

Macailah had been trying to convince Ethan to return to his Astral Projection classes, but with no luck. He didn't want to face his instructor, his classmates and particularly Callie. His *date* with her had been quite exciting for certain. She was the only soul other than Phoebe he had ever experienced spiritual coupling with, and he felt a special closeness to her. But after the carnal display they had put on—him carrying her out of the classroom with her legs and arms wrapped around him like a koala bear on a tree trunk, and the whole class hooting and cheering—how could he ever face any of them again? He would like to couple with Callie for a second time. After all, he still had needs. But he doubted she would ever show up at class again, either.

Ethan's thoughts were interrupted when Macailah suddenly announced, "Phoebe wants to see you."

His heart spiked. His mind raced. "Really?" was the best he could reply.

"Really, confirmed Macailah. "Andrew just passed along her request."

Ethan began pacing around the chalet. Was this good news or bad? Should he agree to this meeting or not? Would she apologize or cast the blame on him like the last time they saw each other? Did she really want him back or was she going to taunt him again? Did *he* want *her* back after what she did with Leonid? He still felt the sting.

"I don't know if this is a good idea," Ethan finally said. "What do you think, *Mom*?"

"Two souls getting together to work things out is never a bad thing," said Macailah. "But it's completely up to you. Do what you think is best."

Ethan paced and pondered a while longer, then said, "Okay. Let's see what happens." As his words were out, he felt both excited at seeing Phoebe again and disappointed in himself for giving in to her request so readily.

"He agreed," reported Andrew.

"He did?" asked Phoebe, a little surprised. She quickly headed for the stairs. "Oh, shit! What should I wear?"

# Chapter 113

Phoebe's plan was to get there *after* Ethan. She wanted him to already be seated at the little Italian bistro when she walked in. She had spent a lot of time in front of the mirror, getting just the right outfit on in just the right way. She didn't want to appear too alluring, for fear of making him suspect she was using her beauty as a weapon again. Yet she wanted to be sexy enough to make sure his libido worked in her favor.

Being there first was fine with Ethan. Rather than having to make an entrance, he preferred sitting at the table in a noncommittal posture, letting Phoebe make hers. Her clothing and body language may tell him how things were and her reason for requesting this meeting. As it turned out, the signals were mixed.

Phoebe looked like she should be walking onto a Spanish gallon. She had on a puffy, long-sleeved white blouse that hung off her shoulders enough to give a peak of cleavage, and drew in tight on her waist to accent her modest breasts. The sheer, satin blouse tucked into the same material of a coal-black skirt that hugged her hips on its way down to end abruptly at mid-thigh. Starting just below her knees were brown leather boots with buckles and medium heels. A rosy coral neckerchief called attention to her exotic pink lipstick. Her honey-blonde hair was pulled back into a low-hanging ponytail, exposing the small, gold hoop earrings. As always, her emerald-green, puppy eyes needed nothing more than a little dark eyeliner.

The small, round table was covered in a red and white checkered table cloth, while silverware lay on solid red cloth napkins. A movie cliché, but effective. When Phoebe took her seat opposite Ethan, her movement caused the simple frosted glass candle to flicker meekly. She smiled warmly at him. He smiled back thinly.

"How are you?" she asked with that soft, raspy weapon that endears her to everyone. She fixed on those sky-blue eyes, already causing stirrings inside her. He was wearing one of her favorite outfits, the teal-colored polo shirt that showed off his nicely-tuned biceps and accented his eyes. She couldn't see his lower half, but assumed the matching shorts and athletic shoes completed the ensemble.

"I'm okay," Ethan replied offhandedly, looking at her face only long enough to speak the words. His eyes then dropped to the candle. His message was sent.

A nervous silence ensued. Phoebe tried to read Ethan's body language, if not his mind. Ethan looked about the bistro, taking note that no one else was there. No surprise. This whole thing was set up by their two mentors, who promised the young couple would not be disturbed. He wondered if they at least would have a waiter. He could use a Jack Daniels.

As if on cue, a handsome, thirty-something Italian, wearing an outfit more appropriate for steering a gondola through a Venice canal—complete with red neckerchief—was bowing at their table, asking if signora and signore would care for a beverage. Never having done this before and knowing very little about libations, Phoebe ordered the only thing she could think of, a *Headlong into a Black Hole*. Surprisingly, the waiter said "Very good" without hesitation. *How did he know Andrew's personal concoction?* She eyed him suspiciously.

Ethan ordered his Jack on the rocks. The waiter bowed and disappeared around a corner.

Ethan still refused to look at Phoebe. Besides not wanting to get entrapped by her beauty, he wished to continue sending the signal that *she* was the one who wanted this meeting, *he* was the one who mostly deserved an apology, so *she* should carry the conversation. Phoebe didn't need to be part psychic to easily pick up on his gambit. She couldn't blame him.

# Chapter 114

"Look, I'm sorry about all this," Phoebe finally said, making her puppy eyes look even sadder. Her gambit.

"Me too," offered Ethan with no emotion.

Phoebe carefully chose her next words. "It wasn't fair of me to torment you back at the cabin like I did. I was deeply hurt by your *thing* with Callie and I wanted to hurt you back."

Ethan sat silent for a few moments, recalling how Callie had made it impossible to resist. "Yeah," he said sarcastically, "you women use your femininity like a weapon."

"I know we do," replied Phoebe apologetically.

"We men can't control our urge to make love with you, to indulge in your sweetness, your bodies." His eyes locked on hers, he began gesturing with his hands. "We need that softer, gentler connection to balance our aggression, subdue our need to dominate. So, you lure us in with your fantastic faces and bodies and we have no defense."

Phoebe's reply formed instantly in her mind. She knew she shouldn't say it, but the words came out before she could stop them. "Your defense against Callie was supposed to be *me!*"

"And there it is!" countered Ethan. "It's all my fault. I knew you didn't come here to apologize."

"Yes, I did," whined Phoebe, her smoky voice cracking. "But you are as much at fault as I am."

"Some fault, yes," hissed Ethan. "But hardly as much as yours. I was *seduced* by Callie. I was the victim. You seduced Leonid. You were the perpetrator. Big difference!"

The heated dialogue was interrupted by the arrival of their drinks.

"Everything all right here, kids?" queried the waiter. Both parties nodded weakly. "Well, try to keep it down, please. You're upsetting the cooks."

Andrew's attempt to ease the tension with humor may have worked if either of the combatants was listening. He bowed and quietly departed.

"I'm sorry!" whispered Phoebe, her eyes emphasizing her words. "I really am." But Ethan wasn't looking at her. He kept his gaze off to one side. When he didn't reply, Phoebe leaned back in her chair and with a hint of hopelessness sighed, "So, where do we go from here?"

Ethan just shook his head.

"How many times do I have to apologize?" she whined, slapping the table with her hand.

Ethan's head turned back in her direction, his sky-blue eyes hard on her emerald-greens. "What exactly are you apologizing for?" he asked pointedly. "Do you even know?"

"For…what happened," she stammered, choosing her words. "For my part in…our infidelity."

"You can't say it, can you?" attacked Ethan. "You can't say you're sorry for flat-out cheating on me."

"I can, but I wouldn't have cheated, if you hadn't cheated first!" she countered, frustrated, tears welling up in her eyes.

"Callie came after me," hissed Ethan, leaning half-way over the table. "She did what you females do. She flaunted her tits and ass at me and literally jumped on me. I was powerless. I felt terrible about it. I confessed to you. And instead of getting understanding, you strip down to nothing like you and I are going to couple, but instead it's just a tease, punishment. You then announce you're going to do it with Leonid and guess what… you do! Premeditated, carefully planned, *revenge*."

Ethan stood up abruptly, knocking his chair backwards. But instead of sweeping her up in his arms as he did in ancient Rome, he stormed out of the bistro without another word.

244

# Chapter 115

After the two older-selves took their respective younger-selves back to their respective domiciles, they reconvened back at the bistro, sitting at the same table Ethan and Phoebe had occupied earlier. Why waste a good rental? And liquor?

"I didn't expect that," said Andrew, shaking his red head.

"I kind of did," said Macailah, "but I was hoping it wouldn't happen. Ethan is really upset over the whole thing."

"Well, he has a point," conceded Andrew.

"And a temper."

"They both need to forgive."

"Especially Ethan," offered Macailah.

"I don't think either one of them really knows how to," proposed Andrew, throwing back the *Headlong into a Black Hole* that Phoebe had ordered but never touched. "Now that I think about it, none of Phoebe's ten lives has dealt much with forgiveness."

"I have to say the same about Ethan," said Macailah, sampling Ethan's Jack on the rocks. It was smooth. Not much bite. "We've been concentrating more on the basics of merely existing in that scary dimension. It may be time to edge a little more into their spiritual development."

"I agree," sighed Andrew. "Forgiveness…tolerance, those are a couple tough ones for any of us. But so important. I didn't begin to understand it till about my fifteenth life, when I was a Polish Jew in Nazi Germany. And then it took a couple more to truly grasp the cosmic beauty of it."

For the next hour and a couple more drinks—which actually have no effect on E3s, they just like the enhanced taste—the two mentors devised intricate game plans for both their progenies' next lives on Earth. They were to center entirely on one particular year in high school. Together, Andrew and Macailah had tallied sixty of those knowledge-building experiences in that low-humming dimension, each being male and female, husband and wife, mother and father, athlete and handicap, intelligent and slow, gorgeous and ugly, saint and sinner…many times over. And in virtually all those lives the

245

one stage that always provided a vast wealth of experience was the teenage years.

For one thing, most souls rarely came Home before completing at least age twenty, so by volume alone they were much better versed in being a teenager than being say an octogenarian or even middle-age crazy. And with all that curiosity and discovery, raging hormones and changing bodies, puppy loves and heartbreaks, there rarely is any period in human existence as exciting or educational as the post-puberty years.

It was done. The plan completed. Pleased with the concept and its potential outcome, they toasted to its success.

"Here's to forgiveness," said Macailah.

"To forgiveness. May it bring our two children and the love they once shared back from the precipice."

"Speaking of which," queried Macailah. "What's in that Black Hole thing you concocted?"

Andrew drained the last bit of liquid down his throat, set the glass gently down on the table and said, "Two parts vodka, one part vermouth, one part gin, two parts rum, a dash of bitters, an orange peel, two parts tequila, one part triple sec, one part…"

# Chapter 116

As he had ten times before, Ethan lay supine on the bed of gently flowing particles resembling cotton candy in various hues of light purple and violet. He was on his way to April 27, 1950 in Cedar Lake, Iowa, where he would be born as Derek, the only child to a wealthy couple: Dr. Glenn Schroeder, the town doctor/surgeon, and his wife Lisa.

He would be foregoing his Adonis features for this life, other than his blue eyes, which Ethan insisted on against Macailah's wishes. They compromised on toning them down from sky-blue to gray-blue. The rest of his physical appearance would rely on that human body's natural DNA. They already knew Derek would grow up to be a fairly attractive man, despite a heavily-pocked complexion and big ears.

What Ethan and Macailah did spend a lot of time on was Derek's personality. She felt her student-son was old enough now to take a more proactive role in designing his blueprint. This had Ethan sky-high. Ever so tediously they went over the list of features, picking and choosing the kind of person Derek should grow up to be. Macailah usually let Ethan choose first, but she always retained veto power.

When they were done tweaking the double-helix, Ethan felt quite proud of himself for not only getting his feet wet in the aspects of feature selection, but for the difficult challenges he allowed himself to face in this his eleventh incarnation. He didn't realize, nor was he told, that the end result was designed to be almost exactly as Macailah and Andrew had planned.

Two doors down inside the same Birth Wing lay Phoebe in an identical flow of purple particles, also heading for her eleventh life on Earth. Like Ethan and Macailah, she and Andrew had worked together to design the personality of her upcoming life. And she was just as excited to learn how to manipulate the DNA. Her female visage would be quite pretty, because that would play an important part when three lives intertwined later on.

Her destination was also Cedar Lake, Iowa, but her birth date was two years later on March 30, 1952. She would be born as the second child to Elizabeth and John Beecher, who, by the time she was sixteen, would own and operator the Crystal Café, becoming a popular teen hang-out on the small town's main street. Her name would be Kay.

As both estranged lovers simultaneously shot down the birth canal, each to slightly different points in time, they felt excited and anxious to take on the challenges they had set forth for themselves. They knew the probable future that lay before them. They knew how many of the events would transpire. They knew a couple of those events would be terribly traumatic to their human consciousness.

What they didn't know was that all this involved the other. Phoebe thought she was about to experience a life completely separate from Ethan, and Ethan thought the same thing about Phoebe, as a needed break from each other.

But all this knowledge and all this ignorance were academic, because in just a few more seconds neither would remember any of it.

# Part Four—The Iowa Connection

# Chapter 117

Derek Schroeder wheeled his brand new 1966 Corvette convertible into the only remaining parking spot on the west side of the old red brick building. He killed the engine and tossed his hundred-dollar Foster Grant sunglasses on the cream-colored dash.

Hoisting his six-foot, one-hundred-eighty-pound frame out from under the steering wheel, he tucked both feet under his butt on the white leather seat. Then, as he'd seen Troy Donahue or Frankie Avalon or some other teen-dream do in some movie, he placed one hand on the back of the seat, the other beside the door lock, and vaulted up and out of the bright red vehicle, landing like a gymnast exiting the pummel horse.

The eighteen-year-old sauntered toward the Crystal Café's side door, wearing skin-tight wheat jeans and a yellow polo shirt to match his shaggy, bleach-blonde surfer hair cut just above the collar. A pair of size ten feet were wrapped in Converse low-cut tennis shoes. No socks. Tanned ankles.

As usual, Donna Carter had to open the door on the passenger side and let herself out. She was a nice-looking girl, five-foot-six, slender, with natural blonde hair pulled back in a long pony tail, tied with a light-blue ribbon. Her narrow hips were covered loosely in bell-bottomed blue jeans, and the average breasts pushed out from under a white poor-boy tank top. The seventeen-year-old junior purposely took her time catching up to her boyfriend.

Derek opened the heavy steel door, letting out a blast of the Four Season's *Big Girls Don't Cry,* along with a gush of humidity and deodorant. He hesitated a moment while Donna caught up, then she walked a step behind him into the bustling restaurant overflowing with teenagers. Some were eating, many were shouting to be heard above the din, and one couple was doing the twist between tables. A sheet of cigarette smoke hovered about seven feet off the floor, held in place by the under-layer smell of fried foods.

Standing with his hands on his hips, the Cedar Lake High School senior surveyed the scene for a place to sit. There were two stools at the counter, but he didn't like being on display or having his back to people. Moving in farther he spotted an empty booth at the far end by the front door. The pair strolled slowly across the old, checkerboard tile floor littered with half eaten French fries and catsup stains, waving and gesturing to fellow Lakers.

When they slid into the booth, Derek took the side allowing him to face the action. Neither had been in the old main street building before, which at last count was a variety store, long since defunct. Since its recent purchase and renovation, word was out that the Crystal Café was now the main hang-out for all the cool kids in Cedar Lake.

Far from the snazzy country club that Derek's family belonged to, it did have a rustic charm. Each of its seven high-backed, dark-wood booths was garnished with its own punch-button song selector for the Wurlitzer juke box at the back end under the antique analog clock with swinging pendulum. Three black, old-fashioned ceiling fans overhead turned just slowly enough to keep from disrupting the smoky layer. A glass showcase next to the front door offered everything from Juicy Fruit gum to White Owl cigars, both five cents. Beside it was the cash register, currently totaling sixty-eight cents, which co-owner Elizabeth Beecher had rung up for the cheeseburger, fries, Mountain Dew, and three percent sales tax the young man just paid for.

# Chapter 118

"You hungry?" asked Derek, without looking at his girlfriend. He was busy scanning the scene for whatever.

"Just a Coke," replied Donna, craning her head around the booth for the same reason.

They didn't talk any more. Donna checked her lipstick in the compact mirror. Derek fished for a Marlboro from the crush-proof box in his jeans. A waitress suddenly appeared at their table.

"What can I get you two," she asked, with pad and pen at the ready, looking mostly at Derek. She knew who he was. A senior. Played varsity basketball and baseball. The son of Dr. Schroeder. Rich. Not bad looking in a rough sort of way. Big ears.

Derek subtly stuffed the cigarettes back in his pocket and turned to check out what might be inside the white uniform right next to his face. It was tight-fitting enough to reveal a tiny waist, yet loose enough to disguise the truth of her chest. The name tag read "Kay," although it didn't really register.

What did register was when his eyes climbed up to her face.

Derek's heart jumped into his throat. Saying she was the most attractive girl he had ever seen was sadly lacking in description. She had soft brown eyes with a hint of oriental chink that offered obedience to any man in exchange for protection. Her full lips with bubble gum pink lipstick ached to be kissed. She had the cutest little button nose, and her small ears laid flat to her head, exposed by the natural dark-brown hair pulled up in a bun.

But these physical features were only part of what had him instantly mesmerized. There was something else, something intangible. She could have been considerably less pretty, and Derek would have been just as certain she was the girl he was going to marry.

When it appeared Derek was too bewitched to reply, Donna rolled her eyes and said, "I'll have a Coke, no ice."

The five-foot-four, petite waitress turned her attention back to the gawking Derek. "You want anything?" she asked with a half smile. He looked funny with his mouth gaping and those blue-gray eyes focused somewhere beyond the back of her head.

Coming partially to his senses, Derek blinked twice and said, "Ah, I'll have a milk fries and chocolate burger."

Donna glared at him, as if over the top of the sunglasses she also had left in the car.

The cute sixteen-year-old waitress chortled, "Did you mean a hamburger, fries and chocolate shake?"

"Yeah," said Derek dreamily, now locked on her pink mouth.

She scratched the two orders on her pad, and with a "Thanks" spun and walked away. Derek's eyes followed her until she disappeared behind the swinging doors to the kitchen.

"Jesus, Derek," snapped Donna.

"What?"

"Why didn't you just throw her on the floor and fuck her right here?"

"Whadda ya talkin' about?" he jeered in mock innocence. "I was just looking. She's cute, don't you think?"

"Yeah, she's cute," replied Donna sarcastically. "So are about a half dozen others girls in here…including *me*."

# Chapter 119

"Ah, cupcake," patronized Derek, reaching over to stroke the side of her face, "you know I think you're cute." She knocked his hand away. He momentarily glanced back to where the waitress was last seen, then returned his gray-blues to Donna. "I've never seen her before. Who is she anyway?"

"Man, you're really up on things," sneered the junior. "That's Kay Beecher. Her folks own this place."

"Well, I don't recall seeing her at school."

"She's a sophomore. Must be pretty smart. I have her in my algebra class."

The two fell to silence again, Donna filing a few rough spots on her nails, Derek secretly smoking his cigarette. He kept one eye open for Kay returning with their orders, the other for anyone who might squeal on him to the baseball coach for smoking. That wasn't very likely though, since half of the kids in here were smoking, and the place was getting even more crowded by the minute.

As the Wurlitzer started on its second replay of The Stones' "Satisfaction," the order finally arrived. But the server wasn't Kay. It was a tall, hefty man of about forty with thinning blonde hair and a rosy complexion, possibly from working over the grill in the kitchen. His white apron was in need of washing. His brow was damp with sweat. A disappointed Derek assumed it was her father, Mr. Beecher, the owner. He looked too confident, happy, and overworked to be an employee.

"Here you go, kids," he smiled pleasantly, placing the Coke in front of Donna and the hamburger, fries and shake in front of Derek. "Enjoy."

A little concerned that he may have acted so stupidly in front of Kay that she had asked her dad to bring the food, Derek snapped into best behavior mode. "Thank you, Mr. Beecher," he charmed, taking the chance it was indeed Mr. Beecher. "It looks very good." *Why not be pleasant? This man is my future father-in-law.*

When John Beecher left, Donna leaned forward and hissed, "You make me sick!"

"Now what?" groaned Derek.

"Thank you, Mr. Beecher," she mimicked, her blue eyes rolled half way up behind the fluttering lids. "It looks very good, Mr. Beecher. Did your daughter get her cute ass from her mother or you, Mr. Beecher? Do you mind if I screw your daughter in the backroom, Mr. Beecher?"

"Oh, for Christ's sake, Donna," he countered. "Get serious. She's only a sophomore."

"And I'm only a junior and you sure have no qualms about banging me."

# Chapter 120

That night Derek lay on the double bed inside his family's three-room guesthouse, mindlessly tossing a baseball in the air with his right hand and catching it in his left. He could just as easily have stayed in his own bedroom in the main house—a three-story, five-bedroom, five-bathroom, brick ranch with four-car garage, three-hundred-foot asphalt drive-way, and massive playroom in the basement. The entire estate spanned four elongated acres that privately hugged the east shore of Cedar Lake in southern Iowa.

He couldn't shake this feeling he had about Kay Beecher, nor did he wish to. For no logical reason he could think of, he coveted her more than anything he had ever wanted before. More than the Corvette his folks got him for his eighteenth birthday a few weeks ago. More than the in-ground, L-shaped swimming pool complete with cedar-wood cabana and privacy fence. More than this knotty pine guesthouse he asked for two years ago as his own private "playhouse." He wanted it built a hundred feet west from the main house, so if he saw or heard someone coming, he might have time to snuff out a cigarette or get clothes back on himself...or a girl...or both...or all three.

Sure, Kay was cute. But like Donna had said, so were many other girls in Cedar Lake. And the fact was the instant he saw that face, his blood pressure took off for the sky before his mind could even objectify her looks. So what was there about this sophomore that had him thinking about her every minute?

One thing was certain: he hadn't made a good impression this afternoon at the café. That needed to be rectified somehow. Should he just call her up and ask her out? He already had memorized Kay Beecher's number and address from the Cedar Lake phonebook. Should he try to bump into her at school and offer her a ride home? She'd be impressed with his Vet. Maybe he should go a little slower and hit the café sometime alone when she's working. Let her see that he wasn't the spaz he appeared to be. Let her get to know him better. Yes, that was the best idea: go to the café.

His stomach began to knot up in excitement.

With the help of a friend who knew Kay's best friend, the spoiled but amiable Derek learned that Kay was working tomorrow, Saturday, from eight a.m. till five p.m. Since there was the annual May Day band concert in the city park that morning at ten o'clock, he figured that would be a good time to drop into the Crystal Café. Hardly anyone else would be there and Kay would have more time to chat.

# Chapter 121

Derek purposely parked the red Corvette in the diagonal space directly in line with the café's front picture window. This way, if Kay were looking out, she would see him pull in. If not, maybe she would notice it parked there at some point. And if all else failed, when he left he could always rev the 390 horses a few times and then peel out. If she didn't get to see his beautiful muscle car, she could at least hear it.

Wearing his best fitting wheat jeans and a green and tan checkered madras shirt, his no-socks Converse low-cuts stepped through the front door and carried him straight to the lunch counter. With all five stools unoccupied, he slipped into the first one, next to the opening between the lunch counter and the cash register. He spun around. No one was there. He heard female voices to his right coming from the kitchen. Probably Kay and her mother.

Suddenly Kay popped through the swinging doors and glided over to the water and ice dispenser, her back to Derek. She was wearing the typical, all-white waitress frock: a short-sleeve cotton blouse with black trim around the cuffs and collar. It was tucked into a hip-hugging skirt that suggested a darling little butt and reached to just above her knees. Her slightly tan, exquisitely shaped calves were offset by white bobby sox and light-green leather Keds.

Derek took a tense breath and held it.

Kay turned around and placed the glass of ice water in front of her customer. She recognized him. "Hi," she smiled. "Would you like coffee?"

Resting on top of her dark-brown hair—today pulled back in a ponytail—was a white, paper waitress cap, held in place by small black barrettes on each side. Her choice of lipstick was a redder pink than two days ago. And those brown puppy eyes were just as gentle and needy as he remembered.

"Ahem…no thanks," he said, having to clear his throat to get the words out.

"Would you like to see a menu?" she asked mechanically.

"Oh, not really," he replied, trying to keep his eyes gently on hers, rather than locked tight. "Just tell me what's good here."

257

"Everything," she nodded with a sigh and half-grin, having to sing that refrain for about the tenth time since she started working here.

"Are you still serving breakfast?" he queried, relieved that his delivery now seemed more composed.

Kay turned her face toward the kitchen. "Mom," she yelled, "are we still serving breakfast?"

A voice lifted from somewhere back there, "I can do eggs and toast. But no bacon or hash browns. They're put back in the freezer."

Kay turned her attention back to Derek, and pulled her pad and pen from the front pocket of her short, pink apron. Assuming he had heard the report about no bacon or hash browns, she waited with raised eyebrows.

"I'll have bacon and hash browns," said Derek, tongue in cheek.

Kay snickered, crinkling her button nose. That added just one more thing to love about her. His heart banged once hard against his sternum.

"Cute," said Kay, now purposely deadpanning. "Now what can I get you?"

Derek toyed with saying *A room alone with you.* But he quickly thought better of it. He was already ahead with the bacon and hashbrowns quip, ratcheting it up to the sexual level this soon may not go over so well. *Don't be stupid, ace.*

"Two eggs over easy and toast with strawberry jam would be just fine," he said politely.

Katy scratched the order on the pad. "Anything else?"

"Just some orange juice, please."

Kay thanked him with a smile and glided back into the kitchen.

# Chapter 122

Derek waited impatiently.  The five minutes it took to prepare his order seemed like hours.  When the sound of muffled voices and the smell of eggs frying in butter stopped filtering in from the kitchen, Kay appeared with his order.

"There you go," she said, setting the plate on the counter in front of him. "Anything else you need right now?

"Your name is Kay, isn't it?" asked Derek nonchalantly, salting the eggs.

"Ah, *yeah*," she replied, pointing at her name tag.

Realizing he had just gone ahead and said something stupid, to cover up Derek looked up and smirked, "See?  Nothing gets by me."

It worked.  Kay chuckled.  "And you're Derek."

Hearing his name come from those angel lips and tongue was like a heavenly melody drifting in on a gentle breeze. *And, my God*, he thought, *she actually knows me.*

"Yeah, how'd you know?" he asked.

"You're a senior, right?  You play basketball?"

This was getting better by the minute.  She had undoubtedly seen him on the court…in his short shorts and sleeveless jersey, splashing a fifteen-footer or blocking a shot.  She may even think he's a stud.

"Yeah, I guess," he replied with false modesty.  "And baseball."

"Your dad is Dr. Schroeder, right?"

"Yeah."

"He delivered me," said Kay."

"Me, too!" chimed Derek with playful, mock enthusiasm, "And conceived me, too."

They both laughed.

With the ice broken, the two teens engaged in small talk about school, the café, Cedar Lake, his Corvette.  When Kay had to attend to another customer, an awkward situation developed for Derek.  He had long ago finished his eggs and toast.  Plus the second refill of orange juice he ordered to justify staying in the café longer was down to the dregs.  So, when Kay returned front and center to resume their dialog, he was not only relieved, but getting very encouraged.

"So, why aren't you at the band concert?" she asked, taking away his dishes and placing them on the high counter by the kitchen.

"Not really my thing," he replied.

"So, what is your thing?" she asked, leaning back against the water and ice counter, a coy twitch in one corner of her mouth. *What was there about this guy that was so attractive?*

*Man, I think she may actually be interested in me!* thought Derek. *And here's an opening, she wants to know what I like. I could say I like talking to her. No, that would be really lame. She'd laugh at me. So, don't say that. Say something else. Think.*

"Well, I like talking to you," said Derek's mouth before his brain could stop it. *You dumb shit!*

Kay fought and failed to subdue the smile on her lips. A small patch of rose colored her cheeks. "That's sweet," she said, puppy eyes downcast.

*It worked! I'm in! Should I ask her for a date? No, stupid, that would be rushing her. Keep the dialog going. Stick to the plan. She needs to get to know me better first.*

"Would you like to go out some time," Derek blurted. *Damn this mouth!*

Kay immediately started swaying, her faced scrunched. "I don't know," she said with a nervous groan. "I hardly know you."

"Hey, we both had our bottoms smacked by the same doctor," quipped Derek. "What more do you need to know?" *Now that was a nice comeback, dude. You're in the zone.*

Kay laughed nervously, and kept fidgeting. "I don't know....I'm kinda going with someone."

# Chapter 123

There it was. The knife in the heart he hadn't planned for. How could he be so blind? Of course someone this cute had a boyfriend. There would be something wrong if she didn't.

"Oh, yeah?" he posed, mustering all his strength to keep the disappointment out of his tone. "Who is he? I probably know him."

"I doubt it," she replied. He's from Central City (the county seat ten miles to the west). His name is Jack Goodwin."

"How'd you two meet?" Derek's heart just splashed down in his stomach.

"His dad is our produce supplier. He helped with our first delivery over spring break. He goes to college, Southern Iowa."

His heart grabbed hold of the bottom of his esophagus and pulled itself up a bit. Things were looking a little more promising. "A college guy?" tested Derek. "What do your folks think of that?"

"They aren't real thrilled, our different ages and all. But he's really nice and they don't want to cause any hard feelings between them and his dad. He gives us a good discount on milk and eggs."

"So, are you going steady?"

"Oh, no," she twittered. "We've just started going out. For all I know he's dating other girls in college. He's a big baseball jock. There on scholarship."

"Then we could go out some night when you aren't seeing him."

Kay was caught off guard again. She thought quickly. "You're going with Donna Carter, aren't you?"

*Man. This chick is really up on things. But it is a small school.*

"We go out, but we're not steady either," he replied nonchalantly. "We're both free to date others. Life's too short."

The conversation lulled. Derek could sense the chances for a date were slim. He searched for a solution, for the right thing to say. Then a brilliant idea came to him, as if someone whispered in his ear.

"Listen, what are you doing next Saturday?"

"I have a date with Jack," she replied, almost apologetically.

"I assume that's at night, right?"

"Yeah. He's picking me up at seven, after his baseball game."

"Tell you what," Derek said, leaning a little forward, as if on the down-low. "I'm planning a private pool party a week from this afternoon at my house. No dates allowed. Everyone must come stag. Why don't you come? Bring as many girlfriends as you want...*for protection*. You should be home in plenty of time to get ready for your date with *Jerk*."

"*Jack*," grinned Kay, knowing Derek did that on purpose. She liked the idea of the party, but there were some concerns. "I don't think my folks would let me, if there's going to be drinking. Geez, with Jack I have an eleven o'clock curfew. Can you believe it?"

"No booze, no beer," assured Derek. "Just pop and snacks. Swimming. Music. Sun. Relaxing." Kay fell to thinking. "What do you say? It will be a good time."

"Let me ask my mom." She walked into the kitchen. Fifteen seconds later she was hovering behind the chest-high swinging doors. "Will your folks be home?"

"Definitely," he assured. "I could never throw a party otherwise."

Kay disappeared again, this time for only about ten seconds. She walked back through the doors to stand before Derek. "Mom says it's okay with her, if it's okay with my dad."

"Do you think it will be?"

"I'm pretty sure," she nodded, considering Derek's father was one of the richest and most respected men in town, plus their family doctor.

"Great," grinned Derek, keeping his cool and tapping his knuckles once lightly on the counter. "See you at two o'clock Saturday afternoon."

She smiled and nodded, "Should I bring anything?"

Wanting to quit while he was ahead, Derek slipped off the stool and started side-stepping toward the door. "Just some of your friends" he said, his eyes still on Kay. "But not too many. We don't want the whole high school. My pool isn't that big."

"Would three be okay?" Kay asked.

"Perfect," said Derek.

They waved goodbye. He turned and floated out the door, his Converse low-cuts never touching the floor.

Now all he had to do was tell his mom and a couple dozen friends about this party.

# Chapter 124

The hot water streaming out of the shower head felt good on Kay's face and sore muscles. Hopefully its eroding properties—along with Prell for her hair and the bar of Dove for her body—would erase every last scent of her eight-hour shift at her folks' Crystal Café. She doubted if many college guys liked their dates smelling like grease and stale cigarette smoke.

She was looking forward to going out again with Jack Goodwin. He was pleasant enough and easy to talk to, even if he was rather conceited about his good looks and corn-fed physique. She guessed he had a right to be. And so far anyway he had treated her with respect, not trying anything, just a little slap-and-tickle and tonsil hockey.

But this was to be that *dangerous* third date. She wondered if he'd get a little frisky. He wouldn't be that easy to fend off. Her mom's insistence that Kay wear a pettipants girdle probably wasn't such a bad idea after all.

"Bad things can happen," grunted Elizabeth Beecher, helping her daughter squeeze into the elastic chastity bloomer, "when a boy takes off a girl's underpants."

Doing the math, sixteen-year-old Kay knew her thirty-two-year-old mother spoke from experience.

The only real negative about Jack Goodwin that concerned Kay was this strange, gut feeling she had about him that made her a little uneasy at times. In contrast, she found it curious how Derek Schroeder kept bouncing back into her mind. He wasn't as handsome, muscular, or experienced as Jack. And she knew very little about him, just that he was athletic, witty, fun to talk to and came from a rich family. Yet, he too caused a funny feeling. But this one in a good way.

"I approve," said Jack Goodwin from the doorway, as Kay Beecher came down the stairs. She was wearing a white, button-down-the-back blouse tucked into a wrap-around red and green plaid skirt that ended three inches above her cute knees. He kind of noticed her bobby sox and white deck shoes, but totally ignored the silver virgin pin above her left breast. He was glad she went easy on the lipstick and eye make-up. She really didn't need either.

From the other side of fashion sense, Kay and her mother didn't necessarily approve of Jack's bright yellow muscle shirt and mid-thigh, white, tight shorts making no attempt to hide his package. All his extremities were a golden tan from hours of baseball practice at Southern Iowa University. A gold chain with cross dangled just above the shirt, accenting his sunburned neck. A silver linked bracelet with *Good One!* engraved on the name plate hung loosely on Goodwin's right wrist.

Jack might have pulled off the cool-stud image he was trying for had he left on his sunglasses. But when he took them off as he crossed the threshold into the house, Kay bit her lip and her mother hid her face behind the door. The white, non-tanned area around his eyes—framed in contrast by his sunburned jowls and cheeks—made him look like the film negative of a cartoon raccoon.

"Have her home no later than 11:30," Mrs. Beecher called after them, as they walked down the short sidewalk to his forest green, 1959 Cadillac Sedan de Ville with dual bullet taillights on each of its huge sharp tailfins. It looked like a sperm whale out of water.

# Chapter 125

After scooping the loop five or six times, the monstrosity with chrome lake pipes rumbled into the Cedar Lake drive-in right at dusk. Jack parked at just the right spot on the hump to allow maximum viewing, then plucked the silver speaker off its post and hooked it over his partially rolled up window.

"You know what the definition of a drive-in is, don't you?" he asked, as a prelude to what he hoped would happen later, at a minimum. When Kay said she didn't know, he replied, "It's a place with wall-to-wall car-petting."

Kay got it and forced a brief laugh lacking any semblance of humor. Jack wished he hadn't told it. This was a sweet, high school girl, not a seasoned coed. She haunted his dreams. He wanted to bed her more than anything in the world. Now she'd probably be on guard all night for his advances. *Damn!*

Jack had already made a blunder by choosing the double feature "From Russia With Love" and "Goldfinger" at this drive-in over Kay's gentle suggestion of "Alfie" at the Lake Theater. Now thirty minutes later came insult to injury. As the *dum-da-da-dum-dum* of 007's theme song started, Jack leaned forward and thumped his thumb on the steering wheel in rhythm. He then stuck a cigarette between his lips, lit it, looked seductively at Kay and said, "Goodwin. Jack Goodwin."

Kay didn't know whether to laugh or throw up. Out of courtesy, hygiene, and a touch of common sense, she chose the former. Even someone as vain as Jack couldn't seriously think he ranked up there with James Bond.

Trying to get involved in the movie, Kay was reminded why she didn't much care for drive-ins as a whole. The tinny speaker with no bass whatsoever crackled like a cheap two-way radio, and the brake lights of the car in front of them kept flashing on sporadically to wash out their windshield with a red blaze. Kay thought that couple might just as well have a neon sign on top of their car blinking, *We're making out. Now we're watching the movie. We're making out. Now we're watching the movie.*

It annoyed Jack too. He suddenly slipped out of the Cadillac and walked up to tap on the driver's side window. Kay couldn't make out every word Jack was saying, but it was something like, "If you two are gonna fuck, do it in the backseat, not on the brake pedal."

That scored points with Kay. When Jack slipped back in beside her, she nuzzled up under the invitation of his extended arm. "Thanks."

Ninety minutes later, Bond and the beautiful Russian spy—getting ready for bed in the pullman car—reminded Jack he may be running out of time. Kay had to be home by eleven-thirty. He pulled the knob of his headlights out just far enough to illuminate the dash lights and the round, analog clock. Ten-fifteen. He needed to make his move. The car behind him honked its horn. Jack pushed the knob back in.

His right arm still around Kay, he pulled her a little closer and pecked her cheek. She replied by turning her head enough to graze his lips with hers. He parted his and pressed them gently against the soft flesh of her mouth. She kissed back. In went his tongue. Hers stayed home.

# Chapter 126

The tempo of the air rushing out of Jack's nostrils increased to a more heated level, as the kiss became deeper and wetter. His left hand massaged her abdomen through the cotton blouse. Her right hand slid up the side of his face and beyond to run through his curly black hair. His left hand eased up between her breasts for a moment, took the chance, and cupped her right one gently. She didn't flinch.

"You wanna get in the backseat," he breathed into her mouth, as he fondled the magnificent orb.

"Oh, I think we'd better just stay right here," she replied, both softly and firmly.

*Damn again!* This was supposed to be the night…the third date. Well, it could still be done…even if in the front seat. As nonchalantly as he could stand it, Jack pulled Kay's blouse out from her skirt's waistline. Again, no reaction. So, he slipped his hand under it and straight to the right breast again. Not even bothering to touch-test on the bra, he went right under it.

Feeling his warm, large, calloused hand petting her breast and his fingers gently pinching the nipple, Kay began to moan from the pleasant sensation. She brought her right hand back down to the side of his face and pulled him in for another kiss. This was becoming a sure thing for Jack. His breathing was almost off the scale, as his left hand abandoned the breast and landed on Kay's knee. He squeezed. No positive response, but not a negative one either. His hand slid up her warm, silky thigh. Still nothing. One last push toward the promise land and Jack discovered something he had never felt before.

"What the hell is this?" he groaned into her neck, running his hand all over the strange fabric.

"That's my pettipants," sighed Kay. "My mom made me wear it."

Jack freed his right arm from around Kay, and used both his hands to locate and begin pulling down the god awful fortress of refusal. "Well, let's get this thing off."

Kay was torn. In one way she wanted to be free of the girdle, to feel Jack's hands on her bare thighs, hips, and maybe more. In another way, it would probably lead to them having sex and breaking her cherry here in the front seat of an ugly Cadillac in a dirty old drive-in. Not the way she had dreamed it.

She was vacillating between lifting her fanny off the seat enough to allow the removal of the pettipants and keeping it firmly down so he couldn't, when the decision was suddenly made for her. Someone was rapping on the driver's side window.

"Hey, asshole," said the large man's mouth into the gap by the speaker, "would you mind keeping your foot off the goddam brake pedal? We're trying to watch the movie."

The green lumber wagon sat empty in Kay's driveway. It was eleven-twenty-nine. A twenty-year-old college baseball player and a sixteen-year-old high school girl were in a loose embrace on her darkened door step.

"I had a nice time," she said.

"Yeah, I guess it was okay," he said, with no attempt to hide is disappointment.

"Oh, cheer up," she said. "You got to watch your precious James Bond."

Jack pulled her closer. *I'll show you James Bond, alright*, he thought. *I'll give you a kiss and a thrust that will remind you what you missed out on tonight.*

Just as his head dipped forward and down to find her lips, the porch light went on, blasting the hell out of the darkness and mood. Through the narrow vertical window popped the face of Mr. Beecher, grinning sinisterly. His lips weren't moving, but in a deep recess of Jack's mind, he could hear some father saying, "Whatcha up to, kids?"

Deja vu hit Jack like a hammer between the eyes.

# Chapter 127

Just as Derek expected, his mom took care of everything. She was always glad for her only child to have friends over, and especially to take advantage of the beautiful pool area that hardly got used otherwise. So when the guests started filtering in at two-fifteen Saturday afternoon, the slab-stone patio connecting the pool to the house was lined with tables of chips and veggies and dips and cookies and pop and lemonade and ice and cups and plates.

Derek was burdened with the responsibility of picking out the music to drift over the party from the stereo system. He had a stack of records piled high on the changer, everything from the Beatles to Herman's Hermits to Elvis. His mother, however, required there to be no ballads for the inevitable slow dancing they would lead to. When Derek demanded an explanation, she put it so delicately, "Such close proximity could lead to embarrassing situations most boys' swimwear are incapable of disguising." Derek had to admit she had a point.

By two-forty-five almost two dozen teens were eating and socializing around the pool area, pretty much half boys, half girls. Cedar Lake High School had only two hundred and eighty students, so if you didn't know somebody's name, they may at least look familiar. Such was the case at this party.

Being early May in southern Iowa, the air temperature was only in the high-seventies, but the sun was warm and the pool was heated to a perfect eighty-three degrees. The privacy fence and dogwood trees lining the perimeter blocked any hint of a breeze off the sixty-five-degree lake, so by three o'clock half the guests were in the pool, splashing, diving, or throwing Frisbees and footballs.

Derek was hamming it up with four of his fellow jocks about their baseball game last night, but his attention was mostly on Kay, who was presently hanging fifty feet away by the cabana with her three friends. He was surprised she had worn a bikini. That gentle "help-me" face belied her obvious self-confidence. The flowered white and yellow two-piece was modest, the top covering the size B breasts with only a hint of cleavage, while the bottom piece raised about four inches high on the hip, leaving just a peek of cheek from the high-riding behind. She had great legs, perfect posture and a natural light tan from some darker blood far down the ancestral line. She wore simple, white flip-flops.

When Kenny, the right-fielder, broke away to jump in the pool, the boy-girl balance was obtained between the two cliques. Derek strategically and easily turned the conversation away from baseball to the four chicks by the cabana. "Let's go over there and talk to those girls," he suggested. All heads turned in that direction. "It's four on four."

"Who's the blonde in the red one-piece?" asked Joe, the shortstop and best looking of the four boys. "I've seen her around, but she must be an underclassman. Don't know her name."

"She's a friend of Kay Beecher's," offered Derek. "She's probably a sophomore, like Kay."

"Which one is Kay Beecher?" queried Willy, the catcher.

"The one in the bikini with the yellow flowery things," said Derek, then he quickly added, "Dibs on her. You guys can fight over the rest."

"Hey, fellas," cautioned Greg, the tall first baseman, looking pointedly at Derek and Joe, "what about Donna and Julie? They're standing right over there, you jerks."

The two guys rechecked their girlfriends talking to a couple guys at the elbow of the pool. Julie was every bit the homecoming queen: a platinum blonde with a killer body and glowing personality. She and Joe had been going steady for a year, until a falling out three weeks ago. They had made up, sort of, but decided to keep dating options open, since they would be attending different colleges in the fall.

Donna Carter was looking pretty sharp herself in the strapless one-piece of splattered gold and ivory with a French cut high on the hips. Her lean, fashion model body had kept its back to Derek the whole time, emphasizing what she thought of his blatantly-obvious, no-date mixer.

"What about them?" challenged Derek. "This is a stag party."

"Yeah, we're free men," added Joe. He turned his attention back to the new quarry. "I'll take the blonde with the big tits. She's a fox."

# Chapter 128

The other two boys divvied up the other two girls, and the foursome set forth in conquest. Derek led the way and headed straight for Kay, telling his feet not to move too fast. She had been looking mighty fine from fifty feet away, but she was becoming even finer with every forward step. No longer in the café bun or ponytail, her straight, dark-brown hair was now framing her face and bouncing lightly off her shoulders. Sunglasses hid her big brown eyes, but Derek remembered them well.

Her head turned and her mouth inched upward into a polite smile, as her host approached. He was wearing nothing but flight sunglasses, turquois surfer baggies trimmed in white, and an aura of confidence. He'd been pumping iron hard all week, with a final session just minutes before the first guest arrived. He was sure Kay would find his physique passable.

Introductions were made all around, followed by the typical nervous chatter and giggles. Joe and the blonde in red seemed to hit it off and began dominating the conversation, as Derek once again became tongue-tied by Kay's beauty and aura, now so close and so exposed. He could feel the heat radiating from her skin. She, on the other hand, was keeping her left shoulder toward him and her attention more on the group. Derek took that as a signal she didn't want to pair off with him, at least at the moment. He understood. This wasn't a date, just a preliminary, just a chance to show her he was a nice, harmless, *rich* guy.

When all agreed it was time for a swim, the girls placed their sunglasses, flip-flops and pool bags on the nearest glass table under a huge sun umbrella, and inched up to the pool's edge to toe-test the water. Boys will be boys. Kay and the blonde were simultaneously pushed from behind, shrieking in anticipation of a wet temperature change just before splash-down. When they came up, both brushed the hair and water from their faces and admonished Joe and Derek with threats of reprisal. But the two jocks were already on their way with cannonballs directly over the girls, adding new sheets of wetness to the backs of their heads.

While completely submerged, Derek located Kay's bikini bottom, and frog-kicked toward it. She turned in his direction, anticipating the submarine

271

attack that was already too late to avoid. Derek wrapped his arms firmly around her legs at mid-thigh, gathered his feet beneath him, and swiftly stood up. Kay screamed, suddenly finding more of herself above the waterline than below it. Derek relished in the silky firmness of her cool thighs and the softness of her lower abdomen against the side of his head. When she demanded he let her go, Derek released his embrace just enough to allow her to slide slowly down, copping a feel of her pert derriere with his hands and his face brushing lightly against her breasts.

For Derek the sensation was electric. Kay wasn't sure what to think. She was in the clutches of some strong, sinewy arms, belonging to a guy she hardly knew and had just felt her up. He was rich, the party was fun, and those big ears weren't so bad after all. But she couldn't explain the other thing…that strange feeling they had met before, a kinship of some kind. A deep tingling.

She bopped him lightly on the top of his wet, shaggy bleach-blonde head. "Brute!" she said with false sternness, adding a two-handed splash of water to his face.

Derek grinned wide as the chlorinated pool water trickled down across his lips and sparkled off his teeth.

No doubt about it. He was in.

# Chapter 129

The party three days ago was still fresh in Derek Schroeder's mind. It had been a huge success, at least as far as he was concerned. He had a great time with his future bride and she had fun, too. Oh, and she *was* interested, otherwise she wouldn't have agreed to go out with him the next Saturday night. It just so happened her college boyfriend, Jack Goodwin, had a road game in western Illinois that night and a double-header the next day.

Derek slept out in the guesthouse Tuesday night with his copy of the 1966 Laker yearbook that had just come out that afternoon. He had located and studied every photo of Kay Beecher: one in chorus, one in pep club, two in home ec, her sophomore portrait, and two on her junior varsity basketball team, one showing her pretending to pass the ball to someone off camera. The very short skirt of the uniform revealed much of those graceful, slender stems. It was the centerpiece of his self-gratifying fantasy that night. Twice.

\* \* \* \*

The Cedar Lake Country Club was having their monthly dance Saturday night...a very informal affair where members could bring non-members. Shoes and shirts were of course required, but other than that one could wear anything they wished. Kay found the prospect of finally attending a function at the snobby place quite exciting, and even more so since she didn't need to dress up. She didn't own anything considered even close to formal wear. It was a warm, humid night, so she opted for a breezy, sleeveless sundress with wide straps. The crinkle cotton material in lime green with a white lacy hem flared out just above the knees. A pair of white barrettes pulled her dark-brown hair back to show the fake pearl earrings. A matching pair of white leather pumps with two-inch heels and ankle straps completed the ensemble.

Derek went with a cyan polo shirt and white pleated, permanent-pressed cotton shorts, not tight. He didn't like wearing loafers, but the leather soles made it easier to dance in than his signature rubber-soled Converse low-cuts.

273

Again, no socks. People who didn't know better wondered if his folks were too poor to buy him a pair.

With all age groups present, including Derek's parents, the music was a mix of rock-and-roll and big bands. Kay was absolutely adorable doing the twist and quickly learning the Chicken Scratch line dance to the Beach Boys' "Little Deuce Coup." Each slow dance brought the sixteen-year-old to trusting her eighteen-year-old date a little more. By nine-forty-five she was laying her head against his shoulder and allowing her bosom to press lightly against his lower rib cage.

Derek was so lost in love he refused to close his eyes, for fear of waking from the best dream he'd ever had.

"You ready to get out of here?" he asked, laying his cheek on the top of her head, as *Smoke Gets in Your Eyes* by The Platters came to an end.

"Sure," she replied. "What do you want to do?"

"Let's go for a drive around the lake and cool off."

On the way to the dance in his Corvette convertible, Derek had thoughtfully kept the top up to protect her hairdo. She appreciated the courtesy. Now she didn't care how much it blew. "Sounds good," she said. "Can we put the top down?"

# Chapter 130

It was a magical night with plenty of stars and a gentle south breeze. Kay loved feeling the wind course through her hair, and particularly holding her hands high above the windshield to let the night air push against them like it had a life of its own. The gurgle of the Corvette's 427 cubic-inch engine was intoxicating, and when Derek would rap it out on a straight-away, the power surge was erotic.

Half way around the lake's perimeter Derek pulled into the West Overlook, a popular parking place for couples. He followed the gravel road for a quarter mile, winding through the forest of trees and leafy bushes, finally easing the '66 Vet up to the wooden railing put there many years ago mostly as a warning of the sharp drop-off just twenty feet beyond it. Some thirty feet above the water, the ridge was the highest point on the lake, offering a romantic view of the town's lights in the distance, dancing off the expanse of rippled water.

Derek killed the lights and turned to Kay. "Let's get out and sit on the railing," he said. "The view is better."

Kay was both surprised and pleased. Here they were at a prime make-out location, and her date was proving himself to be honorable, trustworthy, and in no apparent hurry to get in her pants. How sweet.

This actually was true about Derek. Kay was the girl he was going to marry. There wasn't the slightest doubt. So there was no hurry. Plus there was the obvious factor that making out in a Corvette was less than practical: no back seat; bucket seats; a console with a stick between them.

The young couple sat on the wooden railing, his arm around her tiny waist, her head resting on his shoulder, both lost in the ambience. It felt particularly good to Kay, but she didn't know why. It was like being on the threshold of a place she loved, a place where she belonged. And this guy she was with...well, it just kept feeling so right.

As Derek maneuvered to kiss her, Kay sensed the approach and shifted her own weight to receive it. It was a gentle, soft, dry kiss. Nothing steamy. Just a tender message of fondness between two teenagers. When it was over, both sighed and returned to looking out across the water.

"See that big white light over there with the three smaller ones right below it," said Derek, pointing in the general direction.

Kay looked along his finger and offered an "Uh-huh."

"That's my house."

"Cool," said Kay. "You'll have to show me the inside sometime. I've only seen it from the outside at the pool party.

Derek wasted no time in getting there.

# Chapter 131

Derek's house was even better than she had imagined. The huge first level had vaulted ceilings and oak trim, with plush light-gray carpeting throughout. All the furniture was contemporary and high quality. The modern kitchen was massive with double islands and black marble countertops. The finished basement was a recreational dream that included a pool table, a ping pong table, two pinball machines, a bar, two television sets, a built-in stereo system and a wet bar.

They batted a few ping pong balls back and forth and played some pinball. But what Kay really wanted to see was Derek's room. So hand-in-hand they went up two flights of stairs to the top floor, down a long hall to a six-panel door with a sign that read *Abandon all hope ye who enter here*.

Kay expected to find it a complete mess, but it was neat and tidy. Derek didn't bother to explain it was none of his doing. She waltzed around the all-boy bedroom, studying each poster: *Carnival of Souls*, John Travolta in *Blow Up*, a red and white Corvette streaking down Route 66, the Beatles, Stones, Dylan. His student desk in the far corner had a portable television with rabbit ears and everything in place. His walk-in closet was full of suits, sport jackets, dress pants, jeans, shoes, more than she could comprehend.

The inspection completed, she sat down beside her smiling date on his double bed. "Man," she sighed, "your bedroom is larger than my living room."

"To tell the truth," admitted Derek, "I don't spend much time here. I don't even sleep here very often."

"You don't?" said Kay, cocking her head at him. "Well, where *do* you sleep?"

By now Derek had his arm around Kay's waist and was gently pulling her toward him. "We have a cool guesthouse out back," he said softly, as he nuzzled her neck. Kay didn't resist. She turned her head toward his and was immediately met with his lips on hers. The kiss was soft and moist. She kissed him back. His tongue stroked hers. Her hands left their supporting role on the bed to encircle his neck. Off balance and still locked in the kiss, their

277

bodies fell naturally to horizontal. Derek twisted his torso to be on top of hers, and forced his tongue as far as it would go in her mouth. She moaned. His hand slid up to cup her left breast. Kay's moan turned to a muffled plea, as she pushed him away.

"Whoa, this is too fast," she breathed, once back in control of her lips. "We need to slow down."

Kay's words belied her desire. It was just something she felt a girl was supposed to say. She didn't want to appear too easy. And his folks could get home from the dance at any moment.

It took all of Derek's fortitude to acquiesce and slide his face away from hers. He settled for gently nibbling on her earlobe. A monster erection was pushing so hard against his zipper he feared something might snap. He kept it pinned down on the bed so Kay wouldn't notice, while still maintaining the embrace.

She turned her head toward him, stroked the back of his head and quickly changed the subject, "I want to see your guesthouse."

While frustrated by the shattered rapture, the thought of having her alone in his private hide-out was perfect. She'd be more willing to allow some petting with no danger of his folks busting in on them. That concept required an extra couple minutes of face-down time on the bed.

# Chapter 132

With her arm around his waist and his around her shoulder, they walked the beaten path past the big oak tree to the secluded guesthouse some one hundred feet from the main house. Derek turned his key in the lock, opened the door, and flipped on the overhead light attached to a ceiling fan.

"How cute," said Kay, walking in ahead of him.

Like the outside, the walls were true knotty pine, but stained to an auburn tan. Paintings of scenery and wildlife hung between the dark-brown casement windows on three of the walls. A couch and arm chair were upholstered in a burgundy cotton-blend, a twenty-inch Zenith television rested on a rolling stand between them. The sectional sound-proof ceiling was off-white with a single I-beam running from one end of the room to the other.

Kay unbuckled and kicked off her shoes to feel the caramel-colored, loop pile carpet between her toes, as she did a three-sixty around the small living area. Beyond it to the left was the kitchen-dinette, and to the right was the door to the only bedroom. Derek started guiding Kay to the right, she resisted and headed left.

"So, you hang out here a lot, huh?" she mused, checking out the contents of the small refrigerator. Besides some pop, fruit drinks, jelly and half a block of cheddar cheese, it was pretty much barren.

"Yep."

"Must be nice to have such privacy. I had to share my room with my little sister until Brad left for college. He'll be back for summer break soon, so she and I will have to double up again."

Derek joined her at the open refrigerator and plucked a sixteen-ounce glass bottle of Pepsi from the center rack. "Want some?"

She nodded, now inspecting the knotty pine cupboards. Crackers, bread, cookies, a bag of M&Ms. Plates and glasses.

He popped open the Pepsi with a church key, grabbed a couple glasses from the dish drainer beside the sink and filled them with ice from the freezer. He then used a folding stepstool to reach far back into the highest cupboard and fetch a half-full bottle of Southern Comfort.

"Good stuff," he said, pouring about two ounces into each glass, then adding the cola. "You'll like it. Not strong at all. Made from peaches."

He handed Kay the glass and she took a cautious sip. "Mmm, that is good," she relayed, taking a bigger sip.

They toasted the fun night and chatted about this and that until the highballs were drained and Kay was feeling good. Derek fixed another round and she drank hers down even faster this time. Derek loaded her yet another one, grab his half-gone second one, and guided her gently into the bedroom.

# Chapter 133

"So thish ish where the mighty Derek geths away from it all," she observed with an awkward sweep of her hand. She stumbled around the sixteen by twenty room with its own back door. She tried to focus on the posters of various NFL, NBA and MLB stars, and the occasional Playboy Playmate. The double bed had a multi-colored, checkered spread and a bookcase headboard filled with magazines, a clock radio and a box of Kleenex. Directly above were dark-brown casement windows with cranks on the sills.

When Kay saw the little attached bathroom, she announced she had to tinkle and disappeared inside it. Derek took the opportunity to peel off his shirt and shoes. He cracked a window and lit a cigarette, his first since late afternoon. He turned on his RCA radio and rotated the tuner knob until soft music flowed from the dual speakers. As an afterthought, he checked to make sure a Trojan was still in place behind the small bulletin board, where his baseball schedule was attached with a thumbtack. He had no intention of using it on his precious future wife, but what kind of man wasn't always prepared? He tore open the foil and placed the exposed condom under a magazine beside the lamp on his nightstand.

Half way through his cigarette he realized there had been no sound coming from the bathroom, not even a flush. He called out, "You okay in there?"

No reply.

Derek took a couple more puffs and snuffed the cigarette out in the ashtray on the window sill. Still quite sober, he walked to the bathroom door and knocked, repeating his question. When there was still no sound, he slowly cracked open the door.

"Coming in," he announced, not sure what he would find.

Kay was curled up in the fetal position, seemingly passed out on the floor. Derek knelt beside her and gently jiggled her shoulder. She moaned, but her eyes remained closed. With the excuse of checking to make sure she had finished her business, Derek lifted the hem of her lime crinkle dress high enough to see her white panties were in place. Further inspection of the toilet revealed unflushed pee and toilet paper. He closed the lid and returned to jiggling his drunken date. Her eyes cracked open halfway, and Derek pulled her up to the sitting position.

"Good morning, sunshine," he grinned. "You feeling okay?"

Saying something unintelligible, her eyes rolled in their sockets and she started to canter sideways in his arms. Still sitting beside her, he slipped his left arm under the crook of her knees, his right arm around her upper torso, and lifted her onto his lap. He then wrestled himself and his hundred-and-five-pound cargo to his knees, and grunted up to the standing position. Her arms dangled lifelessly as he carried her to the bed and set her down. She immediately toppled backwards, her legs hanging over the edge.

Seeing if a kiss would get those eyes open again, Derek angled himself on her right side, bent down and kissed her gently on her parted lips. He thought he heard a slight moan...undoubtedly of pleasure. He kissed her neck and high on her chest. His left hand stroked the side of her face and hair, and then wandered down to make slow circles on her stomach.

"Wake up, sweetheart," he sang. "You don't want to miss this."

Derek stood back up to bury his mouth in the crook of her neck, while squeezing each globe of her behind. Kay let out a soft squeak and brought her arms loosely around his waist. Derek took one short step forward and lowered his darling Kay onto the bed. He quickly slipped his white boxers off, then paused a moment to drink it all in. He was in carnal euphoria and so far in love with the naked creature lying supine on his bed his mind was swirling. He wanted desperately to catalog the moment so it would always be at his memory's beck and call.

The very sober Derek finally positioned himself on top of the very inebriated Kay. Staying on his elbows to avoid putting his full weight on her, he kissed her lips gently and whispered in all sincerity, "I love you, Kay Beecher. I want to marry you."

Kay made another small sound and her mouth curled into a half smile. "I love you, too, *Ethan*," she mumbled so faintly Derek didn't catch the mistaken name. Even if he had, it didn't matter.

# Chapter 135

Derek tried some more foreplay, but the doctor's son was so anxious to join with her he pushed her legs apart with his knees, grabbed the condom from under the magazine on the nightstand, slipped it on with one hand, lowered his pelvic region to hers and thrust his rock-hard member into her. Kay immediately winched and whimpered. She came to her senses enough to feel Derek pounding inside her and his mouth smashed against hers. His breath was hot and tasted lightly of cigarettes. She turned her head to gasp for air and clear her head a little more. The cadence and force of the thrusting increased. His hands were squeezing her gluteal muscles so hard it hurt. Derek's breathing escalated to panting, then to "Oh, God! Oh, God! Oh, God!"

It suddenly stopped. She felt his full weigh collapse on her chest. Her vagina burned, her butt ached, the room spun.

It didn't enter Derek's mind that he had just raped the most precious thing in his life, until she sat up and looked down between her legs. Blood was around her black pubic hairs, on the inside of her thighs, and on the bedspread. She reached down between her legs and dabbed at the red, sticky substance. She then brought her hand back up to inspect the stained fingers.

"What did you do?!" she screamed, a look of horror on her face.

Derek was shocked. "I'm sorry, Kay," he stammered. "I assumed you were doing it with your college boyfriend."

"No we weren't," she spat. "He's a *gentleman!*" She jumped to her feet, and began to sway. Derek reached up to help steady her. "Don't touch me!" she cried, knocking his hand away.

"I don't understand, sweetheart," whined Derek. "I thought you wanted to."

"I did *not*," she howled, staggering toward the bathroom. "How could you?"

She slammed the door. Derek heard sobbing. He was perplexed. He got to his feet and walked to the bathroom door. He could hear the shower running. With a shaking hand he opened the door and stepped in. Her blurred image was cast on the frosted glass door. He slid it open to find her face tilted upward into the full spray, while she soaped her genital area with the bar of Irish Spring. The sight of her naked body glistening under the stream of water was something Derek had imagined while showering here for the past two weeks, each time generating an instant erection. But now…there was nothing erotic about it at all. There was something sinisterly wrong.

"I'm sorry, Kay," he shouted to be heard above the shower pelting her face. "I honestly thought you wanted to make love."

"*Get out!*" she screamed at the top of her lungs, throwing the soap at him and slamming the sliding door shut.

Derek exited the bathroom and slumped onto the bed. He mindlessly lit a Marlboro without bothering to open a window. Guilt came creeping into his stomach and was soon spreading throughout every fiber of his being. How could something so wonderful go so wrong? How could he deflower and blemish someone so pure, so beautiful? Would she ever forgive him? Would she ever agree to be his bride? Would she ever want to see him again?

"What time is it?" demanded Kay, storming out of the bathroom, still buck naked. She was almost sober.

Derek checked the clock on the radio. "It's eleven-fifty," he reported.

"Take me home, Derek. I'm supposed to be home at midnight. Where are my clothes?"

Derek helped her locate all the articles and watched dejectedly as she hurriedly dressed. She grabbed her shoes by the door and didn't even bother to put them on.

"Let's go!" she ordered, already half way out the door.

She refused his hand as they double-timed it along the path to his car. Before Derek could get there, she let herself in the passenger door.

Kay never spoke again, not even a *goodbye* when she slammed it again and hustled up the sidewalk to her house.

# Chapter 136

The next two weeks until graduation were not a happy time for the high school senior.  After dropping off Kay that night he considered driving his Vet into the lake and going down with it.  Instead he went back to the guesthouse to clean his bedspread, but ended up finishing off the rest of the Southern Comfort.  He woke up at three-thirty a.m. on the floor of the bathroom and threw up until five.

The next day he fended off his parents' questions about his state of health, saying he must have eaten some bad shrimp at the dance.  His dad didn't buy it and forced a man-to-man that evening in the rec room.  Since he could never lie to his father, with his head bowed Derek explained everything that had happened.  At its conclusion Dr. Schroeder laid even more guilt on his depressed son with, "You've stolen something from a young lady that she can never get back."

The following Monday's baseball game with Trenton found Derek striking out three times and getting benched in the seventh inning.  In fact, for the remainder of Cedar Lake High School's spring schedule he batted a paltry two-for-twenty-five, dropping his average down from 3.16 to 2.72.  His grades endured the same fate, but his GPA had been high enough to absorb the decline and he graduated with a 3.1.

He ached to see Kay again, to try to apologize again, to see if she was okay.  But he knew it would only make matters worse.  She must be keeping that night to herself, since no one in his circle was acting differently toward him or showing any indication they knew about it.  And her beau from Southern Iowa hadn't shown up to beat his brains in with a baseball bat.  But that didn't negate the fact he had violated her very soul, and she would never forgive him.  Obviously she hated him and wished him dead.

That line of thinking was substantiated when Kay's brother, Brad, came home from Southern Iowa in late-May.  He had always been very protective of his little sister, and he was the only person she would ever confide in.  Brad had detected right away something was amiss.  And while it took some extra and unusual prodding to pry it out of her, Kay did explain the situation…but

287

only after making him promise to tell no one and not go after Derek. When Brad heard the story, it was all he could do to keep from tearing out of the house, finding the sonofabitch and beating the shit out of him. At the very least he should be arrested for rape and thrown so far in prison they'd have to pump air to him. But he honored his precious sister's wishes. For the most part.

# Chapter 137

After their first summer game on the road thirty miles to the north at Carlson, the school bus pulled into the Cedar Lake High School parking lot at ten-thirty p.m. and began disgorging its tired baseball players. As Derek shuffled slowly toward his Vet, he was cut off by an older model, white Ford pickup. The driver's side window was already down and a smiling face with a black crew-cut and dark eyes poked out to greet him. He looked vaguely familiar.

"Hey, aren't you Derek Schroeder," the driver chimed.

Derek nodded.

"How you doing? Did you guys win?"

"Nay, lost in extra innings," replied Derek, studying the guy's face. He remembered him as a football jock one or two years ahead of him in school. But the name escaped him.

"Listen," said Brad directly, seeing no reason to carry the pleasantries any farther, "I'm Brad Beecher, Kay's brother." When Derek took a step back, Brad quickly added, "I'm not here to hurt you. I just want to talk. Kay has a message for you."

Derek's heart was already racing with fear. When he heard there was a message from Kay it leaped up and gave a double thump inside his chest. He took a breath and stepped forward. "What is it?"

"Hop in and I'll tell you."

Derek stepped back again.

"Really, I'm not going to hurt you," said Brad. "Just talk."

Derek didn't move or reply.

"Look, either get in or don't. Makes no difference to me if you don't get Kay's message…"

Derek remained motionless, trying to decide.

Brad put the truck in gear and started to ease away. "Okay, have it your way," he said.

"Hold it," said Derek. He hesitated then walked around the back to the passenger side and climbed in. He dropped his spikes and glove on the floor and looked straight ahead. The pickup took off out of the gravel parking lot.

They drove in silence for a couple minutes, before the two-hundred-thirty-pound, six-foot-two, ex-tackle for the Lakers said, "Kay told me all about that night at your *playhouse*." Derek said nothing, waiting for what may come next. "That was a pretty sleazy thing you did, getting her drunk and taking advantage of her."

Derek held his stare on the glove compartment. "I didn't mean for it to happen that way," he said meekly.

"How *did* you mean for it to happen?" challenged Brad, trying to keep the disdain out of his tone.

"I made us a drink to, you know, relax the mood a little," said Derek quietly. "I was hoping for at the most some petting. I really like Kay. She started throwing the drinks down like a sailor, and I figured, you know, she knew what she was doing...she'd done it before...she could hold her liquor. Hell, she was dating a college guy. We started necking and I felt she was really into it. One thing led to another and, you know..."

Brad jerked the pickup to the side of the road and slammed on the brakes. He reached over and grabbed Derek by his baseball jersey and pulled him toward him. Even at a sizable six-foot, one-hundred-eighty pounds, Derek made the journey like a rag doll. "No, I don't know," spat Brad. "Tell me about it, asshole."

Derek looked hard into the piercing, angry black eyes. He saw mayhem. He sized up the burly man and decided he, Derek, didn't stand a chance. But that was okay. A good beating might feel pretty good, all things considered. Maybe he would even be killed and put out of his misery.

"You said you had a message from Kay," stated Derek rather calmly.

"I lied," hissed Brad.

"You also said you weren't going to hurt me."

"Damn. I lied again."

# Chapter 138

Brad Beecher knew he was lying about the lying. He was just enjoying the pretense of smashing this punk's face in. "You raped my little sister," he hissed, a mere five inches from Derek's face, his breath stinking of whisky and cigarettes. "And the only thing that keeps me from pounding the crap out of you is she made me promise not to. If it was up to me, you'd be lying on the side of the road here with busted bones and bleeding from every orifice, you cock-biting, asshole sonofabitch!" For final emphasis, Brad released Derek with a stiff shove, sending him banging against the passenger door. Derek's baseball cap tumbled into his lap.

The two sat in silence for what seemed like hours to Derek. Brad had lit and finished a Winston without offering one to his captive. He could sure use a smoke, but his Marlboros were back in his Vet.

Brad lit another one, inhaled deeply and asked straightforwardly, "Did you at least use a rubber?"

"Yes," said Derek, barely audible, saddened once again by thoughts of that night.

Brad took another big drag. "Back in the old days," he mused, the smoke bubbling out with each syllable, "my dad would shove a shotgun in your back and make you marry her."

"I'd marry Kay in a second," said Derek to his lap.

"Oh, hell yes, you would," mocked Brad.

"I would. I really would," insisted Derek, still not facing his antagonist.

Brad turned to look at the younger, smaller man. He sounded serious.

Derek continued, "I love her, man. I love your sister more than anything…more than my own life. I loved her the second I saw her in your folks' café. I knew right then she was the girl I was going to marry."

Brad continued studying Derek's profile. This was something unexpected. Brad understood being head over heels in love. He had to leave his heart's desire for the summer. She lived in New Orleans. He already missed the hell out of her.

Brad had an idea. He started the truck, cranked the wheel hard to the left, and accelerated back the way they had just come. When they arrived at Derek's Corvette, he did a one-eighty and parked twenty feet in front of it.

"Nice Vet," he stated. "What's it got?"

"A four-twenty-seven."

Brad whistled. "Really flies, I bet." Derek nodded. "Bet you love it."

"Sure do."

"Do you love it more than my sister?"

Derek groaned, "To get Kay back, I'd give it away in a heartbeat."

Brad tapped his thumb on the steering wheel, thinking. Without a word he rolled his large frame out of the truck and walked around to the back. He rummaged around the large cargo box, producing a gallon can of gas, and brought it up to the open window beside Derek. He held it up for confused young man to see and said flatly, "Prove it!"

Without hesitation, Derek climbed out of the truck, took the can from Brad, and started pouring gasoline all over his car. He walked back to Brad, set the empty can on the tailgate beside him, held out his hand and said firmly, "Got a match?"

With a crooked, incredulous smile, Brad handed the bleach-blonde baseball player his book of matches. Derek walked back to his Vet, struck a match and tossed it onto the car's ragtop. With a loud "Whoomp" the gas fumes ignited and the beautiful 1966 red Corvette convertible with a honking four-twenty-seven engine was engulfed in yellow and blue flames. The searing heat sent Derek back-peddling to the pickup.

"Holy shit!" yelled Brad, pivoting to run for the driver's side door. "Let's get the fuck out of here!"

Derek jumped in and the truck sped away, throwing gravel all over the hapless, burning Vet.

"Woo-wee!" exclaimed Brad, the adrenalin pumping, as he watched the huge fire growing smaller in his rearview mirror. "I didn't think you'd do it."

"I told you I love your sister," said Derek matter-of-factly, sadly watching in the side mirror. Right then the Vet's gas tank blew, sending a huge red fireball and various pieces of automobile into the sky.

Still holding the matches, Derek snatched a cigarette from Brad's pack on the dash and lit it. He took a big drag, inhaled deeply, and blew a stream of smoke at Brad's still-surprised face. "Need any more proof?

# Chapter 139

Derek was gut-shot losing his Vet. But the pain didn't compare to his loss of Kay. At least it seemed to get Brad off his back. The ex-tackle had even wished him good luck when he dropped Derek off at his home that night.

Even Derek's dad wasn't very upset when he heard the play-by-play. Dr. Schroeder used his standing in the community—plus the fact it's not healthy to piss off the town doctor—to get the police to classify the fire as "Vandalism by Persons Unknown." The insurance covered the entire loss minus the $500 deductible, and the good doctor offered to buy his melancholy son a new Vet. Derek declined, feeling he wasn't worthy. But he also needed something to drive to his summer ballgames, so he agreed to a used 1961 brown Pontiac *Tempest*. If they made a car named *Melancholy* or *Depressed*, he would have opted for it. But *Tempest* was the closest thing he could find to match his mood. He made sure it had a small, four-cylinder engine and cloth bench seats. And as the final self-induced punishment, it had to have an automatic transmission! If nothing else, he could drive past the Crystal Café or Kay's house incognito for a while. He didn't know why. For all he knew she was going steady now with Jerk. Seeing them parked in her driveway making out would only shove the knife in farther.

Donna Carter called twice the next week, then gave up. Derek had no interest in seeing her and he told her so. That's probably why she—with the help of some poor farm kid she enlisted with the promise of a blow job—forked a load of prime Black Angus cow manure into his L-shaped pool one night when nobody was home. She called later to take credit, saying she had *found a way to make his pool party worth shit*. His mom made him clean it up...using a rake and then pool skimmer. It was even worse having to clean the wet, stinking manure out the filter every fifteen minutes. It took two whole days. He swore vengeance. And all the while of being around the pool reminded him of Kay standing there in her cute bikini, so innocent, so pure, so about to be abused and violated a week later by Cedar Lake's local perv.

Besides, after Kay, Derek saw no point being with any female. Sex had become a dirty, four-letter word to him. He took down his Playboy Playmates and had no urge to masturbate. He hung out in his guesthouse almost

293

exclusively, coming in the house for meals or to collect some clothes or drop off some laundry.

Sure, being in the guesthouse made him replay that wonderful night turned horrible over and over, but that was the point...more punishment. Besides, seclusion was paramount to him these days. Outside of baseball, he spent virtually no time with his buddies, as they got summer jobs and prepared for their freshman year at college.

He didn't know what he was going to do. He'd been accepted at Southern Iowa University, but had no idea what to major in. Maybe he'd get a job at the marina or a gas station. He should probably leave town. It just didn't matter. Nothing mattered.

# Chapter 140

It was 10:30 p.m., Monday, July 4th, 1966. His folks had gone to the fireworks at the lake. Derek wasn't interested. He didn't deserve fireworks. He didn't even deserve any of the nice clothes in his closet, preferring to stay in his worn-out blue and white plaid shorts and plain gray t-shirt for the past couple of days. He just lay there on his sanctuary's couch, watching Johnny Carson and smoking Winstons, his new favorite. He didn't bother to open a window. The small window air conditioner was circulating the smoke, heat and humidity well enough. Besides, it just didn't matter.

He hated life. He was seriously considering cranking up the gas oven, when someone rapped lightly on the backdoor of the guesthouse.

*It's happening,* he thought. The police were here to arrest him for rape. Brother Brad had urged Kay to tell her folks and they'd gone straight to the cops. Good for her! She deserved to watch her defiler suffer public humiliation and be tossed into prison for the rest of his life, where he would be married to some thick-necked guy named Bubber. No punishment was too severe. The important thing was for Kay to be validated in the eyes of the town, so she could get on with her life, marry a good man, and raise a bunch of beautiful kids.

Derek actually felt some of the burden lift from his shoulders, as he walked slowly in resignation through his bedroom to the backdoor. He thought it must be how the Catholics feel when they confess to a priest. A cleansing of the soul and the doors to Heaven open. Not a bad deal. He wondered if it applied to atheists.

He opened the door and his heart stopped. The breath left his lungs and didn't return anytime soon.

It was Kay.

The last time he saw her face in this setting it was furious, confused, and clouded by alcohol. Now her countenance was closer to when she had waited on him at the lunch counter that day he invited her to his pool party. Congenial, yet cautious. Behind that understandable veil, her brown eyes still held that pure-Kay, heart-melting dependency that made you want to hug her until they bulged out. Her full lips were pursed, her shoulders back and stiff, neither offering any further hint of her mood or intent.

Derek looked past her to see who or what may be there in the dark. Brad, her brother? Jack Goodwin, her jock boyfriend? Her dad with a shotgun? A swat team? Villagers with torches and rakes? Nothing, just the leaves of the surrounding maple trees reflecting each colorful flash of the fireworks over the nearby lake, followed by the delayed report of booms and crackles.

Self-preservation dictated he glance down at Kay's hands. She didn't have a gun, at least not in her hands, which were flat and tight against the sides of her upper thighs. It could still be tucked in her waistline behind her. Or she could have a knife back there.

"May I come in?" she asked cordially, taking her turn to look past him at the cluttered bedroom, mostly to see if someone else, like *Donna*, was there.

It took his numbed brain a few seconds to register the request. "Of course, please do," he finally said, stepping to the side. His five-foot-four, ex-future wife breezed by him, leaving in her wake a slight whiff of her usual, sweet perfume, whatever it was. She was wearing a loose-fitting, white polo shirt with "Kay" embroidered above the left breast and "Crystal Café" silk-screened on the back in much larger blue script. While Derek's gaze naturally lowered to check out her backside as she passed by, tonight he did so strictly to verify there was no outline of a weapon under the loose-fitting, mid-thigh, pink shorts.

Further inspection revealed she had since shortened her dark-brown hair to a pixie cut, and pea-size, gold butterflies kissed each pierced earlobe. On her feet were white deck shoes with pink shoelaces. If she had come here to kill him, she was doing it in a most casual style. She paused in the center of the room, waiting for an offer from Derek.

"Do you want to sit down? A Pepsi?" he asked nervously. Under different circumstances a more confident man in good standing may have offered her some Southern Comfort, as a private joke. This was neither the situation nor the man.

# Chapter 141

Kay glided over to the unmade bed and planted herself daintily just to the left of center on a heap of a white sheet and thin yellow comforter thrown open and rumpled. Derek thanked God he had laundered the stained bedspread, even though little of it was showing at the moment.

Derek had no idea what he should do. He looked around, feeling as if he should ask her permission to sit in the straight-back chair behind him— presently serving as a valet for his dirty baseball uniform. He considered just squatting on the floor.

"Come, sit," she said with the slightest suggestion of a smile, patting the bed beside her.

"Really?"

"Yes, come. We need to talk."

Derek took a deep breath and shuffled over to sit exactly where she had indicated to her right. Afraid to look her in the eye, he kept his gaze on the opened copy of Sports Illustrated lying at his feet on the caramel-colored, loop pile carpet Kay had said felt so good between her toes...that night.

"So, how have you been?" she asked cordially, again giving no indication of her intent.

"Okay," he replied just above a whisper, eyes still downcast. "You?"

"Okay."

With the dialog exhausted, the pair fell silent. Muffled pops and booms drifted in from the lake. From the living room Ed McMahon could be barely heard laughing at every word and gesture of Carnac the Magnificent. Derek had a sudden itch on the side of his nose, but dared not move to scratch it. Kay shifted her weight forward. She took in some air and let it out.

"Look at me, Derek," she said flatly. Once again her tone and inflection revealed nothing.

Derek raised his head, but balked at turning to meet her eyes. After being caught, criminals never like looking at their victims. Seeing his hesitation, Kay reached across and placed the fingertips of her left hand on the right side of Derek's chin and gently turned it toward her. "Please, look at me," she repeated, now with a tinge of pleading.

Like a grade-schooler being chastised by his teacher for some misgiving, Derek obediently looked into her soft eyes, looking back at him. That's all it took. The guilt, the shame, the sorrow…all the emotions he had sequestered inside for weeks erupted to the surface. He dropped his head to her bosom, threw his arms around her waist and blubbered, "I'm so sorry!"

The tears flowed freely, forming wet spots on the polo shirt just above her embroidered name. He expected…no, he *hoped* the steak knife she had hidden in her hair or the back of her bra would any moment now come down hard between his ribs to pierce his heart. He ached for it. It's what he deserved. It's what he knew she wanted to do to the bastard that had raped her and stolen her virginity. There couldn't possibly be even the smallest sliver of forgiveness in her.

Instead, he felt Kay's soft hands caress his head. Then her chest began to quake. She was crying, too. "I'm the one who should apologize," she sobbed.

Her words resonated in his brain, testing a variety of synapses until it found one that verified he had heard her correctly.

Derek slowly brought his wet face up to study Kay's. *What*?! How could *she* possibly be sorry…and crying? Maybe she was apologizing for the murder she was about to commit.

Through her own blurred vision, Kay was just as surprised by Derek's actions and look of confusion. Was he actually this remorseful for that night? She remembered him being overly apologetic, but she had assumed it didn't go much beyond that. She hadn't heard from him since. She figured he'd simply gone on to his next conquest…or back to Donna Carter.

But as she studied this heart-breaking, repentant face, all indications were that this poor guy was riddled with guilt and had been going through hell these past weeks. Out of sympathy, she lightly kissed his warm, moist forehead and drew her arms around his neck. They both tightened their hold on each other and just cried and rubbed and squeezed for many minutes.

# Chapter 142

Derek pulled back a couple feet to look deep into her eyes. "I don't understand, Kay," he whispered incredulously. "How can you possibly be apologizing to *me*?"

Kay took his face in her hands, kissed him lightly on the lips and said, "I shouldn't have gotten so hostile toward you that night. It wasn't that big of a deal."

Derek's reply wasn't brilliant. It wasn't articulate. But it was perfectly descriptive. "*Huh*?"

Kay ran her fingers through his damp, blonde hair and said with a maternal smile, "I realized you were just being a typical, red-blooded American boy. And I certainly did my part in leading you on." She blushed a little. "It was rather fun and flattering to turn you on so much."

Hearing her explanation did little to bring Derek back from the land of the befuddled. "How could you possibly have forgiven me so fast after what I did?" he whined. "I stole your virginity without asking. I took something you can never get back. I took advantage of you. I defiled you. You screamed at me."

Kay released Derek and stood up to move into the living area and the kitchenette. She filled two glasses of water from the faucet and in true waitress fashion brought one to Derek. She drank heavily, gathering her words.

"Yes, at first I was furious with you. But, listen, I wanted to make love to you too. In time, just not on the first date, not wham-bam-thank-you-ma'am. Not while I was buzzed with booze."

"I understand," he said sadly, with bowed head. "I should have respected you more."

"Don't get me wrong," Kay continued. "While you were undressing me, and fondling me and kissing me and lying on top of me..."

"You remember all that?" Derek asked in surprise.

"Sure. I may have been drunk, but I knew what you were doing, what I was doing. And I liked it. I liked the feel of our naked bodies pressing together. When I felt your…er… *thing* push against me, I remember thinking how much I wanted you inside me."

Derek knew if Kay didn't stop talking, there was going to be a replay.

He rose to his feet, keeping his back to her. "Then I broke your cherry," he said to the wall.

"Yeah, that scared me. First the sharp pain. Then seeing my blood all over everything. I freaked. I shouldn't have. It wasn't that important."

"Of course it was!" said Derek, spinning around, finding it safe to face her now. "You had every right to be upset."

"Maybe in the moment," nodded Kay. "But later, a couple days later, I realized losing my virginity wasn't such a big deal. All my girlfriends had already lost theirs, and they seemed okay, even proud of it. I was glad I had lost mine. And it was to someone…someone I wanted to lose it to."

"Why didn't you tell me?" pleaded Derek, now directly in front of her, his hands gently on her forearms. "I've been in agony ever since."

Kay returned the gesture with an extra squeeze. She smiled bemusedly. "Well, it would have seemed pretty forward of me to call you up and say, hey, you know the other night, that night you screwed me and broke my cherry? Yeah, that was kind of fun. Want to do it again sometime?"

Derek snorted and nodded. He loved the sarcasm.

"Besides," Kay continued, moving over to sit on the arm of the couch, "I still had to sort some things out. What were your true feelings toward me? What were mine toward you? For all I knew you just chalked me up as another conquest and moved on to the next."

"Hardly," moaned Derek, recalling the hell of the past six weeks. "All I could think about was you and what I had done to you. I gave up sex. I dumped Donna. I even took down my Playmates."

Kay scanned the bare walls where they used to be. "So you did…" she said, doing a poor job of hiding the pleasure in her voice. Not for the absence of the centerfolds so much as for the departure of Donna.

# Chapter 143

Derek plopped back down on the couch. Neither knew for sure what to say or do next. The air was clearing, but not completely yet. Who should speak next?

"So, what finally brought you here tonight?" he asked, feeling the need for a little more assurance. So far, this had been too good to be true.

Kay slid off the arm of the couch, landing on Derek's left side. She lay her head on his shoulder and affectionately cradled his arm. "When Julie told me your car had burned up, the first thing I thought was you had been in it. I was panicky. I realized I really loved you. I started bawling, losing it."

Derek's heart started pounding. *Did she just say she really loved me?!* He suddenly couldn't breathe. Yes, *I think she really did say it.* The room got very bright. *Should I ask her to repeat it to make sure? No. Just let it lie for the moment. We can get back to it. Just stay on topic.* He cleared his throat, and with the same lungful of air he'd been holding for the past half-minute asked, "Didn't Brad tell you why I torched my Vet?"

"Brad?" she asked, sitting up and twisting to look at him. "Why would my brother know why you did it?"

Derek was surprised Brad hadn't told Kay about that night. Apparently he didn't want her to know he had anything to do with it. Brad had said he'd promised Kay not to hurt him. And being instrumental in burning up his Vet would certainly have implicated him, and incurred her wrath. *Well, Brad,* thought a smiling Derek, *payback time, you asshole.*

"I guess Brad failed to mention he was there when I did it. It was even his suggestion…and his gas."

"*What*?!" gasped Kay. "Why would he make you do such a thing? Why would you let him? This makes no sense."

"He didn't exactly make me do it, and I didn't exactly let him. I did it to prove to him that I loved you more than the car. He didn't believe me when I said I did. This proved it to him…and to me, too, for that matter."

Kay's brown eyes got big and round. Her mouth dropped open. Her body went so limp it naturally slid off the couch and onto her knees on the floor. After a moment of letting it all sink in, she pivoted to be directly in front of Derek, in the slave position. Her hands slipped up to grab the sides of his thighs.

"You…set…your…beautiful…red car…on fire," she whispered, tears welling up in her eyes, "to prove…you *loved* me?"

Derek nodded, smiling weakly.

It all became clear to Kay. It was more than just the sex that night. Derek did it out of love. And if she thought that was the sweetest thing she had ever heard, she needed to wait for only one more moment, because a bigger bombshell was about to drop.

"Shit, Kay," said Derek, as if overstating the obvious, "I've loved you from the first moment I saw you, when you waited on me and Donna in the café. I said to myself right then that you were the girl I was going to marry."

Kaboom! Kay's body went limp again, rolling to one side on her hip, clutching Derek's knees to keep from going completely prone.

"Really?" blubbered Kay, a big smile stretching across her face. "You want to *marry* me?"

"More than anything, baby! I'd do it right here and now, if we could."

Kay's blurry brown eyes bore deep into Derek's, searching for incriminating evidence. Every receptor in her mind, body, and soul said he was completely serious. Her heart rate doubled. Her entire body quaked. Leaping to her feet she dived into Derek, throwing her arms around his neck and smashed her body hard against his. He returned the embrace, squeezing her almost to the point of fracturing a few ribs. They tumbled to horizontal on the couch and stayed locked together for…well, for a long time.

There would be no sexual intercourse this night. No way. Such would be only anticlimactic compared to this spiritual coupling of two young souls, out of their physical bodies, so much in love, finding each other after so long an absence. Caring once again.

*Forgiving.*

# Chapter 144

Before calling everyone else in for the meeting, the two old friends took a few moments alone to relax and reminisce. Dressed in their usual tunics, Macailah and Andrew sat cross-legged on one of the half-dozen beach blankets encircling a small, crackling campfire. Beside them sat a cooler full of beer, wine and margaritas.

The plaid blankets and crackling fire were courtesy of Macailah's skills in creative visualization, patterned from her memory of that one life long ago, when she was a seventeen-year-old, Malibu Barbie-type, and the night she lost her virginity to a beach bum named Buzz.

The cooler full of beer, wine and margaritas was courtesy of Andrew's similar talents and his recollection of being that beach bum named Buzz. Until just now, neither soul had made the connection that they had actually met one time long ago, while incarnate on good ol' Earth-One.

"So, how good I was that night," said Andrew, twisting the cap off a bottle of Bud. "Was I a good lover?" It was so many lifetimes ago, he barely recalled the brief encounter.

"For about a minute and a half you were excellent," she replied, patting Andrew's leg.

Not since the night in that Italian bistro, planning the incarnations for their young wards, had these two imbibed in alcoholic refreshment. And this island in the middle of the night in the middle of Cedar Lake in the middle of Iowa in the middle of the twentieth Century seemed as good a place and time as any to do it again.

Laughing about that past life sent the two waxing nostalgic about many other incarnations, and soon the anecdotes were flying as fast as the cooler was emptying. This just naturally led to what was most on their minds these days: *their two younger-selves*. In far fewer tries than either Andrew or Macailah had needed as fledgling souls, Ethan and Phoebe were now able to separate themselves at will from the human bodies they were occupying—presently Derek and Kay. Always a big step for any young soul, it meant they no longer needed to remain locked up inside the physical shell for the duration of that life, believing they actually are nothing more than that flesh and bone human. The feeling of liberation is most gratifying to the *inner self*.

"Ethan is literally *beside* himself now that he can do that," remarked Macailah. "Pun intended. He keeps jumping in and out of Derek just to prove he can."

"Same with Phoebe," said Andrew. "In fact, did you know she stayed firmly inside Kay while Derek was *raping* her, just to get the full sexual effect?"

"Why, that little vixen," laughed Macailah.

"Oh, that's only the half of it. When Kay's conscious mind got all pissed about it, Phoebe got the hell out of there right quick!"

"Smart girl," replied Macailah flippantly. "Those humans can get so furious over the littlest things sometimes."

Andrew lit a huge Cuban cigar off a glowing ember from the fire, blew a few smoke rings into the night air, and turned pragmatic. "Remember in our earlier lives when we were so young and dumb? If we'd only known we had a seasoned, well-connected soul right there with us, to watch over us, to meet with us every night in our dreams, to make sure what is supposed to happen happens."

"I know," sighed Macailah, looking out across the lake and its shimmering reflection of the town's streetlights. "We were a closed system throughout our waking hours. All we had to do was open our minds."

"Well, it's how we learned," said Andrew. "Look at our Phoebe and Ethan during their early incarnations. Without the slightest clue of possessing an inner-self, they never even considered falling back on intuition or conscience to guide them over the rough spots. Yet, it was that very ignorance that hastened their early development."

"Just like us," said Macailah. "It always works out."

# Chapter 145

"And have you noticed how much braver are kids are these days?" asked Andrew, reaching into the cooler for another Bud.

"Oh, God yes!" laughed Macailah. "Ethan thinks he's ready to take on anything."

"Tell me about it," nodded Andrew. "Phoebe's gotten so cocky she's talking about having some type of serious retardation or being another Stalin in her next life."

"Speaking of which," said Macailah drolly, standing up and smoothing out the back side of her silvery tunic, "shouldn't they have been here by now?"

"Just a second, I'll check." Andrew closed his eyes and tuned into Phoebe's frequency. He had his answer quickly. "Not much longer, she says. She's waiting for Kay to get deeper into REM. She had to get up and pee. What about Ethan and Derek?"

"Same. Just a few more minutes. Too much Mountain Dew."

"Okay. Let's go ahead and call in the others."

The first to arrive around the campfire were the inner-selves of Derek's mom and dad. On their heels came those of Kay's mom, dad, brother Brad, and little sister, for a total of eight inner-selves. Where needed, introductions were made and the bottomless cooler opened. The mood was jovial, despite the relative seriousness of the meeting.

Shortly, in floated Ethan with the astral body of Derek in tow. He set the half-asleep specter of his physical-self down gently on one of the beach blankets and sat down next to him. Ethan waved and smiled warmly at his older-self, Macailah. She gave him a wink.

But when Ethan then noticed Andrew next to her, his forehead scrunched in bewilderment. Before he could ask what Phoebe's older-self was doing here, Phoebe herself—hand-in-hand with a slightly more awake astral body of Kay—floated in. Seeing Ethan, she put on the air brakes and hovered.

"What the hell's going on here?" she gasped, her heart suddenly pounding in her chest. She hadn't seen her estranged lover since their break-

305

up back in the cabin some twenty Earth years ago. She just realized how much she missed him. *Oh, God, how she missed him!*

"What are you doing here...Ethan?" she asked cautiously. Had he forgiven her? And what was he doing sitting beside Derek?

"I was wondering the same thing," piped Ethan, searching faces for some kind of explanation. Why was Phoebe holding hands with Kay? Why was she here at all? Had she forgiven him? Did she want to get back together? *Oh, God, he hoped so!*

As yellow particles of confusion spun around the auras of Phoebe and Ethan, their eyes danced back and forth longingly between themselves, as well as questioningly at their respective greater-selves. Macailah looked innocently at Andrew and shrugged. Andrew looked innocently at Macailah. The group of elders began to twitter; this was going to be fun.

In the meantime, half-asleep astral-Derek suddenly spotted Astral-Kay. He became fully alert and wasted no time leaving Ethan's side and darting for his precious. The two smashed together harder than two cymbals in the 1812 Overture, and sailed off behind a tree, kissing and dry humping in a most audacious and embarrassing fashion. Macailah asked the group to pay no attention.

"Okay," confessed Macailah. "Yes, we tricked you two."

"But think about it," added Andrew. "If either of you had known the other was involved in this Iowa incarnation, things probably would not have turned out as well as they did."

Macailah floated over to come face-to-face with her younger-self. "Ethan, being mad at Phoebe, if you had known all along that she was Kay, you could easily have sabotaged the whole game plan. You might have gotten Derek to lead Kay on, only to dump her hard the moment she fell for him."

Ethan stared off in the distance, pondering the hypothetical.

"Just as you, my darling daughter," added Andrew, kissing Phoebe on the top of her head, "could have made sure Kay never agreed to go to the pool party, let alone out on a date with him. And the whole scheme goes to hell. No date, no date rape, no learning the virtue of forgiveness. One big waste of an incarnation and a great opportunity."

# Chapter 146

While Ethan and Phoebe sat preoccupied with the concepts they were just presented, Macailah turned her attention to the group.

"As we mentioned in the telepathic text we sent all of you, we have a situation here where Kay has forgiven Derek for virtually raping her. That in turn has taught them both how important forgiveness is. Now Derek and Kay are madly in love and want to get married."

The group applauded. Off in the distance Derek lifted his blurry face from Kay's to see what the ruckus was about. But Kay quickly pulled it back down by the ears.

"Consequently, from experiencing, from demonstrating this valuable lesson of forgiveness," continued Macailah, "we think, we *hope* their real-selves, Ethan and Phoebe here, have also learned to forgive, and are ready to make up for cheating on each other back on Earth-Two." Macailah gestured toward the pair, presently sitting an arm's length apart…the closest they had been to each other since back at their cabin. "Is that a distinct possibility, my young souls?"

Ethan looked longingly at Phoebe. Phoebe looked like she wanted to devour Ethan.

"Phoebe," said Ethan, leaning toward her, his tone a mixture of contrition and humility, "I'm sorry for doing it with Callie, and I forgive you for doing it with Leonid. I should have long ago. In this life as Derek, you've taught us the magnificence of forgiveness. You could have had us thrown in jail for rape, but instead you forgave. I'm overwhelmed. And I'm more in love with you than ever."

Phoebe had already turned to Ethan and edged closer. She reached out and touched his face. "My darling, Ethan," she said evenly, tears rolling down her cheeks. "I've longed to hear those words for what seems like forever. I forgive you for making love with Callie. And I apologize for cheating on you with Leonid. You had every right to be mad at me. And I, too, love you more than ever, which I didn't think was even possible."

With that the two entities eased into each other's arms. The embrace then became so fervent, loud applause spontaneously broke out, followed by nary a dry eye on the island.

Hearing the even louder commotion, Derek's curiosity again got the better of him. He lifted off of Kay and began drifting toward that source of this high energy. But this time, instead of pulling him back down, Kay felt herself being pulled toward the group, as well. So, they just let themselves gravitate over to join with their two inner-selves in a swirling embrace.

Soon everyone around the campfire was hugging and blending.

# Chapter 147

As both the fire and love fest cooled to glowing embers, it was time to get down to business. "As we've seen," said Andrew, now taking the lead, "the main goal of these incarnations of Ethan as Derek and Phoebe as Kay was to teach them the importance of forgiveness, which was demonstrated exceptionally well by her forgiving Derek.

"But let me emphasize that this was not *a* goal. It was *the* goal. It was based on a blueprint Macailah and I designed most carefully with much effort and insight. We did it behind the backs of Ethan and Phoebe, and it worked out to virtual perfection. By any means possible, Macailah and I were determined to preserve one of the greatest love affairs ever recorded in archives of The Deep Blue." Applause.

"So, with the primary objective achieved," said Macailah, "the issue we need to address tonight is…" She stopped and looked over at the now-exhausted Derek and Kay, still entwined with each other, hovering directly behind their inner-selves, trying hard to stay awake to hear about this issue that they probably shouldn't hear.

"Phoebe, Ethan," whispered Macailah, pointing at the pair behind them. "Why don't you send your human specters back to dreamy time. It's better they not be present for this."

"They wouldn't remember it next morning, anyway" offered Ethan.

"True. But let's not take the chance. They need to be completely oblivious."

Both inner-selves rotated one-hundred-eighty degrees and placed their hands on the astral heads of Derek and Kay. "Nighty night." The pair flashed away to reenter their own dream dimension.

"It is for the better," nodded Andrew to the group. They all agreed.

"Now, as I was saying," continued Macailah, "with the goal obtained, and with this highly motivated pair of younger-selves Andrew and I have here, we are anxious to move on with their educations. So, the question becomes whether to have Ethan and Phoebe continue on in their lives as Derek and

Kay, where there isn't much more to learn, or to bring them Home in the very near future, so they can take on more challenging roles."

"You're suggesting we kill them off," calmly proposed Joseph, the older-self of Kay's father, Mr. Beecher.

"Yes," said Macailah. "Andrew and I think there is little more to gain for them in this incarnation. We have them on the fast track to becoming E3s. We'd like them to move on…with everyone's approval."

There was considerable buzzing among the greater-selves of Derek and Kay's immediate family, most of them nodding, seemingly in agreement, as expected. After all, to the inner-self of an earth-bound human, dying is nothing to fear. In fact, it's a joyous occasion, as it means coming Home to a much nicer environment and old friends after experiencing something akin to boot camp in a mosquito-riddled hell-hole. And while it can be sad for that soul to leave loved ones behind, and in turn cause a great deal of anguish for those humans, he knows in the big picture it is for the better; the souls of those cherished friends and family members will only grow in wisdom from the experience.

As the buzzing subsided, it was Joseph who announced that everyone was fine with *whacking* Derek and Kay. Kay's mother and father were going to be very heart-broken for the obvious reasons. But conversely, their greater-selves were the ones mostly for it, because their younger-selves had yet to experience the loss of a child, and this was as good an opportunity as any to cross that prerequisite off the Reincarnation Cycle list. It would advance their knowledge and growth considerably.

"How and when?" asked Joseph.

"We don't know yet," said Andrew. "Our current list of exit points shows the earliest one not for about ten Earth years for Derek and thirty-three for Kay. We'd like something much sooner. And we want them to go together. As we have learned from past patterns, Ethan can get a little over-anxious if he has to wait too long for Phoebe to come Home."

Phoebe beamed and gave Ethan and big kiss. "You're so sweet, honey!"

"We will scan the future for possibilities," continued Andrew, "creating one if we have to."

Suddenly there came a new voice from behind the group, apparently just arriving, "Sorry for crashing your little party," she said. "But I have a suggestion."

# Chapter 148

The figure moved to the front of the group to face Andrew directly. It was Phaidra, the older-self of Leonid. "Hi, old friend," she said, spreading her arms.

"Well, hello, Phaidra," chimed Andrew, stepping forward to hug her. "How are you?"

"Oh, you know, just running around, keeping the kiddies in line, like you. How are things going for you and yours?"

"Same as always: living, learning."

"Let's see," mused Phaidra, "I haven't seen you since our collaboration to do that Magens Beach charade…when your Phoebe and my Leonid almost got it on."

"Ah, yes, that was quite the thing," sighed Andrew with a wry smile. "When I asked for your help, I just wanted you to materialize a few apparitions to gawk at Phoebe, to get her believing in her new image, so she could maintain it on her own. I didn't expect your boy, Leonid, to be there, let alone try to jump my girl."

"He'd just got in from being a young, horny pro football player," sighed Phaidra, "who thought sex had been invented just for him. I thought he would stay inside, but he sneaked out on me. I didn't know he would hit on Phoebe like he did. He was certainly infatuated with her looks. She was and still is a knockout. You did a great job on her, Andrew."

Ethan looked hard at his wife, as if seeing her for the first time. She really was beautiful. Phoebe blushed. She was embarrassed having everyone's eyes suddenly on her.

"Thanks, but it's all her own doing now," said Andrew. "And how is Leonid? Has he ever forgiven me for busting his balls?"

"He got over it," said Phaidra. "But the truth is he's never got over Phoebe. His infatuation with her has been relentless."

"Really? I didn't know."

"Oh, it's not so surprising when you consider the poor devil has been thwarted at every turn with your *daughter*. The first one, as you remember, was in old Germany when Leonid was Gunther, the young bronco who was about to bang Gretchen in the hay loft when her father caught them."

Andrew's attempt to hide his mirth was largely unsuccessful. Picking up on it, Phaidra asked with one eye cocked, "That wasn't you with the big knife, was it, Andrew?"

"No, it wasn't me, I promise," he said truthfully. But the concept of neutering Leonid was pleasing.

"Didn't think so. The next time was, of course, when you coitus interrupted him at Magens Beach."

"Of course," deadpanned Andrew.

"Anyway," continued Phaidra, "against my stern advice and really frustrated now, he wanted to try again, this time sliding into Phoebe's DeKalb, Illinois life. He saw the probability that she would miss meeting Ethan and marry a local farmer instead. So, Leonid goes in, grows up to be the farmer, and sure enough he gets Phoebe to marry him. But my hapless horn dog didn't count on my rendering him *ineffective* on the night of his wedding, as retribution for once again not listening to me. So, naturally Phoebe was very disappointed with him and the prospect of life on the farm with no life in the conjugal bed. As we expected, she hurried back to Ethan by taking a header off that ridge into Four Mile Creek."

"Wow," breathed Andrew. "I had no idea that farmer was Leonid."

"Wait, there's more," said Phaidra, rolling her eyes.

# Chapter 149

Phaidra went on to explain that Leonid's next attempt was in his sixth incarnation and what she believes was Phoebe's seventh. They were Fifteenth Century French aristocrats engaged to each other, trying to have sex for the first time. But Leonid always kept getting so excited, he would explode all over her prematurely.

"Your handy work again?" laughed Andrew.

"No, actually, I was going to let him finally have his turn with Phoebe. It was all the aristocrat's DNA this time."

"I *did* know Leonid was in that one," said Andrew, stifling yet another grin. "It turned Phoebe gay, and thereby enabled her to check that sexual orientation prerequisite off the reincarnation list."

"See?" said an exasperated Phaidra, tossing her hands in the air. "Phoebe listens to you and moves steadily along in her development. Leonid doesn't and doesn't."

"I'm really sorry for all Leonid has been through on account of my Phoebe," said Andrew, taking a deep breath and doing his best to turn serious. But his words of condolence were no sooner out than one more episode between Phoebe and Leonid came to mind…the very last one…the one, in fact, that was instrumental in the need to blueprint this whole Iowa incarnation chapter in the first place.

Everyone watched as the puzzled look spread across Andrew's face. He help up one finger and said to Phaidra, "Wait a second…Leonid finally *did* succeed. He got my baby into the Mediatory of the library there at Seth Hall. In fact it was *Phoebe* who seduced *him*. I thought that's all he ever wanted from her."

"I'm sorry to say that only made matters worse," sighed Phaidra. "He was so pumped up to finally couple with her, he…well, it was over shortly after it had started. Leonid felt he could have done much better. So, to get more chances to prove himself as the great lover he thinks he is, now he wants her as a mate, and not just as a one-time bang among the books. With all his other sex partners it's always been hump-and-dump. Not with Phoebe. She has him so mesmerized, he doesn't even want to couple with anybody else."

"Well, that little rendezvous became an intricate part in Phoebe and Ethan breaking up," stated Andrew flatly. "Is he happy about that?"

"Definitely. He thinks he now has a good shot at becoming her steady lover. He's so obsessed with Phoebe, in fact, he's entered her life here in Iowa."

The group murmured.

Andrew had to think a moment. "You don't mean he's the college boy...Kay's first boyfriend, do you?"

"One in the same," sighed Phaidra. "Jack Goodwin."

The group gasped.

"Man, he *is* a glutton for punishment," said Macailah. "He doesn't have a chance with Phoebe (as Kay) now."

The group agreed.

"I know that," said Phaidra. "But *he* doesn't. He thinks he can win her over on Earth, and that conquest will carry over to Earth-Two. After Magens Beach he discovered he can jump into any Earth body he wants with or without my permission. So ever since he has insisted on devising his own incarnations. I could interfere again, but, as you already know, we need to let them make their own mistakes."

"It's how they learn," nodded Andrew and every other older-self there.

Understanding the teacher-student relationship all too well, all the greater-selves around the campfire let Phaidra know it with a mild applause. The slender, bald-headed waif in the floor-length, purple tunic bowed sheepishly. Her ivory skin that normally glowed with a silvery aura had a touch of pink to it.

"So, anyway," she said, "regarding getting Phoebe and Ethan quickly over and done with this Iowa chapter..."

"Yes?"

"I have an idea, if you all would care to hear it."

314

# Chapter 150

It was the dog days of mid-August.  Kay was still working fulltime at the Crystal Café before starting her junior year at Cedar Lake High in a couple weeks.  High school baseball was over for Derek forever, and that didn't really matter.  No college was going to offer even a partial athletic scholarship to a centerfielder with a flagging .272 batting average and a give-a-shit attitude.

 That didn't matter either, because his parents could easily afford to send him to any college he chose, which didn't matter either, because he had decided to wait two years before even thinking about college, so he could stay near his beloved Kay until she graduated.  Then they'd probably get married.  His class ring wrapped in mohair on her finger was a preamble to the engagement.

Speaking of wrapped, if Jack Goodwin wasn't so engrossed in himself, he may have noticed the ring.  But having spun around on the counter stool, he was too busy scanning Kay's backside, as she took the order of the two teens in the second booth.  Since missing their chance of sex at the drive-in, plus just getting back from three months of playing summer college ball for the Saints in St. Joseph, Missouri, he was certain Kay would be very glad to see him.  And this meant there was a high probability they'd be doing the deed on their next date.

Granted, her letters—basically as replies to his—lacked any amorous content…just short blurbs about her work and her mundane life between shifts.  There was even a nondescript "As always, Kay" in the closings.  That was okay.  She'd soon see him sitting on this stool in her café, looking as tanned, toned, and sexy as ever.  And wait until she heard the news about a Chicago Cubs scout talking to him after a game, indicating they were interested.  She'd be so turned on he wouldn't be surprised if she took him in the back and jumped his bones in the bathroom.

Unfortunately, it didn't quite play out that way.  Kay passed the teenagers' order onto her mother in the kitchen, pivoted, and walked with her head down to where she knew a new customer was waiting at the counter.

She was preoccupied with a loose thread on one of her blouse's buttons. She snapped it off and plucked the order pad out of her apron.

"What can I get you," she asked mechanically. When she looked up, the Cheshier Cat smile on Jack's broad, tan face nearly knocked her backwards. She let out a surprised *Oh!* From there her expression turned to scrutiny. When it reached the level of conciliatory, she offered an unenthusiastic, "Hi, Jack."

"Hi, baby," he replied, just as cocky and clueless as always. "Man, it's great to see you."

Kay looked around, searching for someone or something to get her out of the confrontation that was inevitably coming in a very short while. "Yeah, when did you get back from…St. Jude or St. Francis or whatever that was in Missouri?"

"It's St. Joseph, sweetie," laughed Jack, "and just last night. I couldn't wait to see you. Did ya miss me?"

"So, how'd summer baseball go?" she dodged.

You didn't need to ask Jack that twice. "I had a bunch of pro scouts watching me all summer. The Chicago Cubs are very interested. I may get an offer any day. Batted .329 with ten home runs. And this was against top-notch pitching…guys that are definitely going pro real soon."

"That's nice," said Kay unexcitedly, shooting a glance toward the door, praying for a customer to walk through it. But none came.

"So, you wanna got out tonight?" asked Jack, nonchalantly plopping his right forearm on the counter, his *Good One!* silver bracelet clinking against the white Formica.

# Chapter 151

"Oh, I can't," replied Kay, feigning mild disappointment. "I have to babysit my little sister."

"Hmm…well, I could come over and help you."

"Oh, no, my folks wouldn't go for that."

"Let's not tell them," grinned Jack, leaning forward, winking.

Kay just stared at him, eyebrows raised, one corner of her mouth tweaking an inch to the left.

"Okay," conceded Jack, "how about tomorrow night, Friday night?"

"Can't. Busy."

"Busy?" huffed Jack. "Then let's do it Saturday night. Nobody's busy on a Saturday night unless they have a date."

Here it was. The dreaded confrontation. And the bad news for Jack Goodwin. Thank goodness they were in public…her family's café, no less, with her dad in the back.

"I do have a date," Kay stated boldly, gazing hard at his face for the reaction. She had already checked her balance, just in case she had to move quickly one way or the other.

Jack's lips parted, his eyes blinked rapidly. "A date?!" he spat. "With who?"

"You don't know him," Kay said flatly. "He's from here."

"Maybe I do," Jack replied indignantly. "Try me."

"It doesn't matter," said Kay, getting a little testy.

"Hey," said Jack, recoiling, spreading his hands. "I just want to know who my competition is."

"There isn't going to be any competition," said Kay, bringing her left hand out from behind her back to display Derek's class ring. But rather than holding it out like showing off a diamond engagement ring to a girlfriend, she just held it up beside her head for a brief moment.

Jack's eyes bugged out. Then his lips pursed into a grotesque slit. "What the fuck, Kay," he hissed. "I thought you and I were…."

"You and I were nothing!" Kay shot back whispering, leaning into him. "We had a few dates. Then you went off to play ball all summer. Did you expect me to wait around for three months? We weren't even going steady."

"But you wrote to me all summer," protested Jack, on the defensive.

Kay's brown eyes flashed. "I wrote *back* to you…you and your boring letters about you did this and you did that and you had five RIBs and you hit a home run with six guys on base and…"

Jack stammered without getting any words out.

"Meanwhile," she continued, on a roll, "I met a really nice guy who cares about me. He plays baseball, too, but I don't think he's ever once mentioned how he did in a game."

"Okay, okay," offered a pleading Jack. "I won't even talk about baseball again. I promise. Just give me another chance, Kay. I really like you. I thought we had a real connection."

Kay shook her head slowly. "It just won't work, Jack. I liked you, too. But I'm in love with Derek. Really in love. We plan on getting married next year."

Jack sat in dumbfounded silence. His face got red, even redder than his sunburned cheeks. His jaw muscles flexed.

Without a word, he fetched the squeeze bottle of catsup out of the rank and began writing a message upside down on the counter for Kay. He got the "C" in "Fuck" turned around and was too lazy to do anything more than a "U" for "You, but he made his point.

As Kay left to get a wet rag to clean up the mess, Jack Goodwin spun on the spindle and stomped out of the Crystal Café.

# Chapter 152

The 1960 forest green Cadillac with lake pipes rumbled into the Phillips 66 station at four-thirty Saturday afternoon, each tire tripping the bell inside. Derek quickly finished his cigarette and stomped it out on the garage floor. He grabbed the dirty chamois from the dirty water in the rusty washtub and hustled out to the waiting customer.

"Fill'er up with premium, sir?" he asked, as the owner had instructed him to say last Monday during Derek's orientation and first day at work.

"Yeah, and check the oil."

Derek lifted the nozzle from the premium side of the pump, flipped open the Cadillac's protective gas cap door, unscrewed the cap and inserted the nozzle. As the gas flowed, he skipped around to the front of the car and lifted the hood.

"Oil looks okay, he called out.

"Good. Thanks."

After closing the hood, Derek pulled the spray bottle of half-Windex-half-water from his back pocket and commenced washing the windshield with the dirty chamois.

"That your brown Tempest parked there?" asked the driver, leaning his head halfway out of the window and gesturing to the side of the building. He wasn't really interested. He just wanted to start up a dialog. This kid may know something.

Derek didn't need to look. It was the only car there. "Yep."

"What's it got?"

"Nothing. Absolutely nothing."

"Hey, it's got wheels," laughed the handsome young man.

By now Derek had worked his way around to do the driver's side of the windshield. He noticed the occupant was wearing an USI baseball cap. "You play ball for Southern Iowa?"

"Nah, just a big baseball fan," lied the very tan twenty-year-old. "You look kind of athletic. You play baseball?"

"Yeah, used to."

319

"For Cedar Lake High?"

"Yeah," sighed Derek. "I graduated in May. Played this summer. Now we're done."

"I thought you looked a little familiar," lied the driver again. "I went to a couple of your games last spring. I scout sometimes for USI. You played...?

"Centerfield," said Derek, a little surprised. This scout certainly hadn't come to watch *him* play. Joe at shortstop or Willy catching maybe. But not him.

"That's right: centerfield," nodded the driver, as if he knew. To demonstrate he was interested and ready for some conversation, he twisted in his seat to better face the young gas jockey. He then brought a big right hand—with a silver bracelet hanging loosely around the wrist—through the window. "Sorry, but I don't remember your name," he said, offering his hand. "I undoubtedly heard it over the PA system a few times."

Derek shook the guy's hand. "I'm Derek Schroeder."

Jack Goodwin's adrenal glands shot a bolt through his system. He'd come into town on a mission to find all he could about this one particular guy. He didn't have much to go on, just what Kay had leaked: his name was Derek and he played baseball, probably for the Cedar Lake Lakers. Jack had pulled into this gas station just to ask this young attendant if he knew of anybody matching that description. And damned if this may very well be him! After all, how many ball-playing Dereks could there be in this small dump? A couple more subtle questions and he'd know for sure.

"Yeah, nice to meet you, Derek. I'm...a..Leo."

"You from around here, Leo," asked Derek, just making conversation, as he ran the chamois along the driver's side wiper blade.

"Nope, from Central City, born and raised."

The gas pump had clunked off, so Derek slid over to finish up. "So, what brings you to our small burg on a late-Saturday afternoon?"

Jack had to think fast. "Just thought I'd drive over and see how the lake looked. Haven't seen it in a while. Might bring my girl over later. There's that island we used to canoe out to...with a blanket...well, I'm sure you know all about it."

"Oh, yeah," smiled Derek. "Evergreen Island. It's a good make-out spot. Haven't been there myself for a year."

"Oh, you must have a girl," said Leo "...good looking, baseball-playing guy like you."

"Yep," grinned Derek proudly. "Gonna get engaged here pretty soon.

"Well, congratulations," said Jack. "Same with me. My girl's name is Kate…"

"Hey, mine's Kay. Pretty close."

"Small world, ain't it?" said Jack, hoping he could stay calm and pleasant for another few moments. He fished out his wallet. "What do I owe you?"

"$3.90. It took only ten gallons."

Jack gave him four dollars and said to keep the change.

As he pulled the huge Caddy away, Derek called," Thanks, Leo. Maybe we'll see each other again."

"Oh, you can count on it!" hissed Jack, glaring in the rear-view mirror.

# Chapter 153

Kay and Derek came out of the Lake Theater, having just seen "Georgie Girl" on the silver screen. They turned down the first side street toward the parked Tempest. Spotting it, Derek hoped this might be the last time he'd see the brown POS parked and waiting for him. The 1966 Chevelle Super Sport 396 he had let his dad buy for him was due in Monday. He would like to have had another Vet, but both he and Kay didn't want bucket seats keeping them apart while driving. With the SS 396, they were able to get the bench seat option, even with a four-on-the-floor. Kay was almost as excited as Derek about the new car. The Tempest was rusty, noisy and smelled like a filthy oil rag.

"You want to have kids?" Kay asked, as she slid into the passenger's side of the Tempest, its door being politely held open by the love of her life.

"Sure, some day," replied Derek, closing the door then lighting a cigarette. He climbed in the driver's side. "Not real soon."

"Oh, I agree. We have plenty of time. I just think I'd make a pretty good mother...like Lynn Redgrave in the movie."

"I know you would, sweetheart," said Derek in all sincerity. "But I want you all to myself, for a few years anyway."

The brown Pontiac started up on the second try and eased up to the stoplights. When it turned green it took a right onto Main Street.

"What do you want to do?" he asked, giving her knee a squeeze. She sure looked cute in that pink jumper and short-sleeved white blouse. She liked him in his khaki slacks and a navy-blue button-down shirt. They both wore white, low-cut Converses. No socks.

"I don't care," Kay sighed. "Drive through the A&W. Go park at the west overlook. Go to your place and rape *you*. What do you want to do?"

Derek wheeled the car to the curb, slammed it into park, and flipped the half-finished cigarette out the window. He reached over to take Kay's face in his hands, and gave her a big smooch straight on, nose to nose.

"What was that for?" she laughed in surprise.

"Nothing," he said, shifting the transmission back into drive and pulling back onto Main Street. "I just love you, Kay Beecher."

If she wasn't sure before, she was now.  She would have followed Derek into hell after that.

Taking a slow spin through the A&W, Derek spotted Joe's green and white '56 Chevy angled in one of the slots.  He'd seen very little of his best friend and teammate since the end of summer baseball.  The space on the right was open, so the Tempest pulled in.

"What're you guys up to?" shouted Derek under the menu.  His voice had to carry ten feet through the canned music, roller skating carhops, and a blonde in the passenger side.  He turned to Kay and reported the girl was her friend, Julie.

"I know," she replied.  "She told me she was going out with Joe tonight. Sorry.  I meant to tell you."

Both Joe and Julie were already out of their car and at the windows of their respective friends.  The girls chatted about each other's excellent choice of clothing tonight, the boys about cars.

"So where are you guys heading after this" asked Joe, the good looking, well-built shortstop.

"We hadn't decided," said Derek.

"There's that kegger starting up about now at Pelican Park.  The end of summer final fling thing.  Wanna go?"

Derek checked his watch.  It was nine-fifteen.  Kay's curfew was midnight.  He would need at least an hour to make mad passionate love to her at his guest house.  That left a little less than ninety minutes they could devote to the party.  He asked Kay what she thought.  She liked the idea.

"Let's do it."

"Go ahead," said Joe.  "We'll catch up.  Gotta finish our burgers."

# Chapter 154

Heading down the dark Lakeshore Road ten miles from Pelican Park, a pair of headlights came up fast behind them, flashing its brights and honking.

"Must be Joe, said Derek, looking intensely into both rearview mirrors, trying to make out the Chevy's telltale grill in the glaze of white light. "He used to have one headlight dimmer than the other, but he's probably had it fixed by now. All four are bright."

"I think he wants us to pull over," said Kay. "I hope nothing's wrong."

There wasn't much shoulder, but Derek eased over as far as he could, leaving his left side wheels barely on the asphalt, the right wheels on the edge of the shallow ditch. The other car pulled up right behind.

Both drivers got out at the same time and began walking toward each other. Having to still look straight into the bright headlights, Derek couldn't tell who the guy was. He seemed to be the same size as Joe, so it had to be.

"Anything wrong, Joe?" he said, now stopping at the rear of his car, holding his hand up to shield his eyes.

The figure reached Derek's position and put a heavy arm around his shoulders. "Not Joe," he said, leading Derek up to the driver's side of the brown Tempest.

Now better able to see the guy's face, Derek was surprised to discover it was Leo, the baseball scout from earlier at the gas station.

"Leo?"

"Yeah, *Leo*," snorted Jack sarcastically, bending himself and Derek down to peer inside the car. "Hi, Kay," he said with sour honey dripping off his tongue.

"Jack?" gasped Kay. Her tone immediately turned hostile. "What the hell are you doing here?"

"Jack?" questioned a very confused Derek. "I thought you said your name was Leo."

"Leo. Jack. Jack. Leo," mocked Jack, putting Derek into a powerful headlock. "It doesn't matter. All you need to know is I'm the guy who's gonna kick your ass."

"Let him go, you asshole," demanded Kay, sliding over behind the wheel.

Anticipating one of her possible intentions, Jack quickly reached in with his free right hand, turned off the car, and plucked the keys out of the ignition.

"You son of a bitch!" she spat. "Give those back."

"Easy, sweetheart," Jack said menacingly, slipping the keys into his jeans pocket. "If you'll be a good girl, I'll give them back to Dork here, and he can drive away unscathed."

"What the hell are you talking about?" insisted Kay.

"It's real simple," said Jack. "You get in my car with me and be real nice, and your wimpy boyfriend here can drive his weenie ass down the road still in one piece."

"Leave her alone, you cocksucker!" threatened Derek from his non-threatening position.

"Shut up, grease monkey," spat Jack, tightening his hold on Derek's neck. With the added pressure on both his carotid and jugular, Derek's downcast head began getting woozy.

"How about it, Kay? We've had some unfinished business for a long time now. It's not like you don't want to. You've wanted to fuck me since our first date and you know it. Christ, I'm twice the man of this twerp. Think how much better off you'll be with me."

"Not if you were the last man on Earth," she jeered. "You're absolutely disgusting!"

"Oh, that's not very nice," mocked Jack. "Do you think that's very nice, Dork? What's that, Dork? Oh, you can't speak because your windpipe is being crushed?"

"Derek!" screamed Kay. "Are you alright?"

It was true. Derek was unable to do anything other than slap the side of the car, and he wasn't all that far from being unable to breathe. As he reached the point of passing out, his arms flailed weakly at Jack's right wrist and forearm.

"Okay. Okay," said Kay in as calming a tone as possible. "I'll do whatever you want. Just let Derek go. You're killing him!"

# Chapter 155

Jack let up a little to allow some blood back into Derek's brain, but his hold was still secure. Derek wasn't going anywhere.

"Well, for starters," said Jack, laying his free right forearm on the Tempest's window sill and ducking his head a little farther inside the car, "why don't you lift up your dress so I can see what you've got under there."

"*What*?!" spat Kay.

"Just do it, bitch!" shot Jack. "Or your boy here gets really messed up."

Realizing she was out of the options she never had, Kay reached down to the hem of her pink jumper and pulled it halfway up her thighs.

"Higher," demanded Jack.

Kay obeyed, showing most of her light-brown legs.

"All the way," sang Jack. "Don't be shy."

She lifted the skirt until the white of her panties were well visible. "Happy?" she jeered.

Jack leaned in even farther to get a better look. The only available light was that coming from the high beams of his Caddy, bouncing around the inside of the Tempest.

"Gee," he taunted, "seems mommy doesn't make you wear your girdle for little Dork here."

Jack the jerk reached in and placed his right hand high on Kay's heated thigh. In doing so, he unconsciously opened up his stance a little, his crotch now being at a better angle to Derek. He had also loosened his chokehold enough that his captive was able to regain most of his mental and physical faculties.

As Derek locked both his hands together into a double fist and cocked his arms back as far as they would go, he wondered what kind of grade-point average Jack here had in college. It couldn't have been anything much over a point-zero-one, because the stupid shit had left himself wide open.

The double-fist belonging to the ex-centerfielder—who in his final year had tagged eight homeruns over the left-center fence—came upward with all the force he could muster, catching Jack full blast on the underside of his testicles. Derek's parallel, flattened thumbs felt softness at first, followed by the harder substance of pelvic bone.  Whether fact or wishful thinking, Derek thought there was a double *pop*.

Jack immediately released his hold on Derek's neck, doubled up and clutched the area of excruciating pain.  His howl, echoing off the trees and racing across the lake, resembled nothing neither Derek or Kay had ever heard before, even on Wild Kingdom.  The kegger on the other side at Pelican Park stopped a moment in attempted analysis of the plaintive scream.

Jack's knees had no sooner collapsed onto the pavement, than Kay opened the car door with exceptional speed and strength for a one-hundred-five-pound pixie.  It caught poor Jack smack on his nose, rocking him backwards onto the road with a second alien screech overlapping the first.

Kay jumped out of the car and fetched the car keys out of the right-hand pocket of Jack's cut-off jeans.  She cocked her foot to give him a swift kick to the ribs, but thought better of it.  Why risk breaking a toe on this asshole?

"You okay, Derek?" she asked, stepping over the groaning lump to grab ahold of her lover.  "You look a little shaky."

"I can drive," he asserted, taking the offered keys and shaking more blood back into his brain.

When the pair turned to go to the Tempest, they noticed the driver's side door had swung back to being almost closed.  There was a dent right in the middle and what looked like a spot of blood in the center of the dent.

"Oh, Jack," teased Kay.  "Look what you did to Derek's car door.  He's not going to be happy with you.  I hope you have insurance."

Laughing, they jumped into the car, started it up and pulled back onto Lakeshore Road.

# Chapter 156

They hadn't noticed the other car that had been coming up from behind them was now only about one hundred yards back. It flipped its brights up and down.

"That can't be Jack," breathed Kay, twisting hard to look back.

"It's Joe," assured Derek. "There's that headlight dimmer than the others."

Derek slowed way down and motioned for Joe to pull up along side. When the two were abreast and going about ten miles an hour, Julie yelled, "What the hell was going on back there? Some guy was crawling toward a big green Caddie on his hands and knees as you guys were pulling out."

"Tell you later," yelled Derek. "Let's just get to the kegger."

"You sure you two are all right?" yelled Joe. "You sound a little frazzled."

Derek nodded. "We're okay. Let's get going."

He rapped his Tempest up to sixty as Joe's '56 Chevy fell back about ten car lengths.

Unfortunately, that was more than enough room for the forest green Cadillac to come racing up with its lights off and slip in between the two cars. It immediately banged the Pontiac's rear bumper.

"What the hell...?" gasped Derek, looking in the rearview mirrors. Silhouetted by Joe's headlights behind, he could see the black figure of what had to be a very pissed visitor from Central City.

"Jesus! It's Jack," said Derek in disbelief.

The Caddy backed off then bashed into them again.

"You son of a bitch," screamed Kay at the back window. "You're insane!"

Derek floored the accelerator and the small engine did what it could to speed up. But it was no match for the Cadillac, which stayed right on their tail. Joe's '56 mill wasn't much more powerful than Derek's, but he kept trying to get around the Caddy to protect the arthritic Tempest. His efforts were also futile, as Jack kept swinging out into the other lane to block the attempt.

328

As the three vehicles raced down the road in a weaving, tight single file, Derek was frantically trying to study his options. The four of them could undoubtedly take Jack on, but that would have to be a last resort. He didn't want the girls having any part of that, much less getting hurt. They could keep going ninety miles an hour along this dark, winding road until something happened. But that could be somebody dying in a crash. They could try to make it to the keg party, but that was still a good five miles away.

A sign for the upcoming West Overlook shot passed. Derek had no idea why, but he suddenly hit the brakes and skidded up to the narrow entrance. He cranked the wheel to the right and fishtailed onto the gravel road. As he gunned the engine again, a quick check in the mirror showed the Caddy sliding past, its tires screeching in protest. A second later Joe's Chevy was doing the same.

Derek kept accelerating along the gravel lane, but all too soon had to hit the brakes again to keep from smashing into the wooden guardrail. The car stopped just a few feet short.

"What are we doing, honey?" questioned Kay, nervously looking out the back window.

"I don't know," breathed Derek. "I really don't know."

Just then the Caddy with its lights on now came weaving down the lane, slicing through the cloud of dust left by the Tempest. It pulled up behind them and gave the piece of junk a good bump, knocking it forward a few inches. In a couple seconds Joe pulled up on the left side of Derek. Joe jumped out of his car and ran back to the driver's side of the Caddy.

"What the fuck you think you're doing, asshole," shot Joe, his face not a foot from Jack's profile. There was dried blood under Jack's nose and all over his white muscle-man tee shirt.

"Fuck off!" hissed Jack, not bothering to even turn his head. He back up a few feet and rammed the Tempest again, much harder this time and without letting up. The smaller brown car with its brakes locked was pushed through the railing. The Caddie let up again, and the Tempest came to a halt, teetering on the edge of the cliff.

# Chapter 157

"You mother fucker!" yelled Kay, leaning over the back of the front seat, flipping Jack the bird with both hands.

In a moment of crisis, the mind can do strange things. Derek's made a note to have a word with Kay about her language at their earliest convenience. Kay searched her memory for where that phrase may have come from. She didn't believe she had ever used it before. The image of a young, black male, looking at himself in a wardrobe's mirror, flashed across her memory and was just as quickly gone.

Derek knew he should open the door and get both of them out of there. But he couldn't move. It wasn't that he was frozen in fear. Just frozen. Sitting here, teetering on the brink of death, felt so...*right*. It's where they were supposed to be. Kay's frantic animations belied that, because deep inside her conscious mind, she was feeling the same as Derek. This was supposed to happen.

The Caddy backed away, shifted again into low, and made another run at the Tempest. The fatal run.

"God damn it! screamed Joe in the expressionless maniac's ear. Joe grabbed the sedan's support frame and planted his heels to try keeping the lumber wagon from completing its mission. It was too no avail. The two-ton Cadillac smashed hard into the one-ton Pontiac, sending it over the brink.

In the three seconds it took to fall the thirty feet into Cedar Lake, Kay and Derek found each other and hung on with every ounce of strength. Their hearts and minds screamed in abject terror.

The car had canted just enough to land upside down in the water. The jolting impact was cushioned somewhat by the lake itself, but the two inhabitants were still thrown around like marbles in a tin can, knocking their heads hard against the steel ceiling covered only with a thin layer of soundproofing fabric. Water gushed in through the open windows, as the Tempest rapidly sank into the ten feet of water.

Her mind still screaming, Kay opened her eyes to find a beautiful face with emerald-green eyes smiling at her.

"It's okay, Kay," said the familiar, sultry voice. "It's over. You're safe." The angelic apparition reached out her hands. "Come with me now. Let's go home."

All fear drained instantly from Kay. She took the waiting hands and let herself be pulled into the soft bosom of the lovely phantasm. The sensation of love and belonging was euphoric. This was more than a sister. More than a mother. This was her inner-self...her true self. She was once again Phoebe.

Derek's experience was virtually the same, except the god-like face winking at him was definitely a male with very familiar, sky-blue eyes.

"Great job, Derek," it said with arms spread wide. "You did everything exactly right. Now come here big fella and give your real-self a hug."

Derek didn't need any coaxing. He flew right into his true self's familiar embrace of love and affinity. In a heartbeat they became one: the ever-curious, ever-learning entity named Ethan.

# Epilogue

# Chapter 158

The joint service for Derek Schroeder and Kay Beecher at the Cedar Lake Funeral Home was attended by half the people in town. Every store on main street had closed for the funeral. The homicide of two such young people was a horrible tragedy. Things like this just didn't happen in small town Iowa.

At the foot of the chapel's alter stood the two open caskets, surrounded on three sides by dozens of bouquets, plants and wreaths. Hovering directly above were Macailah and Andrew, watching bemusedly as their younger-selves, Ethan and Phoebe, stood beside the caskets, peering with wonder into the plastic faces of their respective dead bodies. This was the first time they had hung around to watch their own funerals.

"You know, Phebes," said Ethan tongue-in-cheek, after he floated over to check out Kay's remains, "the mortician did a good job of capturing Kay's *inner* beauty. She looks just like you."

"Bite me, Ethan!" replied Phoebe. "She looks like a department store dummy forgotten in some dark corner of the warehouse." Phoebe scooted over to Derek's casket. "And you, *Derek*, look like a Halloween mask of Owen Wilson somebody left in the back window of a car too long."

"Why do humans do that?" pondered Ethan, turning philosophical. "The last image the loved ones see of the deceased is usually a grotesque veneer. Why not keep the casket closed and show photographs of when they were at their best?"

"Humans need closure," shrugged Phoebe.

"That's just the point,' said Ethan. "Closure means closing…bringing something to its conclusion. The end of a physical existence is ten times more of a beginning than that entity's birth was. Human beings need to wise up."

"They're getting there," said Phoebe.

Bored with their unearthly dead bodies, both turn around to observe the overflow crowd of mourners. In the front row were the immediate families of Derek and Kay, most crying, others cried out. Above them hovered their respective souls, looking sympathetic for the misery their oblivious, physical selves were going through.

"Oh, that is so sad," lamented Phoebe, gesturing toward her weeping mom and dad, as they clutched each other in shameless sorrow. "They are so heartbroken."

"I know," said Ethan. "I had never seen my dad cry before."

With all of Derek's eighteen years of Earth experiences now a part of Ethan, and Kay's a part of Phoebe, the memories and feelings of those lives were still very fresh in each of their consciousness. So, a great deal of empathy for their recent family members was quite understandable.

"I almost feel guilty..." offered Phoebe, wrapping her arms around Ethan.

"I know what you're going to say," he interjected. "Here we are, happy, in love, feeling wonderful, while our poor human families are miserable."

"Is there anything we can do for them," Phoebe projected up to Andrew. "It's not easy seeing the grief we've caused, even if it is for the greater good."

Andrew joined them by the caskets, glancing over at the family. Doing a headcount, he saw that all but Brad's inner-selves were advanced enough to be hovering outside of their respective physical-selves. "You can go over there and hug their souls," Andrew suggested, "and ask them to give your love and sympathy to their human counterparts."

"Will that message get passed along?" asked Ethan. "Humans are such a closed system."

"It might," said Macailah, joining the group. "It all depends on how receptive the individual human is at the moment. Most are so grief-stricken they have their walls up. But in time it will."

# Chapter 159

Phoebe and Ethan drifted over and embraced each of the family's inner-selves one by one, offering congratulations for their courage in agreeing to go through the devastating pain of losing loved ones at such a young age and in such a violent manner. They asked that their sincerest condolences and love be imparted to the sorrow-stricken human portions, then Phoebe and Ethan floated back to join Macailah and Andrew.

"Well, are you two ready to head home?" queried Macailah.

"Could we hang around just a little longer?" asked Phoebe. "We'd like to see how some of our friends and school mates are reacting to our departures."

"Sure. That's always fun," smiled Andrew.

Sweeping slowly around the chapel, they discovered most of Kay's friends were weeping and consoling each other. Derek's teammates stayed more in control of their emotions, so not to appear too wimpy. The first baseman Derek had considered a friend seemed almost unmoved by his passing. *Oh, well, we weren't really that close anyway.*

The person who looked downright miserable was his old girlfriend, Donna Carter. Phoebe's proclivity for reading minds revealed that Donna was deeply upset for missing out on marrying into Derek's money, plus racked with guilt for dumping all that manure in his pool. Ethan floated over to her in the back of the room, kissed her forehead and said with all sincerity, "I forgive you, Donna. You're really a very nice soul. I enjoyed our time together."

Phoebe applauded. "Proud of you, honey."

"Hey, I'm on a roll with this forgiving thing," piped Ethan.

Two rows in front of Donna were Derek's best friend, Joe, and Kay's good friend, Julie. Julie was still bawling into her hanky, while Joe just sat there stunned, staring into nothing. Ethan could feel a lot of anger radiating from him. He motioned Phoebe over for some more psychic analysis.

"Do you think Joe's planning to take some revenge on Jack?" he asked.

Phoebe tuned in to Joe's inner-self, who wasn't able to dislodge itself from its human quite yet. After all, this was only his fifth incarnation. Ethan and Phoebe had just completed their eleventh.

"He's thinking about it, for sure," she reported. "He keeps replaying that night at the West Overlook. He's frustrated he couldn't stop Jack. But his inner-self indicates no action is planned. It seems there is a high probability Jack is going to be in jail for about twenty years. That should be punishment enough."

"Speaking of which," said Andrew, joining the conversation along with Macailah. "We want to stop by and thank Phaidra for her rather ingenious plan to get Kay and Derek off the planet and back into you guys. Want to come?"

"Most definitely," voiced Phoebe.

"Oh, you bet," said Ethan. "Let's see how horny ol' Leonid likes being somebody's prison bitch for a couple decades."

"Ethan!" scolded Phoebe, smacking him playfully on the top of his celestial head.

# Chapter 160

Andrew told everybody to hang on, and he transported the foursome ten Earth miles west to the county jail in Central City. They found Phaidra hovering above Jack in his cell, smoking a cigarette, talking to somebody telepathically. She was very glad to see them. Thanks and hugs all around.

"I didn't really do all that much," confessed Phaidra. "I just led Jack to Derek's gas station, and suggested he keep an eye on the A&W, since there was a high probability Derek and Kay would drive through the popular teen hang out. His bruised ego and anger took care of the rest, as expected."

"Well, your foresight and nudges were spot-on," said Macailah.

"As were yours," returned Phaidra, "getting Derek to turn into the West Overlook, then to stay in the car instead of jumping out before it went over the cliff."

"Thanks, but that actually was all Ethan's doing. Obviously, he had the closer connection to Derek."

They joined the others moving in for a closer look at Jack Goodwin. Waiting for his bail hearing, the dejected figure had a strip of white tape across his broken nose and two black eyes. He was dressed in county jail orange, lying on his back on the dirty mattress atop the steel cot attached to the cinderblock wall. There was no inner-self hovering above or around him.

"I assume Leonid isn't yet capable of separating," observed Macailah.

"Nope," replied Phaidra. "This is his ninth life, but he's been so wrapped up in himself and pursuing Phoebe throughout his existence, he hasn't learned much of anything. This stretch in prison will do him good. I'll school him in his dreams, and really turn up the training when he comes home in about sixty years."

"Wow," said Phoebe, with a hint of sympathy. "You're going to leave him in Jack and on Earth that long?"

"Maybe. Maybe not. I'll see how he does in his sleep training. And if he learns how to separate from Jack—which I highly doubt—I may bring him back sooner."

"Well, for what it's worth," said Phoebe, "Leonid isn't anywhere as bad as Jack. I've blended with Leonid. And while he's a lousy lover (Ethan snorted), he does have a decent spirit."

"I'll keep that in mind," smiled Phaidra, giving Phoebe a hug. "You're such a sweet soul. I hope he eventually stops pursuing you and meets someone more in his league."

"You and me both," said Phoebe and Ethan in unison.

"Well," offered Andrew, "unless anybody wants to go back to the funeral and listen to some worn out old eulogy, what say we all head home?"

All agreed, and with considerable enthusiasm.

So, the foursome locked up in a group-hug and beamed off across the macrocosm to a log cabin on the outskirts of Chicago. There were ice box cookies to eat, *Headlong into a Black Holes* to drink, and the next go-round on good old planet Earth to plan. There was still so much for Phoebe and Ethan to learn before earning their Earth-Three wings.

# Acknowledgements

Although a work of fiction, this book is based largely on two non-fiction sources.  One is the widely-popular teachings of Seth, a self-described spiritual entity, who—through author and medium Jane Roberts (1929-1984)—had dictated volumes of insights into who we really are, why we are here, and what awaits us after death.

The second is Taylor's earlier work: "Making Sense of It All: Practical Answers to Our Greatest Spiritual Questions," which applied common sense and scientific facts to Seth's teachings to offer a down-to-Earth approach on the purpose of life and the prospect of our afterlife.

\* \* \* \*

Recommended web sites for the many works of Seth works include:
    Seth Network International (**www.sethnet.org**)
    Seth Learning Center (**www. sethlearningcenter.org**)

\* \* \* \*

Autographed copies of all of Taylor's books, including "Making Sense of It All: Practical Answers to Our Greatest Spiritual Questions," can be found at **www.primetimes2.com/books.html**

With a literary career spanning decades and hundreds of feature articles, non-fiction books, and novels, Richard Douglas Taylor's subject matter has ranged from astrophysics to aliens. His imaginative storylines have just the right touch of humor to make them a joy to read and difficult to put down.

## Books by Richard Douglas Taylor:

Novels—
The Brookfield Daughter
The Brookfield Daughter—Sanctuary
Earth-Two
Earth-Two—Game-Changers

Non-Fiction—
Under the Solar/Lunar Influence
How to Know When to Go
Making Sense of It All

*Web site:* www.primetimes2.com/books.html
*Email:* rdtaylor@mediacombb.net

# EARTH-TWO